ENEMY OVERNIGHT

ROBIN L. ROTHAM

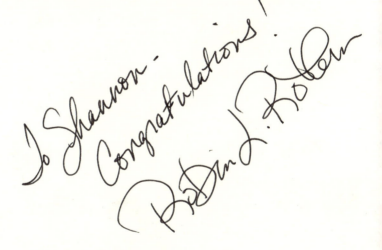

Ellora's Cave
Romantica Publishing

An Ellora's Cave Romantica Publication

www.ellorascave.com

Enemy Overnight

ISBN 9781419961342
ALL RIGHTS RESERVED.
Enemy Overnight Copyright © 2009 Robin L. Rotham
Edited by Sue-Ellen Gower.
Cover art by Syneca.

This book printed in the U.S.A. by Jasmine-Jade Enterprises, LLC.

Electronic book publication June 2009
Trade paperback publication June 2010

The terms Romantica® and Quickies® are registered trademarks of Ellora's Cave Publishing.

With the exception of quotes used in reviews, this book may not be reproduced or used in whole or in part by any means existing without written permission from the publisher, Ellora's Cave Publishing, Inc.® 1056 Home Avenue, Akron OH 44310-3502.

Warning: The unauthorized reproduction or distribution of this copyrighted work is illegal. Criminal copyright infringement, including infringement without monetary gain, is investigated by the FBI and is punishable by up to 5 years in federal prison and a fine of $250,000.
(http://www.fbi.gov/ipr/)

This book is a work of fiction and any resemblance to persons, living or dead, or places, events or locales is purely coincidental. The characters are productions of the author's imagination and used fictitiously.

ENEMY OVERNIGHT
૪૭

Acknowledgements

My books would not be what they are without all of the following people —

The three greatest editors an author could ever hope for — Heather, Mary and Suz, who had her work cut out for her with this one.

My insightful and, when necessary, brutal critters — Sher, Anne, R.G., Red, Feisty, Crys, Kate and Janet.

My support groups, where I go for sympathy and adult conversation — Romance Divas, Passionate Ink and Prairieland Romance Writers.

Sexy Mr. Robin and my beautiful kids, who are learning how to fend for themselves when I'm on a deadline.

VAST, whose music is endlessly inspiring.

And my wonderful readers, whose ~~kicks in the ass, constant prodding~~ unfailing encouragement galvanized me into finally getting Shauss' story down in writing.

I love you all!

Trademarks Acknowledgement

※

The author acknowledges the trademarked status and trademark owners of the following wordmarks mentioned in this work of fiction:

BowFlex: Nautilus, Inc.

Gatorade: Stokely-Van Camp, Inc.

Hershey's Kiss: The Hershey's Company

Independence Day: 20th Century Fox

iPod: Apple, Inc.

Lady Chatterley's Lover: D. H. Lawrence

Mr. Clean: The Proctor & Gamble Company

Olympics: International Olympic Committee

Pepsi: Pepsico, Inc.

Scrunchie: L&N Sales and Marketing, Inc.

Star Trek/Enterprise: Paramount Pictures Corporation

The Stepford Wives: Ira Levin

Terminator: Warner Bros. Entertainment, Inc.

UPS: United Parcel Service of America, Inc.

Zumba: Zumba Fitness, LLC.

"Real isn't how you are made," said the Skin Horse. "It's a thing that happens to you. When a child loves you for a long, long time, not just to play with, but REALLY loves you, then you become Real."

"Does it hurt?" asked the Rabbit.

"Sometimes," said the Skin Horse, for he was always truthful. "When you are Real you don't mind being hurt."

"Does it happen all at once, like being wound up," he asked, "or bit by bit?"

"It doesn't happen all at once," said the Skin Horse. "You become. It takes a long time. That's why it doesn't happen often to people who break easily, or have sharp edges, or who have to be carefully kept. Generally, by the time you are Real, most of your hair has been loved off, and your eyes drop out and you get loose in your joints and very shabby. But these things don't matter at all, because once you are Real you can't be ugly, except to people who don't understand."

—from *The Velveteen Rabbit* by **Margery Williams, 1922**

Prologue

Dayree King had only been driving for twenty minutes when the hairs on her arms prickled to attention. She hadn't felt the whisper-soft charge of flare energy in decades, but she recognized it in time to keep from careening off the road when her husband materialized in the seat beside her.

She tensed, deliberately backing off the accelerator. Ragan's use of the advanced technology spoke volumes about his determination to keep her home and she didn't want to have this argument at breakneck speed.

"Taking the scenic route to the theater?" he asked acidly.

Dayree spared him a wary glance. It was strange to see him in the passenger seat—he always insisted on driving even when they took her SUV.

The greenish glow from the dash did nothing to warm the arctic planes of his face as he stared back at her, and suddenly it was hard to remember what she'd ever seen in either the scientist she'd served with or the lover she'd married. They hadn't had sex since the Garathani settled into orbit six months ago and, as far as she knew, he hadn't slept in all that time.

Once the Garathani forged an alliance with the Terrans and began recruiting females for sexual service, Ragan's devotion to duty, once so appealing in its zeal, had morphed into a fanaticism that bordered on hysteria. That fanaticism was going to cost innocent lives, and though it went against her training—indeed, her very nature—to challenge her mate, Dayree couldn't let Jasmine be one of those casualties.

"I have to go, Ragan."

"Enough of your foolishness," he replied, tugging at the cuffs of his gloves. One would think after all these years on

Earth, he would have developed some tolerance, perhaps even affection, for the planet and its inhabitants, but he still acted as if all things Terran were contaminated with fecal material. "Turn around and I'll endeavor to forget you ever defied me in such a manner."

"I can't let her do this."

"You can, and you will. She's a stubborn, ungrateful little wretch who owes us this, at the very least."

"No." Her fingers clutched the steering wheel convulsively. "She's got to know."

Worry for her beloved daughter was like a wild bird trapped in her breast. It was bad enough that Ragan was infecting their cell with his paranoia and whipping Earth's population into an exophobic frenzy—sending Jasmine in to monitor the enemy's activities armed with anything less than the truth was something she simply could not allow.

Even as they zipped through the moonless night, Jasmine was sorting and packing and making the final preparations for her move to the alliance compound, and Dayree felt almost frantic with the need to get to her. She should never have let things get this far, should never have let Jasmine give up the teaching job she loved for a fight that wasn't hers—a fight that by all accounts wasn't even theirs anymore.

"For the last time, Dayree," Ragan said with exaggerated patience. "The less she knows, the safer she is."

"You mean the safer we are."

Ignoring her barbed observation, he tugged at the black leather cuffs again, obviously preparing to grab her. Never mind that flaring her out with him would leave the unpiloted vehicle barreling into oncoming traffic. Typical Ragan—the cost of such an act, be it in dollars or lives, meant nothing to him.

Her grip on the wheel tightened. Damn it, if he wanted to take her, he'd have to take the car too.

"Are you going to turn this vehicle around and return to the house?" he asked.

"No. I'm going to Denver and nothing you can say will change my mind."

"I'm sorry to hear it," he said flatly. "Your presence will be sorely missed."

Taken aback by his reversal, she blinked. "Well, I'll be home by—"

He grabbed the steering wheel and Dayree's heart jumped into her throat as they swerved sickeningly.

"Ragan, stop it!" She fought him for control of the big vehicle, unable to believe he would put both their lives in jeopardy like this.

Then his foot came down on top of hers, depressing the accelerator slowly to the floor.

"All right, all right!" she screamed over the revving of the engine, terrified by their out-of-control speed. "I'm sorry! I'll go home, I'll stay home, I'll do whatever you say, just stop!"

He jerked the wheel hard to the right and Dayree screamed again when they veered across the shoulder and jumped the guardrail with a horrendous screech of metal on metal. His boot ground into the top of her foot and they bumped blindly down the grassy hill toward the cliffs.

Her mate was killing her.

Before she could pry her frozen fingers off the steering wheel and reach for him, Ragan disappeared in a flare bubble. She slammed on the brake, but it was too late. The bumping stopped and she sailed off the cliff into the chilly northern California night.

She knew it was a long way down when her disbelief had time to give way to anger and betrayal. And then fear—for herself, for the people of Earth, but mostly for her daughter. Jasmine would be alone and utterly unprotected now.

Although it was too dark to see her doom rushing up to meet her, Dayree closed her eyes. She'd die on impact, so at least her death wouldn't be painful.

She prayed Jasmine would be as fort—

Chapter One
The Garathani warship Heptoral
One year later

☙

"You are being dishonest."

Commander Kellen's accusation hovered in the air like a swarm of killer bees, and Jasmine King gripped the edges of her seat with palms that had suddenly gone clammy. Had she really thought she was prepared for a confrontation with this big, pissed-off alien?

"No!" she gasped. "I swear, I've told you everything I know."

The commander continued to search her face as he leaned over the table, and she didn't have to be psychic to know he didn't like what he saw. His stony expression said it all—she'd deprived him of his mate, and for that there would be no mercy. Even if she got off this ship alive, he'd hunt her down and kill her.

Jasmine's breathing quickened and surging adrenaline set up a fine vibration in her joints, but she forced herself to sit there and stare back at him. She'd known this was a possibility. No wimping out now.

God, she had to pee. Nerves had made it impossible for her to eat more than a few bites of the pizza they'd brought aboard, but she'd guzzled enough Diet Pepsi to float a battleship while she sounded Monica out about the state of her sex life. And once Monica admitted she hadn't slept with Shauss yet, Ambassador Pret had swooped in and whisked her away before Jasmine could ask where the bathroom was.

You should have gone before you left the planet.

She swallowed hard, locking down a giggle. If she so much as squeaked now, she'd break.

Kellen straightened, his long tawny hair scattering over his shoulders, his thunderous blue eyes never wavering from hers. "Minister, this female has cost Lieutenant Shauss his chance at a mate. He must be compensated."

"Lieutenant, the female is yours," the Garathani minister replied.

The killer bees gathered to strike. "Take her, Shauss," he said flatly, "and make it as painful as you possibly can."

Jasmine gaped at him. *Take* her?

Her eyes dropped to the scissors she'd just used to cut Monica's hair, but before she could snatch them up, Shauss grabbed the collar of her blouse and hauled her sideways out of the chair.

"No!"

As he swung her around, Jasmine caught a glimpse of Shelley's shocked face and bitterly regretted not getting the little nurse off the ship while she had the chance. She shouldn't have to witness this, especially in her condition.

Fighting panic, Jasmine lashed out sideways with her right foot, but her skirt was too tight—the kick didn't even come close to touching him. Shit, how was she supposed to defend herself against a seven-foot alien whose arms were probably longer than her legs?

Shauss reeled her in closer and Jasmine screamed in growing horror, clawing at his wrist and kicking out at him again. He restrained her with humiliating ease, pinching her wrists together behind her back, and she shuddered at the vibrant energy blazing from his palm. He'd never touched her before, never so much as shaken her hand. Why did it have to happen now? Why this way?

When he ripped her skirt off, she froze, her heart fluttering like it was about to stop altogether. This was all just a dream, another bizarre, stress-fueled dream. She'd wake up any minute and—

His fingernails scraped her hip as he snapped her panties off and panic won. She screamed and jumped and kicked and twisted hard enough to pull her arms from their sockets, but she couldn't break free of his brutal grip.

"Shauss, please don't," she cried.

His boot swept her feet out from under her and she went down hard, barely turning her head in time to avoid landing on her nose.

He followed her down, leaning hard on her wrists, still pinned in the small of her back. The pressure on her bladder made her squirm with a different kind of panic.

"What's the matter, Jasmine?" he asked. "Don't you want me?"

"No!"

"That's funny, I heard you did."

Nauseating heat gushed up her neck into her cheeks and she closed her eyes, pressing her forehead into the smelly blue biologic pad. His mocking observation cast an ugly light on her actions, but damn it, she'd had no choice. Monica had signed on to care for the Garathanis' sexual recruits, not to become one of them, and the fact that she'd turned out to be half Garathani didn't change that. She was an American citizen and, as such, entitled to choose her own mate. She wouldn't get that choice while she was trapped on a Garathani vessel.

Jasmine seized that righteous anger and held on, taking deep breaths to center herself. Monica was free now, and that was all that mattered.

The long, slow buzz of a zipper crawled over her skin like an electric current and she stiffened again. This could *not* happen. If they discovered what she was, her father's life would be in jeopardy. What would happen to her didn't even bear thinking about.

Unbelievably, his grip on her wrists eased for a split second and she took her chance. If Shauss went with her, so be it.

Wrenching one hand free, she reached under her blouse.

He caught her before she even got close.

"What are you up to now?" he said tightly as he rolled her to her side.

The massive erection thrusting from his open uniform made her squeeze her thighs together. "Don't do this, Shauss, please don't!"

"What were you trying to do?"

He used his free hand to push her blouse up and jolted at the sight of the activator taped to her ribs. Then his furious eyes bored into hers. God, he absolutely hated her.

She hissed in agony as he tore the device from her skin and shoved it under her nose.

"Why would you do this thing for Pret?" Minister Cecine looked like a flame-haired Grim Reaper as he loomed over her in his long robes. "Do you have any idea of the kind of pain this death would cause you?"

Every drop of blood drained from her head. "D-death? He said it would tr-transport me out of h-here."

"Miss King, this device is a feyo shell," Kellen said harshly. "It will incinerate you and anyone you're touching from the inside out."

Her world tilted. Oh God, she'd been set up.

"Jasmine?" She flinched at the accusation in Shelley's tone. "You *helped* him?"

"How did he convince you?" Shauss barked, seemingly oblivious to his nudity. "Promises of money? Power? Technology?"

"Nothing!" Jasmine's eyes fell again to his angry, mile-long penis and the appendage emerging above it before skittering to the commander. "He came to me and said that

Monica didn't want to be with you, that she was miserable and had begged him to get her out of here, and I thought it was true because I heard her yelling at you in your office that day before she disappeared! Please, Commander, I swear to God, I was only trying to help her!"

"Where has he taken her?"

"I don't know!"

Shauss rolled her to her stomach again, forcing her thighs apart with his knees, and she squeezed her eyes shut, nearly hyperventilating with the expectation of a vicious rape and the horrors that would inevitably follow.

"Tell me where he took my mate," he roared, shoving the blazing-hot hardness of his cock against her bare bottom, "or I and every soldier on this ship will fuck your ass into useless, bloody shreds!"

"I don't know!" she screamed again. "All I know is they're underground somewhere!"

A loud thump made everyone still, and then Kellen said, "Ketrok hasn't removed her biomet."

Shauss heaved her off the floor and spun her around just as a flare bubble engulfed the commander. Clamping her arms in an excruciating grip, he pulled her up until her toes dangled in the air and his clove-scented breath gusted over her face. "If Monica's lost to me, I'll be back for your ass."

His snarl shattered what was left of her composure and she whimpered weakly as a cold sweat broke out on every inch of her skin. *Oh God, no...*

Her bladder released in a scalding torrent down her legs. The splatter on the biologic pad seemed to go on forever as his gaze dropped to her privates and his expression went from murderous to cruelly amused. "Well, I didn't see that coming."

"Please just kill me," she choked.

He raised one sleek black eyebrow. "And waste a perfectly good piece of ass?" Setting her down, he shoved her toward one of the guards and zipped up his suit. "Don't let her out of your sight, Zannen."

The instant he disappeared in a flare bubble, Jasmine swayed, rubber-kneed and shaking. Only the grip around her abused arm kept her upright. Tears of shame streaked down her cheeks in cooling echoes of the rivers drying on her legs.

"Miss King." The minister's tone was flat as he approached. She couldn't bring herself to look at him but she could just imagine the expression of scorn on his face. God knew she'd seen it often enough on her father's.

"You will remain here," he continued, "under guard until my daughter's status has been determined. Do not create any further difficulties for yourself."

"Your daughter!" Her eyes jerked up to his and suddenly the ambassador's true motive for spiriting Monica away from the ship slammed into her—he planned to forge a political alliance with their leader by claiming the man's only living daughter.

And she had helped him do it.

Jasmine felt sick. When Pret had come to her, she'd considered the possibility he wanted Monica for himself and immediately dismissed it. He was a fussy old diplomat who exhibited none of the brooding sexual hunger all the other Garathani males radiated, while Monica was a belligerent little Goth doctor who loved nothing more than letting the air out of pompous windbags with her verbal darts. She'd drive him crazy within five minutes.

So much for her powers of deductive reasoning. The idea that Monica might be fighting Pret off right now just about killed her. Thank God the doctors hadn't removed her biometric implant yet so Kellen and Shauss had a chance to find her before it was too late. The man was old and thin but he was Garathani-tall and he hadn't just gone through a life-threatening physical transition. If anything happened to Monica, she'd never forgive herself.

"Yes, my daughter—whom I may never have a chance to know now, thanks to you. I suspect she would die before submitting to Pret. So you understand," his pointed look became even more pointed when it drifted below her waist, "why I'll be disinclined to protect you should anything happen to her."

A tremor shook Jasmine as sharp prongs of awareness penetrated her shock. She was mostly naked in front of a bunch of seven-foot-tall aliens who hadn't had sex in over a decade. If Cecine chose to withdraw his protection, Shauss would probably order them all to fuck her to death—after he'd exacted his own personal revenge.

"I'm so sorry," she whispered, quelling the urge to slide a palm protectively over her crotch as more tears rolled down her cheeks.

After staring at her for another agonizing moment, Cecine snatched a roll of fluffy white material out of thin air and handed it to her.

"Clean and compose yourself as best you can." He turned to Shelley. "Nurse Bonham, do you require a physician?"

"No!" Still sitting at the table, Shelley kept her arms wrapped over her bulging stomach. "I just want to go home."

"In due time." He sent stern a look Jasmine's way. "Zannen, see that she conducts herself appropriately until I return."

"With pleasure, Minister."

She pressed her lips together, not daring to look up at the source of the growl as Cecine stalked out.

"Jasmine, what did you do?" Shelley whispered, leaving dark mascara smudges as she wiped her eyes with unsteady fingers.

Jasmine couldn't speak around the tears. And what could she say that she hadn't already? That she was trying to think for herself, to do the right thing, to prove that she wasn't just Daddy's little embarrassment? Her father would say that's where she'd made her first mistake—thinking for herself. She hated that he was right. If she'd just stuck to the mission, none of this would have happened.

But if she hadn't acted, she would have spent the rest of her life wondering if she'd deprived Monica of her one chance at freedom. That was a burden she couldn't have lived with. Period. She'd made the best decision she could based on the information available to her at the time, and now she'd just have to live with the consequences.

Unfortunately, so would everyone else.

She stood up straighter and swiped eyes with her free hand, determined not to act like any more of a victim than she already had. After all, Cecine hadn't withdrawn his protection just yet.

Taking a deep breath, she glared down at the long, hard fingers clutching her arm. "Do you mind?"

"Not very well," came the gravelly reply.

"Listen, you…" She glanced up and gasped, instinctively trying to pull away. Jesus, he looked like Mr. Clean's evil twin, with flat black eyes, bushy black brows, a big pitted bowling ball of a head, and a grid work of scars ringing his thick, tanned neck. She hadn't even realized there *were* bald Garathani, much less ugly ones, but this guy was all that and more.

Her eyes widened—he even had a shiny black ring in his left ear.

"I'm listening, but I'm not hearing anything," he informed her with a smirk.

She jerked her arm. "Let go of me."

His grip tightened for an instant before he relented, and she flexed both arms gingerly. She'd be one big bruise tomorrow. Assuming she was still alive tomorrow.

Taking a deep breath, she unrolled the spongy fabric, which turned out to be a large towel of some sort. She looped it over her hips and then hesitated, glancing around at a half-dozen chiseled faces. They all just stared at her like stray dogs at the butcher shop window, so even though it went against every instinct, she turned her back and leaned over to pat her legs and feet dry, making sure her rear stayed covered. Everything else could drip-dry—there was no way she was wiping her crotch in front of all these males.

When she rewrapped herself and tucked in the corner of the towel at her waist, a guard she recognized from the compound, Ensign Verr, scooped up her skirt and held it out to her. It was completely ruined, the back seam ripped from top to bottom, so she folded it and set it on the table.

Another guard handed over her flats, which she stepped into gratefully. The biologic pad lining the ship's interior was a brilliant innovation, absorbing biological byproducts and returning oxygen and nitrogen to the atmosphere, but she'd had enough of its squishy moistness under her feet.

Of course the bald one tried to hand her what was left of her underwear. The tattered scrap of lace looked ridiculously tiny in his gigantic fingers.

"Keep them as a souvenir," she snapped.

"Thank you."

Her eyes widened when he raised the fabric to his nose. "No! I was—"

Zannen inhaled so deeply she was surprised it didn't disappear into one of his nostrils.

"You're disgusting," she told him.

He grinned widely, baring enormous white teeth. "You're the one who just pissed herself."

Flushing scarlet, she turned away, knowing there was no comeback cutting enough to top that.

"You may as well be seated," Ensign Verr suggested. "You're not going anywhere until we know Dr. Teague is safe."

Jasmine sat, keeping the towel securely around her while avoiding Shelley's reproachful stare. The scissors still lay on the table, a stark reminder of how ineffective she'd been. Why hadn't she stuck those back into her skirt pocket when she was done cutting Monica's hair? She still wouldn't have posed much of a threat to Shauss, but she might at least have been able to take her own life before he outed her as something other than human.

Maybe it wasn't too late. After all, no matter which way this went down, she came out the big loser. She'd either suffer and die at Shauss' whim, and possibly take her father down with her, or go home with her tail between her legs and suffer her father's undying contempt for the rest of her life.

All it would take was one good, hard jab straight up between—

"I'll take these." Zannen's hand covered the scissors and slowly slid them off the side of the table. "Little girls shouldn't play with sharp toys."

Damn it, couldn't she catch just one break today?

Keeping her eyes on the table, she muttered, "Bastard."

"You have no idea. Yet."

Her breath caught at the silky insinuation. He was just waiting for Shauss to come back in a rage and turn them loose on her.

Another tremor shook her. She wanted to stay strong, to face whatever happened to her with courage and dignity, but she didn't know if she could. She'd just about lost her mind when Shauss jumped on her earlier, and she hadn't even really believed he would obey the commander's order, or at least not at first. Now that she knew what was coming, she might be able to handle it if he came back and finished what he'd started. She'd earned his wrath, and the idea of being punished for her sins was somehow acceptable. Honorable, even. If her father became a target as a result, he'd just have to roll with it—he'd known the risks going in as well as she had.

But there was no honor in ending up a *piece of ass* for this ugly brute. The degradation would be unbearable.

He trailed a fingertip along her jaw and she jerked her head to the side, glaring up at him. There was no way she'd let him have her—she'd tear his eyeballs out first.

"Lieutenant," the other man said in a warning tone.

Zannen just smiled and resumed a watchful stance over her.

Too discouraged to deal with Shelley's condemnation, Jasmine rested her forehead on her crossed arms and started praying in earnest.

Please, God, let Monica be okay…

* * * * *

Three days later she was still praying, though her tone had gone from plaintive to aggravated.

God, please let me out of this hellhole!

Ignoring the burning in her biceps and abs, she clung to the bar and pulled herself up in another gorilla chin crunch, and then another, and another, blowing out with every one.

Three whole days! It was just unbelievable. Monica had been rescued, the ambassador was in custody, and the Garathani *had* to believe that Jasmine had been duped into cooperating in the abduction…and yet she was still a prisoner in her own quarters. Why?

All she'd wanted when Zannen and Ensign Verr shuttled Shelley and her back to the surface was to pack up her stuff and watch the Beaumont-Thayer compound disappear in her rearview mirror along with the rest of snowy Montana. Instead, the bastards had ransacked her room and confiscated her laptop, her extension phone and even her cell phone, which was lying dead in a drawer because there was no reception out here anyway. She'd screamed bloody murder the whole time, but they might as well have been deaf for all the attention they paid her.

When they were done pawing through her belongings, they'd locked her in. From that point on there were two guards posted outside her door at all times and her meals were delivered like clockwork by said guards. Except for Noah Beaumont, who'd dropped by to personally deliver her pink slip that first day, she hadn't seen nor talked to another human being since. It was depressing and frightening. What motive could the Garathani possibly have for detaining her?

Shaking with the effort, she finished her last few crunches and dropped to the floor. Thank God they'd left her workout equipment and DVD player or she'd be out of her mind by now. As it was, she was starting to feel like Sarah Connor after her stay in the mental hospital—lean, mean and a danger to herself and others. If they didn't let her go soon, *she* was going to go Terminator on someone's ass.

Jasmine scowled. After her performance on the *Heptoral*, the Garathani would probably laugh themselves silly if she put up her dukes.

She unhooked the pull-up bar with a sigh and shoved it under the bed. Peeling out of her shorts and athletic bra, she eyed herself critically in the bathroom mirror. She *was* lean and mean, more so than she'd ever been in her adult life. Though she hadn't intentionally set out to lose weight, her mother's death had killed her appetite for weeks, and then once she was over the initial shock, she'd decided now was as good a time as any to get back in shape. Isolation and loneliness had become her friends, driving her to move and keep moving, rain or shine. When the weather was decent, she ran for a couple of hours on the compound's quarter-mile track, and when it wasn't, she ran on one of the treadmills in the exercise facility. She'd ordered a BowFlex and the pull-up bar and made it a point to use one of them whenever she watched TV.

Of course she'd eventually had to order a whole new wardrobe to go with her new body, but such were the hardships of getting in shape.

Now three sleepless nights had created dark circles under her eyes and anxiety was etching permanent frown lines on her forehead. She may not intimidate the Garathani, but her biology students back in Denver would probably back slowly away at the sight of her.

The bruises on her wrists and upper arms still stood in stark purple relief against her pale skin, and she rubbed the thumbprint on her left biceps with unsteady fingers. Shauss was the one element of her ordeal aboard the Garathani vessel she had yet to work through. She'd had no trouble consigning Lieutenant Zannen to her mental File Thirteen—she hated him, period. The minister and Commander Kellen had been harder, though she'd eventually accepted having wronged them and paid the price, thereby compartmentalizing her encounters with them.

But no matter how she approached it, she couldn't even begin to sort out the conflict with Shauss. There was simply too much to process and she got agitated every time she let herself think about it. Just trying to reconcile that hate-filled snarl with his typical coolly amused expression made her stomach twist with dread. It would have been horrifying enough to see such a transformation as an innocent bystander, but to know she was the cause of it...

Jasmine dropped her hand and turned away to start the shower, putting him firmly out of her mind. Time enough to plow through all that emotional crap when she was well away from here.

The hot water felt good while it lasted, which as usual wasn't nearly long enough. Afterward she blew her hair dry and pulled it up in a ponytail then dressed for comfort in thin thermals, blue jeans and a baggy ski sweater. Not that she was going anywhere—she just couldn't stand to open the door to a Garathani warrior in her nightclothes. Plus, it was freaking cold on the north side of the building. The Garathani must be hogging all the heat—the offices were always unbearably hot.

She pulled on wool socks and her sheepskin slippers and then glanced at her watch. Almost three hours to kill until dinner.

Sighing, she pulled a DVD out of the rack and popped it in. *Independence Day*—that was a good one. If she couldn't whip some alien butt herself, might as well watch Will Smith do it.

While the previews were running, she grabbed her nasal spray out of the bathroom and stuck it in her pocket so she didn't have to get up for the next dose. She pinched a few dying leaves off her plants and dropped them into the trash can on the way back to the bed. Then she closed the blinds to cut the glare of sun on snow, kicked off her slippers and stretched out to watch the movie...

Coming to on her stomach, Jasmine grabbed wildly for the bed. Adrenaline pounded through her, leaving her shaking. God, she hated waking up like that!

She stiffened as several things hit her at once. She couldn't reach the edges of her mattress. It sounded as if half the candidates were holding a rally right outside her door. The air was suffocatingly warm and humid. And her bed smelled strangely earthy, kind of like—

Her eyes popped open. *Biologic pad*.

Gasping, she pushed up on one elbow and gazed into a forest of ankles. This time she *had* to be dreaming. There was no way in hell she was back aboard the ship.

Someone staggered and she rolled backward in time to avoid getting stepped on before springing to her feet. Holy crap, she *was* aboard the *Heptoral*, in the cavernous transport bay—only this time it was bursting at the seams with women.

What in God's was going on here? The candidates weren't supposed to be beamed up for weeks, and she sure as hell wasn't a candidate.

Grabbing the first arm she saw, she asked, "What happened? Why are we here?"

The boxy blonde looked frightened. "The compound was under attack, so they evacuated us."

"Under attack! By whom?"

"I don't know. Didn't you hear the jets?"

"No, I..." Jasmine frowned. Yes, she'd heard jets, but she'd been dozing off and thought they were part of the movie.

Well that was just fabulous. Was she ever going to get away from these brutes?

She made her way toward the edge of the bay, taking note of her surroundings. There were a dozen or more guards lining the bay's upper tier, watching over the crowd like long-haired cowboys minding a herd of cattle.

She shuddered. *Cattle*. That was an apt analogy for what these women were to the Garathani, who were paying eight-figure settlements to the families of every candidate who accompanied them on the one-way trip to Garathan. Most of them had been selected for their ability to bear the aliens' extra-large offspring, and the rest for their ability to accommodate the aliens sexually. Garathani males couldn't ejaculate unless both their primary and secondary sexual organs were buried to the hilt in a female, which was why they'd come to Earth, looking for women when most of theirs were wiped out by the Narthani biowar virus. While human females didn't have corresponding nooks to accommodate the spurs like Garathani females did, their anuses had proven an acceptable alternative for receiving the finger-sized secondary projections.

Deliberately blinking away the memory of Shauss' spur emerging above his rampant penis, she stood up on tiptoe and looked over the sea of feminine heads for Dr. Snow's white pompadour. The idea that all these women were basically selling their bodies to aliens made her skin crawl. It would be different if they were doing it for love—love made even the oddest matches acceptable—but they weren't. They were letting a computer and some alien committee determine which males they wound up with almost sight unseen. God only knew what the rest of their lives would be like.

And God only knew what hers would be like if she didn't get her *perfectly good piece of ass* off this ship, pronto. She had to find Dr. Snow or Noah Beaumont. If any Terrans aboard knew what was going on, they would.

Her watch chimed. Going tense, she patted her pocket and sagged with relief to feel the outline of her nasal spray bottle. After a quick look around, she pulled it out and inhaled two quick puffs in each nostril before stuffing it back in her pocket. Crap, it was hot in here!

She pulled the sweater off and hooked it over her shoulder before weaving her way through the crowd again. Too bad she hadn't worn a T-shirt instead of this thermal undershirt—she was going to die in this heat.

Twenty minutes later the only thing she'd discovered was that they were locked in. Damn it, where were the medical and support personnel? Between doctors, executives and maintenance, there'd been at least thirty men living at the compound, but so far she had yet to see one of them. In fact, all she'd seen were the candidates, and there was no way she wanted to be included in that cattle call.

"Could someone please tell me what the hell is going on here?" she finally yelled at the top of her lungs.

A handful of female voices echoed the call.

"The minister will address your concerns shortly," a disembodied male voice announced.

"That's not good e—ow!" She tried to jerk away from the fingers pinching her elbow.

"Haven't you caused enough problems?" Shauss growled in her ear.

Her face flamed. Why him of all people? Hadn't she been humiliated enough? "Get your hands off me!"

In an instant, everything around them disappeared into a white void.

"The candidates are already on the verge of revolt," he said, glaring down at her. "The last thing they need is a former compound employee with a grudge leading the charge."

"I'm entitled to a grudge or two, don't you think?" she snapped, trying to pry his steely fingers off her. "You've kept me locked in my room for the last three days. I don't know what you call that on Garathan, but on Earth it's known as false imprisonment and punishable by several years in prison."

"Actually," he said in an informational tone, "unlawful restraint in the state of Montana is punishable by a fine of no more than five hundred dollars or a jail sentence of no more than six months."

She blinked. How the hell did he know that?

"However," he continued, "your restraint was in no way unlawful. You were a confessed accomplice in the abduction of our mate."

"He tricked me and you know it!"

"All the more reason to keep you on a tight leash. Peserin knows who would use you against us next."

"I'm no one's puppet!" she ground out.

His arch look made her want to scream—and cry. Damn the ambassador for permanently wrecking her credibility!

Taking a deep breath, she told him, "I just want to go home now."

"That's not an option at this point."

"What could I possibly do to you from Earth?"

"That's a very good question, and one we would just as soon not have to contend with at the moment. Hence, you will remain aboard."

"That's not acceptable." She slapped at his hand again. "And let go of me, damn it! You're cutting off my circulation."

Her heart went into overdrive when he twisted her arm behind her and jerked her against him. Leaning down, he said, "Miss King, my patience with you wears thin. Hold your tongue until the minister has addressed the candidates or suffer the consequences."

Though she was trembling, she managed to pant, "Screw you."

"Ah, you'd like that, wouldn't you?" She tried to look away, but he grabbed her chin and forced her hot face up to his. Stroking her jaw with his thumb, he breathed into her open mouth, "Were you very disappointed that I left your ass intact?"

Burning with humiliation, she swung a fist at him but he grabbed her wrist and twisted it behind her back with the other. The action arched her body more fully against his and she was startled to feel the hardness of his cock poking at her belly.

"Don't get too excited," he told her coldly. "That's not for you."

"You're despicable," she hissed.

"Be still and listen to the minister."

Although the white void remained, the voices of those around them were suddenly audible, and judging from the whispers, all the women were giving the field surrounding them a wide berth.

"I hope she's okay," someone said.

"Ladies, if I may have your attention, please." Minister Cecine's voice boomed in the open bay and all conversation ceased. "I apologize for your unexpected removal from the planet's surface but time was of the essence. As I was explaining in the auditorium, unknown enemies have been circulating anti-Garathani propaganda to the Earth's major media, and now those enemies have committed an unspeakable act of terror against your planet. Less than two hours ago, six major Terran military bases were simultaneously destroyed by abbarint devices."

"Oh my God!"

"Hush," Shauss hissed in her ear.

Jasmine froze, her heart racing out of control. She tried to wrap her head around the minister's words but nothing could get past the feel of Shauss' silken hair brushing her face. The cool mass felt almost alive as it caressed her cheek. Would it taste as good as it smelled? She could see herself pulling a strand between her lips like a honeysuckle style and delicately skimming its nectar onto her tongue, could almost taste the cloves and honey and fresh, clean—

Crap! Her eyes popped open. What in God's name was she doing?

"Although every component required to synthesize the abbarain molecule is available on Earth," the minister continued after the women's noisy reaction subsided, "Terrans lack the technology to do so, and thus suspicion fell naturally to us. When American bombers targeted the compound, we felt it prudent to evacuate all residents to the *Heptoral*. The compound itself has since been vaporized."

Horror cramped in her abdomen. The compound was gone. Her workout equipment, her plants, her DVDs, her computer...all toast.

And if the Garathani hadn't beamed her aboard, she'd be toast too.

Cecine's voice snapped her back to attention. "Until diplomatic relations have stabilized, you will all remain aboard as our guests. If the process takes more than a few days, we will house you on Garathan until we are certain that you will suffer no undue consequences upon your return as a result of your association with the Garathani."

"What!" She struggled again. "There is no way I'm going to Garathan. I mean it, Shauss—I have to go home."

Shauss didn't respond, and the minister waited for the candidates' dismayed reaction to die down before he went on. "Since mating assignments have not been completed, it will take time to work out living arrangements, but we will endeavor to make you all comfortable and address your most pressing needs. There are Terran physicians aboard to see to your medical care and we can replicate any medications you require."

Jasmine cringed. What about her nasal spray? There wasn't enough left for a few days, much less a scenic cruise to Garathan, and no way could she let them replicate it.

Shauss suddenly released her and the field dissolved. "Your name will be called when your quarters are assigned," he said. "Now mind your manners so I don't have to come back."

He walked off while her brain was still wrestling with the nasal spray problem, saving her the trouble of formulating a withering reply. While it was a relief to have him away from her, and certainly much easier to think, she felt a ridiculous sense of abandonment when he disappeared from view. She did *not* belong among all these women.

Then she noticed them all staring at her and blushed.

"Everything's fine, nothing to look at here," she said under her breath, picking up her sweater, which she'd dropped at some point.

She had to get off this ship or die trying.

Chapter Two

Shauss arrived at the transport pad five minutes before the assigned time. Not surprisingly, Kellen was already there in his polished dress uniform, a ceremonial dagger tucked into the sheath at his waist.

When his eyes dropped pointedly to Shauss' dagger, which he'd carefully not worn since Monica used it to put a hole in him, Shauss said with a wry smile, "I'm feeling adventurous this morning."

"That's good. President Landon's bodyguards likely won't be any more welcoming than Monica was." He nodded at Holligan. "You may power up at will, Ensign."

"Aye, Commander." The flare generator began to hum.

"We could just send him a written invitation on a flaming arrow," Shauss suggested.

"While that would get the point across quite effectively," Kellen said dryly as they stepped onto the platform, "it is the council's wish that we reestablish face-to-face relations before the Terrans can work themselves into even more of a frenzy."

"Get them back in the saddle?"

"Exactly." He grinned. "I'm enjoying the western flavor of your banter this morning, Shauss."

"It seems appropriate to the occasion."

After a moment's hesitation, Kellen sent privately, with obvious care, *"Monica is worried about you."*

"Worried about me? For Peserin's sake, why?"

"You departed rather abruptly after your claiming."

Shauss raised a brow. *"Was I supposed to tap you on the shoulder for a mid-coitus group hug?"*

Kellen directed a speaking look his way but said nothing, which suited Shauss just fine. He had claimed Monica in the mutually agreed-upon manner two nights past and taken his leave when it became obvious his presence would not be missed. What was there to discuss?

"Transport systems at full power, Commander."

"Commence flare, Ensign."

They'd barely been engulfed when the brain-piercing shriek of converging anharmonic flare membranes nearly drove Shauss to his knees. Trapped in the bubble, he had no choice but to clap his palms over his ears and brace himself for whatever awaited them.

Put your head between your knees and kiss your ass goodbye.

He would have sent the thought to Kellen, who stood in a similarly tortured pose, but Shauss couldn't even hear himself over the clash of energy membranes, which meant Empran couldn't pick him up either. Too bad—he wouldn't have minded having that bit of macabre Terran humor holoscribed on his memorial plates.

Six seconds after it had begun, the convergence ceased and they dropped their arms. They had an instant of blessed silence before their transport flare dissolved. Not surprisingly, they weren't in the Oval Office.

Kellen's eyes widened. *"What in Peserin's hell…?"*

Before them, in a harshly lit, low-ceilinged room, a crowd of sweaty Terran females gyrated to the rhythm of recorded music.

"Latin fusion," Shauss replied, nodding toward a banner on the side wall. *"Zumba perhaps?"* Hardly the worst possible outcome of a flare convergence but a startling development nonetheless—and not just for them.

Screams erupted as the females noticed their reflection on the mirrored front wall and scattered like billiard balls.

Sighing, Kellen ordered, "*Holligan, emergency flare-out, if you please.*"

A new flare field engulfed them and the low-ceilinged room disappeared.

"What happened?" Shauss asked.

"Flare deflection at its most benign, thank the Powers," Kellen replied grimly.

"I got that." Shauss stretched his jaw to relieve the stuffed feeling in his ears. "But where did it come from? It wasn't there yesterday."

They arrived back in the transport bay and Holligan immediately powered down the flare generator. "Trouble, Commander?"

"Trouble, indeed," Kellen replied as he stepped off the platform. "Empran, the council is still in chambers?"

"The minister and resident elders are currently in session with the general council," the computer reported.

Kellen strode out the door and down the port corridor at an urgent pace. "There's no way the American government could have developed defensive flare technology so quickly."

Shauss fell in beside him. "They had help."

"Without a doubt. I apologize, Shauss. My miscalculation could have cost you your life."

"Commander, no one could have foreseen—"

"Poppycock. I knew Pret was utilizing alien flare technology. I should have erred on the side of caution and led with a probe."

Shauss swallowed a snicker. *Poppycock?* "You do realize you won't come across as very fearsome using language like that with the Americans?"

"I suppose you would have said *bullshit*."

"That's what our obstreperous little mate would have said."

"Precisely. I can't very well take her to task for using foul language if I'm using it myself."

"Of course you can."

Kellen just smiled.

When they entered the council chamber, they found Minister Cecine and all four resident elders seated at the vast curved table. The twenty-six members of the general council, each seated at his own legislative desk, appeared in holographic assembly opposite them.

"Please forgive the interruption," Kellen said with a bow as all heads turned their way. "If we may have a few moments?"

Cecine addressed the assembly. "Gentlemen, let us adjourn the general session while the high council confers with Commander Kellen."

"As you wish," Braman said. The hologram disappeared, leaving the vast floor of the council chamber empty.

"You aborted your attempt to see the president?" Cecine asked.

Kellen dropped into his seat and gestured for Shauss to pull a chair over from the vacant gallery along the round arena's edge. "Someone aborted it for us. Our flare was deflected."

"Deflected?" Elder Luide echoed in the tremulous voice of the exceedingly old. "By whom?"

"That's the sixty-four-dollar question." When the elders looked at him blankly, Kellen said, "It's from an old… Never mind. It's not important."

Shauss stifled a grin. The commander delighted in the vagaries of American English, and his habitual and colorful use of the language often annoyed the elders, who had little contact with Terrans. If it wasn't included in the cerecom download they didn't want to hear it, much less try to understand it.

Leave it to the high council to fault an officer for his facility with languages.

"We slid approximately six miles from our target coordinates within the White House," Kellen continued, "so the deflection field must shield an area of at least one hundred thirteen square miles."

"You're fortunate to have returned whole," Cecine commented. "Follow exploratory contact protocols next time, Commander, so that I'm not forced to explain the gruesome details of your demise to my daughter."

There was a moment of silence and Shauss assumed they were all doing what he was—imagining him and Kellen arriving on the platform as one big, bloody pile of ground Garathani. Most of the more sophisticated defense systems bounced unauthorized flare bubbles back to their points of origin, while less powerful systems like the one encountered today simply slid them off their deflection field's perimeter. But a malicious few pulled the bubbles, which were almost pure energy, through magnetic netting that julienned everything—and everyone—inside. A reverse trip through the netting effectively minced what was left.

Monica would not be a happy camper if they returned in such a state.

The minister rose and began pacing around the table with his hands clasped behind his back and his crimson robes swirling around his ankles.

"Someone is determined to prevent us from reestablishing relations with the Terrans," he said. "Presumably that someone is limited to Terran energy sources, but we can take nothing for granted. We must operate on the assumption that another race is sharing advanced technology with the American government for the express purpose of sabotaging our long-term objectives here. No other vessels have approached the planet since our arrival, so we must also assume this other race preceded us."

"We can eliminate the Narthani as suspects," Elder Gillim rasped. Taking a deep breath, he continued. "They have no transports capable of traveling this distance."

Shauss was surprised he didn't collapse after such a lengthy speech—Gillim was even older than Luide and hadn't weathered the passing decades nearly as well.

"No." Cecine shook his head, scattering his flaming red hair across his shoulders. "We may have destroyed their long-range vessels, but the Narthani should top our list of suspect races. They're the single largest producer of flare technology after us, and there's nothing to prevent them from joining forces with some other race capable of interstellar travel."

"They've already proven themselves more than willing to commit genocide, which is why we're here in the first place," Kellen said—as if any of them needed reminding.

Kellen had lost his first mate and young daughter to the biowar virus, and the protracted cruelty of their deaths had nearly crushed him. He'd shown admirable restraint in executing the counterattack against the Narthani, but Shauss doubted Kellen would be able to maintain such self-control if anything happened to Monica, his little GaraTer hybrid. Shauss would have been none too happy himself. Just the thought of Monica's near-rape sent a red haze over his vision.

"Exactly." Cecine nodded. "They might view our mission here as an opportunity to take care of unfinished business."

"I'm inclined to believe these attacks are the work of some radical splinter group rather than an official government action."

"I concur, Commander." Cecine turned to the elders. "Let us open communications with Lord Sals and the Narthani parliament. Perhaps they can help us get to the bottom of the matter before any more innocent lives are lost."

"We must also devise some other means of conferring with President Landon," Kellen said. "We can't flare in, and we can hardly walk in. I'm open to suggestions, gentlemen."

Shauss stood, knowing Kellen would be obliged to participate in the general session now that their mission had been postponed. "It might be wise," he suggested, "to take another hard look at everyone aboard the *Heptoral*. Wide-array flares don't discriminate between friend and foe, and Miss King in particular has already proven herself easily swayed by those in league against us."

When the American bombers targeted the compound, there hadn't been time to check IDs. They'd simply herded everyone—doctors, copulative candidates and support staff alike—into the auditorium like sheep and flared them out by the hundreds. Nearly forgotten in the confusion, Miss King and her guards had been the final residents retrieved in a last-minute flare sweep of the compound.

Kellen stared at him for a moment before replying, "Indeed. Consider yourself assigned."

After a quick salute for the council, Shauss headed for the door. *"Empran, research Jasmine King. Download detailed history, including a record of all her communications for the past five years, to my quarters."*

"Affirmative."

His walk was slower than usual as he made his way toward the tranlift, examining his uncustomary eagerness to lay more blame at Miss King's feet. He'd never been so enthusiastic about carrying out an order as he was when Kellen commanded him to attack her. The efficient, almost too-perfect little female had always intrigued him. Something in her eyes, a vulnerability lurking just beneath her finely polished surface, had made him itch to dig into her, to discover what it was she was hiding.

When he'd heard Monica and Nurse Bonham discussing her "crush" on him, he'd felt almost indulgent toward her. Then Monica had disappeared, and the discovery that Miss King was hiding a duplicitous nature rather than any fondness for him had made him treat her more brutally than he might have otherwise. He wasn't just interrogating Jasmine to get

Monica back—he was terrorizing her for his own dark pleasure and drinking in her screams for mercy with unholy satisfaction.

Unreasonable possessiveness had hammered him at the sight of her tender, bare privates—a rather idiotic reaction, considering Terran women depilated at will and a hairless cunt was no indicator of innocence. But the knowledge hadn't stopped him from burning to ram his cock into *her* hairless cunt, to stake his claim on it and warn off potential rivals.

He'd never wanted to fuck a female as badly as he'd wanted to fuck Jasmine King, and he'd very nearly done it. He *would* have fucked her if Kellen hadn't redirected their efforts. Although she appeared to have been victimized by Pret every bit as much as they, something in him had howled ferociously at being denied the opportunity to punish her with his cock. Seeing her lose control of her bodily functions in his grip hadn't eased his physical craving for her in the least. On the contrary, witnessing her abject humiliation had flooded him with a sense of his own absolute power over her.

In that moment, he'd never felt more repulsive. He despised nothing so much as a tyrant who thrilled to another's debasement. He'd given himself a stern dressing-down…and then promptly sprouted an erection the very next time he saw her.

Peserin, what was wrong with him? He'd just reclaimed his mate two nights ago, albeit in the ass. Garathani law didn't specify exactly which orifice a male must ejaculate in for the bond to be finalized, so he'd chosen the one that was least likely to tie him to Monica forever. Theirs was a tentative bond that he honestly couldn't see lasting more than a few months—just long enough for Kellen to find a more acceptable second—but it was more than Shauss had ever expected to have. So why this desire for the confounding, deceitful Miss King?

When he stepped into the tranlift, several males filed in after him.

"Baya Deck," one of them requested.

"This ought to be interesting," another said with a snicker.

Ah, yes—the demonstration was this morning.

When the door opened on Baya Deck, they all crowded out. "Coming, Lieutenant?"

Shauss hesitated and then stepped out. "Why not?"

* * * * *

What in God's name was she doing on the bridge?

Go back to your quarters, you idiot—now, before you get yourself killed!

But Jasmine couldn't move. The object of her darkest cravings stood at his post beside the commander's chair, his beautiful hair falling like a curtain of black-and-blue silk over his shoulders, his hands clasped behind him as he focused on the viewscreen ahead.

Tha-*thump*.

Tha-*thump*.

Tha-*thump*.

The heavy, ponderous heartbeat she'd come to expect whenever they were in the same room kicked in, and she leaned heavily against the handrail, her eyes devouring the leanly muscled back Shauss' sleek uniform did little to hide.

Her throat seized when he glanced her way. He didn't react at all, but his awareness bored into her like a laser probe. He was willing her to come closer, and unable to help herself, she went, although she fought it every step of the way. The other Garathani warriors on the bridge seemed to be oblivious to her presence, but she knew they would watch avidly as Shauss took her, stroking themselves and hoping for a turn with her.

Anticipation made the air thick and hard to breathe, and Jasmine cursed herself yet again. How could the prospect of being taken in front of a roomful of barbaric aliens turn her insides to liquid fire?

As if he could read her thoughts, Shauss' cock began to stir beneath his skintight suit, but he didn't move, didn't look at her.

Her mouth watered as she crowded closer, drinking him in without touching. Lord, he smelled so savory-warm and sweet. She brought her face within a hairsbreadth of his chest, inhaling deeply, and energy buzzed between them. His sculpted lips were an irresistible temptation, but she hesitated. The last time she'd come so close to this man, she'd barely escaped with her sanity intact. If she gave in now, she'd lose herself completely.

Then his eyes captured hers, and the power swirling in their liquid obsidian depths crushed the breath from her chest. If there'd been condemnation in his gaze, she would have crawled away, weeping, and blown herself out the nearest airlock. Instead she saw understanding, caring…

Permission.

A sob of gratitude burst from her as she threw herself at him, instinctively climbing his body in a frantic race to get what she needed. She wrapped her legs around his waist, clutching at whatever she could get a hold of. The tall, pointed ears grazing her fingertips gave her a moment's pause, but then her hands slid into his silky hair and her lips landed on his and suddenly nothing else mattered.

She sucked Shauss' tongue into her mouth and her world ignited in a kaleidoscope of color and scent and dizzying need that made her whimper. God, she couldn't get enough of his tongue! Long and agile, it tasted like hot spiced wine and something more personal, something that sent her pulse skyrocketing. His intoxicating flavor seared through her bloodstream, sparking an instant addiction. The more of him she swallowed, the more she craved.

Agonizing need gripped her abdomen and she groaned as she rocked her hips against his hardness, desperate for the release only he could give.

Then his hands seized her forearms, jerking her away from him, and she strained forward with her mouth wide open in a frenzied attempt to get his tongue back.

His smile doused her passion like a bucket of icy water.

"Now that you've had a taste of me, Miss King," he said, spreading her arms wide to expose her naked body, "let's see what kind of disgusting creature you turn into."

She fought to break free of his hold, to run away and hide, but it was too late—she was changing. Dread cramped her insides as her bones popped and stretched, and her skin rippled into a scaly exoskeleton. It only took seconds for her to shift from a pretty human into a hideous monster, hissing and dripping slimy acid from her yawning, fang-studded mouth.

Shauss shoved her away, revulsion evident in every line of his face and body, and the other warriors all gagged and retched at the sight of her. Burning with shame, she staggered toward the tranlift, only to find Shauss blocking her path. He assumed a fighting stance, swinging a huge, gleaming broadsword over his head with both hands.

"Now you die, alien bitch."

Oh God, he was going to chop off her head…

"No!" Jasmine jerked straight up in the dark, her hand at her throat.

Blankets rustled on the other bed. "What the hell! Are you okay?"

"Bad dream."

"You scared the crap out of me," Portia grumbled.

"I'm sorry." Honest to God, it was like someone had hacked into her brain and planted a Trojan horse that created increasingly bizarre pop-ups every time she closed her eyes.

"Yeah, me too."

Jasmine pressed the button to illuminate her watch face and then threw back the covers. "I'm going for a run."

"You've got to be joking. What time is it?"

"Seven-fifteen. Empran, wardrobe light, twenty-five watts."

Portia groaned. "Oh shit, I just got to bed three hours ago."

"Go back to sleep." Not that Portia needed her permission to do that, since even at the compound, she'd never crawled out of bed before the crack of noon. On paper she was a secretary, or at least she'd started out that way, but in reality she hadn't shown up for a shift at the secretarial pool for months. And yet apparently no one had shown her the door. What she did with all her time in an environment brimming with horny aliens, Jasmine didn't even want to speculate about.

She snagged her Garathani-issued tank suit from the wardrobe and pulled on the light, stretchy garment with jerky movements before stepping into the bathing area. When the light came on automatically, she splashed her face with cold water from the fountain but avoided looking at her reflection. The commander had explained to everyone how the flare fields that had transported them from the surface also functioned as lighting, windows and mirrors on board the *Heptoral*, but he'd failed to mention how the versatile energy bubbles could be used for covert observation.

It was a secret she felt bad keeping from the rest of her fellow Terrans, but if the Garathani really wanted to spy on anyone, raising a stink would only prompt them to replace the reflective fields with invisible fields. Worse, it would draw more unwanted attention to her familiarity with Garathani technology.

After blotting her face, she dabbed a little vanilla on her pulse points. Then she grabbed her nasal spray off the shelf.

The tiny, hollow splash when she shook it made her cringe, but she braced herself, inserted the tip into her nostril and squeezed anyway.

Nothing.

"Come on, come on," she muttered. "Please God, just one more dose."

Apparently God wasn't listening because three more tries yielded nothing but the sweet scent of her medication.

She snapped the cap back on the bottle with a shaky hand. Crap, talk about situation critical! That spray was the only thing standing between her and the transformation of her nightmares. She had two choices now—she could ask to have the spray replicated and hope that whoever handled it was too busy or too stupid to recognize it for what it was, or she could execute her insane escape plan.

Talk about your no-win scenario. Where was Jim Kirk when you needed him?

Taking a deep breath, she bit the bullet. "Empran, where can I get medications replicated?"

"Original replication requires the approval of Commander Kellen."

She sighed. "Of course it does."

Too bad she hadn't gotten the spray replicated two days ago when she was just one of hundreds of hysterical women. Now she'd have to face the commander conspicuously alone and explain why she hadn't gotten in line with everyone else. Hopefully the replication lab was so backed up they wouldn't have time to scrutinize every med that came through.

"Where can I find the commander?"

"Commander Kellen is currently on the Command Deck."

Ugh. The Command Deck would be bristling with Garathani warriors, and since Terrans were only allowed supervised access to that deck, she would have to have an escort. Ugh.

Swallowing a surge of fear, she pulled her suit down and dabbed more vanilla under her arms and in the creases between her legs. Her father had told her it would mask the scent of any pheromones she might emit, so she'd worn it every day at the compound. Fortunately, the steward in the candidates' mess hall had been as accommodating as possible of their dietary requests and hadn't batted an eye when she asked for her own bottle of vanilla extract.

Tugging the suit back up and pulling her jeans on over it, she slipped the nasal spray into her pocket and left behind the gentle snuffle of Portia's snoring. The biologic pad felt gross against the soles of her feet as she strode down the corridor, but it was either go barefoot or wear the Garathani-issue knee-high boots, which were too hot even without her wool socks.

Stepping into the tranlift, she turned to face the door as it closed behind her. "Command Deck, please."

She didn't feel any movement but assumed the car was going down. When the door slid open, her path was blocked by an all-too-familiar mountain of flesh.

Wonderful. Maybe she should just space herself now and get it over with.

"You again," she said in a bored tone, noting the insignia on his collar. "Shouldn't you be out grinding up someone's bones for bread or something, Sub-lieutenant?"

"*Lieutenant* is the proper form of address."

She gave him a brittle smile. "I know."

Zannen's flat black eyes raked over her and it was all she could do not to cover her girl parts with her hands. She absolutely hated being without her bra. "What are you doing down here? Copulative candidates aren't allowed on this level."

"I'm not a candidate and you know it," she said. "Tell Commander Kellen that Jasmine King needs to speak with him at once."

"The commander isn't available. Perhaps you should report to Infirmary Three next week with the rest of the candidates. I understand mate assignments are to resume—"

"I am *not* one of the candidates," she enunciated clearly, "and I do *not* need to report to Infirmary Three. What I *need* is to speak to Commander Kellen. Today. Not next week, not tomorrow—today."

"As I said, he's not available."

Jasmine ground her teeth in frustration. Maybe she should space *him*. She'd scoped out a couple of airlocks and knew how they worked. "This is a matter of life and death, Lieutenant."

The oaf continued to stare and she fought the urge to fidget. No doubt she looked awful, and not just because the evacuee packages hadn't included cosmetics. Sleep was even harder to come by on the ship than at the compound, and when she finally did nod off, her wild dreams left her feeling even more exhausted and frantic. She'd dozed for a few minutes yesterday afternoon and dreamed she was running on the Frisco bike trail, basking in her freedom and trembling with the anticipation of hugging her mother again—waking aboard the *Heptoral* had been such a cruel shock, she'd very nearly burst into tears.

Just remembering that moment made her eyes and nose prickle, and Jasmine immediately turned away. Screw him. He obviously wasn't going to lift a finger to help her, and she wasn't going to stand there and entertain him by bawling like a baby.

His voice stopped her. "You may proceed to the atrium on Baya Deck. Someone there should be able to help you."

She pivoted and stared at him. "Why the change of heart?"

"You did say it was a matter of life and death."

The gleam in his eye and the smug curve of his lips belied his neutral tone, but at this point she had little choice but to go where the brute sent her.

"Baya Deck—isn't access to that level restricted?"

"I'll authorize you."

"How do I get to the atrium?"

"Step back."

When she did, a three-dimensional schematic of the *Heptoral* appeared in the air between them. He pointed to the jagged red line marking her route. "Go left from the command center to tranlift three and take it up two levels to Baya Deck. From there, go right to the second intersection and make another right. The atrium is at the end of the corridor."

She opened her mouth to issue grudging thanks, but another red line appeared on the schematic, branching away from the first.

"Mine is the third door on the left in the opposite corridor, if you don't find what you need in the atrium," he said, his tone dripping with suggestion.

"Not if you were the last male in the galaxy," she replied with a mocking look. Probably not smart to taunt a man she looked squarely in the diaphragm, but her reservoir of sweetness and light was running on empty.

He raised one dark brow. "You wouldn't say that if you'd seen my cock. I'll wager it's bigger than the commander's."

"I'll wager you can't say the same about your brain," she snapped. Lord, the last thing she wanted to think about was Garathani cocks, especially his. "But I'll be sure and tell him you said so."

An annoying grin split his big face. "You do that."

* * * * *

Shauss shook his head absently as he looked at the nude figure on the dais. Only Hastion would volunteer to masturbate in front of hundreds of horny warriors.

"Be careful who you make eye contact with," he warned, *"or someone might take it as an invitation."*

Hastion's ice-blue eyes immediately focused on him. *"The homosexual mating demonstration hasn't been scheduled yet, but I'm game if you are."*

"Bend over then, Ensign."

"After you, Lieutenant."

Shauss chuckled silently. *"Monica might as well give up on that pipe dream. While some may be willing to administer an ass-fucking, no Garathani male would willingly accept one."*

His smile faded at the memory of Monica's finger probing his waste canal. It would be a frigid day in the Inzeled nebula before he allowed anyone else, male or female, that kind of control over him again.

Dr. Ketrok stepped up beside Hastion.

"This is a masturbation probe," he announced, holding up one of the silver spheres in his palm. "It's a myzare probe that has been reconfigured to induce ejaculation by detecting and stimulating the prostate gland."

Shauss shifted uncomfortably. As far as he knew, Ketrok had kept his unwilling role in the discovery of anal orgasm to himself. Hopefully the good doctor would be as discreet about the probe's origins.

"Used in conjunction with manual stimulation of the penis," Ketrok continued, "and applied after spur emergence, the probe has proven to be one hundred percent effective. Since Ensign Hastion has been kind enough to stimulate himself to emergence, he will now demonstrate proper use."

Shauss barely suppressed a snort. Proper use barely required instruction, much less demonstration, but the high council thought warriors might require reassurance that no stigma would be attached to allowing the probe access to their waste canals. Of course most of the council had been dead from the waist down for decades and had forgotten the urgency of unspent sexual energy—otherwise they would realize that no young, healthy warrior would let fear of being shunned by his peers prevent him from seeking release after years of deprivation.

Hastion scooped the probe from Ketrok's palm and turned to display his profile. Reaching behind him, he placed the shimmering sphere against his buttocks, where it immediately began reassembling into its new matrix.

A disturbance made Hastion look up and grin. Following his gaze to the port entry, Shauss sighed. What in Peserin's name was Monica doing in here? The last thing this restless crew needed was exposure to a mature Garathani female, and a gorgeous one at that.

He shot her a look that said *leave*, but she came right over beside him and leaned against the back wall to observe Hastion's display, giving every indication of clinical detachment. Shauss sighed again. Kellen must have let her know he'd returned safely and was trapped in the general session—she'd obviously decided to go on the offensive.

"In the corridor," he said under his breath.

"But I just got here," she whispered back.

"And now you're just leaving."

She ignored him.

"A probe's programming," Ketrok continued, "can be customized to the user's preferences. The size and shape can be modified to mimic one or more fingers, or even a penis. Its programmed functions include heat, vibration of varying speeds and intensities, gyration, and thrusting motion similar to intercourse."

The crowd of macho warriors took a moment to eye each other suspiciously and Shauss looked skyward with a sigh. What was Ketrok thinking, going on about the probe's intercourse functions? Shauss had incorporated the penile matrices not with males in mind, but with some vague idea of using them to torture Monica.

That would teach him to indulge his libidinous impulses in the tech labs.

Hastion groaned, his agitation growing as the probe's sinuous, seductive finger zeroed in on his prostate. The heightened color in Monica's cheeks as she watched told Shauss she wasn't as detached as she liked to pretend — the hardened nipples straining against her wrapsuit told him it was time to get her out of there before she started emitting a pheromone stream that would make it impossible to protect her.

Grabbing her arm, he pulled her into the corridor. "What was so important that it couldn't wait until after the demonstration?"

She shot him a glare. "It could have waited, but you'd have disappeared. Again."

"I never disappear, Monica. Empran is aware of my whereabouts at all times."

"Empran is a cold bitch who lives to fuck with me."

"Empran is a computer," he said as he ducked into a nearby consult room. "She doesn't live, and she certainly doesn't fuck with anyone."

"That's what you—" *Thud!* "Ouch!"

Shauss turned to see her kick the half-open door as she rubbed her forehead.

"God damn it, see what I mean?" she snarled, wrapping her hands around the door's edge and forcing it open far enough to slide into the room. "Fucking cyber-bitch! I swear to God she's out to get me."

He tried not to feel guilty about ordering Empran to make it difficult for Monica to follow him. The computer had obviously taken his orders a little too literally.

Knowing exactly why she was stalking him, he invited her to sit at the consult table.

"You've been avoiding me," she accused as she flopped into the chair.

"I've been busy."

"Busy, my ass. Doing what?"

"Well, you don't think that myzare probe was actually designed with prostate stimulation in mind, do you?"

"So that's your doing, huh? Very original, but it couldn't have taken that long to reprogram it."

"Monica," he said in an eminently reasonable tone, "I do have obligations as an officer of the Garathani fleet, and in addition to my regular duties and modifying the probe, I've been assisting with evacuee management—not to mention trying to track down Pret's accomplices."

"Yeah, and you have a mate you haven't set eyes on since the day we rebonded."

"That was only two days ago, and Kellen and I have both been busy."

"At least Kellen slept with me last night. You couldn't even be bothered to answer my messages." When he didn't reply, she continued. "You just got back together with us to protect me from having to accept another mate, didn't you? Admit it—I was a pity fuck."

His bark of laughter was harsh. "You have the nerve to say that to *me*?"

She recoiled as if he'd struck her. "You're not a pity fuck to me, Shauss," she said in a dangerous voice. "I thought we both benefited from being bonded."

"We do," he said, striving for a reasonable tone. "And I'll take ample advantage of those benefits when time allows."

Monica stared at him for a moment, and then said, "Kellen explained to me about your spur being...the wrong shape for my nook. I didn't know that could happen."

It took every ounce of his self-control to meet her gaze because, to a certain extent, she was correct about his motives for rebonding with them. The realization that her nook was too small to accommodate his unusually wide spur had rung the death knell for any hope that he might one day be on equal footing with Kellen in their bond, but he hadn't wanted to force her into accepting another mate she neither knew nor cared for. He, at least, was a known quantity, and she had professed to love him — though not to be *in love* with him the way she was with Kellen.

Restricting himself to anal sex with her served a threefold purpose. It allowed him to take her face-to-face, with his spur in her vagina. It prevented pregnancy, and thus the possibility of their being permanently bound. And it gave Shauss the illusion of having a part of Monica that was his alone.

And an illusion it was — Monica belonged heart and soul to Kellen, and despite the man's alleged distaste for taking her anally, there was no doubt he would eventually claim every part of her.

"So you understand," he finally said, "that my already-slim odds of finding a compatible Garathani mate were reduced to virtually zero by the biowar attack."

She nodded. "I also understand that the spur situation is just one more reason why you feel like you're a pity fuck to me. But that knife cuts both ways, Shauss. It makes me feel like a consolation prize to you too, someone you have to settle for because your real mate probably — "

"You *are* my real mate." Heaving an exasperated sigh, he reached over and took one of her hands between his. "Monica, I know you believe that you and Kellen have some kind of predestined love, but as a rule, we Garathani don't subscribe to the concept of soul mates. Even before the biowar attack, we tended to mate for expediency, and since then we've had to approach mating even more pragmatically. You are as real a mate as I could ever have expected to have."

She shrugged out of his hold and crossed her arms over his chest. "That's not what you told me in the atrium. You said you couldn't settle for anything less than what I have with Kellen. And yet…" She arched one eloquent brow at him.

Shauss digested that for a moment before replying carefully, "That was…a temporary aberration."

"From which you've now recovered."

The blatant skepticism coloring her tone made him grit his teeth. Peserin, but she was obstinate.

He was casting around for a way to draw her off point when he was paged. *"Tiber to Lieutenant Shauss."*

"Shauss here. What is it, Doctor?"

"There's an unconscious candidate in the atrium port corridor."

"I'm on my way." Shauss frowned as he rose from his seat. What was a candidate doing down here? To Monica, he said, "My apologies, sweet one, but I'm required in the port entry."

"Saved by the bell, huh?" she said, standing as well. "Maybe I'll go with you."

He swept his arm toward the door. "Be my guest. You might be needed."

Chapter Three

☙

Jasmine frowned in her dream. It felt wonderful to be held like a child again, but something wasn't right. "Shauss?"

Unfamiliar voices rumbled around her and her heartbeat picked up as she started to struggle. Or she would have struggled if her body didn't weigh ten times what it normally did.

"You're not Shauss," she mumbled. "Where's Shauss?"

The arms holding her shifted and she gasped at the brief sensation of weightlessness. Then suddenly she was where she belonged.

She sighed with relief, soaking up nirvana with her nose as she snuggled into that solid, masculine chest. If someone would hand her a spoon, she'd gobble him right up.

"Hey, Stepford, can you hear me?" Cool fingers patted her cheek. "Jasmine?"

She stirred reluctantly and frowned. Monica's voice was an unwelcome variation. Time to wake up before her lovely dream turned to another nightmare.

When she managed to lift her heavy eyelids, Shauss was still holding her. Apparently knowing she was asleep didn't mean she could wake on command.

"Will you ever stop haunting my dreams, Lieutenant?" she murmured.

This time his dark eyes held nothing more threatening than a man's inquisitive awareness of a woman, and figuring she might as well enjoy herself before the dream went to hell, Jasmine slid a hand up into his long, slick hair. Noting the absence of Spock ears with relief, she pulled his face down to hers for another one of those delicious kisses.

The minute their lips met, she let her eyes close and drew his tongue into her mouth. His flavor was more subtle this time but no less intriguing, and her breath quickened along with her pulse as longing gripped her insides.

Shauss squeezed her closer to his chest as his tongue circled hers once, twice. When he tried to withdraw, she bit down none too gently to hold him in place and felt his cock surge against her hip.

He tore his mouth away from hers and stared down at her with a frown.

Sighing her regret, Jasmine smoothed a fingertip over the crease between his fine black brows and his grip tightened again on her ribs and thigh.

"Not in the mood tonight, huh?" she asked. "That's okay. Maybe we should just skip the sex and the dripping fangs this time and go straight to the sword. I'm tired of dreading it." She rested her head on his shoulder and closed her eyes again, snaking her arms around his chest and holding him tight. "I've heard that if you fall off a cliff in a dream and hit bottom, you actually die. Does that mean that if you chop off my head in this dream, I'll wake up decapitated?"

The very idea should scare the bejeebers out of her, but somehow it just didn't matter right now.

"Jasmine," came that wry feminine voice again, "what you just said is wrong on so many levels, I don't even know where to start, but if I were you, I'd wake the fuck up."

"Monica?" She opened her eyes again and tried to focus.

"Girl, you are freaking me out. Did you hit your head on something?"

Jasmine frowned. "I don't know. I..."

Then she noticed the spiky-haired blond guy crouched beside Monica. As big as he was, she should probably be nervous, but he didn't look dangerous. In fact, he looked like a ski patrolman, someone she could trust with her life. His clear brown eyes were filled with concern and curiosity as he stared back at her. The lines and creases on his lean, tanned face spoke of both laughter and pain, and yet his expression held no trace of bitterness.

He smiled. "Hello."

"Hi," she said breathlessly. "Do I know you?"

"Jasmine," Monica said, "meet Tiber. He's the one who scraped you off the atrium floor."

"Hmm?" Jasmine blinked at her. "Atrium? What was I doing there?"

"We were about to ask you the same question." The harshness in Shauss' voice made the bottom drop out of her stomach. She hid her face in his chest and tried to hang on to the contentment that was beginning to evaporate with every accelerating beat of her heart. "What sort of life-and-death matter could compel you to intrude on a Garathani sexual demonstration?"

If his tone wasn't enough to make her stomach roll, his words sent the image of a naked warrior through her mind.

"No!" she cried, squeezing her eyes shut tight. She didn't want to remember that.

"Back off, Shauss," Monica ordered. "You're the last person who should be quizzing her after what you did."

"What *I* did?" He sounded offended. "*She* kissed *me*, remember?"

"I wasn't talking about that."

"It can wait until she's more comfortable, Lieutenant," Tiber said.

"I don't know, Doctor," Shauss returned. "She seems quite comfortable to me."

Doctor. Tiber was a Garathani doctor.

She wasn't dreaming now, was she?

"Oh my God!" She tried to bolt off Shauss' lap and the world tilted.

"Take it easy, Jas," Monica said.

Shauss' hard hands grasped her waist. "I've got her."

That's what he thought. Throwing her weight forward, she managed to jerk free of his grasp and tumble onto the padded floor. She scrambled over to a couch and leaned against it, pulling her knees up to her chest. The nasal spray bottle digging into her hip bone made her lightheaded with relief. Thank goodness she hadn't lost it.

"Where am I?" she gasped, breathing heavily. "How long was I out?"

"Apparently not long." Shauss stood over her. "And you're in Atrium Consult Three. Do you need to go to the infirmary?"

"No!" She tore her gaze away and shook her head emphatically. Even though she felt queasy, the infirmary was the last place she wanted to go.

A quick scan of the room revealed no sign of the bald mountain. Good. One less bastard to witness her ongoing humiliation.

Then she groaned and dropped her forehead to her knees. Dear God, she'd just kissed Shauss. In front of *Monica*. What else could she do to utterly screw herself?

"Seriously, Jas, calm down," Monica commanded. "No one here's going to hurt you."

Jasmine made a conscious effort to slow her heartbeat and respiration. Taking stock of her condition, she realized that, except for the dizziness and nausea that were probably to be expected after holding her breath until she passed out, she didn't really feel any different. She certainly wasn't experiencing the kind of intoxication Monica had after a significant exposure to male pheromones. Maybe there was no irreversible damage done after all.

"I'm fine," she said, raising her head with a shaky sigh.

"Are you sure? You look kind of shocky," Monica said. "After what you went through, it must have been an ugly surprise to walk in there and see all those guys."

"Totally ugly," Jasmine agreed faintly. The last thing she'd expected to see when she rounded the corner was a naked Ensign Hastion frantically stroking his engorged phallus. The spectacle had rooted her to the floor for an instant, her face in flames, before she noticed the hundreds of Garathani warriors also watching him. Then she'd taken one breathless step backward and run into a wall of muscle.

"Why were you there in the first place?" Shauss asked.

Jasmine looked at him then, letting her anger flare. "Because that baldheaded ape sent me there."

Shauss frowned. "Zannen?"

"How many baldheaded apes are on this ship?"

His lips quirked, making her heart skip another beat. "Just the one."

"Well, that's one too many."

"You should have left at once," he said severely. "A roomful of aroused Garathani is a dangerous place for a lone female."

"I tried! The jerk was right behind me and held me there, made me watch..." She swallowed, her heart jumping in her throat. God, she'd never been so terrified as when those fingers of iron closed around her upper arms and held her in place. She'd frozen, unable to look behind her. What if it was Shauss trapping her there?

What if it wasn't?

Then Zannen had murmured in her ear, "Leaving so soon? I thought it was a matter of life and death."

Fear of drawing the attention of all the males avidly watching the demonstration had kept her still and silent and, like an idiot, she'd held her breath instead of just breathing through her mouth. The pressure in her lungs had built to intolerable levels, and the last thing she remembered was Ensign Hastion shooting his semen across the stage.

"Why would he do that?" Shauss asked.

She threw her hands up. "Why do you people do anything?"

Feeling steadier, she got to her feet. Definitely better, though she still felt small and incredibly vulnerable next to all the tall bodies in the room. She walked over to look out the window. God, there it was—Earth! It looked deceptively, cruelly close. She started to put a hand out to touch it and then turned away.

"You have to admit he's an asshole, Shauss," Monica said. "When I go down there to see Kellen, he looks at me like something he scraped off his boot."

"Zannen's comportment in the presence of females has always left much to be desired," Tiber volunteered. "But otherwise he's a fine officer."

"You still haven't told us what you were doing at the command center, Miss King," Shauss reminded her. "Did you require some sort of assistance?"

Her fingers slid down to rest over the lump in her pocket. "I, uh, really need to talk to Monica. Alone. It's...female stuff."

Shauss regarded her quietly for a moment and she held her breath again. Maybe he wouldn't trust her alone with Monica.

Finally he gave a short nod and she released her pent-up breath with a gusty sigh. "Thank you."

He looked at her penetratingly for a moment before saying, "You've been ill served by two Garathani officers, and that reflects poorly on our entire race. Ambassador Pret has already been put to death for his treachery." When Jasmine gasped, he added, "Not by us—even in our young and relatively exuberant government, the wheels of justice do not roll quite so quickly. He was evidently executed by his own accomplices."

Jasmine's stomach contracted. The ambassador had *other* accomplices?

"We will, however, see that Zannen is appropriately censured before this watch ends," Shauss finished. "You may rest assured that he will no longer be a nuisance to you."

Thank you didn't seem like quite the right thing to say, so she just nodded.

He stared at her long enough to make painful heat rise in her cheeks before he and Tiber bowed and then left her alone with Monica.

* * * * *

"Lieutenant Zannen, report to Tactical Three."

After a pause, Zannen replied, *"Yes, Sir."*

Shauss strode toward the tranlift, every nerve ending abuzz, every muscle tense. He really should wait and let Kellen handle the ass chewing, but he just couldn't rest until Zannen knew how very off-limits Jasmine King was to him and every other male on the ship. If he lost control and beat the attitude out of the bastard, so much the better — satisfaction like that was worth being stripped of his rank and spending a few months in detention.

She had kissed him. He still could hardly believe it. Granted, she'd done so in the throes of some bizarre dream in which she'd apparently expected him to decapitate her...but she'd kissed him.

He licked his lower lip. Had any mouth ever tasted as sweet? Holding Jasmine in his arms, inhaling the fresh vanilla cream of her skin and tonguing the sweet delicacy of her mouth, had sent his hormones into hyperdrive and suddenly he'd been rock-hard and ready to throw her to the floor and fuck her senseless.

Shauss shook himself. What had he been thinking to respond to her like that — especially in front of his mate and

Tiber, of all people? What had *she* been thinking to kiss him like that?

The female was obviously dangerous and potentially deadly, and neither he nor Zannen nor any other Garathani needed to expose himself to that sort of risk. The sooner Zannen understood that, the better.

He stepped into the tranlift. "Command Deck."

Tiber stepped in behind him. "Some fascinating history between you and Miss King, I gather?"

"Mind your own business for once, Doctor."

"The mental well-being of the crew and passengers is my business, Lieutenant."

"My mental well-being is no more a cause for your concern now than it has ever been," Shauss said impatiently.

"I continue to have doubts about that," Tiber disagreed, "but right now it's Miss King's well-being I'm concerned with."

Shauss frowned, keeping his eyes firmly on the doors. Tiber had been a pain in his proverbial posterior for more years than he cared to remember. During his military intake physical, the doctor had tried unsuccessfully to ferret out the details of his parents' deaths and noted Shauss' lack of cooperation in his reports. As far as Shauss knew, that hadn't affected his career adversely, but then a murky psychological history could almost be considered a requirement in the line of specialization he'd eventually chosen.

Over the years, he'd endured the required annual psychological examinations and managed to stymie Tiber's every attempt to quantify him. Perhaps it was an assassin's natural paranoia, but he could swear Tiber had made understanding *him* his personal crusade—a crusade that Shauss was determined to see fail.

He'd imagined that being reassigned as Kellen's first lieutenant would mean an end to his annual torture sessions with the inquisitive psychological officer, and it had—until this assignment. Now, instead of suffering once a year, he was the victim of spontaneous encounters and casual quizzes at every turn.

Most recently, Tiber had been appointed by Minister Cecine to advise Shauss following his decision to annul the original bond with Kellen and Monica—after all, what male in his right mind would voluntarily sever ties with the minister's daughter and the commander of the *Heptoral*? Pride was of paramount importance to all Garathani males but few would let it stand in the way of such an advantageous alliance.

After hours of intensive questioning, Tiber had reluctantly conceded that Shauss might be one of those few. Shauss had hoped that rebonding with his mates would set the counselor at ease, but if anything, Tiber seemed even more puzzled and skeptical.

Now Tiber had even more ammunition to use in their little skirmishes—Jasmine King.

The door opened on Voya Deck and Kellen beckoned. "Ah, just the officers I was looking for. Come with me."

"I thought you were in chambers with the council all day," Shauss said, sending a message to Zannen to wait for him as he followed Kellen down the corridor.

"Rendal called me out to see this." Kellen stopped and gestured toward the bulkhead. "What do you make of it?"

Shauss frowned as he looked at the biologic pad. A section no larger than his hand was a slightly paler shade of blue than the surrounding pad, and there was a yellowing patch in the center. "I've never seen anything like it. Some sort of nutrient deficiency, perhaps?"

"If so, it's one I've never seen," Kellen said. "Microscience is sending a team down to investigate whether this is some sort of pathology or a naturally occurring process. But I don't like the timing or the placement, here where any of our unexpected guests could have done something to it."

Tiber nodded. "Suspicious."

"Empran, quarantine this block until microscience clears it."

A translucent white shimmer appeared over the bulkhead. "Block Voya-4742 quarantined."

Shauss looked at Kellen. "Since you're out of chambers, how would you like to take Zannen to task for his behavior?"

"Which female has he offended this time?"

"Miss King. Again."

Kellen winced. "Naturally. It couldn't have been some foolish female we could just silence with a threat to mate her with him."

Tiber sputtered. "Commander, that's—"

"A joke, Tiber. Be at ease."

They headed for the tranlift.

"What did you mean by *again*?" Tiber asked.

Pleased by the doctor's ignorance, Shauss glanced over his shoulder. "You're still here?"

"I'm interested in the disposition of this matter."

"You're interested in Miss King," Shauss corrected.

"The thought disturbs you."

Stopping suddenly, Shauss jabbed a finger in Tiber's chest. "*You* disturb me."

"Gentlemen, do we have a problem?" Kellen asked.

"Not as long as Tiber stays out of my head."

Kellen sighed. "Stay out of his head, Tiber."

"As you wish, Commander."

*****

"Have a seat, Jas." Monica flopped down on the oversized sofa and patted the cushion next to hers. She looked so different now. Back when they first met, her hair had been short and spiky and dyed the most god-awful shade of black Jasmine had ever seen. With piercings too numerous to count and the dramatic Goth makeup, she'd looked more like a rebellious teenager than a bona fide physician.

As it turned out, she practically *was* a teenager at the time. To look at her now, Monica's previous immaturity was obvious. She'd gone from pudgy punk to svelte sex kitten overnight, and Jasmine was big enough to admit that she envied her.

Sighing, she perched on the edge of the cushion to keep her legs from dangling like a child's.

"How about a kiss?" Monica offered. At Jasmine's startled look, she grinned and pulled a foil-wrapped chocolate from the pocket of her lab coat. "Sorry, I couldn't resist."

Heat prickling in her cheeks, Jasmine shook her head, so Monica peeled the little morsel and popped it into her mouth. "I'm not mad at you, you know," she said around the lump of chocolate. "For the kiss or anything else."

"Why not? First I almost get you raped by a slimy diplomat and then I put the moves on your mate in my sleep." She put her hot face in her hands and groaned. "God, I can't believe I did that."

"First off, that slimy diplomat fooled you just like he fooled everyone else," Monica said. "I know you heard me yelling at Kellen right before I was whisked away—you'd have been an idiot *not* to suspect I was being held against my will."

Tears of relief burned Jasmine's eyes. "Thank you for saying that."

"I'm the one who should be thanking you. You risked your life to rescue me and I never even stopped by to see how you were afterward. I was just so messed up about Kellen and Shauss, and then the attack happened and the evacuation and everything…"

"It's okay."

"No, it's not." Monica studied her with a troubled look. "From what I saw of your dream life, you're obviously suffering from some kind of post-traumatic stress. Sex and slimy fangs and decapitation? Seriously?"

She didn't have to fake a shudder. "Yeah, it was a real nightmare."

"You're in love with him, aren't you?"

Blindsided, she gasped for air. "No! Monica, no."

"Shelley said you were, but I didn't believe it."

"Damn it, I'm not in love with Shauss!" Jasmine got up and paced. "He nearly raped me, for God's sake! That's a — a very *intimate* thing, and it's only natural for me to be kind of — of *conflicted* about him. I'm still working through it."

"Well, I'm glad you can work through it," Monica said softly, "but Shelley told me you were stuck on him way before that incident."

Feeling trapped, Jasmine stopped to stare out the flare window. "Monica, I swear I would never have tried to take him away from you. That's not why I helped Pret."

Monica blinked. "I never thought of that."

"Well, I did. Believe me, I stopped and questioned my own motives every step of the way on this, but I couldn't just stand back and let you be forced into a lifetime of — of sexual servitude if that wasn't what you wanted."

"Sexual servitude?" Monica snickered.

"I'm serious! I thought that if I could just get you someplace safe, we could talk and I'd know for sure…" She sighed. "Some savior I turned out to be."

"I'm sorry. Hell, you really were between a rock and a hard place, weren't you?"

"I was an idiot. But, Monica, even if Shauss were free as a bird and I was madly in love with him, I'd never do anything about it."

"Why not?"

She took a deep breath, hating the lies she was about to tell. "Because I can't have children and the Garathani need all the children they can get."

"Well, that sucks."

"Yeah, it does." That was no lie. It sucked completely. "I was in an accident when I was teenager and the trauma to my pituitary gland triggered early-onset menopause."

Monica stared at her. "No way! You look great."

"Well, my dad's filthy rich, so I got the best care available from the world's top specialists. They couldn't fix the problem, but they put me on hormone replacement therapy and gave me breast implants so that I could live a halfway normal life."

"Implants, huh?" Monica gazed at her chest. "Wow. Usually I can spot a boob job a mile off, but I totally thought yours were real. Not that I've been checking you out or anything."

Jasmine smiled weakly. "I didn't think you were."

"You were smart to go for tasteful over spectacular."

Spectacular looked like it was working out pretty good for *her*, but Jasmine bit her tongue. If she drew any more comparisons between them, Monica might start putting two and two together.

"Yeah, I kind of thought anything bigger would be false advertising," she said instead. Pulling the bottle out of her pocket, she forged on. "Anyway, that's kind of related to reason I was looking for you. I was asleep when the Garathani did their beam-up routine so of course I didn't have a chance to grab anything. It was just by the grace of God I had my nasal spray in my pocket. I really need to have it replicated, but I just wasn't comfortable approaching the Garathani doctors."

"Understandable." Monica held out her hand and Jasmine passed it to her. "What is it? There's no label."

"It's a hormone replacement that hasn't even been approved for human trials in the States yet," Jasmine said. "I may not be able to have kids, but at least I don't have to deal with hot flashes, my skin is still firm, and I'm not at high risk for osteoporosis."

Monica shook the bottle and her eyes widened. "Shit, there's hardly any in here."

"Hopefully there's enough left to replicate." Jasmine shifted uncomfortably.

"Jesus, Jasmine, why don't you wait 'til the last minute next time." She shook it again and frowned. "It would have been better to do it right away. There's a reason they have you shake it before you use it. Who knows what kind of concentration is left in here?"

"The computer told me you were unavailable."

Monica's eyes narrowed. "Empran, why did you tell her I was unavailable?"

"Lieutenant Shauss' orders."

Relief bloomed in Jasmine's chest. Monica hadn't blown her off.

Shauss had, the bastard.

"Well, from now on, I'll set my own availability, if you don't mind," Monica snapped.

"That will require the clearance of Commander Kellen."

"I've got your clearance right here," Monica muttered as she stood up. "Okay, Jas, I'll see what I can do. Maybe Ketrok or Tiber can help me get—"

"No!" Jasmine jumped up too. "I don't trust Garathani doctors."

"Hey, I resemble that remark."

Though her ironic comeback held no heat, Jasmine hurried to say, "No, you were Terran first and I know I can trust you to do everything in your power to get it right."

Monica's features softened. "You can trust them too."

"Please, just do it yourself. I don't want to take any chances."

"I can't promise you that," Monica said with a shake of her head. "I've barely begun my training with their technology. But if I have to ask for help, I'll do everything in my power to make sure *they* get it right, okay?"

Jasmine swallowed. "I guess I can't ask for more than that."

"It'll be all right, Jas. Hey, you doing anything for lunch?"

A bizarre, inedible sandwich alone in my room again. "No. Why?"

"Kellen's locked up with the dusty old guys all day, so I'm eating with Shelley and her husband. Why don't you join us?"

She hesitated. "Shelley was kind of mad at me after…"

"The Pret-napping?" At her nod, Monica rolled her eyes. "She just gets really pissy when she's scared. Kellen said she practically screamed the place down until they brought Mark up here."

"You're sure?"

"Positive. Come on, have lunch with us."

Jasmine was torn. She really should stick to her quarters until her supply of nasal spray had been replenished, but after almost a week of relative isolation, a casual lunch with friends sounded heavenly.

"Sure," she finally said with a tentative smile. "And who are the dusty old guys?"

"The high council. Well, except for my father—it'll be a few years before he fits that description." Monica headed for the door, throwing over her shoulder, "Meet us at noon. Infirmary Three."

* * * * *

"What in Peserin's name were you thinking, Lieutenant?" Kellen demanded.

Shauss noted with satisfaction that Zannen's demeanor as he stood at attention was considerably less insolent than it would have been if *he'd* been the one dressing him down.

"I was thinking she needed to be taken down a notch, Sir," Zannen replied without expression.

Kellen got right in his face, and roared, "I'm thinking your rank needs to be taken down a notch!"

"Do what you must, Sir."

Kellen resumed his pacing.

"Zannen, you are an exemplary warrior. Why would you jeopardize your career for such a petty revenge?" Without waiting for a reply, he continued. "I could possibly understand your behavior if Miss King were a copulative candidate and you, her prospective mate. But she's *not* a candidate, and you're no one's idea of a desirable male."

He stopped and narrowed his eyes at Zannen. "Ketrok tells me you refused the probe he tried to issue you."

"I will spend my seed in a female, Sir, or not at all."

"I'd rethink that position if I were you, Lieutenant. You have an abundance of sexual aggression that needs to be relieved before you can conduct yourself appropriately in the presence of females. Perhaps bringing yourself to orgasm a few hundred times will improve your disposition."

"With all due respect, Commander, you can't order me to perform sexual acts."

"No, but I can ensure that the probe is the only sexual satisfaction available to you for the rest of your life. If you step out of line with a female again on my ship, I'll personally see to it that you never reach the top of any mating roll. Do I make myself clear?"

"Yes, Sir."

"I'm glad to hear it," Kellen said. "Now you will apologize—"

"Excuse me, Sir." Shauss stepped up beside him. "Miss King has requested that he not speak to her again, even to apologize."

Zannen's derisive gaze focused on Shauss. "Who appointed you her protector, little brother?"

"Is that what this is about, some kind of misplaced sibling rivalry?" Kellen asked incredulously.

"No, Sir."

Shauss barely suppressed a snort. Zannen had only focused his obnoxious attentions on Miss King because of him and they both knew it.

"It had better not be. Miss King isn't a piece of meat to be scrapped over by two hungry dogs." He sent a penetrating look Shauss' way. "Especially when one of them already has a premium piece on his plate."

Shauss managed to remain impassive. "I couldn't agree more."

Kellen turned to Zannen. "From this moment on, Lieutenant, you will avoid any and all contact with Miss King. One more point of reprimand in your file and you'll face a disciplinary hearing."

"Understood, Commander."

"Good. I'm due back in chambers."

After he left, Shauss looked into eyes as black as his own. "If you go near her again," he growled, "a disciplinary hearing will be the least of your problems."

Zannen grinned. "You're awfully possessive of a piece of ass that's not even yours, little brother."

"The only thing that makes us brothers is the blood of a poisonous female," Shauss said through clenched teeth. "And if you lay a hand on Jasmine King, I won't hesitate to spill every drop of yours."

Chapter Four

Of all the places they could have met, Monica just had to pick this one.

Jasmine paused and took a deep breath before stepping through the infirmary door. No lights flashed. No alarms went off. No one called for her to be detained.

The air whooshed out of her as she sagged slightly with relief. Then she noticed Shelley lying on one of the beds. At her side stood a tall, slender man with shaggy dark hair and a goatee.

"Hey, are you okay?" Jasmine asked. This was the first time she'd seen Shelley since that awful day in the commander's dining room.

"Yeah." The petite blonde grimaced as she shifted on the thin mattress. "Monica was just checking me over to make sure the twins are, too."

"Oh my God." Jasmine stepped up beside her. "I didn't even think about how being in space might affect the babies."

"They're kicking my ass from the inside, so I think they're doing all right. I, on the other hand, am roasting alive on this ship-hole." Shelley sighed as she wiped sweat off her upper lip. "I had to raise holy hell, but the commander finally brought Mark up. Speaking of which, Jasmine, this is my husband, Mark Bonham."

He held out a hand and Jasmine took it, fighting a grin. For some reason, she'd pictured Shelley with someone a shade less…beatnik. Dressed in a tight black turtleneck and black jeans, Mark looked like he might strike an angular modern dance pose and start reciting brooding poetry at any moment.

"Mark, Shelley's told us a lot about you," she told him, tactfully not mentioning that it was usually bitching about how much his job kept him away from home.

He smiled back, his brown eyes twinkling. "No matter what she said, I was going to propose before I knew about the babies."

Déjà vu tickled the edges of her brain. "Have we met? You seem...familiar."

"Not that I know of. Perhaps Shelley showed you our wedding portrait?"

"No..." Jasmine had kept pretty much to herself and no one had ever shared photos or other personal information with her. Besides, the connection she felt seemed older, more distant.

Before she could pursue it, Monica strolled in. "Hey, Stepford."

Jasmine grimaced. "I hardly qualify for that title anymore."

"Too true." Monica looked at her for a long moment before turning to Shelley. "Ketrok says your pee looks fine, and as far as I can tell, everything's perfect with the babies, but I really wish you'd let him do a scan."

"Hell. No." Shelley shuddered. "You do it."

"I don't know how!" Monica was clearly exasperated. "Shelley, their technology got you here in one piece from the surface in less than a second. I don't know why you won't trust—"

"It's not their technology I distrust, Monica—it's them."

"See?" Jasmine jumped in. "I'm not the only one."

Monica rolled her eyes. "You guys, I've only been practicing medicine on this ship for a couple of days. I can barely figure out how to take your temperature, for Christ's sake!"

"You know how to deliver babies and that's all I care about," Shelley said. "How can we trust them, especially after those military bases were blown up? They honestly expect us to believe there are other aliens on Earth working to sabotage their mission, and that they're responsible for killing millions of people?"

"Shelley, why would the Garathani sabotage themselves like that, especially after all this time?" Monica asked.

"Maybe they got impatient."

"What would any other race have to gain by sabotaging them?" Mark chimed in. "The Garathani are the ones who need women."

"Maybe the Narthani need something," Monica fired back. "Maybe they're still pissed about Kellen's revenge and want to make the Garathani suffer, make sure they don't get any Earth women."

Mark snorted. "Good luck getting anyone to believe that. Commander Kellen had supposedly wiped out the Narthani, and now the Garathani are asking us to believe that he didn't, that he just destroyed selected targets? And assuming he *did* destroy their long-range vessels, as he claims, how did the Narthani get here?"

Jasmine just stared at him, but Monica wasn't so retiring. "Gee, Mark, been thinking about this some, have you?"

He frowned. "My family and I are trapped on a Garathani spacecraft. You'd damn well better believe I've been doing some thinking."

Shelley gasped and slid her hands over her bulging stomach.

"Another one?" Monica asked.

"It's fine, just a Braxton-Hicks."

"Uh-huh. I'm checking you for dilation."

"Oh, do you have to?" Shelley whined.

"Suck it up, you big labor and delivery nurse," Monica said with a grin. She walked over to a table and stuck her hands into what looked like an aqua sponge about the size of a bread box.

Jasmine followed her over for a better look. "What is that?"

"It's a manicurist's dream," Monica explained. "I don't remember what they call it, but it's basically a sterilizing cube. Kind of like the biologic pad that lines the ship, only not so dense. It eats all the organic and inorganic impurities from your skin. The longer you leave your hands in, the cleaner they get. Removes polish and takes care of cuticles and hangnails too."

"Really?" Jasmine stuck one finger in.

"Yup, and if you leave your hands in long enough, it'll eat your nails right off."

Although she wouldn't mind seeing the ragged remnants of her manicure disappear, Jasmine yanked her finger away and rubbed it on her jeans. No telling what else the stupid thing would eat.

As Monica approached, Shelley's eyes widened. "Does that mean no gloves?" Monica only looked slightly disturbed. "Uh yeah. Sorry, Shel—I'm not that wild about it myself, but that's life on a Garathani ship."

Shelley shuddered and looked at Mark and Jasmine. "You two—out. Sorry, honey, but it's going to be hard enough to let Monica examine me ungloved without you in here."

When Mark grinned and opened his mouth, she cut him off. "Don't say it! We don't want to hear about your kinky girl-on-girl fantasies."

"You can wait in Ketrok's lab until we're done." Monica nodded at a door.

Mark stepped up and when it opened, he swept out his arm, ushering Jasmine into the next room.

"So you're a secretary at the compound?" he asked, leaning against a table.

"I was, yes," she said regretfully. Much to her surprise, she'd actually enjoyed working with the Garathani. Except for the obnoxious few like Zannen and Pret, they'd been unfailingly polite, and their admiring glances had been fabulous for her ego. She'd miss that. She loved her students but sometimes they could be just as obnoxious as Zannen. Certainly none of them ever looked at her like —

Jasmine shook herself. Enough of that line of thinking. Now that she was lean and mean, Terran men would probably look at her with every bit as much desire in their eyes as the Garathani.

"Shelley told me what happened," Mark said. "I'm impressed. That took real guts."

Jasmine sighed. "More guts than brains, obviously."

"Don't be too hard on yourself. Things are always more complicated than they seem."

"Tell me about it," she muttered.

He turned slightly and touched the cube on the table with a curious finger. Then he turned fully and pressed all ten fingertips into it. "Let's see if this thing takes care of my hangnails. The air's awfully dry up here."

"Really? Our room always seems too warm and humid." Jasmine watched a little breathlessly, blinking away visions of him screaming in agony as he pulled out bloody stumps.

That was it — she was done with movies forever.

"Do you have a spouse up here too?" he asked.

"No, I'm not married. I room with one of the other secretaries."

"Ah. I'll bet your family's worried about you."

Jasmine swallowed a snort. "It's just my father and me, and he knows I can take care of myself. My mother was the worrier."

"Was?"

"She died in a car accident last year."

"I'm sorry."

"Me too. She was…" *All I had.* Her throat got tight and she turned away as she finished, "Great."

After a moment, she felt his hand squeeze her shoulder, but he said nothing, a move she found remarkably astute for a man. Shelley had trained him well.

The door opened. "All done," Monica announced. "Let's eat. I'm starved."

* * * * *

Jasmine wallowed naked in a mountain of potting soil, rolling around and rubbing its mineral-rich blackness into her skin and her hair and her mouth. She found a raw steak and dredged the bloody morsel in soil before eating it with her bare hands. *God, so delicious!* But she still needed more.

Then she saw Shauss kneeling on the fertile ground, the streaks in his black hair glowing iridescent blue under the Garathani sun. Sweat trickled down his throat as he prepared the soil for planting with his bare hands and she licked her lips, desperate to taste it. To taste *him.*

That's what she needed! She needed Shauss to take her, to grind her into the mountain with his big hard body, to split her open and fill all the empty places inside her with soil and seed and sweat-dampened flesh…

"Shauss, please!"

She woke to the harsh sound of her own desperate groan and lifted her head, panting raggedly in the absolute dark. Her hips continued to grind against her dream lover, reaching in vain for satisfaction. She could still smell him, and it was driving her crazy.

"Oh crap." This was bad. This was very, very bad. Obviously she must have gotten a major whiff of pheromones while she was out yesterday. God, she had to get out of here before it was too late.

Please don't let it be too late!

Portia stirred in the other bed. "Are you okay?" she asked in a rusty voice.

"Sorry, just another weird dream," Jasmine said breathlessly, unnerved by the cravings that still clawed between her legs and in her belly. Lord, she was hungry!

Propping up on trembling elbows, she pulled her hands from under the pillow and illuminated her watch face. Five o'clock. She rolled to her side as she threw back the blanket. She couldn't wait for Monica—it was way past time to carry out her insane escape plan.

With her stomach still growling, she stood up, and said quietly, "Empran, wardrobe light twenty-five watts."

Milky light instantly seeped from behind the wardrobe doors. Stripping off her nightgown and dropping it on the bed, she made a quick stop in the bathroom to relieve herself and splash on a liberal coating of vanilla then returned to the wardrobe on legs that vibrated with anxiety. She pulled the exercise suit out of the sanitizer and then paused. Crap. She hadn't sanitized her only pair of underwear—she couldn't bring herself to put them in the sanitizer overnight like Portia did, so she'd intended to sanitize them first thing this morning.

Her hesitation lasted only a second—there was no way in hell she was going commando. Setting her chin, she suited up and yanked up the zipper with a decisive flick of her wrist. Screw it. At this point, day-old underwear was the least of her problems.

"Are you sure you're okay?" Portia asked, propping up on one elbow. In the dim light she looked ripe, rumpled and sexy, her breasts lush and heavy-looking over the blanket. How could she be so unconcerned about her nudity on a spaceship bristling with humongous, sex-starved alien males?

"Hey, if something's wrong—"

"I'm fine, Portia, really." Jasmine shut the wardrobe, leaving only enough light for her to find her way to the door. "I just need to get out of here."

Portia's "Well, if you're sure…" followed her out and she let the door slide shut behind her without answering. There was nothing left to say, really, but she felt kind of bad about not saying goodbye, since it was conceivable they might never see each other again.

She stalked down the corridor, her skin practically crawling with the need to be free of this ship and its inhabitants. Lighting in the ship's common areas was synchronized with the compound's to keep everyone's circadian rhythms on track, and the watery light soaking into the blue walls created a predawn effect so peaceful she almost expected to hear birds chirping.

Keeping her eyes and ears open, she headed toward the tranlift at the deck's core. Movement in a connecting corridor caught her attention and she stiffened until she realized it was just Shelley's husband. He meandered down the hall away from her, one hand behind his back and the other trailing along the wall, and she felt a spurt of sympathy. He must be going as crazy as she was to be out walking the decks at this hour.

She passed without greeting him, careful not to involve anyone else in her reckless scheme.

As expected, the only guard in evidence was at the tranlift. He followed her with his eyes but said nothing as she stepped up to the automatic door. When it opened, she braced herself and stepped inside.

She didn't even bother looking when she stepped out of the tranlift on Voya Deck. There were guards stationed at every tranlift, and by now she'd done enough reconnaissance that they were used to her running laps around the deck at all hours.

The women's exercise facility was already a hive of activity. She took a few minutes to stretch, more out of habit than anything else, and then grabbed a small towel from the rack in the entry and draped it around her neck.

Snagging a hydration bottle from the shelf, she popped the lid on her way out the door. It was hard to swallow past the nervous constriction of her throat, but she chugged some of the tepid pink liquid anyway, shuddering as it went down. The hydration fluid was supposed to be the Garathanis' answer to Gatorade but for some reason the taste reminded her of semen.

Clutching the bottle in her left hand, she started down the corridor at a slow jog, trying not to think about what she was going to do. Which was die, probably, but she'd do just about anything to avoid having everyone look at her like Shauss had in her dream.

When she neared the escape pods, dread pooled in her belly. What was it going to be like in there? When she and Portia were escorted to their room, they'd been told the pods were like lifeboats and they should find their way to one in the event of some major disaster. There was always a guard posted outside the pod bay, and only he could grant them access. They hadn't specified how that happened, but reading Garathani had its advantages—Jasmine knew the electronic screen by the hatch read a palm print to authorize entry.

Any fool could row a lifeboat, so it stood to reason that very little training was required to operate the pod itself. Hopefully she'd just be able to step in, push some kind of emergency jettison button and let the on-board computers take care of the rest. But even if that went as planned, an infinite number of things could go wrong from there. Her odds weren't good. The Garathani could call the vessel back remotely, or blow her out of the sky before she reached safety—assuming she could even get past the ship's energy shields.

She slowed as she rounded the corner. Rats! Ensign Hastion was guarding the escape pods this morning. Why did it have to be someone she liked? He was always pleasant and never leered at her—although the sight of him jerking off in front of all those men had taken some of the shine off his appeal.

Her heart rate escalated again and it was all she could do to keep her pace even. She wanted to run like hell, but where would she go? Back to her quarters to await her doom?

After her fourth lap around the deck, she deliberately picked up the pace. When she passed the escape pods, she let the bottle slip from her sweat-slicked fingers.

"Oops," she said breathlessly. Turning, she saw Hastion bend over to pick it up and took her chance. Praying like crazy, she executed a side kick just as he looked up.

Though her heel slammed into his nose with a meaty crunch, he staggered but didn't go down, so she launched a spinning back kick. This time her heel connected with his cheekbone, snapping his head to the side. He stared at her blankly for a second and then his dead weight fell over into a bloody heap against the wall.

Dead weight.

"Oh my God!" she whispered. "Please be okay, please be okay!"

Snapping out of her terrified reaction, she rushed over and laid her fingers on his neck. Thank God! His pulse seemed strong and steady, so she'd probably just broken his nose and knocked him out. She would never have forgiven herself if, in her rush to save herself, she'd killed someone else. Even if he was Garathani.

"I'm sorry," she breathed, wiping a blood-soaked hank of long brown hair out of his face with her towel. This close, she could hear the air bubbling in his streaming nostrils. She hated having hurt him. Her martial arts training was supposed to be used for self-defense, not to attack the unsuspecting and gallant, but she'd really had no choice. Again.

Taking a deep breath to steady herself, she looked up. *Yes!* The scanner was right over his head. Maybe the gods were smiling on her after all.

She dropped the towel and grabbed his right wrist in both her hands, hauling his arm up as high as she could get it, but his fingers didn't quite reach the scanner. Bracing her legs farther apart, she threw more muscle into it, but his palm barely brushed the bottom edge.

"Shit!" Now what? The man weighed two-fifty if he weighed an ounce—there was no way she could lift his whole body up.

Breathing hard, she stepped back to assess the situation. He needed to be sitting up straighter.

"Great," she muttered. How was she supposed to accomplish that? His weight was already against the wall.

"Okay, Ensign, time to lie down for a minute." Since he was already leaning slightly to his left because of her tugging on his arm, she pushed him the rest of the way over, hoping like hell she was strong enough to get him upright again. Once he was on his side, she dropped to her knees and tried to push his hips toward the wall, but he was too heavy.

"Damn it!"

Sinking onto her butt and offering a silent apology to the unconscious guard, she leaned back on her hands, planted one foot on his low belly and the other over his crotch, and gave a mighty shove.

Hastion's low groan made her scramble backward, heart pounding in her throat, but he didn't move. After a breathless moment, she could see that her push had done the trick, so she got to her feet and approached him again. She could only see one way to get him back up. Straddling his head with her feet, careful not to stand on his hair, she laced both hands around his neck and pulled straight up.

His neck muscles stiffened under her fingers, but she reacted too late. His arm flew up and then the lights went out.

Chapter Five

Now that the moment had finally arrived, Tiber was almost frozen with anticipation. He sat naked at the end of his bunk, eyeing the probe with something akin to disbelief. After so many years of searching for a solution to their sexual crisis, it had come down to something as simple as stimulating the prostate.

Ketrok had claimed the discovery was a result of Pret's experimentation with a dildo, but Tiber knew better. He'd been there the day Ketrok called a gathering to witness the verification. Pret had squealed and looked utterly shocked when Ketrok forced the artificial penis into his rectum, and then he'd screamed for a full minute with the relief of shooting his semen onto the floor. That was unquestionably his first orgasm in at least a decade, if not his entire life, and nothing Ketrok said would convince Tiber otherwise. Shauss, on the other hand… Something about the tense way he'd held himself during the verification, as well as the furtive look in his eye, said he'd played an integral and very intimate role in the discovery.

Someone had invaded Lieutenant Shauss' rectum, making him orgasm, and the knowledge was enough to drive Tiber wild with curiosity and arousal. Had that someone been male…or female? Monica was a physician — would she do such a thing? Surely the commander wouldn't…

Shaking his head to clear the forbidden images, Tiber set his jaw and began stroking his phallus, which was already rock-hard. Less than two weeks ago, he'd have said he would be stroking forever because he'd certainly tried that often enough, especially in those first few years after Nelina's death. As one of the rare Garathani males who'd previously enjoyed satisfying intercourse whenever he wanted it, getting used to going without had been especially trying, and he'd stroked himself raw at first, trying in vain to find release.

Eleven years. He was almost afraid of the effects release after all this time might have. What if he stroked out from the sheer relief of it? Garnam would find him when he got off duty in a few hours, lying on the bunk with the probe bulging from his waste canal.

But at least he'd die with a smile on his face.

His erection was so hard it hurt, and his spur was beginning to rear, so Tiber reached over and grasped the probe. Holding it carefully, he leaned on his side and set it against his naked hindquarters. *"Empran, commence masturbation probe basic program."*

The probe immediately began to snake between the cheeks of his buttocks. He rolled to his back and felt it settle even further inside him.

The sensation was delicious. His belly was already tightening with excitement, and the gentle vibrations were translating themselves all over his body. Pouring some of the lubricant Ketrok had provided into his palm, he began to stroke the fiery rod between his legs with gentle tugs.

He instinctively tried to focus on his lovely Nelina, but instead, Jasmine King rose up to haunt him. The feel of her resting in his arms had been an unexpected, if short-lived, blessing. Her scent, an unusual combination of vanilla and spice, had tortured him long after Shauss plucked her from his arms. Just knowing such a female was on the *Heptoral* now made him want to go after her, but he couldn't. She wasn't a candidate, and even if she were, he wouldn't try to claim her. He'd loved and lost a wonderful mate and still had two sons and a daughter to show for it—other males younger than he deserved a chance to find the same.

When his palm slid over the head of his penis, Tiber nearly choked on his need. Thanking the Powers he was alone, he gripped the throbbing shaft and groaned in genuine pain.

Peserin, but he needed release so badly. If this didn't work, he would probably be forced to the new court of last resort, letting Ketrok probe him manually until he ejaculated. Peserin knew he wouldn't be able to sleep in this condition.

Stroking more urgently, he dug his heels into the mattress and began to arch upward with each pass of his fist. His spur erupted fully from its hollow and he stroked without thinking, his mind drawn inevitably back to Jasmine King. He could still see her on Shauss' lap. The fan of her long, dark lashes fluttering against her pale cheek. The smooth, rhythmic movements of her jaw as she thrust her tongue into Shauss' mouth. Her long, artistic fingers running through Shauss' hair with leisurely abandon.

The two of them had looked beautiful together—perfect for each other in fact—but oh, what he wouldn't give to feel those elegant fingers scraping over his own scalp. And down his back. Over his buttocks. His scrotum...

"Empran, increase vibration."

He moaned pitifully at the excruciating tightening in his belly. But still no orgasm.

"Add thrusting motion."

Finally the probe began to undulate over an exquisitely sensitive spot. Heart jerking in painfully fast beats, he began thrusting his hips in a synchronous rhythm with the probe, and within seconds felt the burning tingle at the base of his spine, a sign that ejaculation was imminent.

Peserin, yes!

Tiber imagined himself mounted behind the tiny Jasmine, penetrating both of her tender Terran orifices, and breathed, breathed, breathed...

Boom! Release rammed into his entire body like a lightning bolt, and he cried out harshly as semen flew everywhere, landing on the blanket, his hand, his chest, his mouth. Laughing out loud, he wrung every ounce of pleasure he could from the release and then lay there gasping, savoring the strong vibrations still rocking his waste canal.

Why in the name of all that was mighty hadn't they discovered this before? To think of all the years he and all the other Garathani males had suffered through!

Then he laughed again, licking a drop of semen from his lip. The last time he'd tasted his own ejaculate, he'd been pleasuring Nelina with his tongue. It was unfortunate he couldn't remember her taste as vividly as he did his own right now, but the sound of her passionate cries would be with him forever.

He rolled to his side and slid his fingers over the probe. What an unimaginable relief! No doubt males all over the ship were writhing and shouting in their quarters. He wouldn't be the only one reporting for duty tomorrow morning wearing a drunken grin.

"Deactivate probe." As the sphere slid free of his anus and dissolved, Tiber shivered with delight at the forbidden sensation. He would definitely be wearing a drunken grin in the morning.

But at the moment he needed to relieve another need.

"Waste unit", he sent as he rose from the bunk.

The unit slid down the wall immediately and he sighed again as he waited for the constriction of his vessels to ease enough to allow a healthy urine stream.

He thought of Dr. Teague's insistence that males experiment with anal intercourse. It was a disconcerting idea, and yet it might be perversely appealing to some, after what the bygone era of females had subjected their males to. Females had always been free to partake of each others' pleasures, for it stood to reason that females were better versed in what pleased females. The same option had never been available to males, however, and as far as he knew, that inequity had never really been questioned because there would be no point in it. They could tease each other into infinity, but they could never please each other the way females could.

That was no longer the case. How would the council handle the inevitable same-sex liaisons that would arise as a result?

"*Dr. Tiber to infirmary three for a medical emergency.*"

"*Empran,*" he sighed, "*your timing, for once, is impeccable.*"

* * * * *

When he entered Infirmary Three, he saw Hastion leaning against the bed and diagnosed the broken nose at once.

"What happened?" he asked, heading directly for the regenerator cabinet.

"Miss King tried to make my nose an innie instead of an outtie," Hastion said in a nasal tone.

"An innie?" Tiber paused with his fingers on the handle, frowning at Hastion. "What in all the planets is an innie and why would Miss King want to—"

Then he saw the slender bare feet on the mattress behind him.

"She knocked me out," Hastion said wryly. "I felt it only fair to return the favor."

"You struck Miss King?" Tiber slammed the door and rushed to the bed. "Move!"

"Oh, don't look so offended," Hastion grumbled, moving aside. "I was barely conscious at the time—I doubt I did her nearly as much damage as she did me."

Tiber drew in a sharp breath at the sight of her. Even slack-jawed in unconsciousness, she was a bounty of loveliness.

"Ensign, you are lower than the pad under my boot," he growled, sliding his hand under her chin and turning her head carefully. His fingertips measured her pulse as he examined her. "And just how did this slip of a creature manage to inflict so much damage on you?"

"Typical feminine wiles," Hastion said sourly. "She dropped her bottle and when I bent to pick it up for her, she thanked my face with the sole of her foot. Twice."

"Why?" Her injury didn't appear too serious, but Tiber wasn't happy that she was still unconscious.

"Maybe I looked thirsty and she wasn't in the mood to share." Hastion leaned against the bulkhead and sighed. "Peserin, but my face hurts."

Glancing up, Tiber had to agree the ensign had taken the worse beating. "Go lie down. It looks like you might have an orbital fracture as well as a broken nose."

"After I've spoken with the commander. He's on his way."

"Fine." Tiber focused on Jasmine King once more. "Empran, image and assess this subject's head injuries."

"Commencing cranial scan." Seconds later a holograph of the female's skull appeared above her head and he studied it with interest. "No fractures detected. Level two trauma to left temporalis."

He frowned at an anomaly in her septal structure. It almost looked as if she had a fully developed bilateral vomeronasal organ. Most Terrans had them unilaterally at birth, but by the time they reached puberty, the organs had regressed to such a degree they could be considered vestigial.

Of course the so-called Halethoid mutations were occurring with increasing regularity as Terrans' physiology finally overcame the adverse effects of Sol's light, and this might very well be one of those developments. He'd have to examine the scan more closely later.

"Brain trauma?"

The image switched to physio mode.

"Level two-minus."

"Empran, assess the ensign's facial injuries."

As he suspected, Hastion's nose and cheekbone were fractured. "You lost consciousness?"

Hastion grimaced. "Not for long."

A low moan made him look down. Brushing the loose hairs from her forehead, he asked, "Miss King, can you hear me?"

She moaned again and turned her face into his palm. Her smile as she nuzzled him made Tiber's chest contract like he'd just been spaced. He was fighting for breath when her lashes fluttered, and then eyes bluer than an Ethrian sunset blinked at him before a frown furrowed her brow. "My head hurts."

"I'm not surprised. You've got a slight concussion." His voice sounded disturbingly breathless.

"Where am I?"

"You're in Infirmary Three, aboard the *Heptoral*."

She looked around and her eyes widened. "Oh my God."

"There's no need—"

Before he could reassure her, she'd knocked his hand away and rolled off the other side of the bed. She tried to stand up and Tiber reached over the mattress to catch her before she fell over, but she stumbled back against the next bed.

"Don't touch me!" She hung on to the edge of the bed, blinking rapidly. Sweat broke out on her upper lip as she panted. "I think I'm going to be sick."

"That's the concussion, Miss King," Tiber said softly as he rounded the foot of the bed. "You need to lie down. Nobody's going to hurt you."

"No! I want to see Monica." She dropped to her hands and knees and lowered her forehead to the floor. "Please, just get Dr. Teague."

The infirmary door slid open and Commander Kellen strode in. His gaze darkened as it zeroed in on Hastion. "Ensign Hastion, report."

Lieutenant Shauss strolled in behind the commander and his dark eyes settled immediately on Miss King. There was that proprietary air again. Tiber's hackles rose.

Hastion sighed before reporting, "Miss King attacked me, Sir."

Kellen's eyes widened as he took in the ensign's condition. "The hell you say! For what reason?"

"I don't know, Sir."

"Well, what were you doing at the time?"

"Standing guard outside the Voya escape pods."

"And she launched an unprovoked attack."

"Well, Sir, she was running laps around the deck, which Ensign Beral reports is not unusual. She dropped her hydration bottle, and when I bent to pick it up for her, she kicked my face in."

Kellen stared at him for a moment before glancing at Jasmine, who hadn't looked at any of them yet. "Apparently you subdued her."

"Once I regained consciousness," Hastion confessed gruffly.

Kellen brushed past him and crouched beside her. "Miss King, I hope you have a good reason for assaulting one of my warriors."

"Go away," she said into the pad. "I want to talk to Monica."

"I'm afraid that won't be possible unless you tell me why you attacked Ensign Hastion."

"I didn't want to hurt him." Her muffled voice was flat. "I just wanted to go home."

"Go home?" Shauss repeated incredulously. "Surely you didn't intend to steal one of the evacuation pods?"

"Yes, I did!" Her head snapped up and she glared at him. "Can you blame me?"

Kellen closed his eyes for several seconds and Tiber had the distinct impression he was counting. Then he opened them and looked at Tiber.

"Her condition?" Kellen asked.

"Bruising and low-grade brain trauma."

"Does she require treatment?"

"I'd like to administer ferilyde, but she won't let me near her."

Kellen focused on Miss King once more. "Miss King, if you wish to suffer the effects of brain trauma while we discuss the consequences of your actions, so be it, but if I were you, I'd accept the ferilyde treatment, just in case you'd like to speak in your own defense."

Then he said to Shauss, "Escort her to Tactical One when Tiber is finished with her. Don't take your eyes off her until then."

* * * * *

Garathani medicine was a thing of beauty, she admitted reluctantly. After permitting the painless ferilyde injection at the base of her skull, she'd felt a hundred times better within seconds. Any other injury to her skull would just have to heal on its own—there was no way she was subjecting herself to computer scans of any sort.

When she entered the tactical room, escorted by Tiber and Shauss, she was too focused on the occupants to give the room more than a cursory glance. It was unnerving to find the ever-annoying Zannen standing guard inside the door. The skin on the back of her neck prickled as she walked past—no doubt he was tracking her with his black gaze the way a buzzard eyes a wounded calf.

And, oh Lord, Minister Cecine had been brought into this and he didn't look happy about it. He stood by a window with his arms crossed over his chest. Kellen sat at a long table, which was surrounded by at least a dozen chairs.

"Please be seated." Commander Kellen gestured to the chairs opposite him

"I'd rather stand if it's all the same to you."

He nodded. "As you wish."

She was grateful for Tiber's presence beside her. She could practically feel concern emanating from him.

Kellen didn't wait for the minister to sit before he launched his offensive.

"Miss King, you have made it eminently clear that you cannot be trusted to supervise yourself," he said. "I've discussed this with the minister and we see only two alternatives. You may spend the rest of your stay with us in the detention bay or join the ranks of the recruits and take mates to supervise your activities."

Well that was a no-brainer. "I'll take detention."

"Very well," Kellen said. "Be aware, however, that there is no privacy in a detention cell. You will be confined by a transparent containment field at all times. You'll eat, sleep, bathe and use waste facilities in full view of the guards, and your activities will be recorded by Empran. You will have no visitors. You may exercise only within the confines of your cell. Your access to Empran will be restricted to entertainment files."

Jasmine's hands got clammy as she stared at him. "That's ridiculous. Even death-row inmates on Earth get to leave their cells for an hour a day."

"Death-row inmates on Earth do not have the potential to end thousands of innocent lives in the blink of an eye."

"I wasn't trying to hurt anyone," she said in an uneven voice. "I just wanted to go home."

"Be that as it may, you could very well have killed yourself and everyone aboard this ship in your ill-advised escape attempt. You have no training and no experience operating an escape pod."

Jasmine bit her lip. It hadn't occurred to her that she might be risking any lives but her own.

"And for all I know," the commander continued, "you intended to crash it into the *Heptoral*, kamikaze style."

"I wouldn't do that!"

"So you say."

She swallowed her arguments. He had no reason to believe her and every reason to doubt her. But, good Lord, under guard twenty-four hours a day, and they'd be able to watch her bathe and use the bathroom... Would their pheromones reach her through the containment field? Did it even matter now?

"Commander, there has to be some other way," she said desperately.

"As I said, you may take three Garathani mates who will assume responsibility for you in continuous shifts."

She gaped at him, her mouth working soundlessly. *Three?*

"Yes, three," he said. "That way one of them will be guarding you at all times."

"Neither of these options is acceptable," she declared.

"Miss King," Minister Cecine thundered, "you are lucky to have any options at all, considering the peril you placed my daughter in."

"Why don't you just beam me back to the surface? I'd be out of your hair forever then. You'd be happy—I'd be happy."

"At this point your happiness is of little interest to me. What is of interest is the safety of the people on this vessel, and your returning to the surface with whatever information you may have gleaned here is not an option."

She looked away from the minister, knowing her protests would, as always, fall on deaf ears. Licking her lips, which were suddenly bone dry, she asked carefully, "Would I have to…"

"Have intercourse with them?" When she gave a jerky nod, Kellen said, "It would be advisable for your protection. If they don't each claim you at least once, you would be open to a situation like the one you helped put Monica in."

"Just once? That would be enough?" She swallowed hard, trying to blink away images of herself being bent over and used repeatedly by three huge aliens. The curling sensation in her stomach was *not* arousal. It wasn't.

Kellen watched her inscrutably for a long moment before answering. "Miss King, the laws of our new order specifically prohibit females from refusing their mates sexual congress unless they are pregnant or otherwise physically incapacitated."

Her first instinct was to object, but the commander's thoughtful tone made her hold her tongue while he continued. "However, given the circumstances, the council might grant you a special dispensation from that requirement, provided you agree to cooperate fully with each initial claiming—and by fully, I mean *enthusiastically*. If these males voluntarily relinquish their right to take you at will, I'll expect you to make that one time worth their while."

Well, that was better than nothing. "Who would choose these mates?"

"Any male may petition to be your primary mate," Kellen said. "Upon approval by the council, he, in turn, would select secondary and tertiary mates."

"I don't have any say in the matter at all?"

"If you have some preference, Miss King, now would be the time to voice it, but I can't make any guarantees."

Her face flamed, knowing Shauss was watching her.

"And when this crisis on Earth is over, I'd get to go home, right?"

"When and if the crisis on Earth is resolved to our satisfaction, and when and if you are deemed to be no longer a threat, you would be given the option to dissolve your bond and return to your home planet."

Jasmine bit her lip. God, this was crazy. The idea of having to have sex with not one but three of these giants was enough to make her babble like an idiot. But at least she'd have the possibility of escaping at some point. In a cell, under constant surveillance, she'd have no chance.

"So how will this work? Do you show me a list of potentials or something?" she asked uncertainly.

"Two males have already filed petitions to mate you."

She stiffened. "What? Who?"

"Lieutenant Zannen's petition preceded Dr. Tiber's by roughly one second."

"No," Jasmine said immediately. "N. O. No. There is no way in hell." She glared at Zannen and nearly screamed at the look of lustful triumph on his face. "I'd sooner be mated to an ape. A whole herd of apes. In fact, I'd rather be spaced. Seriously. Just point me to the nearest airlock and I'll show myself out."

"Don't be afraid to tell us how you really feel, Miss King," Kellen said dryly.

She glared at him. "I *really feel* Dr. Tiber would be a much better choice."

"Your preference is duly noted." Kellen froze, staring at Shauss with a strange expression on his face. "There is an urgent matter which requires my attention. These proceedings are on hold until tomorrow morning. Ketrok will stand guard over her until midnight. Shauss, I trust you'll take the next shift?"

"Of course."

He was going to kill that baldheaded ape.

Shauss watched Jasmine's colorless face as Tiber led her away and ground his teeth in rage when Zannen winked at him before following them out.

"Shauss."

He turned to find Kellen staring at him. "I wouldn't be too concerned about Zannen at this point. Neither he nor Tiber can claim Miss King."

Shauss raised his brows. "Why not?"

"When the minister gave her to you to interrogate, Empran recorded the claim." Kellen paused and then gave him an enigmatic smile. "You, my friend, have two mates."

Chapter Six

Monica cornered him again right outside his door. "You're not really going to let that asshole have her?"

Shauss edged past her to enter his quarters, still trying to wrap his head around the idea that Jasmine King was officially his.

He almost grinned at the image of his head warping and stretching to accommodate such a concept. English might be a frightfully inconsistent language that required daily updates to his cerecom download, but it was also quite entertaining, especially when it sprang from Monica's sharp tongue.

"Zannen might be the best choice to keep her and everyone else aboard safe," he said neutrally.

The instant he understood the implications of Kellen's statement, the urge to keep Jasmine out of his brother's hands had gone to war with his honor. How could he bow out of his bond yet again, force Monica to accept another mate, for the sake of a Terran female—especially one who showed a marked predisposition to deceit, conspiracy and violence?

Monica followed him inside, looking around curiously. He glanced around as well—the only thing his surroundings revealed about him was an intolerance for clutter.

"Shauss, seriously, you can't do that to her. If you do, I'll be so pissed, I may never sleep with you again."

"Let me see if I understand this correctly," he said as he settled onto his couch and folded his hands across his stomach. "If I don't claim Jasmine, you'll never sleep with me again. If I do claim Jasmine, you'll never sleep with me again. Isn't that what's commonly referred to as a Catch-22?"

She settled beside him with a disgruntled sigh. "Well hell, it's not like you'll be missing anything, since you don't sleep with me anyway."

Ah, hoist on his own nobility. Or was it his pride again?

"And it's just temporary, right? When all this mess gets straightened out, she can go home…" Her gaze intensified as she added significantly, "If she wants to."

"Why wouldn't she want to?"

"Don't play naïve with me. You know, or at least suspect, she has feelings for you. Kellen told me what you said to her during your *interrogation*." She made a face. "I can't believe you were so cruel to her."

"Indeed, so why would she want to be mated to me?"

She rolled her eyes. "Again with the naïve crap. Shauss, you heard her yesterday morning. Who did she call for when she was out of it?"

"I was a familiar face."

"So was I, but you didn't hear her calling out for me, and you certainly didn't see her laying a liplock on me."

He couldn't argue with that.

"I'm far from an expert on matters of the heart, Shauss, but it looks to me like she might be less frightened of you than of her *feelings* for you. And call me crazy, but I think she might be a better match for you than I am. It's obvious that there's something pretty powerful going on between you two that has little or nothing to do with fear."

He opened his mouth to speak but she interrupted. "You know I care about you. A lot."

"You don't love me anymore?" he asked with a half smile.

"About as much as you love me," she countered.

Shauss scrubbed his palms over his face. He felt great affection for Monica. He really *should* love her, and if he had an ounce of sense, he would. His life would be so much simpler if he could just settle for her leftover passion.

"You gave me my first kiss, Shauss, and that's something a girl never forgets," she said earnestly. "If you loved me and wanted to stay with me forever, I'd be totally happy to keep you. But we both know that's not how it is, and you can't leave Jasmine to that ugly fucker's tender mercies just to protect me from having to choose another mate."

"How is forcing her to mate with me any better than forcing her to mate with him?"

"At least with you I know she'll be getting someone who knows how to give pleasure as well as receive it. And I trust you to choose a second and third who'll do the same."

"Meaning you trust me not to choose Zannen?"

"Exactly. You'd never choose someone you couldn't control."

His hackles rose. "You think I couldn't control Zannen?"

"Please," she snorted. "Not without a fight, and you and I both know you want something a little…different."

"Oh?"

"Oh," she affirmed flatly. "You'll want absolute control over every member of your bond, no matter how temporary it is. In fact, I wouldn't be surprised if you fucked whatever guys you chose just to show them who's boss. But even if you could wrestle that bastard into submission, for some reason I just can't see you fucking him."

Shauss fought a grin and lost. Perhaps he'd underestimated her awareness of his needs—even without knowing Zannen was his brother, she'd certainly divined that he could never fuck the bastard.

"Have you always had this fixation on males fucking each other?" he asked.

"I don't understand why all you guys are so resistant to the idea," she insisted. "It's the perfect solution to your most immediate problems."

"And I suppose if all the males in the universe dropped dead overnight, you'd hook up with Miss King?"

"Damn straight. She's hot," she shot back. When he gave her a startled look, she said, "Hey, you're the ones who turned me into a slave to my libido."

Then she looked as if a thought struck her. "Oh hell—how do you feel about children?"

"In what context?"

"I mean having some of your own."

He studied her for a moment, and then said, "The Andagon house spawned numerous heirs to its legacy, and I feel no desire to continue the Frantere name. Why do you ask?"

"Frantere? Is that your name, Shauss Frantere?"

"It's my father's family name. I'm a first son of the family Frantere, but I hail from the third house of Andagon, which descended through my mother. In America, the two names would probably be hyphenated so I'd be Shauss Frantere-Andagon."

"How weird is it that I didn't even know your full name until now?" Then she turned serious again. "Anyway, I asked because Jasmine wasn't a candidate and she's never been evaluated. She's...very slender, Shauss, and her pelvis looks pretty narrow. It would be a miracle if she could carry a Garathani baby."

"I'd already assumed contraceptive measures would be applied, since Jasmine hasn't agreed to more than a single mating with each male." Not that he was bound by any such restriction—or at least any more bound than he allowed himself to be—but he had no desire to tie her to him permanently with an unwanted pregnancy. No child deserved that.

"I can't believe you'd settle for just once."

"I've managed it with you," he pointed out indelicately.

"Thanks for the reminder, but this is different and you know it."

It *was* different, and obviously more complicated than Kellen had explained to her.

"Monica, with you I have friendship at the very least. What do I have with Jasmine King? What if we prove utterly incompatible and she returns to Earth? I'll have given you up for nothing."

"Sometimes you just have to take a chance." When he hesitated, she added, "Just talk to her before you make up your mind. Kellen says I'll have three months to select another mate. Hopefully this mess with Earth will be straightened out by that time, then Jasmine can go home and you can just step right back into our bond, if that's what you both want."

"What if you've already selected another mate?"

"Then you'll have to settle for third place," she grinned.

He digested that for a moment, and then said, "I could live with that."

"Bullshit. You can't even stand to be second."

He stared at her and she stared back. They both knew that even should his claim on Jasmine turn out to be temporary, if he vacated this bond, he wouldn't be back. Their friendship would remain just that—friendship.

* * * * *

He was there, standing outside her cell as she lay on her bunk. It was too dark to see his expression, but she could feel his concentration focused on her just like she had in her dream. She knew *he* knew she was awake.

Or maybe she was dreaming again. It was hard to tell in the surreal setting of the Garathani ship.

"Miss King."

She pulled the blanket more securely around her and closed her eyes tight. If this was a dream, she was better off not answering. Shoot, even if it wasn't a dream, she was probably better off not answering. After all, what did they have to say to each other? She was about to spend some quality time with three of his king-sized cohorts, and if she survived, she'd head back to Earth. End of story.

"No matter whom you're mated with, you've no need to be frightened," he said gruffly. "Kellen wouldn't allow you to be harmed."

Her anger spiked. "He didn't seem to have any problem with your harming me."

"On the contrary, he believed I wouldn't carry through with my threats."

"He doesn't know you very well then."

After a moment, Shauss said, "Apparently not as well as you do."

Her heartbeat skittered. He *would* have followed through with his threat, not that it mattered. "Why are we having this conversation? I'm tired."

"Because I'm curious. Empran, deactivate confinement field."

Jasmine's eyes popped open as Shauss walked into her cell, determination clear in every line of his body. He stopped beside her bunk and held out his hand. Her eyes followed it up his arm to his shoulder and finally to his face. Her heart raced even as her cheeks flamed. Somehow she knew he was curious to find out if what he thought he knew of her feelings was true. It wasn't clear why—his ego didn't appear to need boosting, and there was bound to be nothing in it for her except more humiliation.

But even as her brain screamed at her to roll over and ignore him, her hand reached for his. She shuddered with reaction to his warm, dry skin as he helped her rise. She longed for and dreaded this experiment in equal measures.

"Shauss, please."

The echo from her erotic dream startled her and she tried to pull away, but his hand tightened while his other hand slid behind her head.

"Please what?"

"Please don't do this to me," she said weakly, clutching at his tight-fitting uniform. "It won't help anything!"

"That remains to be seen," he murmured. He leaned way down and she turned her head just in time to avoid his kiss. His mouth slid down her cheek to the hollow under her ear and her heart skipped a whole handful of beats when he pressed her body against his.

"Oh God," she whimpered against his chest. "Why didn't you just leave me back at the compound to die? It would have been better for everyone."

His hand forced her face up. "Stop feeling sorry for yourself and take what you want."

He didn't have to tell her twice. She went up on her toes as he came down and then his lips landed on hers.

Tears squeezed out from under her eyelids as emotion erupted from every cell in her body. Her mouth opened on a sob and Shauss drew back long enough to shush her. Then he dropped gentle kisses along the tortured curve of her lip as she tried to hold back her anguish. This was so wrong! He was her enemy, her captor, her interrogator and near-rapist. He'd literally scared the piss out of her, for God's sake.

So why did his kiss taste like...home?

A low wail escaped her, but he just kept kissing her lips, drawing their edges between his like he was testing her flavor.

She pounded his shoulders with clenched fists and he responded by settling in for a deep, tongue-filled kiss. Lord, this had better be a dream—her nose was running, and that wasn't how she wanted him to remember her any more than she wanted him to remember the pee running down her legs. All *she* would remember was the symphony of joy that welled up to wash away the knowledge none of this would last. She had this moment, this touch, this one deliberate, wide-awake taste of the beautiful alien who could never be hers.

She was barely conscious of Shauss walking her backward and lifting her until his body crushed hers into the padded wall. The hard ridge of his cock straining between them thrilled her out of her mind, and she thrust against him without thought, wrapping her legs around his waist.

He lifted his head slightly and pressed his lips to each of her eyelids in turn as tears continued to rain down her cheeks. "Don't cry, *aramai*."

"I can't believe I'm doing this," she choked. Then she remembered. "Oh my God, Monica! I can't do this!"

She shoved at him and he stepped back, letting her drop to the floor and stumble away. "I don't know why you did that, but I hope you're satisfied."

God knew she wouldn't be, mated to that bald-headed ape and whoever else he chose to inflict on her.

"Not yet," he murmured. "But I will be."

* * * * *

There were way more people than she'd expected when Tiber and the guards escorted her into the council chambers through a side door. The commander, the minister and four old men she assumed were council members sat at a curved table at the head of the oval room, holding a quiet discussion, and a couple of dozen warriors sat mute in a gallery at the back. Zannen stared at her from the front row, his face devoid of emotion, and she fought back the urge to scream at him as her skin tried to crawl from her bones.

Shauss and Hastion stood in the huge open area in front of the table, their expressions equally unreadable. Ugh. Nothing like facing your accusers in front of your judge and jury.

Hastion's lips curved in a rueful smile as she and Tiber joined them. Though he looked much better than he had yesterday, the brownish-yellow tinge of fading bruises still marred his eye and nose.

Cringing, she glanced at Tiber. He'd been strangely silent, which was really making her nervous. She wished she'd had a chance to talk with him privately, but being under guard had eliminated any chance of that. The jerks who'd taken over for Shauss wouldn't even face the other away for her to use the toilet, so she'd held it all night. When Tiber showed up at the crack of dawn, he'd taken one look at her and ordered them to turn their backs so she could relieve herself. For that alone she could have kissed him. Then he'd had them escort her to a room with a private shower and given her a grooming kit and ten minutes to clean herself up. That's when she knew she'd made the right decision.

After her inexplicable encounter with Shauss, she'd spent hours tossing and turning in her bunk, weighing her options under his silent, watchful eye, knowing there was no way she could escape now. As closely as they all watched her, she probably couldn't even get close enough to an airlock to space herself, so suicide was out too.

Sometime near morning, she decided it was up to her to make a bargain she could live with. If she had to agree to take Zannen as a second or third mate in order to be awarded to Tiber, so be it. He'd been nothing but kind to her, and if the look in his eye was anything to go by, he was attracted to her. He was far from unattractive himself, and the fact that he was a physician hopefully meant he had taken an oath to do no harm, as Terran doctors did. Even better, he was a psychiatrist, which meant he would have some understanding of her position and perhaps not pull out his dagger and slit her throat when he found out how completely she'd deceived them all. If he was her primary mate, he might actually protect her.

Tiber escorted her to the spot right in front of the table, and though she was covered more completely than yesterday, being the center of so much masculine attention made her feel utterly, glaringly naked. It didn't help that she was braless *and* commando now, in addition to having no makeup. That was her only complaint about Tiber's service—when he'd taken her dirty clothes and given her this full-body suit, he'd failed to return her panties. Did she have anything left to call her own?

Minister Cecine turned, focusing on her, and she had the insane urge to grab Tiber's hand and hold it like a scared little girl. Then again, her palms were clammy and shaking—he was probably better off not touching her.

"Good morning, Miss King," the minister said, unsmiling. When she acknowledged him with a short nod, he continued. "Before we proceed, let me reiterate that our objective in requiring you to take mates is not to punish you for any misdeeds but to keep you and everyone aboard safe. That being the case, I had intended to grant Tiber's petition to be your primary mate on the condition you both accept Zannen as second."

Jasmine's heart fluttered. There was a really big *but* at the end of that statement and she doubted it meant happy things for her.

"However, I must now formally deny both their petitions on the basis of a preexisting award."

"What?" Jasmine frowned, looking back and forth between Cecine and Tiber. Tiber didn't look surprised at all, which made her stomach sink. "What are you talking about? What award?"

"Miss King, Empran recorded Lieutenant Shauss' unconditional claim the day I awarded you to him."

She felt herself sway. "Shauss? Are you talking about when he—he—" *Nearly raped me* rang in her head but she couldn't make herself say it. "Interrogated me?"

He dipped his chin in assent.

"But he's already got a mate."

"Garathani law is still evolving," he explained. "Though it specifies that all males are required to share their mates, until this morning it included no language prohibiting males from mating with two females, which meant we weren't alerted to the conflict until I tried to award you to Tiber. Lieutenant Shauss has consented to terminate his bond with my daughter in order to finalize his claim on you, and the council has already approved the annulment."

She looked at Shauss and joy squeezed her chest. He would give up Monica for her.

Then dread squeezed her chest even tighter. Shit, when he found out exactly what he'd given up Monica for, he would be livid.

"Shauss, you can't," she said faintly. "You can't throw away what you have with Monica for one time with me."

"Perhaps I should clarify, Miss King," Cecine said. "The award I made was recorded without condition, which means that, although his secondary and tertiary mates must initially observe the one-time claiming requirement, Lieutenant Shauss is under no such constraint. You are bound to him and obliged to acquiesce to his demands for sexual congress until such time as he rescinds his claim—assuming he ever does."

She gaped at him. "I have to have sex with Shauss? *Forever?*"

"For the rest of your life, yes—or his, whichever is shorter. If he decides to keep you beyond the initially agreed-upon period, your bond would be converted to a traditional bond and your secondary and tertiary mates would acquire the customary mating privileges."

"No," she said. "Shauss, Monica is Garathani. She's the minister's daughter, for God's sake! I'm just a puny human. You can't possibly want to give her up for me."

He looked at her impassively. "I have my reasons, which I'll gladly discuss with you at length after the ceremony."

"But I'm not worth it—I can never give you children!"

"That's of no consequence to me."

Jasmine wrung her clammy hands. Oh God, oh God—this couldn't be happening. "Shauss, please don't do this. I'd rather have Tiber. Really."

"Minister, if you please." Tiber's voice was strong and everyone froze. "I wish to challenge Lieutenant Shauss for the right to claim Miss King."

Shauss' jaw hardened to stone at the hope on Jasmine's face.

"Perfect," he said coldly. "I've been looking for a way to get you off my back. Killing you ought to do the trick."

Jasmine immediately stepped between them, putting her arms out as if to protect Tiber. "Shauss, no!"

"That would be unwise, Doctor." Kellen rose from his seat, no doubt preparing for violence to erupt—which it very well could, Shauss realized, if Tiber didn't back the fuck off *his* female.

"Commander, she doesn't wish to be mated to him," Tiber replied implacably.

"She doesn't wish to see you die, either, I suspect."

Shauss seized Jasmine's upper arm. "*Empran, privacy field.*"

When they were enveloped in a solid white flare bubble, he looked down at the female trying to wrench out of his hold.

"Tell him to withdraw the challenge, Jasmine," he said in as mild a tone as he could manage. "Tiber knows I'm a trained assassin and any challenge between us would almost certainly end in his death. Are you willing to let him pay such a price after what we shared last night?"

"Last night was a mistake!"

"No, last night was finally some truth between us." She jerked in his hold again, but he persisted. "I have nothing but the best of intentions in claiming you. I would give my life to protect you."

"Oh really? And who's going to protect me from you?" she demanded, trying to pry his fingers off her arm.

"You have my word that no harm will come to you while you belong to me." He leaned down and brushed his nose over her temple. She smelled lovely. Placing his lips against the shell of her ear, he breathed, "And you do belong to me, Jasmine King. You can't deny that."

When she didn't reply, he slid his hand behind the delicate stalk of her neck and tilted her head back until it rested in his palm. He would like nothing more that to free her rich brown hair from its elastic band—the ponytail made her look oddly innocent and there was nothing innocent about what he wanted to do to her.

He scraped his teeth over her earlobe and felt her shudder.

"You scare me to death," she finally whispered.

He raised his head.

"I know, and part of me wishes I could change that." Watching her closely, he added, "On the other hand, a certain amount of fear can be a good thing between a dominant male and a submissive female."

Her reaction was immediate and unmistakable—flags of color rose in her cheeks as her pupils expanded and her breathing grew rough. "I am not submissive!" she cried. "When are you going to get it through your thick head that I am not now, nor will I ever be, anyone's puppet? I have a brain, damn it, and I can think for myself."

"I never said you couldn't. But when it comes to this..." He rubbed his thumb gently over the pulse in her throat and she swallowed, looking at him with such despair and longing, Shauss felt his own throat tighten. If he let her go now, before they'd explored whatever might exist between them, they would both regret it for the rest of their lives.

"Perhaps we can arrive at a compromise," he proposed.

After a heartbeat, she asked, "What kind of compromise?"

"I am prepared to surrender my unconditional award before the council if you, in turn, will agree to give yourself to me without reservation until it's safe for you to return to Earth."

She chewed her lip for a long moment. "You won't hurt Tiber?"

"Not if he withdraws the challenge."

"And you'll let me go home when this is all over?"

"If that's truly what you want."

"It is," she said with finality. "I'm going home as soon as the commander gives the okay."

"That's a chance I'm willing to take." He captured her lips and sank into her with his tongue, delighting in the sweet, fruity taste of her. As he'd hoped, she leaned into him with a moan, and he took full advantage. Sliding his hands down around her waist, he lifted her higher and trapped her against him. She wrapped her arms around his neck as they kissed and he shuddered at the feel of her fingers combing through his hair. It wasn't the delicacy of her touch so much as the awareness of her desire for him that set his blood on fire.

He was going to fuck her. Over and over and over, by Peserin's sword, he was going to fuck Jasmine King until she couldn't even remember another male, much less desire one.

He let his hands slide down to her thighs and pulled them up until they bracketed his waist. *"Empran, cancel privacy field."*

"It looks to me like she wants him," Hastion's voice rang out.

Jasmine jerked her lips away from Shauss' and shoved at his shoulders, fire blazing in her cheeks. When he let her slide to the floor, she felt the stiff rod of his cock and the fire blazed even hotter.

"You jerk," she muttered, wiping the back of her hand over her mouth and trying to look anywhere but at the huge tent in the front of his uniform.

Shauss didn't bother wiping the shiny evidence of their kiss from his lips. "Why don't you tell them about our agreement, Jasmine?"

Although his tone was pleasant, his eyes darted to Tiber, reinforcing the *or he dies* message. Damn it, why couldn't it have been Zannen who challenged Shauss? She'd step back and watch him die with a smile on her face.

Jasmine stared at him for a minute before turning to Tiber. "I appreciate your trying to protect me, Tiber, I really do, but I want you to withdraw your challenge. Shauss has agreed to let me go home when it's safe if I…" She licked suddenly dry lips. "If I give myself to him without reservation until then."

"Is this true, Lieutenant?" the minister asked.

"Yes, Minister."

Tiber frowned. "Jasmine, are you certain?"

She took a shuddering breath. "Yes."

"He frightens you."

"That may be, but I don't want you to be hurt or killed because my head's a wreck."

"I can take care of myself." He sounded offended.

"I'm sure you can," she assured him softly, "but please drop the challenge. For all our sakes."

He hesitated before nodding at Cecine. "I withdraw my challenge."

"I'm pleased to hear it," Cecine replied. "Lieutenant, have you selected your secondary and tertiary mates?"

"Second will be Ensign Hastion."

Zannen snorted. "Because he did such a fine job of containing her yesterday."

If the bastard had had any hair, Hastion's look would have scorched it right off. "She won't catch me unawares again."

"And tertiary?" the minister prompted.

Jasmine held her breath, praying *Please not Zannen, please anyone but Zannen!*

When Shauss looked at her and said Tiber's name, she nearly fainted with relief.

"I told you I would protect you," he murmured.

Cecine stood. "Council members, please cast your vote on formalizing the conditional bond between Jasmine King, Lieutenant Shauss, Ensign Hastion and Dr. Tiber."

Although no one said a word, the minister said, "A unanimous vote in favor. Empran, announce the amended award." Then he focused on Jasmine. "Miss King, your medical records indicate that you are no longer a virgin, and Empran's research leads us to believe you've had sexual contact with at least four different Terran males. Is this correct?"

Cheeks burning, she nodded stiffly. What business was it of theirs how many men she'd slept with, anyway?

"Since you're not one of the candidates, and therefore have not undergone a compatibility evaluation, I'm ordering an examination prior to claiming. Presumably you'll be able to take your mates without difficulty, but we would be remiss in letting them have you without ascertaining your fitness to mate."

"But—"

"My daughter will perform the examination."

Jasmine closed her mouth and nodded. Exactly what she'd been about to ask for. *Please, Monica, have my spray ready!*

"Now one last technicality to attend to is the matter of protected claiming periods. As a result of Pret's attack on my daughter, the general council has amended the law regarding initial claiming of a female. As before, primary males have one Garathani day, or twenty-four point four Terran hours, to finalize their claims before claim protection is forfeit. Secondary males now have two days and tertiary have three. This gives smaller Terran females the opportunity to recover from any discomfort claiming may cause before being subjected to further claiming."

"Minister, I respectfully request *juranin* status." Zannen's announcement provoked gasps and murmurs of conversation.

"The hell you do," Shauss growled. "She's not Garathani."

"Even so, I am within my rights both as a family member and a rival for mating privileges."

Jasmine's eyes widened. What in the world were they talking about? And whose family was he a member of?

"But *jurana* is archaic!"

Zannen went nose to nose with Shauss. "So is the declaration ritual, little brother. That didn't stop Commander Kellen from performing it last week."

Jasmine gasped. How in the world could the classically beautiful Shauss and that brawny bastard possibly be brothers?

Without taking his eyes off of Zannen, Shauss said, "Minister, you cannot allow this."

"Actually," Cecine sighed, "I must. He *is* within his rights under the law."

Jasmine jumped when Shauss slammed a fist on the table. "Then the law should be repealed!"

"Perhaps, but for the moment it still stands."

Then the minister stood and scanned the chamber. "Unless there is some objection from the council, I'm granting Lieutenant Zannen *juranin* status."

When no objections were raised, he addressed Shauss but looked at Jasmine with a troubled expression. "Lieutenant, may your bond prove worthy of what you've sacrificed for it."

Chapter Seven

"So this is a little awkward," Monica said, leaning against the exam table.

"Just slightly." Jasmine could barely look at her. God, how had this happened? "I am so sorry, Monica. I can't believe—"

"Jasmine, relax."

"Relax?" Jasmine repeated incredulously. "I just swiped your mate and you want me to relax?"

"You didn't swipe my mate. Well, you did," Monica corrected with a wry grin, "but not the one you think you did. I actually kind of had my eye on Hastion for our next second."

"Oh my God, you mean I swiped both of them?"

"No, just Hastion. Shauss was more like a gift." When Jasmine gaped at her, Monica hurried to say, "Don't worry, I was pretty sure he was going to claim you anyway, but when Kellen told me what was going down, I just gave Shauss a little nudge to make sure you didn't get stuck with that bonehead Zannen."

Jasmine felt dizzy. "Oh my God, Monica, you pushed Shauss to claim me?"

"No, I encouraged him to do what he needed to."

"Oh my God," Jasmine repeated, heat blazing in her cheeks. And here she'd thought Shauss was taking her because he wanted to. "What did you tell him?"

"I didn't betray any of your confidences, if that's what's worrying you. Shauss only rebonded with us to protect me from having to choose another mate, so I made it clear I didn't need his protection."

"Oh my God."

"Will you quit saying that? Jesus, I thought you'd be happy."

"Happy! I have to have sex with Shauss *and* Hastion *and* Tiber."

"Gasp! You have to fuck three incredibly sexy aliens—a fate worse than death."

"It's not funny!"

"Well, excuse me for saving you from that hulking bastard."

"Monica, the minister was going to make *Tiber* my primary mate, not Zannen."

"Tiber? But I thought…" Monica blinked. "Did Shauss know?"

"Yes, he knew! Tiber challenged him for me and Shauss threatened to kill him if I didn't agree to…to…"

Monica stared at her for a minute and then a huge grin split her face. "I knew it! Shauss is stuck on you too."

"You just don't get it, do you?"

"What's to get? Not only are you going to have unlimited wild monkey sex with the guy you're in love with, but you get to take a flaming-hot exhibitionist and a sensitive doctor type for a bonus test drive. What is the big fucking deal?"

"I'm not in love with him!" Jasmine shouted. "And you want to know what the big deal is? I'll tell you what the big deal is!"

"Well, lay it on me then!"

Jasmine paced between the exam tables, clasping her hands behind her hips to still their shaking. She couldn't believe what she was about to do, but she just had to. She couldn't take facing all this alone.

"Tell me something, Monica." She stopped, staring at the newly buxom doctor. "Is your Hippocratic oath still in effect now that you're no longer human?"

"There's no reason to get ugly," Monica snapped. "I'm just as human as I ever was, and yes, my oath still means everything to me."

"And what about the rules of doctor-patient confidentiality? Are they still as important to you?"

"Of course."

"No *of course* about it," Jasmine insisted. "You're no longer governed by the laws of the United States."

"Yeah, but I'm still governed by my conscience."

"So if I talk to you about a medical condition you'll keep it to yourself."

"I already told you I didn't betray your confidences to Shauss, and believe me, I really wish he'd known about your menopause before he agreed to anything." It was Monica's turn to pace. "I did point out how you're built and told him it would be a miracle if you could carry a Garathani baby, which technically is true, but I only did that because I was pushing him to protect you and I didn't want him to go into a bond with you, anticipating the pitter-patter of little extraterrestrial feet."

She stopped and looked Jasmine in the eye. "But I repeat, I *didn't* betray your confidence."

"Well, thank you. But if I told you about something else, something more serious…"

"Jasmine, you're pissing me off," Monica growled. "Yes, of course I'd keep it to myself. Unless it was contagious or something, if it put others' lives in danger."

Ah, now there was the catch. If Monica thought she might put others' lives in danger, she'd feel compelled to tell Kellen.

"Monica, I swear I'm not contagious or dangerous in any way, and I need your promise that you won't reveal what you learn about my condition to anyone. *Anyone*, and that means Kellen and Shauss too."

"You've got it, already! Now tell me."

Jasmine searched Monica's face. "You know the nasal spray I asked you to replicate for me?"

"Yeah. It's on my to-do list for this afternoon."

"Great." Jasmine wiped her hands on her legs. "But it's not really for menopause."

Monica's gaze narrowed. "So why did you tell me it was? What's it really for?"

"It really is a hormone complex." Jasmine took a deep breath. "But it's designed to suppress part of my endocrine system."

"Say what? Why?"

"Please promise me you won't go crazy."

Monica rolled her eyes. "Would you just spit it out, for God's sake? What's wrong with you?"

"The truth is…" Jasmine braced herself and looked her square in the eye. "I'm Narthani."

* * * * *

"Well, this is…rather unexpected," Tiber commented as they waited outside the infirmary.

"Indeed." Shauss still couldn't believe he'd said Tiber's name. Of all the warriors he could have chosen… Verr, Holligan—Peserin's hell, even Zannen would have been better. He was strong, ruthless and more than able to keep Jasmine in line, as well as protect her from threats. That she couldn't stand him was only a point in his favor—with his singular lack of interpersonal skills, there was no way Zannen would ever be able to talk her into further sexual contact after the initial claiming. And despite Monica's assessment of his malleability, he *could* be controlled, probably much more easily than Tiber.

But no, Shauss had doomed himself to months—and potentially the rest of his life, if Jasmine could be persuaded— with the ship's wily psychiatric doctor. *Why* was a mystery only the Powers could fathom. And he hadn't even negotiated terms with the man! If he'd been thinking ahead, he could have offered Tiber third position on the condition that he settle for the initial claiming and not press for more, and Tiber would have accepted for no other reason than to protect her from Zannen. Now he was free to woo her as he pleased during his guard rotations.

Shauss was going to have to establish his dominance over all involved in the bond immediately.

"I could have let you challenge me," he told Tiber.

"You could."

"You'd be dead by now."

"Probably."

"So why did you challenge me?"

"Because she needs a champion."

Shauss stiffened. "*I* will be her champion."

"That remains to be seen."

"Tiber, do not make the mistake of trying to usurp me."

"I wouldn't dream of it."

"In this bond or in Jasmine's affections," he specified.

Tiber's brow rose. "You assume Jasmine's affections are yours to lose."

Shauss looked away, his jaw clenched. Tiber's determination to zero in on his weak spots obviously hadn't lessened in the slightest. Beating his troublesome ass into submission was going to be a real pleasure.

* * * * *

Monica's jaw dropped. "What the fuck do you mean, you're *Narthani*?" When Jasmine shrugged apologetically, her eyes bugged. "Jesus Christ, do you realize the position you're putting me in? You're Narthani! You're the—"

"Enemy. I know." Jasmine sighed. "Now do you see why I was so careful? I had to be sure you wouldn't take this straight to Kellen. God only knows what they might do to me if they find out."

Monica recoiled. "*Do* to you? Jasmine, the Garathani aren't barbarians. I don't think they'd do anything to you unless…" Her eyes narrowed.

"I promise you, Monica, I had nothing to do with Pret beyond what I told you. Honestly! I would never have helped him if I'd known what he had planned. I was just as much a pawn as you were."

"That's not what's worrying me. The big picture says that there are aliens at work on Earth besides the Garathani, and now you pop up and say, 'Hi, I'm Narthani!'" She winced. "Holy shit, Kellen will have my ass if I keep this from him."

"I know, and I'm sorry, Monica, but please don't tell him." Jasmine looked her in the eye, laying bare all her fear and hope and uncertainty. "I'm begging you."

"Why should I trust you?"

Looking away, Jasmine swallowed. That was the question, and it would always be an issue. Not only was she Narthani, but she'd already helped a rogue Garathani perpetuate felony kidnapping on one of their females, albeit innocently. Nothing she did or said could convince anyone that she harbored no ill will toward them.

Her stomach clenched. The gamble hadn't paid off. She was probably about to be incarcerated, interrogated, maybe even executed. The possibilities spun in her head until she wanted to vomit.

"Jasmine! Snap out of it!"

Monica was waving a hand in front of her face.

"Hey, I'm not saying I'm going to turn you in. I just want to hear your story before I put my life and the lives of everybody on this ship into your hands." She gestured to the desk in the corner. "So have a seat and talk to me. Please."

That was something, anyway, and a very reasonable request.

Taking a deep breath, she began her tale. "I was thirteen when I found out the truth…"

* * * * *

Bumping up over the curb into her yard, Jasmine steered her bicycle around the side of the house and into the backyard. She was a half-hour late and didn't look forward to the lecture she'd get if her father was home. He was so paranoid and overprotective, she was about to smother. Mom would probably let it slide though—she'd always been cooler than Dad.

Squeezing the hand brakes, she slid to a stop by the garage door and peered inside. Rats! He was home. Fifteen minutes minimum of pure torture was headed her way.

Sighing, she dismounted and grabbed her backpack off the handlebars then leaned the bike against the garage. A heartbeat later she changed her mind and used the kickstand— Dad hated it when her bike handles left scuff marks on the siding. He was almost as anal-retentive as he was paranoid.

Anal-retentive. Jasmine grinned. She'd read about that at the library and thought it fit him just perfectly. The ultimate anal-retentive control freak.

And just think, in five years she'd be eighteen and could move out on her own, away from him and his crazy ideas. They were going to be the longest five years of her life.

She punched in the security code without looking and then shoved her key into the lock. Their doors were always locked whether they were home or not. Stupid. Nobody else on this block locked their doors unless they were gone overnight or out of town for the weekend or something.

Turning the key, she slipped into the kitchen and automatically reset the alarm. The backpack landed under the bench by the door and her grass-stained sneakers weren't far behind. Jasmine padded to the fridge in her socks and opened the door, looking for something to fill the noisy cavern of her stomach. Cheerleading was hard work, though she was lucky enough to be too tall to throw around. She'd hate that, having to trust one of those turkeys to catch her. Especially when a routine was new, the guys tended to drop as often as they caught. *Ow.*

Grabbing a can of diet soda and the carton of cottage cheese, she kicked the door closed. Two minutes later she was sitting at the table, enjoying her guilt-free little snack when her father walked in.

"You're late."

"I know," she mumbled around a bite. Swallowing quickly, she added, "I'm really sorry, Dad. Cheerleading practice ran late and I—"

"Come to the den at once. Your mother and I have something to discuss with you."

"Uh, okay." She scooped up one last big spoonful and shoved it into her mouth before snagging her soda. Jeez, what was up with him? He was acting even weirder than usual. He looked funny too. His hair looked like it hadn't seen the business end of a brush since the light bulb was invented.

Her mother was already there, sitting on the couch with a worried look on her face. That wasn't good.

Jasmine took the chair her father pointed at, carefully setting the soda can on a coaster. Her father sat beside her mother, directly across from her.

Without preamble, he said, "You have developed blemishes on your face."

Heat bloomed in her cheeks. All this drama because she was getting zits? "Gee, Dad, thanks for noticing. I swear, I'm washing my face every—"

"Your hygiene habits do not concern me at this time. What concerns me is that your body has begun maturing."

"Well, thank God!" Jasmine rolled her eyes. "I was beginning to think I'd never grow up."

"Child, this is a very serious matter. There is a reason you have not matured at the same rate as the other girls of your acquaintance."

Jasmine frowned. "What do you mean?"

"You're not human."

Well. Okay. That was special.

"Um, you're kidding, right?" She grinned at him uncertainly. Halloween was just three weeks away. Maybe he'd finally discovered what a joke was and had decided to play one on her. *I'm not human. Uh-huh, pull the other one, Dad.*

"How often have you known me to jest?"

Right. Jasmine swallowed. "So if I'm not human, what am I?" Not that she believed any of this crap.

"You're a species closely related to Terrans, but considerably more evolved."

Oh God, he'd finally done it. Her father had officially gone off his rocker.

Jasmine snagged her soda and stood up. "I don't know what I've done to make you act like this, but consider me punished, okay? I'm going to my room now. Call me when it's safe to come down."

"Sit. Now."

She knew better than to ignore that tone of voice. Flopping back into her chair, Jasmine took a long swallow of the soda without looking at her parents. Her father wanted to talk, fine, she'd let him talk. That didn't mean she had to listen to his bullshit.

Her mother sighed. "Jasmine, sweetheart—"

"I will handle this, Dayree."

Jasmine looked up in time to see her mother's eyes flash at his imperious tone. "She's as much my daughter as yours, Ragan, and I'll thank you to remember that."

Turning to Jasmine, she continued. "Sweetheart, this is going to be hard enough for you to digest without shutting us out. Please just listen and try to be accepting."

"I'm all ears."

Her father's eyes narrowed, but he didn't comment on her sarcasm. "I think this will be simplest if I lay the facts out for you in chronological order," he began. "Officially you are a Terran citizen. You were born right after Dayree and I arrived for a long-term assignment on Earth. Our mission was to immerse ourselves in a Terran population and study them. Dayree was what Terrans would call an anthropologist and her mission was to study their culture and customs. My multi-discipline background enabled me to study the physical characteristics of the various races."

Jasmine cocked a brown at him. "Okay, so if you're not human, what are you?"

"We are Narthani, of the planet Narthan in the Peserinar star system."

"I've never heard of the Peserinar star system."

He smiled with mock indulgence. "Please, name all the star systems you've heard of. I'm interested to hear how far-reaching your knowledge of astronomy is."

Heat flowed into her cheeks. All she knew about the stars she'd gleaned from her infrequent encounters with *Star Trek* reruns. She wouldn't make herself look any more ignorant by trying to name the ones she'd heard there.

"Ragan, there's no need to make fun of her."

"She's too arrogant."

"She's a teenager."

"Exactly. Now if you'll allow me to continue...?" Her father looked at her mother expectantly and she gave a grudging nod. "Our mission was scheduled to last for approximately ten solar years, but a series of global disasters made it impossible for us to be recalled."

Jasmine digested that for a moment. "So you're stranded here."

"Exactly."

"For how long? Not that I believe any of this," she added quickly.

"Indefinitely."

Her stomach churned. "So why are you suddenly telling me all this now?"

"Because your body is beginning to mature and there are certain choices you must make."

Her eyes widened. Oh God, what were they trying to tell her? Was something going to be wrong with her? Was something *already* wrong with her?

Holy crap, she was an alien!

"No." She shook her head wildly and stood up again, slapping her hands over her ears. "I don't want to hear any more. I don't believe any of this. I don't know why, but you're lying to me and I want you to stop it. Stop it! Now!"

She ran up the stairs to her room without looking to see if anyone followed her. Slamming the door as hard as she could, Jasmine threw herself onto her bed and buried her face in her pillow, sobbing.

It wasn't long before she felt the loving sweep of her mother's hand across her back. Hiccupping, she turned over. "Mom, please tell me it isn't true. I'm not an alien, am I?"

"I'm afraid it's all true, sweetheart. Your father and I are Narthani agents, and you…" Her mother brushed Jasmine's damp bangs out of her eyes with gentle fingers and sighed. "Well, you're just as alien as we are."

"But why?" Jasmine wailed, burying her face in her mother's breast. "It's not fair! I don't want to be an alien. What's going to happen to me? Am I going to turn into some kind of freak?"

Her mother squeezed her hard. "Of course not! But Jasmine, your body is preparing to undergo some major changes and I think you would be wise to consider what your father has to offer."

"What do you mean, *major changes*?"

"He's kept close track of your growth statistics, and from his calculations it appears that when you complete your maturation phase, you will be well over six feet tall. Closer to seven feet, in fact."

Jasmine drew back in horror. "What! I'm going to be a *giant*?"

"Well, you're going to be very tall, anyway," her mother said dryly.

"But you guys aren't that tall!"

Her mother chewed her lip a moment before saying, "It's all a matter of genetics. Both your father and I are shorter than the average Narthani—the smallest in both our families, in fact. You inherited taller genes."

"Oh my God, I *will* be a freak! Nobody will ever ask me out on a date or want to kiss me or have babies with me..." She trailed off with a gulp. *Oh my God, please don't let this be happening!*

"That will not be the only difference between you and Terran women, my dearest heart," her mother said softly.

"Now what?" Jasmine groaned, bracing herself. What could be worse than being seven feet tall? "Am I going to grow an extra head or long, dripping fangs or something?"

"No, but you will have an extra orifice in your...private area."

"Huh?" Jasmine blinked. "Are you talking about a vagina? I already know about that from health class."

"I'm talking about your spur nook."

She blinked harder this time, a blush creeping up her neck again. She'd felt pretty mature, tossing out the v-word as if she'd been saying it all her life, but now she felt like the world's biggest jerk. "Do I even want to know what that is?"

"I don't think it's anything you need to consider at length right now. But my point is, if we don't intervene, you will soon become dramatically different from most of your Terran companions."

Jasmine latched on to one word. "Intervene? What are you talking about? Can you keep me from changing?"

"That's what your father was trying to tell you, Jasmine. He's synthesized a pheromone blocker that will prevent your body from maturing any further."

"Keep my body from maturing." Jasmine stared at her, her mind cranking away. If her body didn't mature any further, that would mean... "Are you saying I'll never grow up at all?"

"Your brain will continue to develop normally, but your body will remain as it is now."

Dazed, Jasmine said, "You're saying if I take this blocker Dad made, I'll never have any boobs."

"Not naturally."

Jasmine shook her head, unsure what to make of that and unwilling to figure it out at the moment.

"And I'll never get hair in...those places."

Her mother shook her head.

"And I'll never get my period. And I'll never have babies..."

"Yes, that's exactly what it means."

Jasmine started to shake with the force of the emotion rising in her throat. "Mother, this isn't fair," she said in a deadly voice. "How could you do this to me? I don't want this! It's not fair!"

Her mother's eyes filled with tears. "I know, baby, and I'm so sorry. So sorry..."

"Yeah, well a fat lot of good sorry does me! I'm screwed if I take the blocker and screwed if I don't. I'm basically screwed here, is what you're telling me. Right?" The anger built and built inside her until she wanted to scream with the pressure of it. "You and Dad got to have your marriage and your baby, but what do I get, huh? I get stuck with the consequences, is what I get!"

She jumped off the bed and ran to her dresser, opening the top drawer and pulling out her diary. "You know what's in here?" she demanded, tearing open the tab without unlocking it. "This is full of all my stupid hopes and dreams, and you know what?"

Jasmine rushed into her bathroom. The light was still on from this morning, which would really piss her father off if he knew, but screw him. She stood over the toilet and started tearing pages out of her diary with shaking hands, wadding them up and dropping them into the toilet as the tears streamed down her face.

"These are my hopes and dreams now, Mother," she choked, slamming her fingers down on the handle and flushing the balls of paper. When the bowl was empty, she closed the lid and sank to her knees, resting her head against the edge. "There they go, right down the toilet. I hope you're happy."

Chapter Eight

Monica leaned back in her chair. "Jeez, I'm sorry, Jasmine. That really sucks."

"I didn't tell you to get your sympathy."

She grinned. "Yeah, you did."

"Okay, maybe I did a little," Jasmine admitted.

"So you've been using the nasal spray all this time?"

"Up until I left home. Once I wasn't exposed to my father's residual pheromone stream, I didn't need it. I only started using it again when I hired on at the compound."

"So you were at the compound…why, exactly?"

"Because I had this stupid idea I could keep an eye on the Garathani and judge for myself if they were as evil as my father always claimed," she sighed. "You see how well that turned out."

"Why did you tell me this now?"

She hugged her knees, and said, "Because I'm scared out of my mind and I don't know what else to do."

Monica narrowed her eyes. "You know, Jas, if you're a spy, you're pretty damn inept."

"Great. That makes me feel much better." Swallowing, she asked, "Does that mean you'll keep this to yourself?"

"I will, but I really wish you'd tell Kellen. I'd trust him with anything."

"The commander might not be too bad, but, Monica, how do you think Shauss would react to the news that he traded the minister's daughter for an inept Narthani spy?"

Monica winced. "Not well. He's pretty volatile—not to mention proud."

"He'd kill me—but only after he made me suffer for making him look like a fool. Then he'd go after my father." Before Monica could speak, Jasmine said, "Don't deny it. You know it's true."

"Any other surprises you want to spring on me?" Monica asked with a long-suffering sigh.

"As a matter of fact…"

"Oh Jesus, now what?"

"Breast implants weren't the only surgery I had." When Monica's brows flew up, Jasmine blushed. "The doctors operated downtown to make me look normal, and it would be nice to know if I'm going to pass inspection or if Tiber's going to take one look and send me to the brig."

"What in the hell did they do?"

"They implanted a prosthetic clitoris."

"You've got to be kidding! It doesn't work, does it?"

"No, I couldn't be that lucky. But as far as I know, no guy has ever suspected I was anything but a human woman."

"So you've been with guys? I mean, as beautiful as you are, I doubt you could be a virgin, but you never know."

"No." Jasmine sighed. "I mean, yes, I've been with guys and no, I'm not a virgin. And thank you, but I don't feel very beautiful right now."

Monica rolled her eyes. "Oh please. You're gorgeous and you know it."

"It's an illusion, Monica. I'm not real. Hell, I even have dental implants to replace two teeth that have fallen out in the last few years."

"Well, you look plenty real to me. And to Shauss, if his claiming you is anything to go by." Then her eyes widened. "Jesus, you must have been scared shitless when he pulled his interrogation act on you."

"That's putting it mildly. I don't think anything about my appearance would have given me away, but it was always a possibility. I don't know all that much about Narthanis or Garathanis. For all I knew, he could have smelled the difference in me."

Monica stood up. "Well I was going to examine you anyway to make sure you can accommodate a Garathani male, so I'll take a gander and see if anything jumps out at me."

Jasmine blinked hard to clear the mental image of a toothy alien mouth jumping out from between her legs and biting Monica's face off. What in the world had made her watch so many sci-fi movies when she was growing up? It only made her that much more fearful.

"Is it possible I won't be able to?" she asked as Monica moved down the cabinet opening doors.

"Definitely. Tight can be stretched, but shallow's a problem. If he can't go deep enough, his spur might not get in on the action."

Hope blossomed. "Hey, can you just tell them I'm not big enough?"

"I could, but they'd probably want my report verified by one of the Garathani doctors." When Jasmine sagged, she added, "Besides, wouldn't you have to go to detention then?"

"No doubt." Jasmine shuddered. "Thank God I didn't get awarded to Zannen. He claims to be better endowed than Kellen."

"I'd like to see that," Monica snorted. "But you know how guys are. He's probably just compensating for a Vienna sausage."

Although she giggled, Jasmine couldn't help but soften slightly at the idea Zannen's overbearing attitude might stem from some deep personal insecurity. There was obviously no love lost between him and Shauss.

"Oh Jesus, now I know you're not a spy—you actually feel sorry for that prick."

"I do not." She bit her lip, and then asked, "Did you know he and Shauss are brothers?"

Monica paused in her search of the cabinets and blinked at her. "Excuse me?"

"Zannen called him *little brother* and Shauss didn't deny it." It was still almost impossible to believe. Shauss, with his pleasantly chiseled face, two-toned hair and long sleek muscles, was breathtakingly beautiful. Zannen couldn't have been less beautiful if he'd tried—his rough-hewn facial features were arranged in a perpetual scowl, and even his bald head seemed to bulge with monstrously overdeveloped muscles. The only things they appeared to have in common were those impenetrable black eyes and the ability to scare the wits out of her.

"No fucking way." Monica stared at her for a second and then burst out laughing. "God, I'm such a dork—there I got all warm and fuzzy because he told me his last name." She shook her head. "You guys are perfect for each other—I can't think of any two people who are better at keeping secrets."

"Well, now you know all of mine." Jasmine sighed. "Monica, thank you for trying to help me."

"Trying? Aha!" She pulled out a hospital gown and tossed it to Jasmine. Turning to face the table, she plunged her hands into the sterilizing block. "Why does it sound like you doubt my chances of success?"

Jasmine quickly changed into the gown. Then she swallowed hard and voiced her greatest fear. "It might be too late already. I might already have been exposed to too much pheromone to ever go home."

Monica looked over her shoulder. "Would that be the worst thing ever? Call me crazy, but I really think there could be something amazing between you and Shauss. Maybe you should just let it happen. They'd probably think you're a GaraTer like me."

"And live a lie for the rest of my life? No thank you."

"Like you weren't living a lie on Earth?" She pulled free of the block and gestured toward the exam table.

"I don't really belong anywhere, but Earth is the closest thing I have to a home."

"On the other hand, you love Shauss."

Jasmine tensed as she lay back and Monica helped guide her feet into the stirrups. Her life sucked. "Quit saying that! He'd kill me if he found out what I am."

"You don't know that."

"Monica, even if he didn't kill me outright, do you really think they'd let me go home if they knew I was a full-blooded Narthani capable of carrying Garathani children?" When Monica didn't answer, she went on. "No. They'd force me to transition and use me for breeding."

Monica shook her head but let it go. "Okay, I officially hate you."

"What? Why?"

"You're still bare. Sorry if this is TMI, but I could hide a small SUV in my lovely new bush."

That startled a laugh out of her, and then a sigh. "Something else to look forward to if I transition."

"Well, for better or worse, you pass muster." Monica plunged her hands into the block again as Jasmine dressed. "The scarring is minimal and women's labia are all as unique as the women themselves. I wouldn't even have noticed if I hadn't been looking for it and I examine women every day."

"Could you feel my nook?"

My nook. She tightened her ponytail to cover her cringe of embarrassment. It was the first time she'd ever said those words out loud. In fact, she'd never talked about her body at all before. When she was sixteen, her mother had explained about the nook that tunneled through her pubic bone—and how her clitoris was hidden deep inside. Already resigned to never knowing the joys of motherhood, Jasmine had been deeply dismayed to learn she could never experience sexual pleasure, even by her own hand, without piercing the veil of skin covering her nook and thus revealing herself as an alien.

"Not really," Monica said. "But then I never noticed mine when I was growing up either, so the hymen must be pretty solid."

"So how soon can you get my nasal spray replicated?"

"Oh Christ, I don't know. It'll be a miracle if I can do it without tipping off one of the doctors—they're always hanging around the labs, so it might take a day or two."

"Do you think they'd notice if I stuffed cotton balls up my nose?" Jasmine asked with a sigh.

Monica's eyes widened. "Hey, that's not a bad idea. Empran, talk to me about insertable nasal barriers…"

* * * * *

"What in Peserin's name is taking so long?" Zannen demanded.

He and Hastion had joined them outside the infirmary door less than ten minutes ago and already Shauss wearied of him.

"I would imagine Dr. Teague is trying to reassure her patient," Tiber replied. "That's what I would be doing."

"You're welcome to return to duty, Zannen," Shauss added sourly.

"I will, after you claim her. Assuming you do," he added.

Shauss stared at him. "You must be insane. Why wouldn't I?"

Zannen just stared back impassively.

"You would be wise to maintain that silence," Shauss told him. "One word during the claiming and *jurana* terminates. Understood?"

"Fear not, brother. I have no intention of depriving myself of the pleasure."

Shauss waited, feeling a twinge of uncertainty. In the space of a single day, his life had changed dramatically. He was now mated to a tiny Terran female who feared him, and he had to claim her today to keep Zannen from jumping all over her.

The door opened to reveal Monica. "Come on in, Shauss." Her eyes widened when she noticed the others. "And company."

He saw Jasmine immediately. Her face turned a deep pink as they all filed in, and she glared at Zannen before turning accusing eyes his way.

"What's he doing here?" She sounded slightly congested. Had she been weeping?

"I'll explain in a moment," he told her. "Monica?"

"I guess congratulations are in order." She glanced at Jasmine apologetically before telling him, "Jasmine meets the criteria for a copulative candidate, but just barely, so you'll have to be careful and take your time."

"Excellent." Turning to his new mate, he bowed slightly and then held out his hand. "Jasmine."

She looked at him hesitantly and then lowered her eyes before sliding her slim, cool fingers into his. Possessiveness roared through him even as tension knotted his gut. Peserin, but it would be all too easy to damage her. He'd have to keep himself under tight control, not an easy task in light of how much he wanted her delicately curved body.

"As I suspected," Monica said, "her pelvic girdle is tiny, so even if she doesn't return to Earth, reproduction is definitely out."

"I thought she was barren."

She gave Jasmine a startled look.

"It's okay, Monica—I told them I couldn't have children." Then Jasmine looked at him. "She was bound by doctor-patient privilege not to tell you about that."

"No such privilege applies between mates."

Monica's eyes narrowed on him and he thought she was going to challenge him. Instead, she said mildly, "You weren't mates when she told me."

"We're mates now, so you *will* keep me informed of her health status."

Monica put her fists on her hips. "Shauss, *you* will remember that you're not the boss of me and never were. And please keep in mind that this isn't a permanent mating. Jasmine intends to go home when this is all over."

While clearly meant to caution him against becoming attached, Monica's reminder only highlighted why they would never have worked as permanent mates. She was too willful, even if it was for his own good.

Rather than goading her, as he was wont to do, he merely tipped his head in assent.

"I'm glad we understand each other." She gave him a searching look and for a moment he thought she would say more. But then she smiled, and said simply, "Congratulations, Lieutenant."

Her formality caused him a brief pang of loneliness and regret. "Thank you, Doctor. For everything."

"You're welcome."

"Kellen has ordered a dinner this evening to honor the occasion. I hope you'll attend?"

"I wouldn't miss it."

Jasmine's fingers tightened on his. "Shauss, you still haven't explained what Zannen's doing here. Or the other two, for that matter."

He hesitated before saying, "They'll escort you to our chambers."

"But—"

"You're safe with them, Jasmine. I'll be there directly."

After they'd left, he asked, "Has she been weeping?"

"No. Why?"

"She sounded congested."

Monica twitched. "Uh, right. Her allergies are acting up, but I gave her something so she should be fine in a few minutes."

Shauss relaxed slightly. "You're certain she's able to accommodate me safely?"

"Shauss, as long as you don't spank her first or otherwise kink out on her like you did certain *other* parties," she said with an arch look, "Jasmine will be fine."

* * * * *

While Hastion walked beside Jasmine, Tiber and Zannen took up flanking positions behind them. Hastion's face no longer looked like he'd gone ten rounds with King Kong but she still felt bad.

"I'm sorry I hurt you," she said.

He snorted. "Not as sorry as I am."

Jasmine bit her lip.

"Be at ease, female," he said. "The pain has all but disappeared and the lingering humiliation is no more than I deserved for letting my guard down while on watch."

A glance at his face revealed a wry grin and she relaxed a little.

"I'm still sorry. I always kind of liked you."

"If that's what you do to males you like, I'd hate to see what you do to those you don't," he said with a mock shudder.

She glanced over her shoulder. "Put *him* in front of the escape pods next time and I'll show you."

Zannen's bark of laughter made her jump but oddly, he said nothing.

"Where did you learn to fight like that?" Hastion asked. "Did you have brothers to defend yourself against?"

"No, no brothers or sisters. I took martial arts classes."

"You don't look dangerous."

"I'm not unless I'm backed into a corner."

"As you are now?" Tiber prodded.

Jasmine didn't know what to say to that. To tell the truth, she wasn't sure she'd be able to keep from utilizing her fighting skills, such as they were, in the coming hours. She was frightened, and if her reactions during Shauss' attack were anything to go by, instinct might kick in before her conscious mind even registered a threat.

"I'll try not to hurt anyone."

"We'll be prepared this time," Hastion said dryly.

"Are you all right?" Tiber asked. "You sound as if you've been crying."

Jasmine tensed. Her nostrils and sinuses were now lined with a thin, oxygen-permeable membrane called galathene barrier. She'd had to snort up a pile of clear, shiny powder and chase it with a squirt of saline to activate it. Just the memory of that creeping feeling in her nose as it gelled made her shudder. The slight stuffiness was supposed to subside within minutes, but apparently it didn't get that memo.

"Um, yeah, but I'm okay now," she said, feeling only a little guilty. Anxious to move on, she asked, "So what about you, Hastion—do you have brothers and sisters?"

"I had two brothers and a twin sister, Aylee," he said as they stepped into the tranlift. "My eldest brother had my mother and sister assassinated and was eventually executed for his crimes."

"How awful for you!" Jasmine gasped.

"I was but a babe at the time, so I barely remember any of them. My father remated to a lovely female whose loss I felt much more keenly when she succumbed to the biowar virus."

Empathy and guilt wrung her guts like a fist, and she raised a trembling hand over her stomach. Her people had done that to him—deprived him of yet another mother. How could they possibly justify ending so many lives? How could her parents have?

When the tranlift door opened on Ayerra Deck, they started down another corridor and eventually entered a bedroom that was a lot bigger than the one she shared with Portia—and it even had a window, which Jasmine walked directly to. Anything to keep from looking at the bed.

"Shauss' quarters, I assume?" she asked Tiber.

"And yours now."

"Apparently we won't all be cohabitating?"

"The ship's living quarters weren't designed to accommodate polyamorous mates, so Hastion and I will maintain our own quarters for now."

Well, that was a relief.

"If we were on Garathan, we'd all live together?"

"Yes." He opened a drawer in the massive cabinet. "We moved your few personal belongings while you were in examination."

Jasmine peered inside and was thrilled to see her panties and the bottle of vanilla right on top of her clothes. She snatched up the bottle at once.

"I hate being without my cosmetics and perfume," she explained as she dabbed some on her wrists and neck. It was silly how much safer she felt being able to take this one simple precaution. If there weren't three alien males watching her every move, she'd bathe in it.

Tiber smiled. "Ah, I'd wondered what that was for."

The door opened and she bit her lip, dropping the vanilla back in the drawer as her heart immediately began its Shauss dance.

"We arrived unaccosted," Hastion reported.

Shauss' brow crooked in amusement. "No surprise, since Zannen is the only one I might expect to accost you."

"True."

"That will be all for now."

After the others left, a flowering plant in a lovely ceramic pot appeared on the table by the flare window. Jasmine gasped. It was a *Jasminum sambac* in full bloom.

"I understand you have an affinity for flora." Shauss propped his shoulder against the wall by the door and crossed his arms.

"It's absolutely gorgeous," she breathed, leaning over to inhale the flowers' heady fragrance. The hint of fresh soil made her stomach cramp with hunger and she backed away quickly. Good Lord, she hadn't had an episode of pica since she was a child but it felt like it was about to make a resurgence. "Where in the world did you get this?"

"The ship's terrarium."

Her eyes widened as her heart raced. "The ship has a terrarium? Really?"

He smiled. "It does indeed. I take it you'd like to see it?"

"See it?" she breathed. "I'd like to live there." God, she'd missed plants and flowers and trees. The compound had been situated on a vast, barren parcel of land with plenty of visibility, so even when there wasn't snow up to her chin, being outdoors hadn't held much appeal.

"That's not possible, of course, but you're welcome to spend time there when our schedules allow." He straightened and stepped over to the wardrobe. Opening one of the doors, he removed a small, flat box and held it out to her. The logo of an exclusive jewelry store was embossed on the lid. "I have another bonding gift for you."

She froze. Gifts. The man was giving her gifts. When had he found the time to go shopping? *How* had he been able to go shopping? It wasn't like a seven-foot Garathani warrior could browse the shops inconspicuously.

Licking her lips, she said, "Shauss, this bond is temporary. When the situation on Earth is resolved, I'm going home."

"I'm aware of that. Open it, please."

Feeling like a total fraud, Jasmine reluctantly took the box and peeled off the lid. Inside, on a bed of white velvet, lay a chain of delicate gold jasmine flowers.

She swallowed convulsively as she blinked back tears. "I can't accept this."

"You can and you will." He picked up the necklace and moved behind her. "Lift your ponytail out of the way."

She obeyed even as she protested, "I don't deserve it."

He slid the chain around her throat and fastened it. It was a choker. "I added the locking clasp myself and I'm the only one who can take it off you."

Her pulse went weak and thready. It felt as if he'd truly claimed her, especially when he pulled out her scrunchie and combed her stubbornly straight hair over her shoulders with his fingers. The sensation sent shivers down her back.

Turning her to face him, he asked, "Aren't you going to thank me?"

"Thank you," she whispered. "For the plant too. I love it. I love them both."

He slid a finger under her chin and tipped her face up. "Surely you can do better than that."

Her heart cracked. The amusement that had been missing from his expression since she'd helped the ambassador was back, only now it was...warm. Almost affectionate.

"Shauss," she choked out as she reached for him. Fortunately he met her halfway so she was able to get her arms around his neck and bury her face in his strong throat as he squeezed her trembling body against him.

God, this deception was going to tear her apart. Everything in her wanted to just blurt out the truth, but three things held her back—loyalty to her father, respect for her mother's memory, and the knowledge that if she confessed now, Shauss might not take her. And she wanted him. Oh, how she wanted him! If he found out about her afterward, it wouldn't matter so much if he pulled out that broadsword and lopped her head off—she would at least have tasted him and known the passionate strength of his long, lean body.

Swallowing her tears once more, she pressed her lips to his throat and felt his pulse leap.

"My mouth is up here," he murmured.

She smiled, feeling calmer as she slid her face through the silky fall of his hair. "Mine is down here."

He ducked and claimed her in a kiss that stole every thought from her head. Without breaking contact with her mouth, he tugged her arms from his neck and pushed them behind her, clasping both her wrists in one hand. When his other hand cupped the back of her head so that he could feed from her mouth, she whimpered at the helplessness flooding her.

Only one thing could have made the experience more sensually complete…

Scent.

Jasmine King's was absolutely divine—rich, creamy vanilla and a definite hint of musk that sent a knife of pure desire through his balls.

Shauss slid his mouth down the vulnerable column of her throat, licking and sucking and trying to glean all the flavor there was of her on the way to his destination. Letting go of her wrists, he reached for the tab of her zipper and tugged.

Jasmine put her hands on his chest. "Um, are we going to do this now? I thought you had twenty-four hours."

"The sooner I do it," he said against her collarbone, "the less chance some fool will try to preempt my claim."

"Would someone really do that?" she asked doubtfully.

"Pret stole Monica."

"Yes, but she's Garathani. I'm just…me."

Shauss frowned. "Jasmine, I'm not certain why you doubt your value as a female, but you need to get over it for your own safety. There are few males on this ship who wouldn't knife their own brothers for the chance to mate with you."

She swallowed audibly. "Oh, okay. So then we do need to do this now."

"Wouldn't you rather get it out of the way so that you can concentrate on this evening's dinner?"

"Probably," she confessed, sliding her hands over his hard pectorals with a sigh. "I just…"

"You just what?"

"Forget it. It's nothing. "

Deciding it would be in his best interests not to challenge her now, he sucked her into another kiss, relishing the honeyed sweetness of her lips as he pulled her zipper down to her navel and slipped his palm into the humid opening. She tensed but then relaxed when his palm coasted around her ribs to rub her bare back.

As the kiss grew more heated, she squirmed against him, plucking at his uniform to draw him closer. Shauss slid his hand from behind her neck and dragged it down the opening in her wrapsuit, pausing between her plump breasts and savoring the ragged beating of her heart before curving it over her ribs. He let his thumb brush the small, hard point of her nipple on his way past and she gasped but didn't object.

Nonetheless, he continued on around and let both his hands rove the delicate ridges of her back under her suit.

Breaking the kiss, she said, "Shauss, please!"

"Please what?"

"Please hurry!"

"We have plenty of time, *aramai*."

"I don't care!"

"Such impatience," he chided, taking a mock bite of her chin. "Who is here to please whom?"

"Is this a trick question?" Her breathing grew ragged. "Aren't we...here to please each other?"

"Indeed. And you do please me very much simply by breathing. However..." He firmed his voice. "That's not what I'm talking about."

A frown furrowed her brow.

"Who belongs to whom, Jasmine King?" he pressed, threading a hand into her hair and pulling her head back to face him. "Whom do you need to please in order to get what you want?"

She sighed, leaning her cheek on his palm. "Shauss, please don't ruin this. I told you, I'm not submissive. I never was and I never will be. Just ask my father," she added. Then she straightened, her eyes widening as if she'd swallowed a *firi* bone.

He watched her carefully for a moment before saying, "Tell me about your father."

Impossibly, her eyes went even wider. "Now?"

"He seems to have some bearing on our current impasse."

"Hardly," she snorted. "He and I just...don't get along. He's impossible to please and I'm tired of trying. End of story."

"Ah, now that tells me all I need to know." He tucked her hair behind her ear. "I'm not your father, Jasmine, and I'm far from impossible to please."

"You want to control me."

Without denying it, he countered, "I want you to trust me."

"Trust you to do what?" she cried, pulling away from him.

He let her go. "To please you."

"To please...*me*. Right." Shaking her head, she pulled the front of her wrapsuit closed. "You're talking in circles."

"It *is* a circle, really—an exchange of power that pleasures everyone involved."

"But how can it be an exchange if you get all the power?"

Shauss paused, struck by how much he wanted her to understand. "Because that power," he said softly, "is a gift only you can give me. It's not a gift if I have to take it by force."

She gazed up at him, yearning, fear and indecision clear on her features.

"Do you want what I have to give you?" he asked.

"Yes!"

"And I want the gift of your submission. So tell me, Jasmine...whom must you please in order to get what you want?"

After a moment, her eyes darkened. "You. I have to please you. I *want* to please you."

"Very good, *aramai*," he said, satisfaction seeping into every part of him.

"*Gentlemen,*" he sent, "*the time has arrived.*"

"Why do you keep calling me that—*aramai*?" she asked as he slipped his warm hands back into the opening of her suit and pulled her against him.

"It's a very beautiful flower native to my homeworld." Brushing a kiss over her lips, he added, "If you'd like, you may call me *mellors*."

"What does that mean?"

He grinned. "Well-hung gardener."

Jasmine giggled nervously. "Mellors was the gamekeeper, not the gardener, you goof."

"I don't know—he seemed fairly adept at making Lady Chatterley blossom," he insisted, skimming his hand from her back to her hip and around to her belly.

She froze, waiting breathlessly for him to head south. Hope and fear warred within her—would he make her blossom? Would he feel her nook?

That lovely, long-fingered hand slid down as he kissed her mouth again, and she whimpered. God, how she'd dreamed of this. She tried to let everything else fade into the background as she tasted him again, wanting nothing more than to let down her guard and sink into the moment completely, to soak him up like a sponge.

His lack of scent frustrated her but she tried to content herself with slipping her fingers into his hair. It felt cool against her hot flesh, and she moaned as she sifted through it over and over while his tongue played intimately with hers. Oh, it felt so good, so perfect. The skin of his face was so smooth compared to the men she'd known.

Then both his hands skated roughly over her breasts to her shoulders and pushed her suit down her arms. Jasmine stiffened at the realization her fake breasts were about to be on display, but she tried to continue with the kiss, tried to comfort herself with the silky tickle of his hair over her shoulders as he leaned over her. Surely with hair like that, he couldn't be bad enough to truly hurt her if he found out what she was.

Don't kid yourself. He'd already shown his ruthlessness to her.

Instead of terrifying her, the reminder made her tummy flutter. *That* terrified her, to be turned on by the memory of his brutality.

Shauss pulled his mouth just a hairsbreadth away from hers. "Don't be frightened," he whispered. "I will never harm you."

"If I please you," she stipulated.

He pulled back a fraction. "I will never harm you. Period. You *will* trust me."

He went to pull her sleeves off and she resisted, instinctively covering her breasts with her hands. The action slid the stretchy fabric right back up over her shoulders.

Apparently deciding she was reluctant to be the only one naked, he stepped back and pulled down his own zipper. After he stepped out of his uniform, he stood there for a long moment and let her look at him. She'd convinced herself that the memory of his cock was exaggerated by the terror she'd experienced, but no—she'd remembered it exactly right, long and straight and deep red against the pale flesh of his muscular belly. Though they'd barely done more than kiss, he was fully erect.

She should be quivering with fear at the thought of taking that immense column of flesh inside her body. Instead her mouth watered.

"Touch me," he whispered.

Sucking in a shaky breath, she reached out with one hand and trailed her fingers down the hardness of his breastbone, delighted that the black hair there was just as smooth and soft as the hair on his head. When she glanced at him, Shauss was staring down at her, and the intensity of his gaze made her return her attention to her fingers, which had made their way almost to his navel. Some instinct made her dip her index finger into that intriguing hollow. He sucked in a breath, and she glanced up again.

"Don't stop there."

Her heartbeat was loud in her ears when she continued down his rock-hard abdomen. When she threaded her fingers through the crisp black curls above his cock and tugged, he grunted. Smiling, she let her palm slide over the head of his cock and held it there, intrigued by his slick heat. She slid her palm in tiny circles, spreading his lubricant around. It sucked that she couldn't smell him, it really did.

His long, long legs made servicing him on her knees impossible, so she leaned over for a taste.

"No," he said, restraining her head mere inches from his cock.

"But I want to," she pleaded. "Please." Oh Lord, she was desperate to consume something of him, *anything*.

Grasping her forearms, he hauled her upright. "Not this time."

When he shoved the suit off her shoulders again and tugged it off altogether, she covered herself with her hands. She'd never felt all her implants so keenly, and even after Monica's reassurances, she couldn't help worrying that he'd notice she wasn't a real woman.

"Would you like something to help you relax?" he asked in a low voice.

It was a tempting thought but she couldn't risk taking something that might loosen her tongue. "No. Can't we just get it over with?"

"Garathani females enjoyed hours of foreplay, and I was under the impression that Terran females had a similar preference."

"Well, normally that would be true," she said tentatively, licking her lips. "But in circumstances like this, the longer you drag it out, the more nervous I get."

"Have you forgotten your promise to give yourself to me without reservation?"

"Excuse me, but I just tried to go down on you and you refused," Jasmine reminded him tartly. "I think I've done my part."

"Well, I intend to see that you orgasm at least once before I penetrate you," Shauss said. "You're very small and should be as loose and wet as possible." He looked over her shoulder. "Perhaps a penetab is in order?"

An instant later he held his hand out and something that looked like a large lavender pearl appeared in his palm.

Startled, Jasmine turned. "Who are you talking to? Is someone in here?"

He looked at her sharply. "Ah, that's right—you know about observation flares."

Jasmine's throat seized. Oh crap, someone *was* there.

"I'd hoped to spare you this, but perhaps it's for the best. As your mates, Hastion and Tiber are responsible for witnessing the initial claiming."

She stared at him, absolutely aghast. "You mean they're watching us?"

"Yes. But only the first time."

"You should have warned me!" Blushing twenty shades of red, she snagged the spread off the bed and she wrapped herself in it before demanding, "Tiber, Hastion—show yourselves. Now."

Her other mates appeared out of thin air, sitting side by side on the couch.

"God, this is so embarrassing! How long have you guys been here?"

"Not long," Tiber said without moving from his spot. "Be at ease, sweet Jasmine. We are merely here to protect you."

"From what?"

"Your claiming must be witnessed, and as Shauss explained, that duty falls to Hastion and me. Without a witness, the claiming isn't officially recognized and you might wind up with another—" his brow quirked up as he looked to his left, "less desirable mate."

Jasmine's eyes widened. "Oh no. Don't tell me…"

Shauss sighed. "Zannen has demanded *jurana*, a mating ritual in which one or more *juranin*, typically family members—or, as in Zannen's case, rivals—witness the initial claiming."

"You mean he's been watching us too?"

Zannen appeared on Tiber's left and more humiliation heated her cheeks as she realized she'd begged to suck Shauss' cock in front of the baldheaded ape.

"No. Absolutely not. He's got to go."

"Unfortunately it's his right to be here, and since the minister has confirmed it, so it will be. If any of the three of us fails to finalize his claim within the protected time, Zannen will be here to assert his own claim."

"You mean he'll try to…"

Shauss shook his head. "He won't just try. He *will* fuck you."

Chapter Nine

The words *fuck you* resonated within her body, taking her breath away, but she stood her ground. "Over my dead body."

"I suspect he wouldn't let that deter him," Shauss replied with a nasty glance in Zannen's direction.

Jasmine sent a nasty look of her own. "Don't get your hopes up, Lieutenant, because it's never going to happen. Ever."

The big oaf just sat there and grinned at her.

Jasmine's nerves jangled. Well that was just great. She was about to have sex with one alien in front of three others — her mother would be so proud.

"I promise, you won't know they're here. Zannen isn't even allowed to speak or he'll lose *juranin* status."

"Yeah, right. Believe me, there's no way I'll not know."

Even as she said it, the room and all the men in it disappeared. Her breath caught in her throat. She and Shauss were enveloped in a flare image of a flowery mountain meadow. The warmth of early afternoon sun rained down on her.

"Does this help?" Shauss asked.

"I don't know. Can they see us?"

"Yes, but as I said, I'm going to make you forget they're even in the same star system."

Shauss tugged the blanket out of her grasp and Jasmine automatically covered her breasts and mons with her hands, her heartbeat thundering in her ears.

"You're extraordinary," he murmured.

"Can you get rid of the illusion, please?" It was unnerving knowing the other men could see her and she couldn't keep an eye on them.

"You're certain?"

"Yes."

The room appeared again.

Her stomach muscles jumped when his hand grazed over her waist and slipped around behind her. He pulled her close and covered her mouth with his, and she worked to get back in the mood, running her hands up his chest and wrapping her arms around his neck again.

Then his fingers tickled her bare mound. Before she could pull away, she was startled to feel something cool slip between the lips of her sex. His fingers pushed it inside her and she gasped when it began to tingle immediately.

She broke away from his mouth, breathing raggedly. "What is that?"

"It's a penetab."

He guided her backward to the bed and lowered her without any apparent effort.

A low moan made her turn her head. Hastion was leaning forward with his head between his knees.

Tiber put a hand on his back. "Are you all right?"

"Actually, no. I'm feeling nauseated and my head is pounding," he said in a muffled voice.

"I'm not surprised, considering the extent of your injuries," Tiber said. "Why don't you return to your quarters and rest. I'll have Empran observe your vital signs to ensure your brain injury isn't more serious than was first diagnosed."

"I should be here."

"Zannen will suffice as witness," Tiber assured him.

Jasmine bit her lip as Hastion left. She'd really done a number on the poor guy.

The pearl chose that moment to catch fire inside her. "Shauss!"

"Now you're getting ready for me, aren't you?" he said with a wealth of satisfaction. He settled on the bed beside her and reached down between her legs. She tried to roll away but he began a slow, firm massage of her mons that did nothing to ease the burning inside her.

When she looked toward Tiber and Zannen, agonizingly aware of their presence, Shauss took her chin and forced her gaze back to him. "Forget them. They have nothing to do with us right now."

Forcing air into her tight lungs, she said, "I'll try."

He leaned down and licked her mons. "How is it that you're so smooth?"

"Laser hair removal." She laughed nervously. "Monica was green with envy."

Shauss chuckled too. "I'm sure. Garathani females generally aren't allowed to remove body hair."

"Why not?"

"That's an explanation best saved for another time."

He tried to ease her thighs open but she couldn't let him in. He finally managed to snake his tongue into the notch at the top of her mons, and while it aroused her on some level, Jasmine had to force herself to lie there with her hands over her breasts, staring at the iridescent blue ceiling and pretending to enjoy it. Every time his tongue flicked over her "clit", she jumped, not in arousal, as he must surely think, but in apprehension.

The thing he'd put inside her made her feel like she had a bladder infection.

"Shauss, please," she said desperately.

He frowned. "You don't seem wet enough."

"This first time, could we *please* just get it over with?"

He tried once more to spread her legs. "Stop resisting and relax. I don't want to hurt you."

"I'm trying!"

After a moment's hesitation, he said, "Is it time to get out the restraints?"

She stilled, staring at him as genuine excitement finally flashed over her skin. It was crazy, but she'd suddenly never wanted anything so badly.

"Look at the pulse jump in your throat," he murmured. "And your pupils are expanding."

She just stared at him, her heart thumping.

His slow smile sent her stomach into freefall. "I'll take that as a yes."

Oh Lord, what was she getting herself into here?

"I hadn't planned to introduce this element to the equation quite so early," Shauss said, rising from the bed. "But perhaps we should start out as we intend to go on."

Opening a cabinet, he removed a pair of leather cuffs.

"You're taking an awful lot for granted," she said in a tremulous voice as he fastened one of the cuffs around her wrist. Lord, she was trembling all over.

"Oh?"

"What if I don't enjoy it?" Yeah, right. Like that could happen.

"Then we'll try something else. Have you never done this before?" he asked, fastening the other cuff. When she gave a quick negative shake of her head, his smile deepened. "You don't know how glad I am to hear that."

He clipped the cuffs together in front of her then grabbed both her wrists without warning and dragged her up the bed toward the head of the bed. She didn't even have time to struggle before he fastened the clip to a silver ring over her head. Her eyes widened as she took in four similar rings attached to the headboard. She hadn't even noticed them before—they looked decorative.

"Look at her breasts," Shauss said, stretching out beside her. "They're augmented with implants."

Jasmine gasped and immediately tried to jerk her arms down to cover herself, her heart thundering. This was a horrible idea. Naked, naked, naked—she'd never *been* so naked.

"I don't understand why Terran women feel the need to improve upon nature's bounty," Tiber murmured.

"Nor do I." Shauss leaned over her face. "You must have been extremely small before the surgery. Delicate. And yet every bit as beautiful, I'm certain."

That's what he thought—he hadn't seen her with rolls of baby fat and no breasts at all.

She squeezed her eyes shut, shuddering when he raked his teeth over her earlobe.

He started kissing her neck and shoulders as he moved over her, sliding a knee firmly between her thighs. His hands pushed them wide open.

"Now where were we?"

Settling on his belly between her legs, he held her nether lips open wide as she bucked with discomfort. "You're going to come for me so you might as well resign yourself."

She tried, honestly she did. The way he licked and sucked at her tender flesh felt really, really good, but the longer he did it, the more tense she got. Surely he would notice that her "clit" wasn't swelling or twitching or doing whatever it was real clits did. None of her human lovers had ever noticed or cared, but they'd never concentrated so completely on her, never picked up so quickly on every little detail.

When his tongue slid deep inside her, she whimpered. Jeez, he had a long tongue, and oh, the things he could do with it... Nothing had ever felt so good as that sinuous squirming and fluttering in such a sensitive place.

She writhed uncontrollably, fighting a scream of frustration. Why her? The sexiest man ever created, arguably the reigning grand master of oral sex, was focusing all his powers on her...and she couldn't come! Why *her*, damn it? *Why, why, why?*

He backed off, provoking both relief and disappointment. Then his long fingers resumed the quest for her orgasm, sinking deep, twisting, searching while his mouth went to work in earnest on her "clit".

Her nervous tension felt ready to explode, and using it as a substitute for sexual tension, she writhed and bucked under his touch before stiffening her whole body.

"Oh God, yes!" she cried, doing Kegels like there was no tomorrow. Embarrassment even added some heat to her cheeks, and by the time she collapsed onto the mattress, she was actually kind of proud of herself.

When she finally looked at Shauss, he was watching her with narrowed eyes. "That was quite a performance."

Shauss imagined his face was just as red as hers. Jasmine couldn't have come up with a better way to humiliate him if she'd tried. She was fortunate he'd picked up on her act—if Tiber or, Peserin forbid, Zannen had pointed it out to him afterward, he'd have been livid.

"Oh God, I'm sorry," she groaned. "There's just no way I'm going to come with them watching."

"Jasmine," he said in a stern tone, "if you ever try to fake an orgasm with me again, you'll be punished."

"Um, punished how?"

"Test me and find out."

When she hesitated, it occurred to him that a bit of punishment might actually help her achieve orgasm—Peserin knew Monica had derived considerable pleasure from having her cunt spanked. But Jasmine wasn't Monica and he couldn't assume she would react the same way to the same things.

It was a tempting thought though.

"I'll behave," she finally said.

"I'm glad to hear that. However, I think you deserve a bit of punishment for this one." He flipped her onto her stomach. Reaching into the bedside table, he pulled out the tube of lubricant and squeezed some onto his index finger. She squirmed as he slid it between her buttocks.

"Uh…"

"Don't worry, I'm not about to fuck your ass. Yet," he added darkly, squeezing his finger into her tight anus without giving the little chit time to adjust. She'd earned more discomfort than that, and he was about to see she got it. "Merely preparing you for my spur."

Straddling her legs, he grasped her hips and pulled her up until he could set the head of his cock against her vagina. "If you become alarmed or are truly in pain, you have but to call me Mellors and I'll stop."

"Mellors," she repeated with a frantic nod. "Got it."

He gritted his teeth and slowly worked his cock into her hot, tight cunt, his heart racing with excitement.

Mine.

She whimpered and continued a half-hearted struggle until he was seated completely. Then she was still. The sight of her bowed before him, her long slender back heaving, her tangled hair concealing her face, and her hands clenching and unclenching in the bedding, satisfied him like nothing ever had. She was a beautiful little submissive.

He slapped her buttock and she cried out.

"Are you going to fake another orgasm?"

"No!"

He slapped the other one and relished the deep pink tinge rising on her pale skin.

"Are you absolutely certain?"

"Yes!" she choked out.

Believing her, Shauss withdrew with care and fucked her slowly, rocking his hips forward and back in a sensuous rhythm as need coiled in his gut. Peserin, but she was tight! The friction was almost unbearable, but he felt the evidence of her excitement easing his way. Sliding his hand down, he was gratified to note the abundant slickness coating her petals now. He caressed her, toying with her and enjoying the throaty moans that burst from her throat.

All too soon his knees began to shake with urgency, the urge to flood her with his seed rapidly consuming him. He thrust faster and faster, his body on fire, sweat rolling off him in sheets.

His spur began to emerge and he stopped, breathing harshly. By all the powers, he didn't want to come before she did but he wasn't sure he could resist.

"Here comes my spur," he grunted, spreading her buttocks. He slid it into her as carefully as possible, and her broken groan drove his arousal even higher, making it hard to maintain any semblance of control. Though he stayed with her as long as he could, Jasmine never seemed to get any closer to orgasm, and his failure to please her was bitter medicine to swallow.

Not wishing to torture either of them any further, Shauss braced his hands beside her shackled arms and battered her with short, hard strokes designed to finish him off quickly. The rush took him without warning and he shouted, filling her with his seed even as he resented the lack of primal satisfaction that should have accompanied such an intense release.

She lay beneath him, unmoving, and didn't look at him when he moved off her.

"Gentlemen, have you seen enough?"

* * * * *

Still shaken and aroused, Tiber reported to Infirmary Three to work on the mate assignments, which recommenced next week. Monica was at the replication station.

"Empran, can you not fuck with me for once?" she said.

Tiber leaned against the bulkhead with a grin. He needed a little more time to collect himself, and it was always amusing to watch Monica interact with the computer. For some reason, Empran exhibited an uncharacteristic propensity for obtuseness with her.

"I am not programmed for sexual activities," Empran replied.

"Just tell me how this thing works."

Empran activated a holochart in front of Monica's face. "Read the directions."

"Hello, they're in Garathani!"

Tiber barely suppressed a snort of laughter.

"What language would you prefer?"

"English, you misbegotten pile of factory seconds!"

The holochart blurred and reformed in English.

"Thanks," Monica said grudgingly. "Leave the image up until I cancel it."

"Affirmative."

After reading further, she said, "Okay, this seems simple enough."

She placed a spray bottle into the replication chamber, and ordered, "Evaluate."

A chemical structure appeared on the replicator monitor, but Monica's head blocked his view.

"This vessel was designed to deliver one hundred twenty metered sprays, each containing hundred milligrams of aqueous suspension," Empran reported. "It is fabricated from a toxic polymer that that may not be replicated. However, I can produce an identical vessel in an approved non-toxic polymer."

"Wow. Okay, great. Is there enough of the suspension for you to replicate it?"

"Affirmative."

"Awesome. Do your thing, then."

"Commencing replication."

Monica leaned back in her seat and put her hands behind her head. "You know, Empran, if you were this helpful all the time, I might actually start to like you."

"Be still my hard drive."

She straightened comically and it was all Tiber could do not to laugh out loud. "Excuse me?"

"Be still my hard drive," Empran repeated mechanically.

"Okay, where the hell did that come from? I mean, I talk to you like you're a bitch, but you're just a machine—aren't you? You couldn't have come up with that on your own."

"I'm an artificial intelligence, capable of learning and applying that knowledge," Empran replied. "Having been programmed with no logical response to your statement, I calculated the odds of your being sincere based on our past interactions and used contemporary Terran literature to formulate an appropriate reply."

"Yeah, well, it—" Monica sounded like she was choking. "Sucked," she finally gasped before bursting into belly laughs. "But it was pretty damn funny."

"Thank you."

"You're welcome."

Tiber decided to approach her. "What is that?"

Monica screeched and jumped. "Jesus, don't sneak up on me like that."

"I'm sorry. What are you replicating?" He leaned closer to the screen. The structure was somewhat familiar. "It looks like some sort of hormone."

She stood up, blocking his view again. "That's exactly what it is. One of the candidates needs it to regulate her cycle, but the label was unreadable and she didn't remember the name of it. "

"Do you require any assistance?"

"Nope, I think I'm done." The replicator doors slid up and she removed both bottles. "Yay! I was way past ready to be useful again."

"I'm impressed with your initiative. I'd think most Terrans would be intimidated by our technology."

"Well, I'm not exactly ready for brain surgery," she grinned, tucking one bottle into the pocket of her lab coat and shaking the other. "On the other hand, I could program my VCR without reading the instructions, so I guess I've always been a technological whiz."

She took the lid off and sprayed several squirts into the air. "Priming," she explained, capping the bottle and dropping it into her pocket. "Well, it looks right to me. Guess she'll let me know if I've screwed up."

"I'm certain it's fine."

"Glad to hear it. Empran, end program." After the screen cleared, she walked toward the door, mumbling something about observing in the infirmary. At the last second, she turned. "See you at dinner tonight?"

Tiber smiled. "I look forward to it."

Chapter Ten

Seated at the commander's dining table hours later, Jasmine wondered if her painful blush would ever subside. She'd had sex with Shauss in front of Tiber and Zannen, and no doubt everyone in the room knew it. If she hadn't broken the bones in Hastion's face, she'd have had sex in front of him too. Of course, if she hadn't broken the bones in Hastion's face, she might not be in this position in the first place.

She was excruciatingly conscious of Shauss' arm draped over the back of her chair, of his fingertips skimming from her shoulder to her neck and back again in an absent but unmistakably possessive gesture.

"What would you like to drink?" the steward inquired.

It was tempting to ask for a double shot of tequila, especially with Zannen brooding at her from the end of the table. Who the heck had invited him, anyway?

Deciding it was better to keep her wits about her, she said, "Just water, please. Lots of it."

"You look awesome," Monica commented.

"I concur." Tiber's face reflected genuine appreciation. "You're incredibly lovely, Jasmine."

Her blush deepening, Jasmine lifted her arms, making the diaphanous sleeves of her violet-toned floral minidress shimmer. The scooped-out neckline displayed Shauss' golden choker and way more cleavage than she was comfortable with. But at least she had on underwear—she'd appreciated the lacy black thong almost more than the dress.

"Gifts from Shauss." Which she in no way deserved.

Monica's brows rose as she turned to Shauss. "You had all that lying around?"

"I shop online."

"I didn't know UPS delivered to the stratosphere."

"Technically, we're—"

"Joking, Shauss, and don't try to distract me with another astronomy lesson. So how did that stuff get here?"

"I...collected it."

The steward deposited a glass of water in front of Jasmine and she lifted it for a long drink, wishing she'd thought to ask for ice. She expected Monica to press Shauss for more details and waited for them with interest, but instead Monica swung back toward the commander and gave him a pointed look.

He sighed. "My love, why are you giving me the hairy eyeball?"

Water gushed from Jasmine's nose as she choked with laughter. Tiber came behind her and held her arms up high while Shauss pounded her on the back.

"Are you all right?" Shauss asked when the spasms subsided.

Jasmine nodded, swallowing for a couple of seconds as she wiped her face with her fingers. Why in the world didn't the Garathani use napkins?

She managed to squeak "The *hairy eyeball*?" before erupting into peals of laughter again.

"He's freakin' adorable, isn't he?" Monica tried to look annoyed but the love shining in her eyes spoiled the effect. "So why haven't you *collected* anything for me?"

As servers settled three large platters of food on the table, Kellen leaned back and watched her with amused affection that sent a knife of envy straight through Jasmine's heart. "Would you like such adornment?"

"Hell no. I wouldn't mind having an iPod though."

"Monica, Empran's music files are extensive."

"Thanks, but I'd rather hold the technology in my hot little hand. Doesn't it worry you to rely on Empran for every little thing?"

"No more than it worries you to rely on the internet."

"Hey, the internet can be a scary place. Lots of hackers out there."

"I believe Empran's security protocols are up to the task," Kellen said dryly.

"That's what everyone believes until someone hacks their system."

Jasmine watched the interplay between Monica and the commander, totally blown away by how comfortable they were with each other after such a short time together.

The knife twisted in her heart. She and Shauss would never feel that kind of connection. It was stupid to have imagined for even a moment that it was possible. After today's claiming, he'd probably figured out what a deal he *wasn't* getting and decided to send her back to Earth when the two species had ironed things out.

Why did he have to be the only male in the solar system who considered her orgasm Job One?

"Jasmine, you're not eating," Shauss said.

"I'm not really that hungry."

He considered her for a moment. "Would you prefer a plate from the candidates' menu?"

She blinked. When would she learn not to underestimate his perceptiveness?

"Please," she murmured gratefully. The Garathanis' preparation of Terran dishes wasn't exactly haute cuisine, but it beat the heck out of their native dishes.

"You mustn't hesitate to express your nutritional preferences," he said.

A moment later a fork and a plate of salmon, rice pilaf, and broccoli were placed before her.

Monica gasped. "How come she gets a fork?"

"Terran meals are served with Terran utensils," Kellen explained in a patronizing tone. "Ask nicely and you may have one too."

Uh-oh.

From the silence at the table, Jasmine figured she wasn't the only one bracing for an explosion, but Monica just narrowed her eyes at him. "Give me a fucking fork. Please."

Kellen's lips twitched. "I suppose that will have to do for now."

He nodded and the wary steward dropped a fork onto her plate from an unseemly height, splashing tiny drops of brown sauce on her pale gray suit.

"Thanks a lot," she muttered.

Fortunately the steward was shrewd enough not to say *You're welcome,* and everyone tucked back into their meals.

"Eat."

Shauss' tone made Jasmine look up and her pulse quickened at his stern expression. When she didn't move, he leaned closer, and whispered, "Eat or I'll feed you. The choice is yours."

Dismayed by the tickle of desire in her belly, she picked up her fork and ate.

Tiber could hardly take his eyes off Jasmine as she nibbled at her meal. She was exquisite with her thick brown hair swept up to display delicate collarbones and Shauss' golden gift. Several loose tendrils framed her oval face, and although she wore no cosmetics, her cheeks glowed with color. Every time Shauss fingered the clasp at the back of her neck, her breath caught audibly and her blue eyes widened with awareness.

"You're not looking so hot, Hastion," Monica said suddenly. "Something you ate?"

Startled, Tiber turned to examine Hastion. Monica was right—he was unusually pale and sweat dotted his upper lip.

"I think he's allergic to females," Zannen drawled. He'd been silent all evening, nursing his ale with a surly expression that discouraged anyone from trying to draw him into the conversation.

As if they'd rehearsed it, Hastion and Monica said simultaneously, "Fuck off, Zannen."

Hastion sent her a wan grin but Monica was too busy glowering at Zannen to notice.

"I don't like this." Tiber stood up. "Let's get you to the infirmary for observation tonight and we'll do further studies in the morning to determine if your injuries are more severe than diagnosed."

Hastion rose too. "You stay and enjoy the festivities. I'll find my own way there."

"Are you sure?"

"I'll escort him," Zannen said, getting to his feet.

"Don't do me any favors."

"Don't worry—I need a break from wearing my happy face anyway."

After Zannen followed Hastion out the door, Jasmine said, "Good Lord, if that was his happy face, I'd hate to see his grumpy one."

"He's just jealous," Shauss assured her.

And no doubt horny, after what he'd witnessed that afternoon—a condition Tiber could heartily relate to. What kind of fool would put himself through a ritual like *jurana* and refuse to seek release from one of the probes?

After a lengthy pause in the conversation, Jasmine asked, "So why aren't females allowed to remove body hair?"

"Now there's a question I'd really like to hear the answer to," Monica declared.

Much to Tiber's amusement, Kellen sighed. "Actually, you probably won't like it."

"Well, I already knew that—otherwise you would have explained it earlier. I'm guessing it's some sort of payback for centuries of matriarchal tyranny."

"Some might think so," Kellen acknowledged, leaning back in his chair and gently swirling the ale in his goblet. "Our females typically abhorred body hair. Not only did they find it aesthetically unpleasing, but it facilitates the radiation of pheromones, which females were loath to be influenced by. While they ruled, both sexes routinely employed long-term growth inhibitors. When males came into power, we dispensed with such foolishness."

His tone dared Monica to object, and for a moment she looked like she might. Instead, she challenged him again. "So how do you account for your baby-smooth faces?"

"Inhibitors are still allowed for facial hair, and should you develop any, I'll gladly help you dispose of it."

"That's big of you," Monica said sourly.

"Be grateful you're allowed to keep the hair on your head," Kellen told her with a grin. "Most of us males were required to keep ours at an inch or less."

"Which explains why so many of you have long hair now," Jasmine said.

"Exactly—although an unfortunate few, like Zannen, had their heads permanently epilated as punishment."

Jasmine frowned. "Zannen's bald because a woman made him bald? That doesn't seem fair."

Tiber couldn't help smiling. Now that she didn't have to worry about taking Zannen to mate, she obviously felt she could afford to show him a little sympathy.

"I'm sure it seemed eminently fair to the female he offended," he said dryly.

"And I'm sure he deserved it so quit feeling sorry for him," Monica added with a severe look at Jasmine.

"Actually, my love, he was punished for his role in the Crunus Uprising."

Tiber gaped at Kellen. "I had no idea."

"He was only fifteen at the time," the commander explained, "so it doesn't appear in his military record."

Sliding his gaze to Shauss, Tiber sent, *"You never mentioned this in our sessions."*

Shauss' expression didn't change. *"You never inquired."*

"What's the Crunus Uprising?" Jasmine asked.

"It was a failed rebellion that occurred during the Crunus Capture." He looked back and forth between Monica and Jasmine's blank faces and sighed again. "I tend to forget you know nothing of Garathani history. The Crunus Capture is the reason the Narthani attacked us in the first place."

"You captured one of their leaders or something?"

"Actually, Garathan captured one of Narthan's moons in an incredible confluence of natural events. Both planets orbit Pesera on slightly different inclines, and every few thousand years, they pass quite close to one another. This time, Crunus was between them and also happened to be at its apogee, or the point in its orbit at which it was farthest away from Narthan. The alignment of Narthan's two moons Crunus and Lomar conspired to allow Garathan's gravity to draw Crunus into a retrograde orbit. The gravitational forces splintered Lomar and sent debris raining into Narthan's atmosphere for weeks afterward."

"Well, that was hardly your fault, was it?"

"No, but as a nearly limitless source of crunite, Crunus was vital to Narthan's economy at the time and our leaders weren't as sympathetic to the resultant natural and economic disasters as they could have been. They ousted the settlement of Narthani miners in a short but bloody conflict and claimed ownership of the moon and all its resources."

"Damn evil females," Monica mocked under her breath.

"I didn't say that."

"You didn't have to."

"Perhaps not. But just so you know," he added with a self-satisfied smile, "once males seized control of Garathan, we reopened diplomatic negotiations with the Narthani and ultimately forged a partnership in the Crunus mines. Now that Crunus orbits Garathan, Narthan is too far away to routinely utilize the crunite, but their miners are paid fairly and the planetary government receives regular dividends from the sale of the crunite."

"Damn angelic males," Monica muttered again. "So what does all this have to do with Zannen's head?"

"Well, during and after the capture, magnetic storms knocked out communications on Garathan, creating a window of opportunity in which males could attack females without being overridden by the imperatives encoded in their cerecom implants. Some males were successful—others were not. But ultimately the uprising failed and all involved were punished. The only reason Zannen wasn't executed for his crimes was that he was a minor. Instead, he was made a field slave. All his hair was ripped out by hand and then his head soaked in a follicular atrophic for several days to prevent regrowth."

"That's barbaric," Jasmine breathed.

"Indeed. Afterward, he was tattooed from head to toe with slave labels. The labels have since been removed, but nothing can reverse the damage to his scalp."

"No wonder he acts like such a prick," Monica said.

"Don't feel too sorry for him," Shauss replied. "Believe me, Zannen takes great pleasure in being a prick."

"Is that any way to talk about your own brother?"

Shauss didn't even blink at Zannen's voice. "You expect me to sing your praises?"

Monica focused on Kellen once more. "Okay, so getting back to the topic at hand, if body hair radiates pheromones, wouldn't you be better off letting us remove it?"

"You're not going to let this go, are you?"

"Only because it doesn't make sense. Aren't you afraid my radiating pheromones will make some half-crazed male jump me?"

"We have numerous safeguards in place to prevent such an occurrence."

Monica snorted. "You know, if you guys would quit being such homophobes and fuck each other, you wouldn't have to worry about pheromones at all."

"Why in Peserin's name are you so determined to see males mate with males?" Kellen asked, clearly exasperated.

"I just don't understand why men who are so desperate for sex would let pride stand in their way."

"You believe that pride is all that prevents us from satisfying each other?"

"Yup."

"Monica," Shauss finally said in a silky tone, "if you're so convinced that switching teams is easy, why don't you—what's the term?—put your money where your mouth is?"

Intrigued, Tiber looked at Monica in time to see her grin slip. "Say what?"

"What's going on in that devious head of yours, Shauss?" Kellen asked.

"Monica told me that if all the males in the world suddenly perished, she'd have sex with Jasmine."

Interest stirred in Kellen's eyes as he turned to stare at Monica. "Did she now? I didn't know you swung that way, my love."

"I don't," she said carefully. Then she added, "Normally."

"But you'd make an exception if you had to," Shauss pushed.

"Shauss, you're a bastard," Monica said, but he noticed she was fighting a smile. "And yes, I could switch teams if the need arose."

"Prove it," he challenged. "Kiss Jasmine. And I don't mean a peck on the cheek—I mean a full tongue kiss that lasts at least a minute."

When she turned to Kellen, he held up his hands defensively. "Don't look at me—I'm a homophobe, remember?"

She stared at Jasmine for a long moment, and Tiber didn't bother to conceal his interest as Jasmine stared back.

Do it, he urged them silently. Because she knew it aroused him no end, Nelina had occasionally brought a submissive female to their bed and played with her for hours while he watched. He'd give anything to be tortured like that again.

When Jasmine turned pink and dropped her gaze to her plate, Monica said, "No problem."

She got up and rounded the table. "Stand up, Jasmine."

Tiber's groin tightened at the air of command about her and he thanked the Powers that Hastion had insisted he stay.

Shauss heard Jasmine swallow and then she looked up at him. Satisfied beyond measure that she was waiting for his direction in front of his insufferable brother, he said, "By all means."

"The pheromone level in here is going through the roof," Monica murmured. "I thought you guys resented it when women pleasured each other."

"Only because we never got to watch," Kellen said.

"And when we did, we were sent away unsatisfied," Shauss added. "But that won't be a problem tonight."

He grinned when Zannen groused, "Not for you."

"There's always the probe."

Zannen speared him with a look. "I prefer fucking to being fucked, if it's all the same to you."

Jasmine stood up. Monica towered over her in an almost aggressive stance, her long blonde-streaked hair falling carelessly over her shoulders, her tight wrapsuit hiding nothing of her considerable feminine assets. Jasmine, barefoot and delicate in the ultrafeminine dress, looked every inch the submissive as she stood with her eyes cast down and her chest rising with every rapid breath. Shauss almost expected her to drop to her knees before his former mate.

"Look at me, Jas." When Jasmine looked up, Monica asked, "Are you okay with this?"

Jasmine nodded.

"How much have you had to drink?"

"Just water," Jasmine murmured.

Monica looked at Kellen and then took Jasmine's face in both her hands and kissed her without hesitation. Their mouths opened and it was obvious that Monica was plumbing Jasmine's with her tongue. The sight was unbelievably arousing, and when Jasmine whimpered and leaned into her, resting her hands on Monica's hips, Shauss' cock turned to a fiery pillar of stone.

But Monica gentled the kiss almost at once, wrapping her arms around Jasmine and rubbing her back. Shauss began to feel a prickle of concern that was dangerously akin to jealousy.

Chastising himself for the fool he was, he forced the feeling down. After all, it had been he who insisted they kiss in the first place.

Monica finally backed away, dropping a few more gentle kisses on Jasmine's lips and cheek before holding her tight.

"Sorry," she whispered when she pulled away. "Are you okay?"

Jasmine looked troubled. "I'm fine."

"Dare I say it?" Shauss asked.

"Fine. You told me so. Happy now? Sit, Jasmine." When Jasmine obeyed, Monica frowned and picked up her glass to sniff the contents. "Are we sure this is just water? Her pupils are completely dilated."

"Monica, have you ever heard of subspace?" Shauss asked.

Monica's eyes narrowed. "I take it you're not talking about how Captain Kirk phones home?"

"No, I'm talking about the state of a submissive's mind when she's deeply affected by being dominated."

She looked between the two of them with keen speculation. "Holy shit, Jas—you're into that?"

"Apparently." She sounded like she was having difficulty talking and Shauss looked at her sharply.

"No wonder you two are so attracted." Monica shook her head. "Shauss is a total Dominant."

"I'm not the one who dominated her just now, Monica," he said, once more fighting off his unaccountable jealousy. "I believe that honor went to you."

Her mouth opened in shock. "But I—you—" Then she looked chagrined. "Holy shit, I didn't mean to."

"That's just who you are, my love," Kellen said. "A very dominant female who enjoys being dominated in bed occasionally."

"Occasionally," she snorted. "More like daily."

"It's a dirty job..." Kellen's lips quirked.

Monica smirked at him before focusing on Shauss. "But if I was dominating her, doesn't that still mean she's under the influence?"

"No doubt she's under the influence of several things, not the least of which is her desire to please a Dom." *Or a Domme*, he thought sourly. "But none of them render her unable to make an informed decision."

Monica looked unconvinced, so Shauss asked, "When Kellen dominates you, who ultimately has control of the situation?"

"He does, duh. That's why it's called domination."

"If you failed to become aroused or were genuinely frightened, would he continue to dominate you?"

"Probably not."

"You don't think your fright or lack of arousal could excite him, make him even more determined to force you?"

"Only if he was an utter asshole, which he's not."

"You trust him to stop when you really want him to."

"Yes," she blew out on an exasperated breath.

"So you hold the ultimate control of the situation."

"I guess so but..." She looked at Jasmine with concerned eyes.

"But...?"

"Jasmine is more sensitive than I am," she finally said. "And you're nowhere near as agreeable as Kellen."

"In other words, she's a doormat and I'm a bully."

"That's not what I said."

"Jasmine, would you kiss one of the elders if I asked you to?" Shauss inquired.

She shuddered. "No. Way."

"What if I wanted you to kiss the commander?"

Jasmine's face reddened and she thought for a minute before saying, "Only if Monica really wanted me to."

"Which I don't."

Kellen's eyes twinkled as he lifted his glass for a swig of ale. "Come now, Monica—surely what's sauce for the goose..."

"Will cook your gander but good," Monica shot back with a stern look.

Kellen just smiled. Shauss didn't know how he accepted her castigation so complacently. He'd have her over his knee, begging for mercy.

"So Jasmine, how do you feel about having kissed Monica?" he asked.

"I...I'm not sure."

"Think about it. Do you feel shame? Disgust? Like you're going to regret it in the morning?"

"No, not at all. I feel..." Tears welled in her eyes and she stood up. "Excuse me."

She fled into the head.

"Way to go, asshole," Monica scolded him before following her.

* * * * *

"Jas, I'm so, so sorry!" Monica wrapped her arms around Jasmine's shoulders from behind and bussed her on the temple. "Me and my big mouth."

Jasmine gave a choked laugh, still trying to hold back an imminent sob storm. "It's okay."

"No, it's not! I had something to prove to those guys, and not only did I prove exactly the opposite, but I hurt you in the process."

Jasmine leaned back against her shoulder and sighed. "No, that's not it at all. Seriously, I can't remember the last time I felt this relaxed, this...free." *This loved.* That was what she couldn't say. For the first time since her mother died, she felt loved. It was a pain that hurt *so* good.

A tear streaked down her cheek. "You know what I am, Monica. I mean, my God, you've even done a complete pelvic on me, so you've seen *exactly* what I am. And yet you kissed me and held me like it didn't—" She swallowed a sob, and choked out, "Like it didn't matter to you at all."

"It doesn't!"

"I miss my mother so much." Jasmine couldn't keep it in. "She was the only person in the whole world who ever really knew *me*, loved *me*, you know? And since she died, I've been so totally alone." She wiped her eyes. "It's just really scary to know there's no one at your back."

"I know," Monica said. "And you're not alone anymore, no matter what happens. Remember that."

Jasmine turned and faced her. "I want you to remove the galathene barrier."

"Okay. I got your spray replicated, so tomorrow—"

"No." Jasmine shook her head. "I mean now. Tonight."

"Will the spray take effect that quickly?"

"I don't want it."

Monica stared at her. "What are you saying?"

"Monica, you were right when you said I was living a lie on Earth, and now I know I'll never be able to go back there and take up where I left off. I'm just...done with it. All the barrier and the spray are doing is postponing the inevitable. My life on Earth is over, and I don't want to go back to that room with Shauss tonight and be fake again. I can't."

"Oh my God, you *do* love him."

She nodded, no longer able to deny it. "Do you ever think that some things are just meant to be?"

"Yeah, I do," Monica said firmly. "Would you believe I knew Kellen's name before I knew he even existed?"

Jasmine's eyes widened and her heartbeat picked up speed. "Really?"

"Yup. I had a dog named Kellen, bought a house in Kellen Gardens, and even scribbled Mrs. Monica Kellen in the margins of my notebooks when I was in college. I never realized it, but I was waiting for him, and the first time I saw him, something inside me recognized him."

Jasmine felt something settle inside her.

"I've had these odd little visions all my life," she said softly. "I dream of myself working in a garden, only it's a different me. I have curly hair down to my butt and I'm wearing an earth-mother dress, and I'm pregnant and absolutely thrilled about it. And working beside me, just beyond my line of sight, is someone I love more than my own life."

Taking a deep breath, she finally admitted the truth to herself.

"The first time I saw Shauss, I knew it was him—and yet not. I felt like I'd been duped. I'd walked through the door expecting this gentle watercolor lover, and then the door slammed behind me and I was trapped in limbo with the darkest, most terrifying man in the world." She swallowed hard. "It was like a countdown on my life had begun, and the harder I fought it, the more inevitable it became—like he was my destiny, and my destiny was my doom."

"Holy fucking shit. What did you do?"

Jasmine smiled weakly. "I kept typing and he walked right by. But from that moment on, I felt like I was living on borrowed time."

"Christ, and there I thought you were the Stepford secretary."

"I had to do that, Monica. I had to paint on that perfect face and sculpt this perfect body and dress in those perfect clothes and put on my best mechanical act. It was the only way to stay sane. But when I wound up on this ship and Shauss stripped off my clothes and made me fight and scream, it felt...weirdly right, like I'd taken one giant step closer to my perfect doom." She looked Monica in the eye. "And now I feel like I have to take the next step. Maybe the last step."

"Oh my God, I'm getting goose bumps. Are you sure about this?"

"Yes, I'm sure. I know it sounds crazy, but just knowing that you're here, that you know and care about the real me, gives me the courage to face it. Deep down, I need to be with Shauss more than I've ever needed anything. Just once I need to be with him as myself, no matter what it costs. I need to breathe him in and soak him up and just...*wallow* in him. I don't know what will happen to me afterward, and frankly, at this point I don't care. I just want one real night with him to remember after he finds out."

"But—"

"He will find out." Jasmine looked at her. "It's only a matter of time. And he's not the type to just forgive and forget."

Lord, remembering his "interrogation" in the commander's dining room just about gave her hives now. He wouldn't hold back this time.

"I won't let him hurt you."

"Don't jeopardize yourself, Monica—this is between him and me."

"You think he and Kellen won't wonder how I missed the signs of Sparnism?"

"I already told you, I had an accident as a child and developed early-onset menopause. Period. It's a bona fide condition, Monica. Look it up."

"I know." She hugged her again. "I'm afraid you're right—he won't be very understanding. But I'll do everything I can to make him understand. He'll come around eventually. I have a good feeling about you two."

"That makes me feel better."

"Okay, let's go peel this crap out of your nose."

* * * * *

Shauss deeply regretted having let his need to best Monica override his sensitivity to Jasmine's needs. When the two females walked through hand in hand and headed for the infirmary to treat her headache, Monica's eyes reproaching him with every step, he kicked himself for being all kinds of fool. Tiber's offer to accompany them was politely but firmly rebuffed as well, and Shauss cursed himself for not showing more understanding and compassion after he claimed her.

When they returned, he pulled Jasmine into his lap and tried to feed her a few more bites of her meal, along with a goblet of white wine to help her relax. He didn't like feeling so inadequate. First he'd failed to induce her orgasm and then she'd turned to Monica for emotional comfort. Knowing that Monica had access to parts of his mate that he didn't, bothered him immensely.

Once dinner was done and they stood up to leave, Monica and Jasmine shared a lengthy hug. Shauss tensed at the worried look in Monica's eye. It was almost as if she didn't want to let her go, as if she were sending Jasmine off on a long and dangerous voyage from which she might not return.

"She'll be fine," he said, disturbed that she would think him less than capable of taking care of his mate.

"I'll be fine," Jasmine reiterated.

Monica nodded.

As they walked, Jasmine's hand seemed to practically vibrate in his. She was so far from the Stepford creature Monica always accused her of being, so full of pent-up energy, he barely recognized her. And yet he wouldn't have her any other way. He was beginning to realize he was much closer to seeing the real Jasmine than she'd ever intended to let him and the idea was arousing.

When they entered his quarters, he turned to her. "You might as well make up your mind right now that you're going to orgasm because we're not done here until you do."

"Well then," she said, licking her lips nervously, "I think it's only fair that I explain why that might be difficult."

When she hesitated, he kissed her delicately. "You don't have to be afraid—you can tell me anything."

"I've only had one orgasm in my life," she explained hesitantly.

"Is that so?"

Excitement burst through him. She was all but a virgin. He led her to the chair and pulled the clips from her hair. Waiting patiently for her to explain, he started brushing the luxuriant mass in long, even strokes.

"My...my clitoris isn't all that sensitive, and no matter how much attention you pay it, I won't come. The one time I had an orgasm, it took the guy's pubic bone slamming against mine for a very long time to make it happen."

After digesting that for a moment, he said, "I wish you'd told me earlier."

"Well, it's hardly the kind of announcement you make in front of a crowd."

"Touché." He smiled. "My apologies—you're absolutely correct and I'm absolutely an ass. You're telling me now and that's what matters."

She sagged a little and smiled over her shoulder. "I'm glad you think so. But that still leaves us..."

"Mating in a position that won't satisfy you."

"I'm sorry."

"So little faith," he chided. In reality, he was getting very excited. He had to believe that a big part of why she had difficulty orgasming was her "head game". She'd admitted she'd never been restrained before during sex. She was just beginning to uncover her submissive nature, and she hadn't been able to relax enough in front of the other males to really give in to him mentally.

Tonight, she would. Tonight, he would dig deep into his treasure trove of Terran toys and plunge her into sensation the likes of which she'd never known. She would come for him, over and over.

Chapter Eleven

"As you probably noticed," Shauss continued, opening one of the cabinet doors, "I've indulged my domination fetish with a collection of Terran bondage equipment."

"Like the cuffs," she said tentatively.

"Yes, like the cuffs. Because of the ship's construction, I'm limited to restraints that don't need to be attached to walls or a ceiling."

"Um, okay." She was without a clue as to what he was talking about.

"How much exposure have you had to the D/s lifestyle?"

"None."

"Then even the mildest of bondage gear will seem rather extreme to you."

They'd passed that a long time ago, but she didn't say so.

"I want to free you," he told her. "Free you by binding you so that you're unable to resist what I have to offer you."

Her heart sank. Would he restrain her again before she got what she wanted?

"Shauss…" She looked at him beseechingly.

"Tell me what you want."

"I want to touch you first. I want to touch you and smell you and taste you. Please."

He deliberated for a moment before saying, "I suppose that can be allowed, with one exception—you will not take any portion of my genitals into your mouth."

She almost pouted. "But why?"

"Take it or leave it, Jasmine."

She wavered. It was tempting to try to restrain *him* in the bondage equipment. She wanted to go down on him, darn it — that was her favorite part of sex and she was good at it.

"Will you ever let me?"

The way he said "Perhaps" made her doubt it. He looked almost suspicious.

"Is it so hard for you to believe I enjoy giving oral sex?"

"Frankly, yes. The women of our planet made no secret of the fact that the idea disgusted them. I'm fairly certain most Terran women only offer it because their males enjoy it, and if it were up to them, they would choose not to do it."

"So the only reason you tasted me was because you thought I'd enjoy it? Did I disgust you?"

"No!" he exploded. "You have a fascinating taste and I'm eager to drink my fill of you."

"Then why is it so unbelievable that I feel the same about you?"

He stared at her. "You're every bit as stubborn as Monica when you want something, aren't you? Do you need to be punished for it?"

She bit her lip, feeling a naughty tickle in her belly. She wasn't being very submissive at all, but she only had a small window of opportunity and she wanted to experience as much as she could of him in the time she had. But the idea of being punished by Shauss revved her engine in a very perverse way.

"If you wish to wear that dress again, you should remove it."

He turned to his cabinet again so she slowly pulled the dress over her head and stood there with it in her hand. She felt hot and prickly all over to be standing there in only the thong.

"You may hang it in the wardrobe," he directed. "Although I didn't originally intend for you to act as my submissive anywhere but in the privacy of our quarters, this evening has convinced me you might feel more comfortable under my guidance even in public settings. Am I reading you correctly?"

She thought about it for a moment before saying, "Maybe."

In theory, the idea made her hackles rise. She was an independent woman who could take care of herself and make her own decisions, thank you very much. But in practice, she'd loved deferring to him, being guided and petted by him in front of Kellen and Monica. She'd felt cherished and had loved pleasing him. It was the first party she'd ever really enjoyed and felt free at. Typically she only felt comfortable at parties when she had an assigned job.

She wasn't sure how to react to this dependence on him.

Shauss brought out a handful of black leather items and a shiny black bar, and like a light switch, the clinking of metal on metal instantly shut down conflict in her head.

He tossed it all on the bed. "You may undress me if you wish."

Thrilled, she pulled down his zipper very slowly and carefully so as not to catch any skin and then pushed the fabric over his shoulders and down. She dropped to one knee to pull his feet out of the uniform, looking up at his already-erect penis with longing.

"You know better." He stepped away to drop his uniform in the sanitizer and then sank onto the couch, his hands behind his head and his knees splayed. "I'm yours to explore within the agreed-upon context."

Still on one knee, she hesitated, shocked by the impulse to cross those few feet between them on all fours. She would keep a watchful eye on his face, and while he was distracted by the seductive stretch and roll of her catlike body, she'd pounce, capturing his long, steely cock in the cage of her razor-sharp claws. He wouldn't dare move or even voice an objection while under such a threat, and she would be free to settle at his feet and consume him at her leisure, savoring the musky flesh between his thighs for hours while he sat there sweating...

"Unless you've changed your mind?"

Startled out of her fantasy, Jasmine shot to her feet. *Seductive*, she snorted. As aesthetically pleasing as she might be in her own synthetic way, she'd never been particularly seductive.

Approaching the couch with perverse reluctance, she perched beside him. It seemed so unreal to have him at her disposal. She devoured him with her eyes first. His silky black chest hair was a stark contrast to his pale skin, but it was so very masculine it gave her shivers in all kinds of places.

"What's this?" she asked, tracing a finger over a two-inch scar on his abdomen. When he didn't answer, she looked up. "I'm sorry—touchy subject?"

"Monica stabbed me," he confessed. "With my own dagger, no less."

"Oh my God, you're kidding!"

"I wish I were. She was none too happy to find herself mated to us—at first." His grin was so satisfied, so happy and tender, Jasmine's heart shriveled instantly. He loved Monica. God, he loved Monica and she'd taken him away from her.

"Don't worry," he said, pulling her against him. "She did me no permanent damage."

"I'm glad," she whispered against his chest. She kissed her way down his torso, silently begging forgiveness and vowing to make every minute of their time together worth it for him.

"Peserin!" he swore when she nuzzled his scrotum, inhaling deeply. God, he smelled so absolutely delicious, she did it again. Sliding her tongue down to his perineum, she licked a broad swath over his tightening sac all the way to the base of his penis.

"Enough," he said roughly, picking her up by the wrists as he stood, ignoring her whimper of disappointment.

Setting her on the end of the bed, he ordered, "Scoot back and lie down face up."

When she did, he fastened the leather cuffs around her wrists again and clipped them to two widely separated rings on the headboard.

When he reached up with a blindfold, she protested, "But I want to see you!"

"You've seen me. Now I want you to go beyond what you see and just feel," he said.

Sighing, she settled into the blindfold. She heard more clinking and something was wrapped around her thighs just above the knees. Then Shauss pushed her legs far apart and attached something to hold them in place. She was effectively spread-eagled on the bed, and the realization sent her pulse racing.

The sight must have affected him too, because his spicy scent suddenly grew very strong. Jasmine soaked it up, breathing deeply. If she was going to suffer the consequences of pheromone exposure, she might as well reap all the benefits first.

Excitement suffused him as Jasmine relaxed before his eyes. He'd acquired all this equipment with the intention of experimenting on one of the common-use copulative recruits, a surprising number of whom had expressed interest in bondage and domination, but he'd never dared dream he might use it on a mate. Or at least he hadn't until Monica responded so explosively to being restrained and punished.

Bondage was definitely in their lives to stay.

He pinched one of the flowers from Jasmine's plant and started stroking her with it. Starting at her wrist, he trailed the delicate petals down the vulnerable flesh of her inner arm into her armpit. She gasped, writhing as he continued over her collarbone and up the other arm. Following a similar circuit, he then started at her ankle and dragged it up her thigh. After swirling it over her belly for a while, laughing softly at the way she twitched and squirmed, he pulled it down her other leg.

When he took it to the soles of her feet, she screeched, breathless with laughter, and tried to kick him away, but he grabbed her ankle.

"Ticklish feet," he said. "I'll have to remember that."

Though he had to sprawl one knee out to accommodate his aching balls, he continued to torture them both with the flower, enjoying the sounds of her pleasure mingling with his own increasingly ragged breaths. Peserin, but she was a passionate little handful.

"Are you comfortable?" he inquired, trailing the flower over first one small, tight nipple and then the other.

"Um...not exactly," she moaned, earning a smile she couldn't see.

"I appreciate your honesty."

When the bloom started to fall apart, he tossed it aside and set about following the same path with his tongue, keeping his eyes on the faint trails as they dried on her skin. The sense of ownership they inspired was overwhelming, as though he were marking her with his saliva.

The memory of her saliva cooling his skin made him wonder if she'd experienced a similar reaction. His jaw hardened at the idea—he would never be any female's possession—but he had to admit the velvet swipe of her tongue on his scrotum had aroused him almost beyond sanity.

He focused on tasting every inch of her skin, and by the time he reached her nipples again, she was moaning, begging him to take her. Instead, he feasted on her firm breasts, plumping them with his palms, squeezing and massaging until she sobbed his name.

"Am I making you so very miserable, *aramai*?" he murmured against one hard, wet nipple.

"Yes, you beast!"

"That's good." Very good, considering how very miserable he was becoming.

He scissored his teeth over the tiny bud and she screamed, bucking hard. The knowledge that she thrived on a bit of erotic pain was hell on his already-suffering cock. Ignoring it, he gave the other nipple the same treatment and reveled in her hoarse cries for release.

Sliding farther down on the bed and planting his elbows inside the triangle created by the bar, he lowered his head to lavish time and attention on the ultrasmooth mound of her cunt, immensely gratified to find copious amounts of slick moisture sliding from her. He lapped it up while she writhed and begged him to stop.

Her clitoris did seem less responsive to the stimulation than her nipples were. He'd rather expected the opposite to be true in light of her breast implants, but his knowledge of Terran female genitalia was limited and mostly secondhand. No doubt pornography was as unrealistic as Monica claimed and he shouldn't base his expectations on its images.

"Please, please," she whimpered.

"What do you want, Jasmine?" he asked. "You have to tell me."

"I want you!"

"What do you want of me?"

"Your...your cock," she gasped. "I want it inside me."

When he unfastened her wrists and turned her over, she moaned, "No!"

"I'll take care of you," he assured her, linking her wrists and attaching them to the headboard. Pulling her up to her knees, he braced his legs outside hers to help compensate for the difference in their heights and slid deep into her cunt. He rode her slowly at first, holding her hips in his hands and pulling her back as he thrust forward, making sure his scrotum ground against her clitoris with every penetration. It was eminently clear from her groans and pleas that she enjoyed being handled this way, so he took his time, savoring every nuance of her surrender. Her back was beautiful, her narrow ribs expanding and contracting in deep, shuddering breaths as she undulated with him. She was utterly at his mercy now and reveling in it, trusting him to provide whatever it was she needed.

And what she needed now was *more*, so he increased the power of his thrusts, driving into her and then withdrawing slowly, his pace deliberately controlled and controlling. The more broken her cries became, the more determined he was that she would orgasm.

He stopped suddenly, drawing another agonized "No!" from her. He fancied he heard an echo of the same from his cock.

Dropping his hands to the mattress, he braced himself over her back and took rough possession of her exposed ear, claiming every ridge and groove with his tongue before savaging her lobe with his teeth.

"I've got endless endurance, Jasmine," he rasped, hoping it was true. "I'll fuck you all night if that's what it takes."

"Then do it!" she screeched, her voice muffled by her arm.

Sliding his hands into the creases between her thighs, he lifted her until her knees left the bed. She hung limply in his hold while he drove into her from a deeper angle, pounding her until his balls ached. His spur erupted, but the angle of his thrusts didn't allow for the dual penetration, which was just as well.

When the broad, flat spur glanced off her perineum, she squeaked, and Shauss froze, worried he'd injured her.

"It's okay," she gasped. "Oh God, please, please…"

Still concerned, he let her dangle for a moment, his chest heaving with arousal and exertion and frustration. Peserin, what if his testicles couldn't strike her hard enough to…

Strike her.

The image that particular phrase conjured made his cock surge inside her, and a wicked smile curved his lips. Despite Monica's admonishments against spanking and "kinking out", she'd never failed to come in a spectacular fashion when subjected to either. Perhaps it was time to see if Jasmine was similarly bent.

Letting her knees drop back to the mattress, he leaned forward and unhooked the clip holding her to the headboard.

"I told you I couldn't come," she moaned. "Quit torturing me!"

"Patience, my mate."

Suddenly lacking patience himself, he shoved his rampant cock back into her cunt and drizzled saliva over the sweet pink pucker of her anus. Jasmine barely had time to stiffen at the sensation before he was driving his spur into her, and her squeal excited him beyond endurance. He tugged her upright and yanked off the blindfold, lifting her bound wrists until he could duck into the circle of her arms. She immediately seized two handfuls of his hair.

"Careful," he murmured. "I can pull hair too."

Hunching over her back, he wrapped his arms around her and fucked her for his own pleasure while he prepared her for hers.

"*Empran, flare reflection,*" he ordered.

When their reflection materialized, her eyes were squeezed shut in a furrowed frown so he had a few seconds to watch her unobserved. She was still concentrating too intently, still trying too hard. She needed to let go. Hopefully viewing the raw carnality of their reflection would affect her as deeply as it did him. Peserin knew the sight of her thighs, forced wide by the toys he'd bound her with, and her bare pussy, open and glistening with the proof of her need, was enough to nudge him over the edge.

"Open your eyes, *aramai*," he whispered. "Watch me fuck you."

She stiffened and flushed scarlet at the sight of them. "Oh God."

Wasting no time, he slid his right hand down her side and over her abdomen, fingering her retiring little clit. "Beautiful, isn't it?"

She moaned pitifully. "Shauss, I—"

"Brace yourself, *aramai*."

He struck before she could obey, catching her squarely on the cunt with a stiff blow designed to ache rather than sting.

Jasmine let out a choked cry. "Shauss, what the hell are you doing?"

If he weren't so damn close to the edge, he would have laughed at the disbelief on her face. Dismissing her outraged cries, he slammed his palm onto her hot, wet flesh again and again, keeping time with his ferocious thrusts. His fingertips caught his balls more than once, but the pain only added to his pleasure.

She screamed, squeezing her eyes shut as she ground the back of her head into his chest.

He didn't let up on her. "You want me to stop?"

"Yes!" she sobbed. "God, it burns!"

Of that, he had no doubt. Her tender labia flamed bright pink with the force of his slaps—but they also dripped with the slickness of her arousal.

"Come for me, then."

She writhed in his hold, tossing her head back and forth, mumbling something almost unintelligible. *Need it harder…?*

Curling his fingers into a fist, he delivered, peppering her cunt with rapid-fire blows and praying to every Power in the universe that he could hold out. His body was ablaze with the need for release, but surely her need was just as great.

Jasmine jerked and her frantic eyes met his. "Oh God, here it comes," she panted.

Shauss nearly whimpered when her body bowed and splotches of deep red rose in her chest and neck. *Peserin, let it be so...*

"Oh shit!" she said tightly. Then she burst into a low wail that escalated to a hoarse scream as she wrenched in his hold over and over again.

The contractions around his cock were impossible to resist.

"That's it, *aramai*," he grunted as fire exploded in his loins. "Let it come."

His own release had never been so good.

Chapter Twelve

His father's genitals were missing.

They'd been on display in the stasis field not ten minutes before—he'd looked when he walked through the foyer on his way to the kitchens. He always looked. The neatly severed flesh, though perfectly preserved, was a sight that he couldn't help but stare at with both awe and bowel-twisting fear. What his father had done to earn such a punishment, no one would say, but it must have been something deadly evil.

Shauss looked around cautiously before stepping closer. The energy that usually hummed from the crystal pedestal was absent, which meant the security perimeter surrounding it was probably down.

Probably.

He put a long, narrow boot on the first step and paused. Nothing. Usually he didn't make it this far before Boydon was grabbing him by the arm and forcibly escorting him to the yard. Maybe it was a trap, a test of his ability to adhere to the dictates of the BayaDesri. The stasis zone was forbidden to all except she who created it, and she had an army of servants to ensure that her commands were obeyed.

Shauss hesitated, looking around again. Something told him this wasn't a test at all, but a sign of larger forces at work. The air didn't feel right and it wasn't wholly because of the electrical storm crackling outside the house's thick-hewn walls. Nor could it be attributed to Crunus' unusual proximity, the excitement and anticipation of which had consumed the entire valley for weeks.

No, the atmosphere was replete with malice. Dripping with it. Shauss' palms were damp with the weight of it on his skin.

Two more steps and he was standing on the dais, his toes a respectful distance from the tectonite ring marking the leading edge of the security perimeter. Wiping his hands on his pants, he reached up with one finger, going slower the closer he got. Hopefully if there were any energy left in the perimeter, he'd feel the whispers in time to draw back before a major jolt shouted down his arm.

Booming thunder made him jerk backward with a gasp. His heel went over the edge of the dais and only wheeling his arms and bowing his back kept him from tumbling backward down the steps. Righting himself with a shaky laugh, he shrugged off the sudden tension in his shoulders before approaching the perimeter once more.

A faint sound made him pause and look down the corridor. Was that a scream?

Sparing the pedestal a regretful glance, he leaped from the dais to the flagstone floor and let his long legs eat up the corridor as quietly as they could. Instinct took him to his mother's chamber door.

He pressed his palm to the reader and was surprised when there was no response.

"Arbitran?" he asked quietly.

Silence rang in the corridor.

The server had never failed to respond to his voice command. Never. It had refused him entry or exit on occasions too numerous to count, but it had never just...ignored him. This was becoming too unnerving.

A grunt and the sound of scuffling seeped from behind the door and his sense of urgency mounted. Raising his knuckles, he rapped on the door. There was no response.

Something was going on in there, and instinct screamed that he needed to be inside. Knowing it was forbidden to enter without permission, he shook as he depressed the manual entry tab and pushed open the chamber door.

It was hard to make sense of the sight that met his eyes. His father knelt over his mother's waist. She was kicking and bucking and scratching at his leather-clad legs, eyes wild as he shoved something into her mouth with...

A scabbard?

Yes—his grandfather's battle sword gleamed on the floor beside them. But what was in her mouth?

"What's the matter, Elona?" his father snarled into her face as he twisted the scabbard with both hands, forcing the object farther down her throat. "Is the taste of my phallus as offensive as you always imagined?"

Horror prickled over Shauss's skin. *His genitals were missing.* He knocked his father off her and tried to pull the chilled flesh from her mouth.

The horror turned to outright shock when he realized it wasn't his father's genitals, but his own—and it wasn't his mother beneath him, but Jasmine. He was thrusting into her throat and she was sucking his throbbing length even as her eyes bulged with panic. He tried to stop, but it was so good and he was so close, he simply couldn't pull out. He prayed he would finish before he killed her...

Shauss jerked awake only to find his cock really was in someone's mouth. Reacting instinctively, he slapped her off him and rolled to his feet, breathing hard.

"Empran, full lighting," he ordered.

The instant illumination revealed Jasmine holding her cheek, her eyes filled with tears.

"I'm sorry," she croaked.

Horrified, he sat on the side of the bed and grabbed her into his arms. "No, *aramai*—I'm the one who's sorry."

"You told me not to do that, but I just..."

"That's no excuse for striking you in the face. There's never any excuse for such behavior. Ever." He held her tight, rubbing her back, sick at the memory of his palm hitting her delicate face. "But I was dreaming about an incident from my childhood and my mind somehow…incorporated you into it."

When he said no more, she reached up to stroke his hair back behind his ear. "Can you tell me about it?"

He sighed and turned into her hand, planting a kiss in the middle of her palm. "It's an ugly story, but perhaps it's better for me to share it so you understand my aversion to receiving oral sex." *Or at least part of it.*

When she nodded encouragingly, he settled his back against the headboard and pulled her against his side.

"My mother was the BayaDesri of our region, a regional governor second in authority only to the Desri of Garathan," he started, rubbing his chin in her hair. "She was first mated to Boydon and they had Zannen, but after her second pregnancy resulted in a stillborn son, testing revealed that Boydon was unable to sire daughters. She consigned him, and Zannen along with him, to the farm barracks and took my father as mate."

"How cold!"

"Yes, but my study of Terran history shows a similar desire for male progeny."

"True."

"At any rate, the BayaDesri was none too happy when I arrived, but then she had my two sisters and thus her need for female heirs was satisfied. As was the norm for Garathani mothers, she showed little interest in me. I was my father's responsibility and I saw very little of her during my formative years."

"That sucks," she said. "I can't imagine my mother abandoning me to my father's care."

"That was just the way of things then." He rubbed his chin against her temple. "As a child, I was aware of the undercurrents that pervaded our house, but I didn't understand them. Boydon told me long after the fact that once my mother had the daughters she desired, she wanted no more children and refused to allow my father to spill his seed inside her. She would drive him to the breaking point, take her own pleasure, and then send him away. Being the proud female she was, she refused to allow him surcease with another and back then we didn't know about prostate stimulation. He was an angry, frustrated man and she delighted in goading him because she had nothing to fear from him. Like Empran, the house server could have him in neural restraints before he could take a step in her direction, and she slept with her quarters under security."

"What a power trip that must have been for her."

"No doubt. But one night, when she was in the throes of her pleasure, he managed to insert himself and ejaculate inside her." He paused before saying softly, "She had him castrated."

*****

"You're disgustingly fit this morning," Tiber accused as Hastion jogged on the cardio platform.

"Usually that's something doctors would be happy about," Hastion said, not the least winded by the brisk pace.

"Not when I'm trying to figure out what's wrong with you."

"That does always seem to be the way of it."

"I should have come with you last night and run more scans."

"*Dr. Tiber,*" Empran said, "*report to Infirmary Three for a level-four medical emergency.*"

"*Flare me there immediately,*" Tiber replied.

When he appeared in Infirmary Three, it was hard to make sense of the scene that met his eyes. Monica and Ketrok appeared to be having a tug-of-war with a blanket while one of the Terran doctors pulled on Ketrok's waist.

Monica saw him. "Tiber, help me get this thing off him!"

"Peserin, get it off!" Ketrok grated. "It's killing me!"

The pregnant blonde nurse, dressed only in a patient gown, leaned against one of the beds, screaming hysterically.

Cold sweat broke out on Tiber's neck. "What is it?"

"The fucking pod thing!" Monica yanked the blanket off to reveal Ketrok's hands lodged in a steripod.

Hastion appeared right beside Tiber. "What in Peserin's hell…?"

"Lean over!" Tiber yelled at Ketrok. "Get it on the floor."

When Ketrok obeyed, grunting with pain, Tiber put his boot on the pod and grasped Ketrok's shoulders. "Pull!"

Dr. Snow, his arms still around Ketrok's waist, leaned back hard trying to pull him free. When their effort failed, Hastion and Monica each put a foot on the pod and grabbed one of Ketrok's arms.

They all staggered back as Ketrok's hands ripped free of the block and Tiber gasped. Holy Powers, the flesh was all but gone!

Ketrok's eyes rolled back and he sagged to his knees.

"Empran, contain this steripod and energize stasis chamber," Tiber barked.

When a containment field materialized around the pod, the four of them carried Ketrok's limp body into the stasis chamber and laid him on the nearest bed. As soon as they were all clear of the chamber and the door closed behind them, Tiber activated the stasis field. Ketrok was instantly encapsulated in blue light.

"What the fuck happened?" Monica breathed, staring at him through the observation port.

"I have no idea. Empran, full pathology scan," Tiber ordered, checking the chamber's readouts to make sure it was functioning properly.

"Monica!" came a pitiful cry.

"Oh shit, Shelley!"

Tiber turned. The nurse was in Hastion's arms, her eyes closed and her face bloodless.

"I think she fainted," he said.

"I didn't faint!" Shelley's eyes opened, dilated and glassy. "I just got dizzy. Jesus, that block tried to eat Dr. Ketrok!" She let her forehead rest on Hastion's bare shoulder again.

"Put her on the bed," Monica ordered.

"I'm fine," she insisted. "He's the one who needs help."

Commander Kellen appeared.

"Monica, are you all right?" He pulled her into his arms. "What's happening to Ketrok? Where is he?"

"That steripod." Tiber nodded toward the cube on the floor. It must have come from Ketrok's lab because the infirmary pod still occupied its customary place on the work table. "It *did* try to eat him. His hands are..." He shook his head, feeling slightly dizzy himself. "I've never seen anything like it."

"Where is he?" Kellen repeated.

"In stasis," Hastion said. "Go look at his hands. They're...destroyed."

Being in the commander's arms seemed to be the trigger Monica needed to let go of her control and she began to shake visibly.

"I was just standing here talking to Shelley when I heard this awful scream. I turned around and Ketrok was stumbling toward me with his hands stuck in that block." She sucked in a shaky breath, tears spilling down her cheeks.

"Hush, Monica." Kellen pressed his lips against her temple.

"Hamburger." She gulped. "They look like fucking hamburger." Closing her eyes, she rested her forehead on his chest.

"What is his condition?"

"The damage is catastrophic," Tiber said grimly. "It will take several weeks to regenerate the tissue."

"Do you have any idea what caused it?"

"I'm waiting for initial scans, but the pod is obviously contaminated with a virulent pathogen of some sort."

"Notify Shauss and get microscience in here. We need to figure out what it is before it hurts anyone else."

"Oh God," Shelley groaned. "I think I'm in labor."

* * * * *

Jasmine's eyes widened in horror. "How awful!"

Shauss nodded pensively. Remembering that first glimpse of his father's severed flesh still curled his stomach. "His preserved genitals occupied pride of place in the main foyer of the house, locked in a stasis field that only she was allowed to approach. It was definitely a message, not just to my father, but to all the males of the House—indeed, of the region."

"I can't believe that was legal!"

"Technically, it wasn't, but there wasn't much to be done about it. One had to go through channels to lodge complaints with the Desri, and the BayaDesri was one of those channels."

"So complaints just got tied up in red tape."

"Exactly. My father became an exceedingly bitter, silent man after that. Boydon told me that nine months later, my mother delivered a baby boy who was officially declared stillborn, but she took great satisfaction in reporting to him that the doctor had let the child bleed out at the umbilicus. Thereafter, my father was like a man possessed. He seemed never to sleep, rarely ate, was always muttering to himself.

"Finally, during the Crunus Uprising, when main power systems were out and the server was down, he took his severed genitals from the display and shoved them down her throat. I happened upon the scene and tried to save her, but the flesh was wedged too deeply." He looked down at her. "That's what I was dreaming about, and somehow your face became superimposed on hers."

"I'm so sorry," she said. "What happened to your father?"

"He locked me out of the room and ended his own life with his father's sword so that I wouldn't have to witness his execution."

"Oh Shauss…"

"Perhaps it was all for the best. Boydon raised me, and though Zannen and I fought like tigers most of the time, I was well taken care of."

"Why do you hate each other so much?"

Shauss reflected for a moment. "Hate might be too strong a word. Full-blood brothers fight even under the best of circumstances, and ours were hardly that. He resented what he perceived as my privileged life in the house, and that resentment only increased after he lost his hair and was designated a slave. He's always been jealous of what I had."

"And what did you resent?" she asked softly.

He gave her a startled look. "I didn't resent anything." But even as the words left his mouth, he wondered about their veracity.

"Lieutenant Shauss, report to Infirmary Three at once."

"My apologies, but I've been summoned." He rose and dressed quickly. "I'll return as soon as I can."

* * * * *

When he walked through the door, Tiber said curtly, "I'll report after we avert the most immediate crisis. Nurse Bonham is in premature labor."

Shauss nodded and got out of his way, frowning at the implication there was more than one crisis.

Kellen and Hastion stood by the stasis chamber window. Although Kellen was in uniform, Hastion wore only shorts and a surgical top. Shauss raised his brow at Hastion's attire but said nothing.

Opening the medical supply cabinet, Tiber withdrew two bottles.

"Trilimin is highly effective at halting labor and algicort will stimulate surfactant production in the fetuses. Both can be easily administered transdermally." He held up the small transdermal dosing button. "I would advise implanting a biomet unit so that we may monitor the patient's vital functions without confining her to the infirmary."

Monica stroked Shelley's hair back. "Are you good with him helping us?"

Shelley, white-faced and obviously in pain, merely nodded. "Where's Mark?"

"He's on his way," Monica said.

When Kellen beckoned, Shauss stepped over to the stasis chamber. What he saw through the port made him shudder. Ketrok's hands looked like they'd been skinned. Even from here, he could see bare bones and shredded tendons.

"What in Peserin's hell did this?" he murmured.

"That steripod." Kellen nodded toward a pod on the floor.

When Shauss approached it, Monica cried, "No, Shauss, don't touch it!"

"Easy, sweet one." He crouched to stare at the steripod. "Even if I were inclined to touch it, the containment field wouldn't let me."

"Empran's preliminary analysis indicates it might have been contaminated with a genetically engineered virus similar to the one infecting the pad on Voya Deck," Tiber said.

"Similar, but with a deadly difference," Shauss pointed out. "The pod looks completely normal."

"All steripods are in containment until they're cleared by microscience," Kellen said. "Access to the infirmaries is restricted until we pinpoint the cause of this incident. We must assume sabotage until it's proven otherwise."

Once he'd shown Monica and Dr. Snow how to prepare the medications and applied an infused button to the nurse's upper chest, Tiber moved to the sink to wash his hands.

"What is Ketrok's prognosis?" Shauss asked, rising.

"Stasis appears to have halted the progress of the infection." Tiber dried his hands on a surgical towel. "After microscience determines the pathology and an effective course of treatment, I'll remove him from stasis and apply regeneration gloves. He'll probably have to wear them for several weeks while the nerves and tendons regenerate."

He pumped a squirt of Terran sanitizing gel into his palm with a grimace of impatience that Shauss understood and could sympathize with. During their rotations on the planet's surface, they'd all had to rely on less-than-efficient Terran technology in order to limit the Terrans' awareness of their own technology. The less Terrans knew about them, the better off they all were.

Watching Tiber rub the gel into his hands, Shauss suddenly felt an icy trickle in his belly. It could have been Tiber whose lean hands were savaged by the steripod. Tiber's well-modulated voice screaming hoarsely. Tiber's amiable features contorted in agony. Why that should disturb him, he couldn't say. Only yesterday, he'd have felt a stab of satisfaction at the idea of Tiber suffering some freakish but survivable accident. Now, however...

He frowned, unnerved by the knot of cold anger burning inside him. Perhaps the protectiveness he felt was a natural outcome of being primary in their bond. Now that he thought of it, he'd be similarly disturbed if it were Hastion lying there.

"Commander." Dr. Snow left Shelley's bedside and approached them, his wrinkled face almost as white as his hair, his usual expression of arrogance noticeably absent. "I'm humbled by your medical technology. Injuries of that degree would probably have resulted in amputation on Earth. It pains me to think that the overzealous response of our government will deprive our citizens of such incredible advances in medical science."

"Yes, well, it pains me too," Kellen said, "but until such time as the powers that be are willing to reopen communications, there's not a lot I can do about it."

"Damn Republicans," Snow muttered. "At any rate, I just wanted to personally express my admiration and gratitude. I hope you'll allow us to learn all we can while we're aboard."

Kellen nodded. "That is our desire, as well."

As the doctor returned to Shelley's side, Monica said under her breath, "He's a registered Republican, you know."

Even as amusement pulled at his lips, Shauss yanked her against him in a brief but heartfelt hug. Peserin, it could as easily be her in the stasis chamber! Why hadn't that occurred to him earlier?

Breathing deeply in an attempt to regain some equilibrium, he murmured, "I've never understood this system of different parties within the same government."

Monica grinned up at him. "Who the hell does?"

* * * * *

When Shauss stepped quietly into his quarters, Jasmine was sitting at the table, sucking the tip of her finger. He was gratified to note that, though he hadn't ordered Empran to confine her, she hadn't tried to leave.

As she pulled her finger free of her lips, he moved to alert her to his presence but stopped when she dipped her fingertip into the soil of the potted plant and then returned it to her mouth. She sucked it clean and returned it to the plant yet again.

"You must be very hungry indeed," he said.

She started and a flood of scarlet ran up into her cheeks.

Shauss cocked his head to the side as he stared at her.

"Um…" She stared back for a long moment, a few grains of dirt still clinging to her lower lip before saying in a low voice, "I like dirt."

"Excuse me?"

"I like dirt," she repeated more loudly with shaky defiance.

Warmth flooded his chest. "I like you," he told her.

She smiled. "I like you more."

He smiled slowly. Strolling over to the table, he picked up her hand and brought it to his mouth to suck her soil-coated finger into his mouth. He moved his tongue around, enjoying the natural flavor. "So you like soil."

"For some reason it reminds me of you," she said, her voice breathy.

"Should I be offended?"

"Not at all. I've always loved the taste of soil. It's earthy and fresh and clean. I'm always puzzled when people think dirt is…dirty. To me, it's totally natural."

Shauss stared down at her, startled by a spurt of longing for the home he'd forsaken. Some of the happiest moments of his childhood had been spent playing in soil while his father worked.

He leaned down and laid his open mouth on hers. The taste of soil between their tongues wasn't the least bit out of place, and he spent long moments savoring this tentative, sweet connection between them. It was becoming apparent that they were anything but incompatible.

Pulling away, he held her chin and examined her cheek. A very faint bruise shadowed the bone. "I wish like hell I hadn't done that. It hardly seems fair that I get kisses from your dreams, while you get a slap in the face from mine."

"At least you didn't chop my head off," she said. "And it really was my fault. You'd made it clear you didn't like that, but I just…wanted to taste you."

"You truly do enjoy it."

Pink surged in her cheeks. "Yes," she whispered.

"Perhaps we can enjoy that activity together."

He drew her to the bed and pulled her clothes off her before divesting himself of his uniform. Lying back on the mattress, he ignored her slight resistance and maneuvered her until she was sitting on his chest.

She looked over her shoulder at him. "I'd rather just concentrate on you."

"Or I could turn you around and just concentrate on you," he threatened, flexing his hands on her thighs.

"Ogre," she replied without heat, leaning down to wrap her hand around his rapidly hardening flesh.

"Get used to it."

With one more solemn look over her shoulder, she lowered her head and swirled her tongue around the head of his cock.

Shauss broke into a sweat. Peserin, but she was hard to resist! When Monica had pleasured him this way, she'd done so almost...methodically. Looking back, he realized it was her first time and she must have been relying on whatever information she'd gleaned from her studies to guide her. She had sucked him with single-minded determination to prove a point, something she'd accomplished with humiliating ease.

Anxiety shimmered in his gut at the memory and he tensed. He hadn't hesitated to let her go down on him—he had thought he'd watched enough Terran pornography to have completely disassociated fellatio from the brutal act his father had perpetrated on his mother. But when Monica took control and forced him to ejaculate, the vision had come screaming back in vivid detail, and he'd very nearly snapped her neck. It had taken him hours to regain control of his rioting emotions.

A soft mewl brought him back to the present and he relaxed almost immediately. There was nothing methodical or calculated about Jasmine's touch. She worshipped his cock as though it held the very key to her existence, laving it with her tongue, nibbling it with her lips, and administering gentle suction as she dew it deep into her throat. Her hands were busy as well, sliding over his thighs and tugging at his tightening scrotum, squeezing his balls until he thrust upward uncontrollably and then easing him with a tender massage. All the while she whimpered and moaned like she'd never known such pleasure.

It dawned on him then that sucking him was the only pleasure she was experiencing.

Ashamed to have lost himself in her caresses for so long, he tugged her knees over his shoulders and pulled her back. She slipped her hands under his buttocks and dug her nails in, unwilling to give up her prize, so Shauss reached up and grabbed a pillow, stuffing it behind his head to accommodate the difference in their heights.

When he parted her flesh delicately with his thumbs, she stilled for an instant and then resumed her attentions with an intensity bordering on desperation. He knew she wanted him to ejaculate in her mouth but he wasn't ready to give her the kind of control that came with her fingers in his waste canal. Besides, he wanted to enjoy the lingering torment while he returned the favor.

Craning his head forward, he drank in the scent of her arousal with fierce satisfaction. There was no doubt she desired him just as fiercely as he did her.

Overcome by the need to devour her, he wrapped his arms around her hips and buried his face in her sweet cunt, loving how she moaned and squirmed in his hold. He would love to make her come this way but he didn't want to make her feel inadequate by trying to force the issue. Perhaps as they grew to know each other and developed more trust, they could find ways to help her orgasm more readily.

It wasn't long before her smell, her taste and her ardent attention to his cock had every inch of his skin in flames. Ignoring her protests, he turned her until they were face-to-face and kissed her wildly.

When he pulled back for air, his chest heaving, she kissed his throat. "Oh God, Shauss, I love you so much," she breathed.

Power and elation blasted through him as he claimed her mouth again. She was his!

Pushing her back into the mattress, he spread her thighs and plunged into her. He knew he'd have to turn her when his spur began to erupt, but right now he wanted to face her, kiss her, enjoy her.

She writhed and moaned beneath him, clawing his back as she tore her mouth away from his. "I love you!"

In that moment, Shauss knew he would never tire of hearing those words.

Lacing his fingers over the top of her head and resting his chin on them, he held her in place as he sank deeper and deeper under her spell, thrusting and thrusting and rapidly losing his mind. Fire gathered in his balls, drawing them up tight, and he gritted his teeth, trying to hold back his burgeoning spur. Jasmine was going to come this time, he could feel it, and he didn't want to turn her until it happened.

The fire raged out of control, searing its way up his spine and raising chills all over his body. His spur bumped her and she moaned frantically. Reacting purely on instinct, he let it ram her again and again, as desperate for her orgasm as she was. The reverberation sent shockwaves through his cock and his balls and even his ass, and he choked on his own cries. Peserin, he was so close! *They* were so close!

Suddenly Jasmine arched up against him, raking his back as she screamed again. "Yes, oh God please, yes!"

Her cries sent him into a frenzy of powerful thrusts, and the feel of her convulsing around him was all it took to send him spinning over the edge into oblivion. He shouted unintelligibly, forcing himself as deep as possible to spew his seed where he wanted it to grow.

Utterly drained, he lay over her, rubbing his chin in her hair. When he rolled to the side, he noted with satisfaction that she was just as drained as he was, her eyes closed, her breathing shallow and rapid.

Then he saw the blood staining her cunt and thighs.

Chapter Thirteen

Tiber jerked in surprise when Shauss appeared naked, holding an equally naked and apparently unconscious Jasmine in his arms. His flaccid phallus and thighs were smeared with blood.

"Oh hell, what happened?" Monica demanded.

"She's bleeding between her legs," Shauss told her roughly.

Tiber led him to the nearest exam table. "Perhaps her menses has commenced."

"No. We were mating face-to-face and my spur…" Shauss swallowed. "Tiber, I lost control. I injured her."

Tiber gaped at him for an instant and then turned to Jasmine, who stirred as Shauss laid her down.

Her eyes opened. "Tiber? What happened? What am I doing here?"

"You've been injured."

She looked blank and then her eyes widened. Obviously realizing she was naked, she tried to cover everything with her hands.

"I need to examine you," he said gently

"No."

"Jasmine—" Shauss started.

"I'll do it." Monica's tone brooked no argument.

Tiber hesitated, the fine hairs rising all over his body. Something momentous was happening here. He knew it with every cell in his body. But what?

"Of course," he said reluctantly, taking a step back, "she would be more comfortable with a female physician tending her."

Jasmine bit her lip, and then said, "Please. Can I have a gown or something?"

Tiber immediately grabbed a gown from the cabinet and passed it to her, surreptitiously studying the bloodstains on her thighs.

Monica raised a brow at them. "A little privacy, boys?"

When they stepped into Ketrok's lab, a memory detonated in his brain, knocking the breath out of him. Was it possible…?

Turning to Shauss, he found him stepping into his uniform, which he must have summoned via Empran. "We need to observe them. Now."

* * * * *

Monica examined her carefully. "Well, you got what you wished for. Was it worth it?"

Unable to say it convincingly, Jasmine nodded. Neither of them spoke as Monica went to work, using a clear gel and some kind of gun-shaped instrument to heal the torn tissues surrounding her wide-open nook.

"Well, that's about the best I can do with the training I've had."

"I'm sure I'll be fine," she said as Monica helped her up. "It feels like nothing ever happened."

Monica paused and then looked her in the eye. "The bioscience team detected a virus infecting the steripod."

"What?" Jasmine stared back, totally baffled by the change of subject. "What are you talking about?"

"Shauss didn't tell you?"

"Tell me what?"

"That sterilizing cube you touched in the infirmary literally ate the flesh off Ketrok's hands this morning."

Remembering her vision of Mark pulling bloody stumps out of the block in Dr. Ketrok's lab drained every ounce of blood from Jasmine's head. "Oh my God."

She swayed. Monica caught her before she fell and helped her back onto the bed.

"Oh my God," she said again. How close had she come to actually getting eaten by that thing? She'd laughed it off when her mother told her she was psychic, but now she was beginning to wonder.

"They think it's a genetically engineered virus, and apparently spots of a similar infection are showing up on the biologic pad in general access areas."

Jasmine stared at her in shock. *A genetically engineered virus.* The words chased themselves round and round the inside of her head, their implications too horrible to contemplate.

"Do they have any idea how the cube was infected?" she asked sickly.

"Most likely by someone touching it the last three or four days." Monica's stare never wavered. It challenged her, demanding an explanation.

"You think I did it." Jasmine's voice was as flat as her heart.

"I don't know what to think here, Jas. Everything in me says, 'No way, she couldn't have done this' but…"

Licking suddenly dry lips, she said, "I swear, I would never do anything like that."

"I really want to believe you."

"What are you going to do?"

"Jasmine, someone infected the steripod and the pad, and it's a pretty good bet they did it deliberately." The statement hung between them like a loaded gun.

"So I'm tried and convicted?"

"No. I'm just saying that it's a pretty big coincidence."

What could she say to that? Monica was right—it was too terribly coincidental to be a coincidence. A cold fear spread in her stomach as she thought about her father. She hadn't heard from him in months. He could be anywhere, doing anything, and not only did he have the means and the motive to create such a virus, but he might even have the connections to get it aboard the ship—he'd arranged for her job at the compound easily enough.

Would he have gone through with a plan like this, knowing her safety was on the line? In his fight against the Garathani, was she expendable?

"Your face tells me you're thinking of someone who might have been involved in this," Monica said.

Jasmine hesitated a split-second too long before answering, "No."

"You're lying." Monica got right in her face. "Jasmine, if you know of other Narthanis who might have had something to do with this, you need to come clean now before someone else gets hurt."

"*Other* Narthanis!"

Jasmine gasped and whirled around.

Shauss looked ready to kill.

Chapter Fourteen

ಐ

"Shauss, oh God." *Oh please, no.* Jasmine felt fragile as spun glass. The way he was looking at her right now was worse than anything she'd ever dreamed, and after what they'd shared last night and this morning, the pain was infinitely worse. Her heart quaked with what she was losing.

She gathered the flimsy gown behind her with a shaking hand, chiding herself for her foolishness. What had she thought was going to happen when she refused the pheromone blocker—that he would just blindly accept that she was one of the hybrids?

"Something you forgot to tell me, Jasmine?" He didn't sneer. In fact, he was just about dead in both face and voice.

"Shauss…" she said desperately.

Tiber stood beside him, looking stunned. "You're Narthani?"

Jasmine took a deep breath. "Yes."

Shauss stalked all the way around her. Then he bellowed as he struck out with one foot. The table flew across the room and crashed into the wall.

Jasmine flinched and made herself as small as possible as he continued to circle her, breathing so heavily he reminded her of a bull pawing the earth. *God,* she prayed, *please let it end quickly.*

"I'm sorry," she whispered.

The commander appeared out of a flare bubble. "What do you mean Miss King is Narthani?"

"She just confessed it," Shauss spat.

Monica said, "Shauss, don't hurt her."

He immediately got in her face with one finger, "You!" Visibly reining in his wrath, he drew a loud breath before saying, "You stay out of this."

Monica held her ground. "I'm serious, Shauss. Don't you hurt her."

Shauss pointedly ignored her. "Permission to treat Jasmine King as a hostile, Commander?"

"Granted," Kellen said grimly.

"Monica knew about her," Shauss said as he continued to stalk Jasmine. "In fact, she was helping her to deceive us. Tell him, Tiber."

"Dr. Teague was replicating a hormone complex yesterday. I couldn't place the chemical structure at the time, but now Empran has verified that it was a pheromone blocker. Miss King is a Sparnite—or rather, she's *infalone*, which is the Narthani term for delayed development."

"Monica, is this true?"

Jasmine kept her head down, watching him without looking. When he went behind her, where she couldn't see what he was doing, it was torture.

"Yes," Monica said, "it's true but— No!"

Shauss struck. He grabbed Jasmine's arm and stripped the gown off her, yanking it painfully out of her clenched fingers.

"No!" Monica shouted again, crowding between them and throwing her arms around Jasmine. "Stop it! Shauss, listen to me—"

"Get your mate out of my way," he grated.

Monica's arms went limp around Jasmine and she collapsed to the floor.

"No!" Jasmine screamed, fighting Shauss as Kellen leaned down to scoop Monica up. "Oh God, what have you done to her? Don't hurt her! This is all my fault, not hers—please, Commander, don't hurt her!"

She was relieved when Monica spoke. "I swear to God, Kellen, if anything happens to Jasmine, I'll never forgive you."

"Frankly, *sziscala*," he said in a dangerous tone, "it's my forgiveness that should concern you."

The minister walked in, followed closely by Hastion, Zannen and at least a dozen others she didn't recognize. Her nightmare was coming true—she was completely naked and surrounded by enemy warriors.

"Miss King has confessed to being a Narthani agent." Kellen looked like he was barely holding on to control himself.

"All concessions granted Jasmine King in her mating bond are hereby rescinded," the minister said in a dispassionate voice. "Lieutenant Shauss, as her primary mate, you're authorized to extract whatever information you can from her and then dispose of her in any manner you see fit."

Monica cried, "No! Father, please!"

"That's enough, Monica," Kellen said. "You can't help her now." He looked at Shauss and then they disappeared in a flair bubble.

"Keep me updated, Lieutenant." The minister whirled and walked out, leaving behind his contingent.

"I have to commend you, *aramai*," Shauss said. "You're very good. Even after your first deception, I fell for your act completely." He let go his excruciating grip on her arm. "Get on your knees."

Jasmine swallowed a ball of nausea and dropped gracelessly to a kneeling position, her heartbeat drumming in her throat. Although the atmosphere was sultry, as it was all over the ship, she shook as if freezing.

When she gathered the courage to look up, he snapped, "Head down."

He nudged her knees apart with the toe of his boot. "Cross your hands behind your back."

Oh God, she was about to die, and that would probably be the easiest part of this.

With her head bent in submission, Jasmine looked at the blood and semen smears on her thighs and saw Shauss' beautiful body arching over hers. Felt his hips anchoring her, spreading her, grinding her into the bed. Smelled the heady flood of his pheromones. Heard their mingled shouts of satisfaction. She'd let go completely, showing him everything she was, and in return he'd lost his vaunted control, sharing everything lovable in him.

Now he would exact revenge by showing her the true depths of his brutality.

Tears of dread and perverse excitement dripped from her eyes, disappearing as they hit the biologic pad between her thighs. Her complete vulnerability was its own terrible reward—she'd never felt so vitally alive as she did at that moment.

It suddenly hit her with crystal clarity just how much she wanted to stay that way. Shauss' pheromones still clung to her skin and nasal passages, and edging into that dangerous subspace, she'd imagined she wanted to go to her death wrapped in the priceless scent of his desire for her. Now that attitude seemed ridiculously defeatist. She had to at least *try* to save herself.

When he reached for her, adrenaline exploded in her veins and she rolled away, jumping to her feet in one smooth move.

"Ooh, you're going to fight me?" he purred. "I do enjoy a challenge—however short-lived."

She didn't answer, too focused on assessing everyone in the room. When Shauss swung a long hand toward her, she kicked it away with a sharp yell and then resumed her fighting stance, bouncing on the balls of her feet with her arms up in front of her.

Yes! She wasn't panicking this time. Without the hindrance of a tight skirt, the self-defense lessons were paying off when she really needed them.

He reached for her again and she blocked him with her forearm, following through with a side kick at his crotch. He jumped back with millimeters to spare and grinned as he grabbed for her again.

This time he managed to snare her wrist and her heart rate skyrocketed. She kicked out at his leg and he grunted when her heel connected with his kneecap. Immediately grabbing her own captured hand with the other, she yanked it free and drove her elbow into his gut with another loud *kiai*, and felt a surge of fierce satisfaction when the air whooshed out of him.

Dancing back, she resumed her stance and waited for his next strike.

"Every blow you land only adds to your punishment, *aramai*," Shauss told her almost casually.

This was ridiculous, really, since there was no getting out of the situation even if she did manage to defeat him. But she just couldn't help fighting for her life.

"It's hard to get any deader than dead, Lieutenant."

He shook his head. "You'll only wish you were dead."

Fear clogged her throat and all she wanted to do was curl up in a ball and cry her eyes out.

Shauss leaned forward and smacked the side of her head with his fingertips then pulled back before she could connect with his arm.

He showed her his teeth in a nasty smile. The bastard was playing with her!

Tears of rage spurted from her eyes as she attacked, advancing on him with a steady barrage of punches and kicks that would have taken down most of her old sparring partners, shouting her *kiai* with every strike. Shauss, however, retreated with so much speed and agility, she never connected once.

"Try a few more kicks," he suggested. "The view of your cunt is spectacular."

His callousness took her breath away.

"I hate you," she said in a thick voice.

There was a long, significant pause before he said in a deadly tone, "So finally we hear some truth from you."

Pain seized her. He thought she'd been lying when she told him she loved him.

Looking into his secretive black eyes, she knew she couldn't die letting him think that. She couldn't leave him thinking she was hard and mercenary enough to fake her feelings for him. If she had to die, she wanted to die as the real Jasmine King—flawed and weak and desperate for the love of a man who hated her.

Although every instinct in her screamed to keep fighting, she took a deep breath and let her trembling legs fold, kneeling with her knees spread and her wrists crossed behind her back. Staring into his startled eyes, she whispered, "I'm yours."

A cyclone of conflicting emotions spun furiously inside Shauss.

"Is that so?"

She continued to stare at him through spiky tear-clumped lashes. "I'm not asking for your forgiveness because I don't think it's in you…but I'm sorry. So sorry."

Because he couldn't bear to look at her anymore, he ordered, "Head down."

She obeyed immediately and a huge sigh shuddered through her. He circled her again, slowly, deliberately, knowing she was watching his boots with wary eyes.

Touching the gold clasp at the back of her neck, he murmured, "I should probably take this off before it's damaged."

Jasmine went stiff but didn't raise her head. "Please don't."

"You want to die wearing my collar?"

"Yes."

Pain lashed at him. He'd wanted her to die wearing it too—many decades in the future. What a fool.

"How touching," he sneered.

When he passed behind her for the third time, he reached over her left shoulder and cupped her right rib cage. Then he reached under her ass with the other hand and heaved her up off the floor by her cunt.

She squeaked and grabbed his forearm with both hands but then hung unmoving in his grip, her heart fluttering against his wrist as he carried her facedown to an exam table. Her warm, fragrant weight in his arms conjured vividly sensual memories, and he hated how much he missed her already. It figured that the one female in the galaxy whose nook fit his spur, the female who fit him in every conceivable way, was a Narthani spy. Would the Powers never stop fucking with him?

Anger and humiliation and pathetic grief made him rough as he laid her across the table. He held her pinned there by the neck, her slender legs dangling limply off the side of the table.

Leaning down, he asked in her ear, "Are you afraid, *aramai*?"

"Yes," she whispered.

"You should be."

"I don't know anything useful, so you might want to just kill me now."

Scraping her earlobe between his teeth, he drawled, "And waste a perfectly good piece of ass?"

When she tensed, Shauss chuckled darkly.

"*Déjà vu*, darling?" He raised up far enough to drag his zipper down slowly. "Don't worry. I have every intention of following through on my promise this time."

She blinked rapidly, her breath coming in short, tortured gasps, but she didn't reply. Shauss had come less than an hour before and was far from aroused in learning of his mate's deception, but only a dead warrior would fail to respond physically to the sight of her laid naked and submissive before him, utterly terrified of the punishment he was about to mete out.

He looked at Tiber. *"Lubricant?"*

Tiber gave him a measured look before striding to a cabinet. He flipped the cap open and tried to hand him the tube, but Shauss held his hand out until Tiber squirted a blob into his open palm. After he worked the chilly gel over his cock, he held out his hand again and had Tiber squirt some on his fingers.

Shauss separated her legs by bracing one knee against the underside of the exam table and slid a finger over the pucker of her anus.

Jasmine squirmed.

"You will relax every muscle in your body," he reproved.

Tiber gave him an incredulous look but said nothing.

Jasmine took another shuddering breath and loosened her fists until they rested limply against the exam table on either side of her head. Her obedience eased the tightness in Shauss' chest. At least something about this falsehearted female wasn't a lie.

With a smug look at Tiber, he pushed one finger deep into her tight little ass and she tensed again.

"Breathe deeply," he ordered. "Make noise, if you must. But do not fight my incursion."

She took a deep breath and then yelped when he slid a second finger in beside the first. He twisted them and watched a tide of red wash up her neck into her cheek as she groaned.

"Whose ass is this, *aramai*?" he asked softly.

"Yours," she gasped.

He withdrew and pushed in three fingers. It was hard to say whether Jasmine's protracted keening as he worked them in and out of her was anguish or desire.

"I have no desire to challenge your authority in this bond," Tiber told him, *"but if you harm her, I'll have no choice."*

Shauss glared at him. All this concern — for a deceitful enemy! *"You'll lose."*

"So be it."

"She's worth dying for?"

"You tell me."

Shauss contemplated Tiber for a moment and then ordered, *"Implant a biomet. You can monitor her vital functions and pain levels."*

Jasmine's labored breathing was the only sound in the room while Tiber implanted the unit under her arm. She whimpered and stirred when it penetrated her skin.

Without further delay, Shauss withdrew his fingers and rested the head of his cock against her opening. "Don't move," he whispered as he let go of her neck to brace his hands on the table above her shoulders.

He penetrated her one slow, agonizingly delicious inch at a time. Peserin, with a grip this tight on his cock, he might not require any additional stimulation to come.

"I'm fucking your ass, Jasmine King," he whispered.

"Yes."

"This is just the beginning of your punishment."

"I know," she sobbed. "Ah God, it hurts!"

He sank even deeper. "And you want more, don't you?"

"Yes!"

"All of it?"

Without waiting for her answer, he hilted, pressing the emerging tip of his spur hard against her tailbone.

"Yes!" she screamed, pushing her torso up off the table and throwing her head back until she hit his breastbone. Her feet flew up against the backs of his thighs to hold him against her.

"I told you not to move." Shauss planted one hand between her shoulder blades and forced her back down to the table but allowed her feet to remain hooked behind his legs. Holding her in place, he began to move, earning a breathy grunt for every inward stroke and a guttural groan for every slow, dragging outward stroke. When things began to get sticky, he reached for the tube and squirted more lube on the rocking shaft of his cock.

He fucked her patiently, deriving brutal enjoyment from both the punishment and the unblinking stares of over a dozen ravenous warriors. Every one of them would sacrifice an eyeball to stand where he did at this moment.

Eventually Jasmine began to squirm and moan. "Please," she gasped.

"Please what?"

"Harder. Please."

He obliged, picking up his pace, slamming his pelvis against her. Her moans became frantic and she pushed up against his restraining hand.

"She's actually enjoying this," Tiber said disbelievingly.

"She's my submissive," Shauss replied, as if that explained everything—which for him, it did. Jasmine King might be the enemy but she was a genuine submissive. *His* genuine submissive, who would suffer at length for deceiving him. While he was tempted to wring her fragile neck for her treachery, he saw no reason to condemn himself to a lifetime of fucking the probe.

Jasmine became agitated, throwing his rhythm off with desperate thrusts of her own.

"By all that's mighty, she's nearing orgasm!"

Shauss ceased all motion. "What do you have to tell me, *aramai*?"

"No!" she screeched. "Please don't stop!"

"Tell me what I want to know and then you can come."

"I don't know anything!"

"You know who you really are."

"So do you." Her voice trembled. "I've told you the truth about everything. My name really is Jasmine King and I'm an American. I was born and raised in Colorado and I consider myself a Terran. My parents may have been Narthani, but I swear to you, I'm a Terran in every—"

"Silence!" Shauss shouted, crowding her harder against the table's padded edge. "Who are your parents?"

"It's all in my records!" she screamed back, panting. Taking a deep breath, she continued. "My parents are Ragan and Dayree King. They were sent to Earth twenty-eight years ago to study the population and evaluate the planet's readiness for contact with a more advanced civilization."

"You mean they followed us to Earth to spy on us."

"No! It was a scientific mission. They were supposed to be recalled after ten years, but no one ever came for them."

Now that, he believed. "Crunus *interruptus*," he speculated.

Jasmine nodded, and just for fun, he leaned all his weight into his hips, grinding the thick base of his cock into her virgin ass. Her squeal of pain was wickedly soothing to his ego.

"And how many Narthani are on Terra right now?"

"Just my dad and me," she whimpered. "My mom died last year in an accident."

Shauss grabbed a fistful of her hair and pulled her head up, twisting it on her neck until his face was millimeters from hers. "Surely you don't expect us to believe that," he breathed in her open mouth. "No operation of this magnitude would be launched with merely two operatives."

"You have to believe me because it's true—God knows I bugged my parents about it a million times and they always swore we were the only ones on the planet. My mother wouldn't lie to me."

"Find Ragan King," Shauss ordered Zannen.

"With all due respect, brother, **jurana** *is still in effect and the secondary claiming period is nearing an end."*

"You still want her? An underdeveloped Narthani?"

Zannen shrugged. *"A fuck is a fuck."*

Too bad. *"Very well. It can wait a few minutes."*

Almost convinced by Jasmine's claims and yet unwilling to chance another deception, he grasped her wrists and slid them behind his neck. In lieu of the cuffs he'd used to secure her in this position last night, he ordered, "Clasp your hands and do not let go."

When she complied, he slid his hands around the fronts of her thighs. Grasping them by their tender inner flesh, he straightened and pulled her up off the table. Leaving her impaled on his cock, he turned, spreading her thighs wide and exposing her dripping cunt to the Garathani males who crowded the room.

"Hastion, your protected claiming time draws to a close in fifteen minutes. If you wish to finalize your claim, free your cock and use it to show your mate the error of her ways."

Tiber's heart thundered with equal parts alarm and arousal. Jasmine's head lolled back against Shauss' shoulder, the golden collar gleaming against her skin. Her pupils were so dilated, the blue of her eyes had nearly disappeared. Her chest rose and fell in shallow panting breaths. If it weren't for the shiny slickness coating her open labia, he would have said she was terrified. And she probably was, but that terror was definitely secondary to arousal.

Hastion stepped forward and Tiber noted the significant lack of bulge at his crotch. He advanced slowly, almost painfully. His face was chalky and beaded with sweat.

"Although I deplore the idea of losing my claim, I might be unable to perform at the moment."

Tiber took a step toward him. "Get to a bed before you—"

Hastion lurched to one side and regurgitated under another of the exam tables.

"Pass out," Tiber finished, rushing to prop the man up before he slumped any farther. Ensign Verr helped him get Hastion up onto the exam table. "It's obvious our scans are somehow overlooking a significant head injury."

"It appears to me he merely suffers from an aversion to female flesh," Zannen said scornfully. "Have no fear, Ensign, I'll take care of claiming the Narthani for you."

"No!" Hastion tried to roll off the table and groaned. "You can't have her, you bastard!"

"Tiber, I hope you're up to the task," Shauss said.

Having spent the previous twenty minutes fighting off an unwilling erection, Tiber now found himself anything but aroused.

"Ten minutes," Shauss prompted. "Then Zannen will no doubt drag her off me and fuck her until she can't walk."

Jasmine spoke. "Tiber, please."

He looked into her dazed, pleading eyes and felt a spark of arousal that was immediately doused by a flood of guilt. Striding over to them, he took her face in his hands. "Are you well?"

She nodded.

"I won't rape you," he whispered fiercely.

"It's not rape if I want you," she whispered back.

"You're being coerced."

"I want to be coerced. I *love* being coerced."

"You're desperate to avoid being bound to Zannen."

Her eyes slid to Zannen and fire kindled in them. "He doesn't scare me anymore. But I *like* you."

Lust tickled his insides once more. "Are you certain?"

She focused on him, and said clearly, "Tiber, please fuck me. Please. I'm begging you."

Tiber heard the rasp of a zipper and turned in time to see Zannen's cock drop out of the front of his suit. The bulbous purple head hung nearly to his knee—obviously he was willing and able to rise to the occasion. Tiber felt a shameful surge of excitement at the sight.

"I really don't think I have room for him," Jasmine said with remarkable calm. "Especially not with Shauss already inside me. Please, Tiber—hurry."

Tiber looked into Shauss' impenetrable black eyes as he pulled his zipper tab downward. Shauss was right—Zannen would take what he wanted however he wanted it. Tiber, on the other hand, felt compelled to beg Shauss to lay Jasmine down and let him have her to himself, both for her sake and his. But it would be fruitless. Shauss had never seemed more unreachable than he did right now.

"But what if she can't take my spur?"

"If she can take mine, she can take yours."

Shauss sounded certain rather than pitiless, and Tiber relaxed marginally. Lowering his gaze, he stroked his lengthening cock while he concentrated on Jasmine's slumberous blue eyes...on lips that were cherry-red from being bitten...on sweet, round breasts that heaved with fear and desire.

Zannen stepped closer, stroking his own monstrous shaft, and Hastion cried out, "For Peserin's sake, Tiber, just claim her. Now!"

He leaned forward and captured her lips in a brief open-mouthed kiss before whispering, "I'm sorry."

Then he grasped his penis and pushed the head into her tiny opening. Her thin, high squeal made him glad he was only half hard. It felt strange to be standing balls to balls with another male, and Shauss' satisfied smile made him feel as if he'd just committed himself to something far beyond his ability to cope with. He felt less like he'd claimed Jasmine than like he'd been claimed by both Jasmine and Shauss. He almost wouldn't be surprised if Shauss grasped his head and kissed him.

Shauss' grin deepened. *"Tiber, your expression is giving me ideas I've never had about another male. Perhaps we'll have to explore your latent homosexual tendencies."*

"Peserin damn you," Tiber whispered as his cock surged to aching hardness inside the incredibly snug haven of Jasmine's cunt.

"Maybe I'll fuck your ass after I've finished with Jasmine's."

"Have mercy!" Tiber wheezed.

He started when Shauss dropped one of Jasmine's legs and grabbed his neck in an iron grip, pulling his forehead against his hard chest. Although he put his mouth against Tiber's ear, he continued to use the cerecom. *"She's not claimed until you spill your seed inside her, so fuck her quickly. If Zannen tears you away before you finish, I'm going to ream your ass in front of all of them while he claims her."*

Tiber hooked Jasmine's dangling leg over his forearm and leaned into her as he thrust deep again and again. Her whimpers fed his arousal and he wanted to sob at her tightness and the knowledge that Shauss' cock was a thin barrier of flesh away from his. Shauss' grip on him never relented and Tiber gave up control completely, bucking inside Jasmine.

His spur erupted and found her nook unerringly. Her scream made him grind to a halt.

"She's fine. Come inside her. Now," Shauss ordered in his ear.

Tiber groaned and barreled ahead, angling his hips for the deepest penetration possible as he reached desperately for release. When Zannen's thick arms slid around his chest and pulled, Shauss locked his grip even tighter, fighting for him, and Tiber erupted with a howl of satisfaction like he'd never felt before, bathing Jasmine's cunt with his seed.

When he opened his eyes and looked at her, he recoiled with cold horror. A single blood-stained tear dripped from the corner of her left eye.

Chapter Fifteen

෨

Jasmine blinked at him. "Why are you looking at me like that?"

"Clear the infirmary," he ordered. Zipping himself back into his suit as all the warriors thundered out, he barked, "Empran, scan Jasmine King for *sbrova* hemorrhagic pathogens."

Shauss' arms tightened reflexively around her. "No," he said hoarsely.

"No *sbrova* pathogens detected," Empran reported.

He and Shauss both let go gusty sighs of relief. Shauss laid her on one of the tables and Tiber covered her with a thin blanket.

"What are *sbrova* pathogens?" Jasmine asked drowsily.

"Display vital statistics and complete blood analysis," Tiber ordered. Wiping the tear gently from the corner of her eye, he showed her his bloodstained fingertip. "*Sbrova* pathogens were used in the biowar attack."

"You thought I had…" Jasmine's eyes widened as she glanced between their grim faces. "I don't, do I?"

A readout appeared on the holoscreen.

"No. Your tear ducts are inflamed." Tiber said. "Hormone levels indicate you're well into the early stages of transition."

"Peserin, she's emitting—that's why she smells so delicious. Why I lost control…" Shauss' frown deepened. "What about the pheromone blocker?"

"I ran out before the demonstration incident," Jasmine said.

"So why didn't our pheromones intoxicate her yesterday?"

"Perhaps it takes time for effects of the spray to wear off," Tiber speculated.

"Actually," Jasmine said hesitantly, "Monica used galathene barrier on me."

"Really." Tiber tipped her head back and peered up her nostrils.

"It's not there now. Monica extracted it last night."

"Ah, yes. She'd replicated the spray by then, but apparently it was too little, too late. You'd already been heavily exposed at the demonstration."

Jasmine looked at Shauss and said nothing.

"You realize, *aramai*, that your punishment is far from over."

"I know."

"What's most unforgivable is that you involved Monica in your deception and now she'll suffer punishment as well."

"I know! Don't you think I feel awful about that?"

"Then why did you do it?"

Jasmine didn't answer.

"Tell me about your father."

Jasmine squirmed a little. "I've already told you all there is to tell."

"Please. Do you think I failed to notice that your *mother* wouldn't lie to you? Obviously you believe your father would, and if a father will lie to his daughter, he is not worthy of her loyalty. So I order you again, tell me all you know about your father."

"Shauss, please don't ask me to betray my only living relative," Jasmine begged.

He grasped her chin. "Jasmine, people are dying. Millions of people died and millions more stand to die if we don't get to the bottom of this conspiracy against us."

"My father wouldn't do that! He considers Earth his home now, just like I do."

"Have you never heard of Hiroshima? Earthlings themselves terrorize their own people with mass murder." Shauss turned to Tiber. "There's only one way to ensure we're getting the truth from her."

Tiber dipped his head in acknowledgement and got a syringe of *corai* serum. It would render Jasmine unable to dissemble.

"What is that?" she asked, trying to squirm away. Tiber didn't hesitate to shoot it right into her neck. "Ow."

"You'll be fine," Shauss said. "Now tell me everything you know about your parents."

* * * * *

After Shauss left to verify her story, Tiber took the time to thoroughly clear away the debris of her clitoral implant, wincing with remorse as he resealed the wounds he'd torn open when he claimed her. Since she was still under the influence of the *corai*, he probed more personally.

"Why would you deliberately choose to remain in an adolescent's body?" he asked as he worked between her legs.

Refusing to look at him, she clutched at her blanket. "It's not an adolescent's body on Earth—not with the implants, anyway. And if I'd matured, I wouldn't have fit in."

"Your mission was that important to you?"

"I didn't have a mission!" She shivered, pulling the blanket around her neck. "Good Lord, why do you even care?"

"I'm simply…curious. And for some reason, I still feel compelled to try to protect you, if I can."

"Don't bother. Look where trying to protect me got Monica. God, I hope she's okay." She sounded near tears again.

"The commander loves her." But even as he said it, he knew that sometimes love could make a man even more violent if such love was betrayed. Which was why he suspected Shauss had reacted so strongly. There was more than ego involved, as evidenced by Shauss' fear at the sight of her bloodstained tear.

"I hope so," Jasmine said. She cringed and put a hand over her eyes. "God, I don't know what you gave me, but I've got a massive headache now."

Concerned, Tiber glanced at her readings. She had a fever and her pain levels were, indeed, increasing.

"Are you having body aches?"

"Well, let's see." She peered at him from beneath her hand. "I just had sex with Shauss, engaged in hand-to-hand combat with Shauss, and then had sex with you and Shauss at the same time, so yes, I'm kind of achy."

Setting aside the regen sealer, he gently laid her legs together and pulled the blanket down to cover her. Removing her breast and dental implants could wait until after the *corai* finished its job. "So if your mission meant nothing to you, why wouldn't you want to mature?"

"Because at thirteen, fitting in was more important to me than just about anything. That's how old I was when my parents told me I wasn't human, and God, I just freaked. I was already kind of an oddity because of my intelligence. I was two grades ahead of the others my age by then, and only the fact that I was…was *pretty* and athletic and a cheerleader kept me from being a complete outsider. Peer pressure is a big motivator for most Terran teens, and I was no different. As far as I was concerned, I was Terran. I didn't want to be Narthani. I wanted to grow up and marry a nice man and have two point four children and drive a minivan and—"

"How can you have two point four children?" he asked, eyes wide.

"It's just a statistic," she said with yawn. "And that's not the point. The point is, in my heart, I was a Terran. That's all I ever wanted to be. If I'd matured into a seven-foot alien Amazon, I would never have gotten to live that life, so I chose to remain...as I was."

Tiber frowned. Seven-foot alien Amazon? Why would she think that? The average Narthani was only slightly taller than the average American. If she actually turned out to be seven feet in height, she would be taller than ninety-nine percent of Narthani females. Surely the Narthani would send spies who were better able than that to blend in with the population.

"Empran, how tall are Jasmine King's parents?"

"Ragan King is six feet three inches tall. Dayree King was five feet eleven inches tall."

After considering how to approach the matter, he said carefully, "Your parents evidently didn't have any trouble fitting in."

"My parents were both the shortest members of their families, but Dad said I inherited taller genes. Lucky me," she said glumly. "I could have lived with the nook, but not with being seven feet tall."

Tiber's mind raced furiously. Where was she getting this?

Jasmine sighed. "You know, Tiber, I lived my whole life as a lie. From the minute I found out I wasn't human, I was playing a role as convincingly as I could. I focused all my energies on being as human as I could so that no one would ever suspect."

"And now that the role you've had to play has disappeared, you don't know who to be."

She nodded sleepily. "I belong nowhere. I have nothing. I *am* nothing."

He paused and then told her, "When Nelina and my daughter Shrea died, I felt much as you do now. I felt lost and without purpose. But I still had a daughter and two sons who needed me, so I carried on. Eventually I found myself again, and I found new meaning in my life. You will too—if you haven't already."

"If I haven't already?" she yawned.

He tucked her under the blanket and kissed her forehead. "Say goodnight, Jasmine."

* * * * *

"She's definitely transitioning," Tiber said as they watched her sleep. "She's already three inches taller than she was at her last physical."

Shauss frowned. "As tall as she is, I would have guessed her transition must have been progressing slowly for some time."

"I imagine it has—she's lost two of her molars over the years, so I suspect the pheromone blocker wasn't one hundred percent effective. But there may be another explanation for her height. While I was healing her, I asked why she would have chosen to delay her transition and she said that she wouldn't have fit in on Earth if she grew to be a seven-foot Amazon."

"Why would she imagine that? Were her parents extraordinarily tall?"

"Empran reports they were only slightly taller than average Americans," Tiber said. "There's no reason to believe she would be any taller, and yet her parents told her they were short by their families' standards and she was a throwback."

"That doesn't make any sense—the Narthani aren't much taller than Terrans." His frown deepened. "Could she be immune to the *corai*?"

"I don't see how—we can't even induce immunity in our own agents and she fell into a light coma the minute I stopped talking to her." Tiber cocked a brow at him. "Shauss, what if she's not Narthani?"

Shauss gave him a look of wide-eyed disbelief. "Why in Peserin's hell would she profess to be Narthani if she weren't?

If she were going to lie, wouldn't it make more sense—not to mention be a damn sight safer—to masquerade as one of the hybrids?"

"I agree completely, and if we hadn't overheard their conversation, I would have assumed Jasmine was a GaraTer just like Monica. But Shauss, if she's Narthani, then she's the tallest delayed-development case on record. Granted, there have only been seven on Narthan that I'm aware of, but considering she was raised on Terra, one would expect her to be shorter than average rather than taller."

"So what are you suggesting?"

"I'm not suggesting anything at this juncture, but simply pointing out a possible inconsistency in her story."

"What is going on here?" Shauss demanded, raking his hands through his hair as he paced. "Is she deluded by her own lies?"

"Or has she been lied to as well?" Tiber asked. "What if her parents aren't really her parents? Just wild speculation here, but what if the Narthani somehow spied on our reconnaissance team and managed to secure one of their hybrid offspring?"

"Why would they do that?"

"To use as a weapon against us."

"That would explain why Ragan King displayed no fondness for her," Shauss said. "And why he placed her in a hazardous situation."

"Empran, compare Jasmine King's DNA to all Garathani reconnaissance team warriors. Are any of them her father?"

"Negative."

Tiber sighed. "So much for that theory."

"I don't know," Shauss said. "I think you might be on to something here. We need a sample of Ragan King's DNA. I'll speak with the commander about obtaining one."

"Very good idea. Perhaps we'll know more after her transition is complete. Based on her history and current state, I'd say full transition is imminent. I've already started nutritional infusion, and after you leave, I'll deepen her coma and remove the breast implants."

"Leave her under."

Tiber frowned. "Leave her under? You mean leave her sedated?"

"That's exactly what I mean."

"Do you think that's wise? Transition is a rite of passage she might—"

"Tiber," Shauss said in a deceptively mild tone that caused immediate tightening in Tiber's scrotum. "Who is the primary in this bond?"

Fighting breathlessness, Tiber crossed his arms and braced his feet apart as he stared at Shauss. "That is irrelevant. I am the physician in this bond."

Shauss stared back for so long, Tiber might have wondered if he'd become lost in his own thoughts—that is, if he hadn't felt the man's will bearing down on him with a force that was almost physical.

Then Shauss reached out in a very casual way and touched Tiber's cheek with his fingertips. Tiber jerked slightly but stood his ground as those fine fingers moved down and traced his lips. Shauss' black gaze was mesmerizing, and though somewhere inside Tiber was jumping up and down and screaming at him to move, to knock Shauss' hand away, all he could do was stand there and feel.

"Who is primary in this bond?" Shauss whispered.

Tiber swallowed, his heart racing. "You are."

"If I tell you to leave her under, what are you going to do?"

"Leave her under."

Shauss leaned closer. "And if I tell you to take down your suit and bend over this bed so I can work my cock into your ass like I did Jasmine's, what are you going to do?"

Tiber nearly whimpered. Taking a deep breath, he said, "Take my suit down and bend over."

He leaned even closer. "And if I tell you to scream when you come for me, what are you going to do, Tiber?"

This time he did whimper. "I'm going to scream."

His lips within a micron of Tiber's, Shauss breathed, "And come for me."

"Yes!"

Shauss retreated slightly. "That day is coming, Dr. Tiber. Do not doubt it." Then he turned to leave, and Tiber cursed the disappointment that left him feeling weak.

Pausing by the door, Shauss told him, "Leave her under until the worst of it has passed. I saw what Monica went through and I don't want her conscious for it."

* * * * *

The Council convened before the conference with the Narthani monarch.

"Do we believe Miss King infected the steripod?" the minister asked.

Shauss shook his head. "At this point, no. Analysis confirms that the virus' host DNA is not hers."

"Circulate among the doctors you trust and question them about any unusual people touching it," Cecine ordered, adding severely, "That could have been Monica."

"The thought has crossed my mind often," Kellen said.

"And what of Miss King's condition?"

"She has entered full transition and Tiber is maintaining a light coma until the worst of it has passed. After questioning her under *corai* serum, I believe she is utterly ignorant of any

Narthani presence on Terra besides Ragan King's." Shauss paused before saying, "Minister, Empran's projections of her transition growth have led Dr. Tiber to speculate that she might not be Narthani at all."

"What! Why would she lie about that?" Gillim wheezed.

"There seems to be no logical reason, which also leads us to believe she might herself have been lied to by her parents. She believes she will reach seven feet in height after her transition, much taller than either of them."

The minister looked startled. "Peserin, could she be one of the hybrids?"

"That was our first thought, but her DNA isn't consistent with any of the reconnaissance scouts."

"What else could she be?"

"At this point we don't know, but we believe the first step in solving this mystery is obtaining a sample of Ragan King's DNA in order to either confirm or eliminate him as her father."

"What do we know of him thus far?"

"Less than we originally thought, Minister," Shauss said. "He has amassed considerable wealth over the years, the initial source of which is unclear. His companies, however, hold hundreds of technology patents, and it stands to reason that he's been selling minor Narthani technology to the Terrans. Since Terra didn't rely heavily on computers until well after his arrival, it's difficult to determine which records of his past are genuine and which are manufactured. Further, it's becoming apparent that high-level government is involved in the manufacture of some of his records."

"What of his mate?"

"She died last year in an automobile accident. Before her death, she was reportedly a simple housewife. I find the timing of her death rather suspicious though. She died just a few months after we made contact with the Americans. I'm not sure what one has to do with the other, if anything, but there it is."

"And Miss King? Have all aspects of her story been confirmed?"

"So far," Shauss nodded. "Every record we've found indicates that she is what's referred to as an all-American girl-next-door type, extremely intelligent, especially by Terran standards. Her education focused on biology and botany, which initially concerned me because of the pad sabotage, but she holds no advanced degrees and her life has been very well documented. Before accepting a position at the compound, she taught high school science classes, kept a greenhouse full of vegetation, and in fact suffers from a psychological malady known as pica, or more specifically geophagia, which compels her to eat soil."

The minister's brow rose. "That's quite...interesting."

"Indeed. Tiber reports that pica is not uncommon among Sparnites and that transition seems to resolve the compulsion." He half hoped it wasn't true—he'd enjoyed tasting soil on her lips.

"Jasmine and Ragan King apparently did not speak for more than eight solar years after her graduation from high school," he continued. "Only she and her mother maintained contact until we arrived in orbit. When the alliance was announced, her father arranged for Jasmine to take the secretarial position and report on our activities. Her reports that we were doing exactly what we claimed to be doing annoyed him and he stopped answering her calls."

"No father I know would send his daughter into such a situation, much less abandon her to it," Cecine growled.

"Perhaps daughters mean less to the Narthani," Gillim said.

"No doubt, but that's still quite a callous attitude." The minister turned to Kellen. "Figure out the best place to obtain a sample of Ragan King's DNA and send down a small reconnaissance team to retrieve it. If she's one of us, I'd like to know it."

"It will be done."

"Now I suppose we should convene our meeting with Lord Sals."

The door opened and Ensign Verr stepped in. "My apologies for interrupting, but there's a situation developing in atmospheric systems, Commander."

* * * * *

"It's definitely sabotage," Verr said as they stared up at the massive atmospheric generators.

Shauss tipped his head to the side. "What in Peserin's name happened to them?"

It looked as though stone were flowing from the ventilation ducts of two of the generators, and the other four were contained in stasis fields.

"Your guess is as good as mine," Kellen growled. "Empran, analyze foreign substance in the atmospheric generators."

"Analyzing..."

"Is it as hard as it looks?" Shauss asked.

In answer, Kellen grabbed an *oveyon* wrench and slammed it against one of the floes—the resulting clank was loud enough to make them all wince.

"Harder," he confirmed.

"Foreign matter," Empran reported, "is the waste product of a microorganism biologically engineered to consume tectonite."

Kellen's face got as hard as the substance. "Narthanis. They're on the biowar attack again."

"It's fortunate we found this when we did," Verr said. "The stasis fields are holding the organisms in check while allowing the generators to remain in operation. If we'd found this a few hours later, we would have had to evacuate the ship."

Kellen looked at Shauss. "We need to find Ragan King and his accomplices. Now."

* * * * *

The minister opened the remote conference with the Narthani monarch Lian Sals. He didn't look pleased to have been kept waiting.

"Minister, your message was quite a surprise," he said, leaning back in his throne. The royal chamber looked to be filled to capacity. In the chair beside him sat his wife Ferla, a stunning but dour beauty. "To what do we owe this extraordinary honor?"

"It isn't a courtesy call, Lord Sals." Cecine rose from his chair and circled the end of the table to stand in front of it, leaning his hind quarters on the edge and crossing his arms. Shauss smothered a grin. Everything about the minister said *You're in deep shit.*

"Then shall we get right to the point?" Sals cocked a brow. "Or are you just going to send a warship to finish what you started all those years ago?"

"You know as well as I that our attack was warranted," Cecine said sharply.

"I know no such thing. Do you have any idea how much all the innocent people of Narthan have suffered because of your petty revenge?"

"It's nothing compared to what they will suffer if I find out that you're in any way behind the incidents that have been happening on Terra lately."

Lord Sals stiffened. "Incidents? Oh no—you're not doing that to us again. If you try to attack because of something we haven't done, there will be consequences."

"And what say you to the evidence we have that you have spies stationed on Terra?"

"Spies! On Terra?" He burst out laughing. "You must be joking. How would we even get to Terra? We barely have the fuel to reach planets in our own system and can little afford even that."

"Come now, don't feign ignorance. We have proof that you've had at least one team on Terra for almost thirty years."

"Thirty—" His eyes narrowed. "I have only ruled since the attack, Minister. If you will allow me to consult with my advisors…?"

"By all means." Cecine presented his back to the view field when the Narthani emblem came up. "I suspect he's telling the truth, at least as far as he knows it."

"The Narthani are cunning creatures," Councilor Alnack wheezed.

"No more cunning than we," Cecine countered. "And they stand to lose a great deal if we cut off trade negotiations with them again. But based on his reaction, I'm definitely inclined to believe his government had no hand in the attack on Terra's military bases."

The ruler reappeared, looking chagrined. "It would appear that you are correct about our having agents on Terra. It has been so long since they were placed there…"

"Please tell me you didn't forget about them," Cecine asked, brow arching.

"I cannot forget that which I do not know. But there was considerable confusion in the government after your attack and much of the documentation of missions was destroyed. It is pure chance that any of my advisors even remembered the mission."

"I need the details—the number and names of agents, their orders, etc."

"Minister, that may be impossible," the monarch said. "My advisor, Megren, was only peripherally involved in the mission. He knows very little about it, beyond the fact that four pairs were sent."

Four pairs! Shauss's stomach turned sour. Either Jasmine was lying or she didn't realize she'd had company on the planet's surface.

"Then you will investigate, Lord Sals. I must also request documentation on all Narthanis traveling off-planet for the last ten years."

The man looked like he wanted to protest, but nodded grudgingly. "That will take time, but it shall be done."

After his image faded, Cecine turned to Shauss. "Get that DNA sample. Now."

Chapter Sixteen

Her mother had always said a bad situation would look better after a good night's sleep, and as it turned out, she was right.

Jasmine stretched and yawned, feeling absolutely reborn. Amazing what a peaceful, dreamless sleep could do for a person's morale. Even in the predawn light, everything looked brighter.

"Empran, full daylight."

Startled by the masculine voice, Jasmine rolled onto one elbow as the lights came up and had to blink away a little dizziness. Hastion lay on the bed next to hers, hands behind his head, looking like he hadn't slept in days. At least the bruising on his face had disappeared.

"How are you feeling?" he asked.

"Great, actually." Frowning, she cleared her throat.

"Is your throat sore?" Tiber asked from the doorway. His spiky blond hair was flat on one side, as if he'd crawled out of bed and gone right to work.

"No, I just sound kind of funny. Throaty."

He walked over and sat beside her on the edge of the mattress. "Your vocal cords have lengthened."

"My vocal cords? What are you..." Jasmine's eyes dropped to her hands and her contentment evaporated. Her fingers looked like talons. "Oh my God. Oh my God!"

Tiber slid a hand under her chin and pulled her face up. "Be at ease, Jasmine. You're fine."

"Please tell me I haven't changed," she begged.

"Your transition is complete."

"But...how?"

"You were already beginning to suffer the symptoms of transition syndrome, so when you succumbed to the *corai*, we maintained a light coma in order to spare you the ordeal of full transition."

"Coma?" That would certainly explain the dreamless sleep. "You mean I missed the whole thing?"

Tiber nodded. "You missed the whole thing. As of this moment, you are officially a mature female."

It was ridiculous, but for some reason she felt slightly cheated, as though she'd missed the delivery of her own baby or something. While it was nice that she'd avoided the discomfort, she'd passed a significant milestone completely unconscious. "How long was I asleep?"

"Just over five days. Would you like to see yourself?"

She cringed. "No!"

His smile was sympathetic. "It's not as bad as you're imagining. Ketrok learned much from Monica's transition, so we were better prepared. Of course you still need to gain a significant amount of weight, but that will come with time."

Finally realizing she was naked beneath her blanket, she wrapped it around her before trying to sit up.

"Slowly," Tiber cautioned, keeping a hand on her bare shoulder.

Jasmine kept her eyes closed until the worst of the dizziness and nausea had passed. The breasts under her arms didn't feel all that different from her old ones.

"How tall am I?" she whispered.

"Six feet nine inches. It's possible you'll grow another inch or so in the next few months, but that should be it."

Her lips trembled. Shit, she was a giant.

Suddenly the need to face what she had become was overwhelming.

"Tiber, could I..." She swallowed. "Could I see myself—in private, please?"

"Certainly." He looked at the wall by the head of her bed and a full-length flare reflection appeared. Then he nodded at Hastion, who rolled off the bed. "We'll be next door when you're ready to talk."

Jasmine just sat there, her heart beating crazily as she tried to work up the courage to look at her reflection. She wished Monica were here to—

Monica!

Crap, she was wasting time. She needed to get this over with and then find some way to help Monica. Throwing off the blanket, she slid off the side of the bed and propped herself up on legs that were as wobbly as a newborn colt's.

"Oh my," she breathed, still clutching the edge of the mattress. She didn't look as different as Monica had after her transition but... "Oh my."

Her hair, which had previously just brushed her shoulder blades, now hung to her waist. It seemed darker, a rich sable that was dull from lack of washing and brushing.

The face was still hers, although her features were now more sharply defined, her eyes deeper and wider-set, her jaw longer and her chin more stubborn-looking.

Jasmine lifted her arms, shocked at how slender they were and yet thrilled at their firm youthfulness. She was less thrilled with the small tufts of brown hair under them but they were nothing she couldn't live with. For some reason, she'd envisioned herself more like a pterodactyl, with fine fragile bones and webbing under her arms. Instead, she looked like a supermodel. An anorexic, Bohemian supermodel, for sure, but at least she still looked human.

And incredibly, she still had tasteful breasts. Her hands trembled as she reached up and touched herself. What had happened to her implants? Were they still there, hiding under the muscle wall, or had someone removed them while she was sleeping?

She let one hand drift down over her bony ribs and taut, concave stomach to the dark brown hair between her legs. Silky and almost straight, it didn't seem all that thick—certainly not enough to hide an SUV in.

A giggle escaped her before a tear slipped down her cheek. That was her in the mirror—the real Jasmine King. If this was as bad as it got, maybe she'd be okay after all.

"So, *aramai*," Shauss breathed in her ear. Startled, Jasmine met his gaze in the mirror. Heavens, she was just a few inches shorter than he was. "Are you ready to end Monica's torment?"

"Torment!" She tried to turn, but he pulled her back against him, twining one arm in front of her to cup her breast and sending the other down lower to cup her mons.

"My, how you've grown," he murmured. Burrowing through her hair, he nibbled at her neck.

"Shauss, stop!" She slapped at his hands. "What do you mean, Monica's torment?"

"While you were sleeping the week away, Monica has been punished every single day."

"No!" Jasmine moaned. "Oh God, Shauss, why didn't you stop him?"

"Stop him?" The puff of his laugh against her neck sent chills down her spine. "I helped."

"For God's sake, why?"

He met her eyes in the mirror. "Because you haven't told me everything you know about Ragan King."

* * * * *

They'd punished Monica because of her.

The responsibility was a crushing weight on Jasmine's chest. She gazed blankly at the flare reflection as Tiber brushed the tangles out of her damp hair, her soul shrinking in horror at the memory of Monica hanging limply in Commander Kellen's arms. What in God's name had they done to her since then? How could the commander, a man who had given every appearance of being deeply in love with his mate, turn against her so cruelly?

Jasmine winced. How could *she* have asked Monica to risk her relationship with him? If she'd seen the two of them together, as they'd been at the celebration dinner, she never would have. The idea that she'd destroyed their incredibly lovely bond was intolerable.

When Tiber paused, she met his pensive brown eyes briefly before looking away. The brushing resumed and she leaned into the strokes with a resigned sigh. He loved her. She could feel it in every tug of the soft bristles on her scalp and in the warmth of the palm he braced on her collarbone to hold her steady, but the knowledge did little to comfort her. He'd been uncharacteristically quiet as he led her to the shower, and he hadn't shown the least sign of arousal when he stripped out of his uniform and soaped her all over. Not that she was in the mood for sex, of course, but the funereal feel of his gentle ministrations unsettled her. She felt like a condemned prisoner being given the last rites.

Surely the Garathani wouldn't have gone to all the trouble to see her through her transition if they intended to execute her…would they?

Jasmine shook herself. What an ungrateful, self-centered bitch. Monica was still suffering because of her, and she was worried about her own future?

Then her fingers drifted to her throat and everything else was momentarily forgotten as grief eviscerated her. Shauss had reclaimed his gift.

"Are you all right?"

Jasmine closed her eyes and nodded quickly, taking deep, even breaths to clear her mind. She couldn't afford to speculate about the numerous and potentially awful implications of the missing choker right now—there was too much at stake. Monica had to be her top priority.

By the time Tiber finished brushing her hair and stepped back, she had herself under marginal control again.

A stone-faced Shauss appeared as if summoned. Without a word, he fastened the leather cuffs around her wrists and the next thing she knew, she was standing in a room she'd never seen before. Commander Kellen was there, and she cringed in humiliation to be naked before him again. Even worse, Zannen stood beside him, looking all kinds of smug.

She flinched when she saw Monica standing in one corner of the room with her feet braced apart and her hands behind her head. She was also naked. Sweat beaded her forehead, her eyes were wide and dark, and her chest rose and fell as if she were running a race.

"Oh my God, Monica!" Jasmine struggled, but Shauss held her arm. Bunching a hand in her hair, he dragged her closer to Monica.

"Look at her ass," he growled in her ear.

Jasmine's stomach dropped. From this angle, she could see that Monica's bottom and thighs were covered with dark red handprints.

That was all it took to shatter her fragile control.

"You bastard!" she shouted at Kellen as tears poured from her eyes. "How could you do that to her? She loves you!" She stopped long enough to scream out her sorrow, and then repeated, "She loves you, you big bastard!"

"I didn't do it to her," Kellen said coldly. "You did when you involved her in your intrigues."

Jasmine sagged in Shauss' arms, sobbing. "I'm sorry! Oh God, Monica, I'm so sorry!"

Monica whimpered then and tears slipped down her cheeks.

"What are you doing to her? Stop it! Please! She doesn't know anything! My God, she can't tell you anything!"

"I'm aware she's told me all she knows," Kellen said mildly. "She's being punished now."

"Please stop. Please, I beg you. I'll take whatever punishment you want to hand out, just please leave her alone. God, she loves you so much and you do this to her," she rambled on. "Please let her go. I'm the one who deserves punishment, not her."

It was then she saw the...the *thing* creeping between Monica's legs. Cold horror prickled over her skin. They were torturing her sexually?

Breaking away from Shauss, she tried to get ahold of whatever it was with her bound hands, but it was odd and fluid and she couldn't get a grip on it.

"Get it off her!" she screamed.

"You can end her punishment, if you like," Shauss said.

Jasmine homed in on him. "How?"

"You enjoy administering oral sex—do so now while you take her punishment," he ordered.

"What?"

He reached down and retrieved the thing between Monica's legs. The odd little blob hovered in his palm for a moment and then disappeared. Then he released the clip holding her wrists together.

"Kellen's held her at the brink of orgasm since he took her from the infirmary. If you want to relieve her suffering, go right ahead."

Jasmine had never been with a woman before and had never given the idea much thought, but it didn't matter. Nothing mattered now except righting *something* that had gone wrong because of her.

Shaking with love and fear for the woman who'd risked so much for her, she dropped to her knees and spread open the silky hair covering Monica's mound. Her inner lips were swollen and red, and Jasmine instinctively leaned forward and sucked them into her mouth, simultaneously sliding two fingers inside. Monica screamed as her back arched.

At the same time, Jasmine felt humming warmth surge into her own vagina and nook. She gasped and jerked away, looking down. Shauss had attached the thing to her and it was filling her, vibrating.

She slapped at it, breathing rapidly, scared out of her mind. "What is it?"

"It's a masturbation probe." Shauss crooked a brow. "Monica's still suffering."

Taking a shaky breath, Jasmine calmed herself and got back to the job at hand. She licked and sucked, pushing her tongue into Monica's nook while she drove her fingers deep and probed for her G-spot. It wasn't long before she felt the firm walls clamp around her fingers. Monica screamed her release, sending a flood of slick fluid over Jasmine's palm.

"Again," Shauss said. "She's been suffering a long time."

Monica's hands were suddenly on her head, pulling her close and grinding her flesh against Jasmine's mouth. Jasmine opened willingly, paying loving penance with every swipe of her tongue and fingers, trying to wipe away the torture she'd caused. Monica jerked and keened above her as she came twice more, bringing tears of relief to Jasmine's eyes.

At the feel of tender hands stroking her hair, Jasmine looked up. Monica opened her mouth, but nothing came out so she leaned down and brushed a brief kiss over her lips, and Jasmine realized for the first time how desperate her own excitement was. She stiffened when part of the probe tickled her anus, but trying to keep it out only let it slide deep into her. She slapped at the probe again, but it expanded, filling her more completely, and the vibrations grew stronger, tightening her abdomen into knots.

"Oh God," she whimpered. It was humiliating but she might actually come.

"Oh no," Shauss said. The probe's vibration remained strong, but it withdrew from her nook, denying her the release she really shouldn't be so eager for under the circumstance. "You're not getting off that easily."

He nudged Monica out of the way and circled Jasmine. "Tell us, *aramai*. How many Narthani are on Earth?"

"Shauss, I've told you over and over, my parents and I were alone there. Now my father is alone there."

"So how do you explain the Narthani monarch's claim that four couples were sent to Terra all those years ago—four couples who have never been retrieved?"

Jasmine froze, dread clamping her stomach. "Four? No, my mother wouldn't lie to me. She wouldn't."

"Pardon the interruption," Zannen said with exaggerated politeness, "but Hastion's protected time is drawing to a close."

Tiber looked around and saw Hastion leaning against the wall behind Jasmine, pale and sweaty and looking like he was actually going to regurgitate again. What in Peserin's hell was wrong with him?

"You can't do it, can you?" Zannen exclaimed with a grin.

"You're not getting her. I'll kill you first," Hastion said, wiping the back of his hand over his mouth as he straightened.

"Is that before or after you stop to puke your guts out over kissing a female?"

He staggered toward Zannen. "Shut up!"

"Perhaps you should go back to the atrium and masturbate for all the warriors again. You seemed to enjoy that."

"I've had more than enough of your shit, Zannen," Hastion growled. "Shut the fuck up before I shut you up."

Zannen crossed his arms over his chest. "Shut me up. I dare you, sissy boy."

Hastion howled with fury and launched himself at Zannen. He was nearly a match in height, but he lacked the width and depth, the thickness and hard muscle that was Zannen.

"Hastion, no!" Jasmine cried, trying to rise. "He'll kill you."

Shauss gripped the back of her neck and held her in place.

Concerned that this charade might be too much for Hastion in his current state, Tiber moved to step in but Shauss stopped him. "It's their fight — let them fight it."

Tiber frowned but held himself in check. He expected Hastion to yield in short order, but his condition seemed to actually improve as the fight progressed. The two rolled along the wall locked in a furious embrace, each trying to get the upper hand. Zannen was stronger, but Hastion was quicker, and every time it looked like Zannen had him, he managed to duck away and attack from a different angle.

Their acting skills impressed the hell out of Tiber...until it dawned on him that Hastion was genuinely enraged and trying to remove Zannen's head from his shoulders. He managed to leap onto Zannen's back and get a chokehold on his neck, sticking like a burr, until the larger man slammed backward into the bulkhead to knock him off. Zannen turned and grinned as a bug-eyed Hastion slid to the floor, but Hastion's breath finally rushed back with a hoarse gasp, and then he barreled toward Zannen again.

Zannen was ready for him. He grabbed Hastion and swung him back into the bulkhead. Hastion tried to duck out of his grip but Zannen wrapped both arms around his waist and threw all his weight onto Hastion's back, taking him down. Hastion's breathing was harsh, almost sobbing, as he tried to scramble away, but Zannen pinned his neck to the floor.

The pose was unexpectedly sexual and Tiber's loins tightened. It looked for all the world like Zannen was fucking Hastion.

"Do you yield?" Zannen gasped.

"Hell, no!"

"Well, you've got him," Shauss drawled. "Now what are you going to do with him?"

Hastion tried to jerk away and Zannen tightened his hold. Hastion's groan didn't sound like pain, exactly…

"I suppose killing him would be a bad career move," Zannen said with a tight grin.

"Without a doubt." Shauss' tone made Tiber look at him and then do a double-take. The man's eyes were positively alight with speculation. "Why don't you fuck him?"

Hastion groaned again, and arousal and alarm seized Tiber's stomach with equal ferocity. What in the name of all the planets was Shauss thinking?

Zannen looked stunned, and then angry. "*Fuck* him? Brother, have you lost touch with your sanity? Males don't fuck each other."

"Terran males do."

"Yes, well their species is dancing merrily down the road to self-destruction as well, but we feel no compulsion to follow their example in that regard."

"It was just a thought," Shauss said with a grin. "Hastion now has an impressive hard-on and I get the distinct impression he's aroused as hell by your dominating him."

"Shauss, shut the fuck up!" Hastion gasped desperately.

Zannen grabbed a handful of his hair and jerked hard. "What say you, Hastion? Is that what your problem is—you need to feel a cock in your waste canal?"

"I'm going to kill you both," Hastion swore. Then he stiffened and then groaned. At first Tiber wasn't sure what was going on, but then he noticed movement in Zannen's arm. Peserin, he was feeling Hastion's privates!

"He *is* hard as stone," Zannen murmured with wonder and no little satisfaction.

"It's the adrenaline," Hastion groaned. "For Peserin's sake, you're hard too!"

"Naked females do that for me." Zannen released him and stood up. "And now I intend to have one. No offense, Hastion," he added.

He walked toward Jasmine, opening his suit as he went. His long, thick cock was indeed prepped and ready to go.

"Shauss!" Jasmine gasped.

Shauss' measured look as he stared down at her wasn't reassuring.

"Tell us about the other Narthani on the planet's surface and Tiber and I will try to protect you from him," he said. "Otherwise, we accept him as third—and I'll warn you right now, Zannen hasn't come in almost fifteen years, so he'll probably fuck you around the clock for weeks."

Jasmine's heartbeat tripled and her breath came in fast gasps. "But I don't know anything! Oh God, they told me we were alone—all alone! Why would they lie to me? Oh my God, why would my mother lie to me?"

Shauss curved his hand under her chin. "Choose now, Jasmine. Hastion's time will officially expire—"

"My mother wouldn't lie to me!" she screeched.

"Now."

Tears slipped down her cheeks. "Shauss, no. Please."

"Ah well. That's too bad. We'll miss your company sorely." He crouched down in front of her and wiped her tears with his thumb. "Now compose yourself and promise me you won't fight him."

She sucked in a shaky breath. "How can you ask that?"

"Whom do you wish to please, Jasmine King?"

"You but—"

"I'll be displeased if you fight him. I'll be displeased if you don't serve him as well as you served me."

Stunned, she stared at him. "You really want me to...?"

He merely cocked a brow at her and she finally sagged in resignation. She didn't understand, but apparently she didn't need to.

"I won't fight him," she whispered. "I promise."

"Very good, *aramai*. Serve him well and hopefully you'll be in decent shape the next time I see you." He kissed her forehead and another tear slid down her cheek. Then he stood up, leaving her to deal with Zannen on her own.

God, this sucked! Every instinct told her to glare at the ugly bastard, to scream invective at him and fight him with everything she had. Instead, she kept her head down and prepared to accept and pleasure him the way she would Shauss. But there was no way she'd let him master her. No way in hell. In fact, by George, she would master *his* miserable ass. It was a given that he'd never experienced oral sex, and once she'd treated him to the mind-bending pleasure of her mouth, he'd be on his knees begging for it. For her.

The very thought of it made her lips curve in a smug smile.

"Awfully submissive, isn't she?" Zannen rumbled as he approached.

"My submissive," Shauss replied. Jasmine felt ridiculously thrilled by the satisfaction evident in his voice and only slightly guilty about her plans for Zannen, who meandered around her with flagrant disregard for his bobbing monster cock.

He finally stopped beside her and she held her breath. "Very pretty," he said. "But I'd rather have that one."

Shauss gaped at his brother, his heart still pounding with pride and affection for Jasmine, and no little concern that Zannen might ignore Tiber's ban on intercourse and shove that obscene tool into his mate. What was the man doing? This wasn't part of the plan—not that anything was going according to plan today.

When Monica realized Zannen was pointing at her, she shook her head wildly, gesturing with her hands.

"Is that so?" Kellen asked, stroking his chin, apparently oblivious to his mate's distress. "Are you sure? You've seen for yourself she's far from submissive."

"I always enjoy a good fight before I fuck," Zannen reported.

Monica hopped over and grabbed Kellen's arm, shaking it with both hands, and he patted her absently. "Well, she'll give you that, no question. And it seems only fair that you have her, since she conspired to deprive you of Miss King—in fact, that's how Shauss wound up with Miss King when she conspired to deprive him of Monica." He focused on Monica. "But I think Monica had someone else in mind, didn't you, my love?"

Monica looked at him warily before nodding.

"You're very easy to read these days," he explained.

Monica held up her middle finger. "Read this, you big jerk."

She looked surprised when the thought actually emerged from her mouth.

"Unfortunately," he continued as if he hadn't heard her, "I'll have to veto Hastion as our second. Not only is he still suffering from the injuries Miss King inflicted on him, but he's too submissive."

"What? But you said you were going to look for someone with a more submissive nature than Shauss," she argued.

"My love, just about every male on this ship has a more submissive nature than Shauss. He's something of a control freak and requires a submissive who can trust him to give her everything she needs." He towered over her with his arms crossed. "Make no mistake, Monica—I am the Dominant in our bond, and as such, it's my responsibility to give you what *you* need. Not what you want, but what you *need*. Those two things do not always coincide, and I would be doing you a grave disservice if I were always to give you what you wanted."

"But—"

"You must learn to trust me to give you what you need."

"But—"

"What you need is another mate who will keep you safe from yourself and others when you're out of my sight, rather than a toy to play with, a submissive male to manipulate and order around."

"But Kellen—"

"You need a mate who won't be annoyed by the fight in you but will enjoy bending you to his will just as much as I do, day in and day out."

"No, I—"

"You, my love, need to accept that you are an alpha female, and while you may be dominant to all other females, and perhaps even a few males, you *will* be ruled by the males in your bond.

"Therefore," he went on before she could break in, "I will let any male in this room who is dominant enough to take you—" his gaze zeroed in on Zannen, "keep you."

"What!" She started as Zannen strolled toward her, shrugging out of his uniform, his cock now so engorged, it pointed straight at her. "Okay, I get it. I'm not supposed to keep secrets from you. I get it. I'll tell you everything from now on, I promise."

"I don't believe you," Kellen said with a smile. "If you think it's the right thing to do, you'll lie to my face."

She gritted her teeth and backed toward the wall. "God damn it, Kellen!"

Zannen toed off his boots and kicked out of his uniform, then proceeded to stalk her, every bit as naked as she was.

"I think Zannen got under your skin the instant you met him. Peserin knows you've complained enough about him."

"Because he's a prick!"

"You're looking at his cock. Admit you want it."

"I do not!"

"See? You're lying already. You're so aroused you can hardly think of a plausible lie."

"Aargh!"

Zannen grabbed her around the waist and she fought him, growling and scratching at his shoulders as he heaved her into the air.

"You fight like a girl," he said with a grin.

"I am a girl, you baldheaded prick!"

"That one fights like a warrior." He nodded toward Jasmine. "Perhaps she can give you some pointers."

Monica hauled back and slapped him hard across the face.

"Do it again," he said.

She stared at him for a moment before saying, "Aw, fuck it!" She grabbed his head and kissed him wildly, tearing at his lips with her teeth as she dragged her palms over his scalp.

Zannen slammed her into the wall. Then he reached down and took hold of his cock, and Shauss winced when he nailed her with a thrust that made her scream like a jungle cat. It was a good thing Jasmine had made her come several times—Zannen really was a huge bastard, and he gave her no quarter as he rammed her over and over.

Her ankles locked behind his waist and she tore her mouth away from his to scream, "Oh God, yes! Fuck me, you bastard!"

"She actually wants him."

Shauss looked down to find Jasmine's eyes dilated with disbelief and arousal.

"So it would seem," he murmured. His head still reeled with his brother's sudden change of course. If it had been anyone else, Shauss might have suspected Zannen was bowing out of *juranin* for the sake of brotherly harmony. Or that he doubted his chances of usurping Hastion in their bond. Or that he had decided to advance his standing by pursuing Monica.

But Zannen had never done anything for the sake of harmony, and he'd been dead certain only an hour ago that Jasmine would be his the instant Tiber's moratorium on intercourse with her was lifted. And while his brother took pride in being a superior warrior, he didn't give a damn about status and never had. He'd told more powerful people than Kellen to kiss his big, hairy ass.

As hard as it was to believe, Zannen preferred Monica to Jasmine.

Shauss shook his head. Incredible. Perhaps his brother wasn't as envious of him as he'd thought.

Nevertheless, making such a public bid for Monica was bold even for Zannen.

"Whose idea was this?" he asked Kellen.

Kellen grinned. *"Does it really matter?"*

His cryptic question was its own answer—Kellen had done a little behind-the-scenes maneuvering.

Shauss grinned. Poor Monica still had no idea what she was dealing with.

Zannen ducked his head and sucked one of Monica's nipples into his mouth, pulling hard, and she screamed again. Apparently tired of her nails raking ribbons of flesh off his shoulders, he seized her wrists and pinned them to the wall over her head. Just as it occurred to Shauss to wonder if she could accommodate him completely, Zannen tipped his hips, deepening the angle of his thrust, and drove his spur up into her nook.

He should have known Kellen would leave nothing to chance this time.

Impossibly, the animalistic fucking grew more intense, and arousal made it difficult to breathe evenly. When Monica sobbed out her release, Zannen buried his face in her neck and went wild in her, choking with the agony of his need, and Shauss' scrotum contracted in sympathy. He'd never thought the sight of his brother's buttocks flexing in a frenzied copulative cadence would turn him on, but seeing Zannen lose all semblance of control pleased him in a host of ways. He had to admit, the brute knew how to claim a female.

Even after the storm of his release abated, Zannen continued to lean into Monica with slow, short thrusts, panting harshly as he licked and sucked at her neck and shoulder.

Monica, meanwhile, hung limply over his shoulder. Shauss thought she'd passed out until she licked a bead of sweat off Zannen's back, and sighed, "God, you bastards can fuck."

"I'm just getting warmed up," Zannen said.

Kellen took a handful of Monica's hair and tipped her head back. "I'm getting a little warm myself." Then he kissed her as if Zannen were nowhere in the vicinity.

"That makes three of us," Jasmine murmured.

Shauss slipped a hand into her hair. "I'm sorry, *aramai*, but your need must go unsatisfied for the moment."

She looked up at him with a question in her eyes, but he was pleased when she held her tongue.

"Not because you're being punished, but because you've just emerged from your transition and Tiber insists you be given twenty-four hours to recover before any of us may penetrate you."

She frowned at him for a moment and then her eyes widened. "You set this up, didn't you? Hastion was never going to claim me and neither was Zannen. You were testing me."

He leaned down and kissed her lips. "And you passed in a grand style, my beautiful submissive."

Not that he'd expected anything else. Monica admitted during her punishment that Jasmine had declined to use the replicated nasal spray, deliberately exposing herself to his pheromones, and the knowledge had at once eased him and turned him inside out with desire.

Speaking of which…

"However." He looked at Tiber. "I'm also feeling the heat."

Tiber straightened away from the bulkhead, his expression wary.

"It may have escaped your notice, Doctor, but while you were finding your release in Jasmine last week, I was left unsatisfied." He pasted a stern look on his face as he strolled toward Tiber. "And since you're being recalcitrant about letting me have her now, I think I'll have you instead."

Chapter Seventeen

Tiber froze, his heart thumping hard and his mind churning. "But I'm her physician. What would you have me do—harm her by allowing you to take her too soon after her transition?"

Shauss stopped directly in front of him. "If you did that, I'd have to beat you to a bloody pulp and then fuck you without the benefit of lubricant."

"Then why are you punishing me for keeping her safe?"

His grin was indulgent. "Because I can."

"You're not seriously going to fuck another male?" Zannen asked as he let Monica slide down to the floor. Tiber couldn't help grinning when she rolled her eyes and ran her fingers through the abundant secretions sliding down her legs before wiping her hand on the bulkhead pad.

"Of course I am," Shauss replied, "and perhaps Hastion after him, if I'm still feeling the need to work off some aggression."

"Ha! I told you you'd fuck every member in your bond," Monica crowed, crossing her arms as she straightened.

"Maybe I'll have some fun with you after I'm done with Hastion."

She narrowed her eyes. "You're not my mate anymore."

"Oh, but I think Kellen will allow me certain privileges with his little playmate if I dangle a carrot."

Monica gave him a confident smirk. "You don't have a carrot he wants."

"No, but he has one you want," Kellen told her with a rueful grin. "And while my main concern is giving you what you need, I'm certainly pleased to give you what you want when it's good for you."

"Me?"

"Yes, you." Shauss walked over and stood behind her, looking over her shoulder at the three of them. Tiber's heartbeat sped up. "Look at my bondmates. Aren't they gorgeous?"

Monica licked her bottom lip as grudging excitement lit her gaze. "Yes, they are."

"Which toy would you rather Kellen gave you—an iPod or submissives to play with once in a while?"

She didn't answer, but Tiber saw her swallow, saw her breathing grow deeper.

"You enjoyed standing over Jasmine, forcing her face into your cunt while she made you come. You'd enjoy doing the same to Tiber and Hastion. Of course, there would be no intercourse between non-mates, but think of the fun you could all have pushing each other's boundaries."

She reached up and pulled his head down to say against his ear, "But who's going to push *your* boundaries, Shauss?"

He turned and brushed his lips over hers. "My boundaries are fine where they are, sweet one, but thank you for your concern."

Tiber squirmed when her gaze focused on him. "I want to watch you fuck Tiber."

He returned her look with a penetrating stare of his own. If she thought he was a simple submissive, she would be in for a rude surprise when their play sessions started. He'd done a little research over the last few days and realized he was what Terrans called a switch. He might play sub for her, but first he was going to exact revenge for this moment.

He looked at Shauss. *"You don't really expect me to just bend over and take it in front of your brother, do you?"*

Shauss deliberated before allowing, *"As a rule, I expect you to do what I tell you without question, but just this once I'll allow you to put up a respectable fight before I take your ass."*

"*Thanks so much,*" Tiber said dryly.

"*Think nothing of it.*" Then Shauss crossed his arms and said aloud in a tone that brooked no argument, "Tiber, take down your suit and bend over the back of that couch."

Tiber looked at him for a long moment. Shauss had a few things to learn about him too, but not in front of his brother. Crossing his own arms and bracing his feet apart, he said, "Make me."

"Two of my very favorite words," Shauss said, unzipping his suit.

Much to Tiber's abiding shame, the fight was over before it had really even begun. They circled each other naked for all of five seconds before Shauss went for the kill. Literally.

Unable to speak, hanging upside down over Shauss' shoulder in a Molbissian death lock, Tiber sent, *"I thought you were going to let me put up a fight!"*

"*I said a respectable fight,*" Shauss replied, turning. "*There was nothing respectable about that.*" At his first step, Tiber's eyes widened—that he was still alive and could feel his extremities in this position was a testament to Shauss' lethal skill, but he desperately needed air.

"*Can't breathe!*"

"*Wait for it...*" When they were in front of the couch, Shauss braced his legs apart and loosened his grip on Tiber's thigh, supporting it from underneath.

Tiber wasn't too far gone from lack of oxygen to realize what the younger warrior was about to do. He stiffened in terror, squeezing his eyes shut as Shauss crouched and flipped him over the back of the couch.

The facedown landing nearly burst his spleen and he gasped into the cushion before moaning, "Ouch." His toes hurt too from crashing into the pad. It was a miracle none of them were broken.

"When are you going to learn not to challenge an Ayeran assassin for physical supremacy?" Kellen asked in a voice dripping with amusement.

Tiber sighed. "Not soon enough, apparently."

A shock of icy liquid drizzled into the crease between his buttocks and Tiber bit back a gasp as he squirmed. Shauss' powerful hand landed on his lower back, holding him in place, and then at least four fingers invaded without warning.

He couldn't stifle a grunt as pain bit his ass. Make that six. Twelve. Hundred. He hissed, grinding his teeth in agony. Holy Powers, how many fingers did the ruthless young pup possess?

"Peserin's hell! Aren't you even going to kiss me before you kill me?" Tiber sent, only half-joking.

"A couple of fingers never killed anyone. Perhaps I should spank you. Monica loves this particular position."

Monica snorted. "Love isn't the word I'd use."

"There's only so much I'm willing to take in front of other males," Tiber growled at Shauss.

"Limitation noted. And the same is true for me. Physical affection will be displayed only in the privacy of quarters."

"This doesn't qualify as physical affection?"

"This qualifies as your claiming. In the future, only Jasmine and Hastion may be present when I fuck you."

Those slick fingers gouged deeper, provoking all sorts of humiliating noises from Tiber's throat and finally, *finally,* rekindling the fires of arousal in his loins. *"Agreed."*

"Commander, I hope you have no similar plans for me." Zannen's tone clearly threatened mayhem if the commander should happen to have such plans.

"You may rest assured, Lieutenant, that your ass is the very last black hole in this universe I'd be interested in exploring."

Hastion's bark of laughter drew a smile from Tiber.

"The feeling is mutual," Zannen replied evenly.

"I'm glad that's settled." Shauss withdrew his fingers. "Now be quiet or leave."

"I'm leaving," Zannen declared, much to Tiber's relief. "Hopefully there's enough ale aboard to make me forget everything I've seen today."

Watching him walk out, Shauss felt a curious lightness of spirit. Zannen's parting comment had been decidedly arid, but the indulgent look that accompanied it was almost...brotherly.

He was ashamed to admit that the root of their past conflicts might have had less to do with Zannen's jealousy than with his own. After the Crunus Uprising, Zannen still had a father because Boydon had loved him and chosen protecting him over attempting to seize power. Shauss' father, however, had chosen revenge and then suicide, leaving him to face the world alone.

It was a sacrifice he'd resented for too long. His father had tried to give him the very life he had now, as master of his own bond — indeed, his own destiny — rather than the slave of some ruthless female. How could he resent that?

He ran his hands over Tiber's muscular flanks, painfully aroused but uncertain how to resolve it. The few times he'd imagined fucking a male, the particulars had been rather blurry. As far as he could tell, both roles had definite drawbacks. The male suffering the indignity of penetration was rewarded with orgasm, while the male who did the penetrating enjoyed a rush of power but couldn't orgasm.

It hardly seemed fair that Terran males endured no such dilemma. No matter who fucked whom, both could orgasm.

"Losing your nerve?" Tiber prodded in a breathless rumble.

Shauss abandoned the logistics of the matter and forced his slick cock into the smartass.

"What do you think?"

The only reply was a hiss of pain. Shauss grinned tightly. What did it matter if he came? He was topping Tiber once and for all.

"Who's claiming your ass?" he asked as he withdrew, just for the enjoyment of hearing Tiber say it.

Tiber groaned before firing back weakly, "Who's asking?"

Shauss forged inward again, darkly thrilled to hear the breath whistle from the good doctor's lungs at his incursion. He skimmed a hand up Tiber's back and rubbed it over his silky blond head. Then he grabbed a handful of hair and turned his head forcibly to the side.

"Your primary bond mate is asking." Laying all his weight down and wedging his cock deep, Shauss nipped at Tiber's earlobe before repeating his question. "Now tell me, Dr. Tiber, who's fucking this nice, tight ass?"

"Shauss!" Tiber wheezed.

"Very good. And why are you letting me fuck you?"

While Tiber mulled it over behind his tightly closed eyes, Shauss sucked on his earlobe and found the texture quite different from Jasmine's. Tiber's skin was thicker, rougher, but tasted every bit as fascinating. This whole experience was fascinating in the extreme and he found himself wondering how Garathani males had lived so many centuries without experimenting with one another.

Perhaps they *had* and were simply too ashamed to admit it. The Powers knew he would have been just weeks earlier. Or perhaps they'd have feared for their lives if their indiscretions were discovered. They would definitely have had cause in decades past. If the ruling females had learned of such experimentation, they would have executed the culprits as swiftly as they did males who coupled with inappropriate females.

Whatever the reason for the taboo on male homoerotic activity in Garathani history, he was fiercely glad to see it end.

"Because it feels right," Tiber finally admitted softly.

Shauss' heartbeat, already pounding, kicked up a notch. Being buried in Tiber did feel perfectly, exquisitely right—just as being buried deep inside Jasmine did.

Lifting his head, he found her kneeling in the same position he'd left her in. She watched them with dark eyes, her cheeks flushed and her nipples tight with arousal, and even from here he could smell the sweet, heady musk of her pheromones.

Kellen was seated on another couch with Monica cradled on his lap, and both observed with similar interest.

Hastion stood propped against the wall, his face pale and dotted with perspiration.

It was an interesting non-nuclear family he'd managed to acquire in a very short time.

"Shouldn't you be in the infirmary?" Shauss inquired of Hastion as he ran his hands down the lean musculature stretched over Tiber's ribs.

"Probably, but the entertainment's better here."

In full agreement, Shauss straightened and grasped Tiber's hips. Before he could move, Tiber held up a probe and Shauss grinned.

"You, my mate, have just earned your orgasm."

* * * * *

Tiber was dismayed by the heat that scorched his neck and ears when Shauss guided Jasmine into the infirmary the next morning. He'd been dreading and anticipating this moment with equal measure for hours. Despite having dived into busywork immediately upon waking, he'd relived last night's surrender at least a hundred times over already. His newly stretched waste canal, which zinged in protest with every step he took, made it well nigh impossible to forget just how thoroughly he'd been claimed, and the empty feeling in his balls and gut reminded him all too vividly of just how hard he'd come.

He wouldn't let himself think about the continuing reminders of just how copiously Shauss had come in the deepest recesses of his rectum.

Tiber cursed silently. Knowing he was blushing made him blush all the harder, and Shauss' slow, arrogant smile only compounded the problem. Peserin, he was the father of grown children and yet his heartbeat fluttered like an adolescent female's!

Ignoring him, Tiber poured all that heat into an open-mouthed kiss with Jasmine and thrilled to the sensual stroke of her tongue against his. When Shauss grasped the back of his neck, linking the three of them, he stiffened — in more ways than one — but managed not to react otherwise to the firm touch.

"I hear you managed to snare yet another Sparnite, Lieutenant."

Ketrok's voice booming from the bed next to Hastion's made Jasmine tear away from him with a gasp.

"Fortune has favored me," Shauss acknowledged with a serene nod, keeping his hand in place. To the casual observer, his touch might appear to be just that, casual and friendly. But

Tiber recognized its two-fold purpose—to remind him of Shauss' dominance and to reassert Shauss' claim on him.

It was tempting to turn the tables, to try to stake his own claim on Shauss, but the sad, exciting truth was that Shauss would probably tie him in a painful knot and fuck him in front of a hundred witnesses as punishment.

"And I." Ketrok glanced at his hands, which were still covered by the thick blue regeneration gloves. "Another minute or two in that steripod and I wouldn't have had any hands to regenerate."

"Dr. Ketrok, I'm so relieved to see you on the mend," Jasmine said, leaning over the bed to kiss his cheek.

The grizzled and graying Ketrok actually blushed, which made Tiber feel considerably better about his own hot cheeks. "Thank you, Miss King. I'm glad to be on the mend."

She sat on the edge of Hastion's bed and put her palm on his forehead. "And how are you feeling this morning?"

"I'm fine, for now," he said, setting aside his frustration long enough grab her hand and plant a kiss on the back. "Tiber can find nothing wrong with me. Nothing."

"I'm sorry," she said.

"As am I. The protected claiming time is now over, and until I'm fit to mate, you are at risk of being claimed by the first male who happens on you unprotected."

"She won't be unprotected," Shauss promised. "Kellen, Zannen and the minister are committed to keeping her safe until this mysterious malady has passed—as is Monica, who can make a grown warrior cry for his mommy," he added with a grin. "Between the seven of us, we should be able to preserve her until you can finalize your claim."

"What are you talking about?" Ketrok asked.

As Tiber explained, Ketrok's expression became more and more thoughtful. Then his gaze slid between Jasmine and Hastion, alight with speculation.

"Miss King looks quite different since her transition," he said.

Confused by the change of subject and the switch to cerecom, Tiber said, "Not all that much. Certainly not like Dr. Teague did."

Ketrok watched him intently. "Look at the two of them, Tiber — Hastion and Miss King."

Tiber did, trying hard to see what Ketrok was seeing. When he did, he felt as though he'd been struck in the chest by a meteor. Opening the link to Shauss and Ketrok, he ordered, "Empran, DNA comparison between Jasmine King and Lieutenant Hastion."

Almost instantly, Empran replied, "Jasmine King and Lieutenant Hastion share twenty common alleles. Likelihood of sibling relationship ninety-nine point nine two percent."

Shauss jerked in surprise and stared at Jasmine and Hastion. "Ho. Ly. Shit!"

Then he burst into belly laughs.

"That would certainly explain his symptoms," Ketrok said.

"What?" Jasmine smiled uncertainly as Hastion frowned at them. "What's the joke?"

When Shauss just leaned against Ketrok's bed and held his sides as he guffawed, Tiber asked, "Hastion, what, exactly, happened to your mother and twin sister?"

Hastion's frown deepened. "They were kidnapped and killed."

Shauss sobered instantly. "How?"

"Well, I wasn't there, but my father told me that he tracked the kidnappers to a vacant distillery and saw my mother lying sealed in one of the tanks with my sister in her arms. When he tried to open the hatch, it triggered a feyo shell that incinerated both of them."

"Oh my God," Jasmine breathed. "That's despicable!"

"Why do you want to know?" Hastion asked.

Tiber looked at Shauss before asking, *"He was absolutely certain your sister was there?"*

"Yes. Father said she was wrapped in her...blanket..." His eyes went wide with shock and he stared at Jasmine. *"By all the Powers, are you saying she's...?"*

"Unless you had another sister, yes – she's your twin."

Hastion opened his mouth but no sound emerged as he continued to stare at her.

"Are you okay?" Jasmine asked, laying her hand on his arm.

That broke his trance and he grabbed her to him, laughing as tears streamed down his face. Jasmine tried to push away from him, but he held her tight, burying his face in her neck and breathing in her scent as if to affirm what he already knew.

"How in Peserin's name did she wind up on Terra?" Ketrok asked.

Shauss raised a brow. *"That's a question I'd like answered myself."*

"What are you doing?" Jasmine demanded, working her hands between them and shoving at his chest. "Hastion, have you gone crazy?"

"Oh Peserin," Hastion breathed. "I don't know how to say this."

"Just say the words," Ketrok advised as both the commander and Minister Cecine appeared in the doorway. Shauss must have summoned them.

"What's happened now?" Kellen sighed.

Hastion looked at him and wiped his eyes with fingers that shook before turning to Jasmine again. Taking a deep breath, he said, "You're my sister."

She stared at him blankly. "What are you talking about?"

"Jasmine, you're my sister." He took both her hands in his. "You're Aylee, my twin sister."

"That's why he's been unable to claim you," Tiber explained. "Like many Terran species, we're often able to recognize family members by their pheromones, and the scent of yours was incompatible with Hastion's reproductive instincts—the thought of mating with you made him physically ill."

"Oh, this just gets better and better," Kellen said.

She pulled her hands away as if she'd been shocked and wiped them on her suit as she stood up. "That's crazy. How could I be your sister? She's *dead*, Hastion. And I'm *Narthani*."

"Actually, Tiber and I suspected you weren't even before you transitioned," Shauss said softly, curving his hands around her upper arms. "You were very tall for a Narthani Sparnite, especially given your parents' unremarkable dimensions. And though common mutations make it difficult to differentiate Narthani DNA from Garathani, the fact that you have now reached nearly seven feet in stature makes your being Narthani extremely unlikely. While you were deep in transition, I took a small team down and collected numerous DNA samples from two of Ragan King's homes. I found only yours and two others, and Empran confirms that neither was in any way related to you."

Remembering how close Shauss had come to being killed on that expedition made Tiber tighten with anger. Someone had prepared for the team's arrival with a powerful explosive device that nearly incinerated them all. If Empran's blast protection system had activated a nanosecond later, they'd all have been lost. The fact that neither of Ragan King's other two residences were wired with explosives told them whoever had planted the explosives knew which residence they were going to first, and the only ones privy to that information were the commander, the high council, and the expedition members themselves.

Jasmine looked utterly lost. "But…but my mother was…my mother. She *was*. She loved me." Her voice broke. "Shauss, she loved me."

Shauss pulled her to him and rubbed her back. "I'm sure she did, *aramai*. But she wasn't your mother. And Ragan King isn't your father."

Tiber's chest ached for her. She'd already lost her mother once, and now she was losing her all over again.

"None of this leaves this room," the minister ordered.

"Agreed." Kellen looked at Shauss. *"Can Miss King be persuaded to keep it to herself for the moment?"*

"I doubt she could be persuaded to even speak of it yet, but I'll convince her of the necessity," Shauss said.

"We need to come up with a plan to draw out the traitor or traitors on the high council," Cecine said in a dangerous tone. "I should have realized when that flare defense field appeared over Washington DC that one of them was in on it."

"I hate to upset her further, Shauss," Kellen said, "but find out if there is any additional information Jasmine can provide to help us find Ragan King."

Shauss nodded, rubbing his cheek against her hair.

"Empran, record an official report that Hastion has finalized his claim on Miss King," the minister said aloud.

"Recorded."

Jasmine looked up, confused.

"That will keep potential rivals from trying to claim you while we're sorting this out," Shauss explained softly. "His bond with us will be annulled when it's safe."

"So does this mean I'm cleared for duty?" Hastion asked.

"Indeed it does," Tiber confirmed with considerable relief. Wondering what he was missing had been driving him mad.

Hastion hopped off the bed. "Then let's go find these bastards."

* * * * *

Jasmine was sick at heart as she lay on the bed, hugging a pillow to her chest. How could her mother have lied to her all those years?

Shauss climbed into the bed behind her and just hugged her close.

"They lied to me about everything," she whispered.

"It would appear so."

"My father used me." Shauss didn't answer, but she felt his agreement. "He really didn't care about me at all. I thought I was just expecting too much, that he was a scientist and a perfectionist and he could just never understand a girl like me, but Shauss…he really hated me," she squeaked before sobs racked her.

"He didn't hate you because he never knew you," he said, kissing her hair and holding her tight. "He hates the Garathani, and it's blinded him to everything good in his life."

She sniffed. "God, it's almost like you know him because you're right—he never saw anything good in anything, except maybe Mom. And there was a lot of tension between them. She was always defending me and doing things to make me happy on the sly. Sometimes he'd get really angry when he found out about the things she'd done for me, and it made me feel so…worthless. Not only that I'd gotten her in trouble, but because he didn't want me to be happy."

"He's not deserving of your tears, *aramai*—or your loyalty."

She sat up. "You still think I'm hiding something about him? Shauss, I've told you everything. I never knew anything important, and you know he would have made sure of that."

"I agree, but you lived together for seventeen years. That's a long time to keep your entire life a secret." He was thoughtful for a moment. "I've been to all three of his homes and they look as though they've been vacant for many months. Was there any place besides the homes and his offices that he spent a lot of time in? Any time at all in?"

"If he did, I have no idea. I only saw him at home. He never came to school functions, never saw the plays I was in, never came to the games I cheered at..." She sighed. "And you know, I was actually glad. He would have put a damper on any event and I knew it. Mom always just handed me a wad of cash and told me to have fun."

"Did you ever travel together?"

"Not very often, and only for business weekends with his..." Her eyes widened. "*Associates*. Shauss, he met with some associates several times a year at an isolated camp way up in the mountains."

He opened his mouth to speak, but she grabbed his arm. "Oh my God, there were four cabins. *Four!* Didn't you say the Narthani sent four couples?"

"I did," he said tensely. "Go on."

Jasmine shook her head, floored at how completely ignorant she'd been. "I never could figure out why he didn't have his meetings in the office like everyone else because those cabins were really hard to get to. They're built around an old mine shaft, and even though he told me to stay out because it was unsafe, he and his associates always seemed to spend plenty of time in there."

"Where exactly was this camp?"

"Oh Lord, I don't know how to tell you exactly where it is. We usually got there on snowmobiles, and once I started on the pheromone blocker, he never took me again." She gave him a determined look. "But I think I could find it."

Chapter Eighteen

The next morning, Jasmine and Shauss ignored Tiber's rigorous objections and flared down to the planet's surface without an escort. In the interests of preserving the element of surprise and avoiding avalanches, they'd foregone snowmobiles in favor of skis, and Jasmine had insisted that guiding one inexperienced cross-country skier over the terrain would be challenging enough. Shauss had agreed. Once they reached the mine and determined whether or not anyone of interest was there, they could either flare out or call for the reinforcements who were standing by in the transport bay.

When the flare field disintegrated, they were right at the boundary between a forest of lodgepole pines and a large, open snowfield that led down into a wide valley. The late-morning sun shone brightly against the blanket of white that still covered the gentle slope. As they stood there, their skis settled into the softening snow.

"Does this look like the right place?" Shauss asked.

"Yes. I haven't been here since I was a teenager, but I distinctly remember that rock face." She used her ski pole to point at a rock face on an opposing mountain that looked like an enormous frowning countenance. "And that stream." She pointed off to her right.

Adjusting her goggles on her face, she looked at Shauss doubtfully. "Are you sure you're up for this? Cross-country skiing can be difficult for those who've never done it."

"You just worry about trying to keep up," he told her with a grin. "Which way?"

"North," she decided. Pushing off, she maintained a steady distance from the tree line. It was slightly uphill, and after a while, the select muscles that hadn't gotten a workout from her daily runs started to burn pleasantly. She'd be sore tomorrow, but right now she didn't care. She was in heaven.

"Oh, how I've missed this!" she cried. "Just smell that air! There's nothing like the smell of a pine forest in the winter. I don't care what kind of purified air that pad supposedly produces on board the *Heptoral*—it's nothing even close to this."

"It's spring."

She threw him a look over her shoulder, surprised to see that he was right behind her. Her transition must still be slowing her down. "It's not spring until I see flowers."

"You and Monica share one trait in common—contrariness."

"It's a woman's prerogative." She glanced back again. He didn't even seem to be breathing hard, gliding along, arms pumping as easily as if he'd done this all his life. "Are you sure you've never skied before?"

"No, but I studied it before we came down."

Great. It had taken her years of practice to become this proficient and he'd picked it up from a book. It was a good thing the Garathani had no plans to emigrate—Earth's athletes would never stand a chance in the Olympics.

"So where did you guys come up with all this gear?" she asked, breathing evenly. The birdsong was thrillingly loud in the hushed mountain altitude. "Did you synthesize it or something?"

"No, our technology hasn't moved in that direction yet."

"So where? Don't tell me you just happened to have some in your closet."

"We appropriated it from a ski shop."

She skidded to a stop and stared at him when he pulled up beside her. "You stole it?"

"We purchased it. They just have no idea who their mysterious buyer might be."

He moved off ahead of her before she could answer and she had to push it to catch up as he went over a rise and down the hill on the other side. "Turn!" she yelled when he picked up incredible speed.

Too late. He caught an edge and tumbled end over end in a spectacular agony-of-defeat moment. When he came to a stop, he was half buried in the snow.

"Shauss!" Jasmine raced after him and skidded to a stop beside his prone body. He wasn't moving. "Oh my God, are you okay?"

"Fuck me," came the muffled expletive from the snow. When he raised his head, his lashes and brows were caked with crystals. He licked his lips, blinking into the whiteness. "Tastes metallic."

Jasmine laughed as she brushed snow out of his hair, half of which had come loose. "Well, that was a pretty dramatic crash. Total yard sale," she grinned.

"Yard sale?"

She gestured up the hill behind him. The snow was littered with his gear—one ski, his goggles, poles and a glove. He pulled his right hand out of the snow and grinned to see the other glove. "Well, I didn't sell everything. And I'm still wearing my pack."

"I'm glad you can see the silver lining here, but damn it, Shauss, that was really stupid!" She rolled her eyes, pushing to her feet. "You could have been killed skiing so recklessly. From now on, you stay behind me and do as I say. Is that clear?"

"I think you're forgetting who's the Dominant here, *aramai*."

"I think you're forgetting who's the Terran here, Shauss." She grimaced. "Former Terran, anyway, and I know this sport and I know this mountain, and I *know* how to get where I'm going in one piece."

Groaning, Shauss struggled to his feet on one ski. "I'll let you get by with the attitude for now, but you're going to pay for it when we get back to the ship."

"Promises, promises," she said lightly.

Turning away, she chastised herself for issuing the subtle challenge. Even if he were inclined to pick it up, now wasn't the time. But he hadn't made love to her last night, although Tiber's ban on sex was lifted, nor had he returned her collar. He hadn't even kissed her, and it was really starting to worry her. Was he punishing her for her deception, or did he just not want her anymore?

Spying one of his skis, she zipped up to collect it and examined it carefully. It didn't look like the safety strap had malfunctioned. "Weren't you wearing the strap?"

"No. I didn't think I'd need it," he said dryly. "Live and learn."

She skied back down, scooping up his other yard sale items on the way.

"No, it's more like learn and live to tell about it," she commented as he reassembled himself and adjusted the backpack. He was lucky it hadn't popped open and distributed all his alien secret-agent equipment.

"Yes ma'am."

They started off up the hill again and this time Jasmine made sure she kept the lead. When they reached a rock overhang, which was laden with a dangerous cornice of crusty snow, she cut a wide path around it. On the other side, she veered off into the trees. The snow wasn't so deep along the path, but it was softer since the sun's light barely penetrated the dense forest of evergreens. They were still moving uphill, and the incline started to become even more challenging.

"This is truly amazing," Shauss said behind her. His breath was deep and steady, like a machine. The man was a machine. He'd taken that spill without a whimper and barely seemed fazed by it.

"Which part?"

"This…"

When he didn't continue, Jasmine came to a stop and looked back at him. He'd already stopped and was looking around in wonder.

"I can't even describe it," he said hesitantly. "We have nothing on Garathan to compare it to. It's so cold, and yet the air reeks of life. It's…vivid. Stark and beautiful."

Jasmine's eyes filled with tears. He'd just described himself. "It is, isn't it? Now do you see why I love this planet so much? I would never do anything to endanger it or those who inhabit it. I have a deep respect for this and every planet—each is precious to its people."

He sighed as he leaned on his pole and looked at her. "Jasmine, I never believed you could be knowingly involved in the attacks on the military bases. Or in the contamination of the pad or the steripod in Ketrok's lab, for that matter—even if you had been working to sabotage the ship, you wouldn't have risked Monica's safety."

"Thank you." Her lip trembled and then the tears slipped out.

Shauss dropped his backpack in the snow. Gliding over beside her, he looped his poles over his wrists and pulled off his gloves and pushed her goggles up over her brow. After plucking off his own and letting them fall to the ground, he took her face between his palms.

"You are an enchanting female, and despite my apparent bent toward erotic sadism, it pained me to respond to your deception as brutally as I did. I derived no enjoyment from tormenting you as an enemy." He brushed his lips over hers and wiped away the tears that continued to skim down her cheeks with his thumbs. "I need you to trust me and I need to be able to trust you."

"You can!" Jasmine dropped her poles and hugged his neck, a task that was much easier now that she'd grown so tall. "I love you, Shauss," she whispered.

"I'm glad to hear it, *aramai*," he murmured, squeezing her tight.

Suddenly embarrassed and annoyed and embarrassed about being annoyed, she broke away from him. Why couldn't she stop saying that to him? It wasn't like he was ever going to say it back.

"We'd better keep moving." She picked up her poles and scooted off up the path at high speed, not really caring whether he kept up or not.

"How far are we from the camp?" he asked after a few minutes.

"Not far. It should be just over that rise."

"Let me go first," he said.

She continued without slowing down. "Why?"

"It could be dangerous."

"Shauss," she threw over her shoulder, "as far as he knows, I'm still laboring under the delusion he's my father, and I *can* defend myself. I could probably just—"

Something snagged her pole and she was jerked off balance. Barely managing to avoid a face-plant in the snow bank, Jasmine turned and glared at Shauss, who held the tip of her pole in his hand. She yanked hard, but he didn't let go.

"Get behind me now or I'll put you there." His look was impenetrable.

Knowing she stood no chance against his brute strength, she stepped off the path with an offended glare and swept an arm out. "After you, Master."

"Ah, now there's a word I intend to hear from you a lot more often," he said as he poled by. Although his statement made her tummy twist, she stuck her tongue out at his retreating back as he powered up the trail.

But her eyes were drawn to the tight buttocks, flexing rhythmically beneath his form-fitting suit, and she sighed with longing. Was she ever going to get her hands on that butt again?

* * * * *

Just before he hit the top of the rise, Shauss halted and waved at her to stop several meters behind him. She didn't look happy about it, but she stopped with a roll of her eyeballs and leaned on her ski poles. Being in her own territory certainly dampened her submissive nature, but rather than irritating him, it made him eager to show her the error of her ways.

She looked sexy as hell in her Terran ski apparel, and if they had more time, he'd pursue making obscene snow angels with her. He'd seen pictures on the internet and thought that would make a tempting image to store for their later enjoyment.

Kicking off his skis and dropping his poles and pack, Shauss did a walking crawl up to the crest of the rise and peered over carefully. The camp appeared to be deserted. No tracks led in or out of any of the structures, and it looked as if it could have been years since anyone had been here. Beyond the four small cabins, he could just see the mine entrance through the scraggly boughs of the trees.

Shauss linked with the server. *"Empran, scan for humanoid life forms and electronic surveillance within a thousand meters of our location."*

"None detected."

Which didn't mean none existed within the mine's entrance, but he would take what he could get.

Skidding back down the hill, he picked up his gear. "It looks secure enough for the moment. Stay here until I signal you."

"Are you sure you trust me out of your sight?" she smarted off.

"You're really dying for discipline, aren't you?" The mere idea was sufficient to give him an incredible hard-on.

"Like I said, promises, promises."

The jolt of annoyance he felt was out of proportion to her comment and he knew it, but he dropped his gear as quickly as he'd picked it up, his breath ragged with impatience and arousal. He was damn well going to *make* time for her to take care of the problem she'd created.

"Take the skis off and get on your knees, Jasmine."

He heard her breath catch. "I don't think so."

"I thought you enjoyed performing oral sex on your Dom."

"Oh, so you're still my Dom? I thought you'd forgotten." She tried to look flippant, but he saw the pain and insecurity in her eyes.

"Jasmine." He pinned her with a stern look. "Allowing you time to fully recover from your transition doesn't make me any less your Dom and you'd do well to remember it. Now get on your knees. I won't tell you again."

Excitement flashed in her eyes, and she licked her lips before whispering his favorite words. "Make me."

She could have taken off down the path and lost him quickly, but she stood there, steam flowing from her mouth in deep uneven breaths, waiting for him to do just that.

Shauss strode toward her without a word. When he reached her, he knelt to remove her skis and then began tossing her accessories carelessly about.

"Hey!" She moved as if to catch some of them, but he held her in place with his hand gripping her forearm.

Once he'd divested her of her gear, he placed his hands on her shoulders and forced her downward. She fought the pressure but he was too strong for her to hold out against. She fell to her knees and he held her there with the one hand on top of her head while his other hand drew down the zipper of his American-issue parka and then the zipper of his uniform. When his rock-hard cock sprang into the cold air, he immediately pulled her face against it.

"Suck," he ordered gruffly. "And since I'm giving you the gift of my cock in your mouth, I want you to make sure I enjoy it."

She whimpered, holding her lips closed for the briefest moment before placing her hands on his thighs and opening to accept his rigid length. The interior of her mouth was hot and humid, a biting contrast to the chill outside. He kept his palm curved over the back of her head for leverage and began thrusting evenly into her mouth, coming into contact with the back of her throat with every push. He spared a fleeting thought for the traumas of the past, but they no longer held any power over him.

Jasmine's eyes watered as she looked up at Shauss, but she managed to restrain her gag reflex and swallow more of him. Oh Lord, how she'd longed for this!

Shauss spread his feet wider and made sure his zipper was as low as it could go. "Do you have any idea how to find my prostate?"

In response, she clutched at his uniform, shaking her head slightly in a negative response. Although that wasn't what she'd meant when she wished to get her hands on his butt again, the idea of touching him so intimately sent whispers of excitement over every inch of her skin.

"You've got long, slender fingers, so it shouldn't be hard for you to find it. Just curve it toward you when you're two to three knuckles in and feel for a knot about the size of a walnut. Rub it hard. That should trigger my ejaculation, and you *will* swallow every drop."

He eased his grip enough for her to pull her head back. She sucked her index finger into her mouth and pulled it out dripping with saliva, looking up at him with trepidation.

"Sometime before it freezes would be good, *aramai*," he prompted.

Tugging at the opening of his suit with her left hand, Jasmine insinuated her right between his legs, under his scrotum. She watched, thrilled when that ruddy sac tightened. The entrance to his bottom was easy enough to find and the tight muscles there seemed to ease deliberately for her passage.

Letting go of his suit, she wrapped her hand around the base of his cock and took him into her mouth once more, loving him with her lips and her tongue, with the hollows of her cheeks and the back of her throat, while she probed his mysterious heat with her finger. His gasps and deep groans made her bold and she eventually she found the knot of flesh he described.

"That's it," he whispered, massaging her head with his strong fingers as she rubbed the knot firmly. "Oh yes, that's it."

Heat blazed from his skin and his harsh breathing was startlingly loud in the quiet morning, and Jasmine had never felt her power over him more keenly. She let her gaze travel up his bare, flat stomach, following the arrow of silky black hair over his chest to his face. His head was thrown back, exposing his strong throat, and everything in her melted. Physically, at least, he trusted her.

"Peserin, harder!" he gasped.

Determined now to taste his seed, she obeyed. The rings of muscle in his anus tightened until her finger tingled with numbness but she kneaded him eagerly, and it wasn't long before he went rigid.

"Now!" He jerked once and she backed up in time to feel the first spurt of his semen hitting her tongue. Growling, he pulled her forward as he thrust again, not stopping until his cock was in the back of her throat. "Swallow it!" he roared.

Unable to do anything else—not that she was inclined to—she went limp in his grasp and swallowed everything he gave her.

Before he'd even stopped pulsing in her mouth, he leaned over and pulled her up into his arms. Breathing in great gusts, he planted an open-mouth kiss on her lips.

"You taste interesting," he murmured.

"Thank you, Master," she replied with a cheeky smile.

He smiled back. "No, thank *you*. That was very well done." Then he set her away from him and fastened himself back into his gear. "Now you're going to stay here until I tell you all is well. Is that clear?"

She gave him a grudging nod. While his praise was nice, it wasn't what she wanted to hear—and neither was the order to cower behind him.

"If I'm not back here in ten minutes, you may assume something has happened to me and it's not safe for you to come in. In that event, you will return to our landing coordinates and wait for a flare-out. Understood?"

She didn't like it, but she nodded again.

After he'd disappeared over the rise, she scooted up to watch him descend. His narrow feet didn't keep him from sinking into the deep snow, but his long, lean legs carried him through it with ease. Although he scanned the area as he descended, he didn't look back until he'd reached the mine's entrance. Even from yards away, she could see his scowl when he spotted her, but she didn't bother ducking out of sight. What was he going to do, come back and spank her?

She sighed as he slipped into the mine, resting her chin on her hands. The camp looked much the same as she remembered it—utilitarian. It wasn't built for fun, but for work, and she'd rarely enjoyed their stays here. Only one of her "father's" associates ever brought his children along, and though Jasmine hadn't minded babysitting sweet little Cara while their parents were powwowing, Mark had been a different story. When he wasn't giving her dirty looks with his beady brown eyes, he was hiding in the woods or trying to sneak off into the mine. She'd spent plenty of afternoons trudging through the snow after the rat-faced little stick boy, yelling his name until she was hoarse.

Mark.

Jasmine jerked straight up, her heart pounding thickly as the name echoed through her head. Oh no, surely not. There was no way Mark Bonham was *that* Mark, was there? Camp Mark had been two or three years her junior while Shelley's Mark was...

She frowned. It was hard to say how old Mark was, but he seemed older. Of course, the fact that he was so much taller than Shelley could have something to do with it, as could the facial hair. And he'd seemed so familiar, though she'd never quite managed to place him.

But if Camp Mark was Narthani, then he couldn't be Shelley's Mark because aliens gave Shelley the creeps. She'd said it over and over — if it weren't for the astronomical signing bonus, she'd never have taken the compound job. She and Mark had plans to build their own house in the Vail Valley after the babies were born and needed a big cash infusion to afford the down payment.

On the other hand, being married to a Narthani would certainly give Shelley a damn good reason to be creeped out by the Garathani. But why would Mark put his own wife — his own *family* — in such danger? Why would Shelley?

No, there had to be another explanation. Shelley would never deliberately jeopardize her unborn babies.

Jasmine rubbed her hands over her eyes, worn out from trying to untangle it all. Realization just beyond her reach hammered on her brain. Something Monica had said about spots of infection in the biologic pad...

In her mind's eye, she saw Mark walking down the corridor in the predawn hours, trailing his fingers along the wall.

And then she heard Shauss' telling her he never thought she'd contaminated the steripod—

In Ketrok's lab.

Her eyes popped open. Shit, she hadn't touched the cube in Ketrok's lab—Mark had. So which cube had been infected, the one she'd touched or the one Mark had touched?

Damn it, why hadn't she picked up on that earlier, when she could have asked Shauss about it? The suspense of not knowing was going to kill her.

She peeled back her jacket cuff and glanced at her watch. Almost eight minutes had passed and he hadn't returned yet. Had something happened to him? What was she going to do if he didn't come back? Could she really go off and leave him alone? She hadn't really thought it would be an issue, with his being some kind of deadly assassin, but he was taking an awfully long time.

Two agonizing minutes later Jasmine stood up and brushed the snow off her suit and then secured her gear at the base of a scraggly pine. No way was she skiing off this mountain without Shauss. It would take her almost an hour to get back to the drop-off point and he was in trouble now. She had to get in there and help him if she could—and the commander needed to know what she suspected. If Mark was sabotaging the ship, he had to be stopped before anyone else got hurt.

She scooted over the rise and waded slowly down the hill. Shauss could punish her all he wanted when they were back on the ship, but right now she was going in.

* * * * *

Shauss crept deeper into the mine shaft, being more careful the darker it became.

A whisper of energy current made him reach for his weapon, but he found himself unable to move. *Neural restraints?* How in Peserin's hell had they gotten his cerecom signature?

"Empran, emergency flareout!" he ordered.

No response.

He fought the restraints until sweat broke out on his brow but his muscles simply wouldn't respond. Fear blossomed in his gut.

"It's no use trying to contact your vessel, Lieutenant."

Flare lanterns on the wall hummed to life and a slender man walked into his line of vision. His heavily lined face was creased into a pained smile as he relieved Shauss of his pulsor and dagger.

Shauss' heartbeat thundered in his ears. "Ragan King, I presume?"

The man nodded. "None other. I presumed I'd catch a Garathani in my little neural trap," he said as he circled Shauss, "but I hardly dared hope it would be you. Strip him and put him on the table."

The chilled air hummed and two more males and a female appeared in the room. One of the men looked somewhat familiar, but the other two Shauss had never seen.

King handed the weapons to the female.

Keep him talking. Buy some time.

Although the cold fear in his belly was bleeding up into his throat, he licked his lips, and asked, "Why did you destroy all those military bases? You killed millions of innocent people."

"Oh, Famen did that," King said with a coy smile. "I just built the bombs."

"I suppose you killed him like you did Pret?" As if there were any doubt. Pret's page was a dead man as soon as his face hit the Terran media.

"Naturally. He'd served his purpose, and after I sent out the video of him planting the devices, he would have been much too recognizable to have around."

Even as the rational part of Shauss said *Just as well*, panic washed over him. He was a dead man—just like Famen. What would they do to him? How could he stand it?

Terrified by his own terror, Shauss grappled for control. Surely someone would come for him. If Empran couldn't communicate with him, a search party would be dispatched...

Unless Empran had been compromised. What if the Narthani had taken control of the ship and jettisoned the crew? What if they were all dead?

The rigid restraints converted to full neural restraints and he collapsed onto the floor. He shuddered when King and the other males pulled off all his clothing.

"What are you doing?" he yelled. "Stop! Leave me alone!"

They dragged him across the floor. It took considerable effort, but they finally managed to hoist him up onto an icy-cold stainless steel table. Shauss' stomach contracted in horror when he saw the troughs running down both sides—it was an autopsy table.

"No! No! Don't put me there! I don't want that!"

Chills racked him. Though he tried to fight the panic as he glanced wildly around at the rough-hewn stone of the mine wall, his pulse raced dangerously and his panting grew harsh. He began to whimper with every breath. Was no one coming for him? Had they all forsaken him, as his father had—left him here to suffer and die alone in the enemy's frigid lair?

Shauss closed his eyes and sucked in a deep breath, reaching for sanity. Mother of Peserin, what was wrong with him? Was this any way to face death?

Focus, damn it! Act like the warrior you are!

Clenching his teeth to keep them from chattering, he said, "Your daughter is about to be executed."

King stepped in front of him, arms crossed over his chest, brow drawn. "Is she, now?"

"He speaks the truth, Ragan," one of the males said. "She was found guilty of high treason this morning for sabotaging the ship. The reason why they're down here is because the pad infection has spread out of control and the other atmospheric generators have finally failed. They're looking for an evacuation site, and they deceived her into revealing the location of this place. She is unaware of her death sentence as yet."

The traitor was revealed—only Gillim had been fed that particular story. Damn the inflexible old bastard!

King continued to frown, and when his shoulders began to shake, Shauss thought he was going to burst into tears. The rumble of laughter that escaped him instead froze the marrow in Shauss's bones.

"Oh, how delicious!" King grinned as the others joined in the merriment. "They're going to execute her."

Shauss stared at him. How could he have spent so many years with a female as lovely as Jasmine and be this coldhearted toward her? The man was a monster.

"Narthani pig!" he spat, trying to maintain the deception and glean more information. "She's your own child!"

King sobered instantly, narrowing his eyes. "She's no child of mine, Lieutenant, and I'll thank you to remember it. She's nothing more than a pawn in our little game."

"What do you mean, she's no child of yours? Whose child is she?"

"She's the daughter of a very noble Garathani land owner."

"So how did you end up with her?"

"Oh, I think that's a story best saved for when she gets here."

"She's not coming here."

"Oh, ye of little faith," King chided. Sliding a hand under Shauss' cheek, he pushed his head over until he faced the other direction. "See? Here she is. Mardo found her trying to follow you into the mine."

Shauss saw Jasmine's slender body slung over the shoulder of a burly male and broke. His beautiful mate was dead. They'd killed her and now he would spend the rest of his life being tortured with cold and pain and loneliness. No one else had ever loved him and now no one ever would.

"Noooooooooo!"

The tormented howl yanked Jasmine out of her oxygen-deprived daze. Everything spun as her captor set her on her feet and she swayed, sucking in a painful breath.

The sight that met her eyes sent shock waves down her spine. *Shauss!* He lay unmoving on a stainless steel table, tears running from his closed eyes as his keening echoed through the mine shaft. What in God's name had they done to him?

"How nice of you to join us, Daughter," Ragan said in an expansive tone.

Jasmine swayed again. What was she supposed to do? There were at least four of them, and the woman appeared to be armed with Shauss' weapon. God only knew what the others were armed with.

She decided to roll with it. "Dad! Thank goodness you found me! I was so worried I was going to be stuck with them forever."

"Well, we couldn't have that, could we?" he asked, strolling over and placing an arm around her waist.

It was all she could do to stifle her shudder of disgust. Shauss continued to moan and babble, and her heart squeezed.

"What did you do to him?" she asked as coolly as she could.

"Oh, I just played on his fears a little," he replied with a smile. "My neural trap does more than restrain its subjects. It also suppresses reason and magnifies emotions exponentially. Right now he has all the analytical capacity of a two-year-old."

Crap! There went any chance of Shauss recovering enough to lend a hand. What the hell was she going to do?

"Oh well, that's…" She swallowed her outrage. "Different."

"I've found it to be quite a time-saving interrogation tool."

Unable to answer that civilly, she just pasted on a vapid smile, and he continued. "Of course I couldn't have used it on the lieutenant if Mark hadn't accessed the ship's cerecom system and sent me the master capture code. He's been a huge help, hasn't he, Siri?"

"He certainly has," the woman replied proudly.

"And you always thought he was such a headache as a child," he mocked, looking at Jasmine with steel in his eyes.

"Mark? You mean Shelley's husband?" she asked blankly.

"Didn't you recognize him?"

"Well, I thought he looked familiar." She shook her head. "He's little Mark?"

"Indeed he is. The dear boy sent me news of all your trials. I'm sorry you were left in the care of the enemy for so long, Daughter," he said. "I tried to get to you after that brute first attacked you, but I had my hands full."

He clucked in mock concern. "And you were forced to undergo your transition, I see. It's unfortunate, but you seem to have weathered it well enough."

"I'm okay." *Okay enough to kick your ass up between your ears, you sick bastard.*

"You're more than *okay*," Ragan insisted. "You're a vision. I had no idea you would turn out so lovely."

"Thank you, Father." Gritting her teeth, she leaned down and placed a kiss on his cheek. "You don't know how much it pleases me to hear you say that."

"Oh really?"

"Yes." She nodded eagerly. "You were always so disappointed in me, and it hurt me badly. I really wanted to please you."

"Oh my dear. I had no idea." He patted her back. "And there I left you on that ship to deal with those dreadful men all alone."

"It was awful," she shuddered.

"Did they rape you?"

She gave him a shamed look and didn't answer.

"Don't worry, child—I can see the answer in your face. But I have something for you to do that will make you feel much better. I'm going to let you exact your revenge for the way the Garathani have treated you."

She smiled uncertainly at him, mentally preparing herself to jump on any opportunity he gave her. "What do you mean?"

He took her hand and drew her toward the table. Turning Shauss' head, he slapped him on the face to get his attention. Shauss quieted, staring as he watched Ragan King with blank eyes.

Her "father" reached onto the counter and lifted a green towel to reveal an array of gleaming surgical utensils.

"What—what are you going to do with those?" she asked.

"I'm not going to do anything," he said holding up a scalpel. Then he pressed it into her icy-cold palm. "You're going to castrate him, just like his mother did his father."

Chapter Nineteen

"Shauss hasn't reported in and Empran is unable to detect him."

Tiber stared at the commander, feeling real fear for the first time in almost twelve years. "Was there any indication of trauma prior to the loss of his signature?"

"None, and he's alive until I have proof to the contrary," Kellen said grimly. "Jasmine's biomet is transmitting so we have their coordinates, but we're unable to breach the flare deflector guarding the mine's entrance. The probe we led with slid several hundred meters. We'll have to land another expedition at the field's perimeter. This field isn't as large, but the terrain isn't easy to cross."

"Commander," Holligan interrupted from the security console. "Verr just found Ensign Beral dead outside command escape pod four."

"Peserin's hell, I knew it. Gillim was the only one told of an impending evacuation." Kellen strode to the weapons safe. "Empran, seal the command escape pods until we get there."

"Command escape pods sealed."

He pressed his palm to the reader, ordering, "Holligan, dispatch a security detail to Councilor Gillim's quarters and confine him until further notice."

"Aye, Commander."

When the weapons safe opened, Kellen removed three pulsars. "Minimal pulse," he said as he handed one to Tiber and the other to Cecine. "We want his accomplice alive if possible."

They headed down the corridor toward the council chambers. The pods were between the command core and council chambers and served to evacuate all of the on-duty command personnel.

When they reached bay four, Ensign Verr was crouching over the fallen guard. Tiber examined him quickly but was unable to determine the cause of death. After he'd flared the victim to the infirmary, he joined the others, taking a defensive position on his knee beside the hatch. His heart raced as he raised his weapon—he'd never been forced to use one against a live opponent.

Cecine passed his palm over the reader and the hatch opened. One by one, they ducked inside the bay, sliding along the bulkhead with their weapons raised. When Kellen dropped to his knee and fired under one of the pods, Tiber instinctively rolled to the floor and aimed in the same direction.

"Empran, confine Mark Bonham!" Kellen ordered, popping right back up and bracing his back against the pod. Tiber remained on his belly, watching a pair of black shoes hover on the other side of the pod.

"Unable to comply."

Kellen raised his brows. "Excuse me? Empran, why are you unable to confine Mark Bonham?"

"Because I am unable to detect Mark Bonham."

"He's right on the other side of escape pod four," Tiber sent. "How can you not detect him?"

"My sensors detect only you, Minister Cecine, Commander Kellen and Ensign Verr in this bay."

"Well that's a new twist. We're going to have to apprehend him the old-fashioned way." Kellen waved his weapon.

Tiber rose and circled the pod in the opposite direction. When he risked a glance around the pod's nose, he saw only Kellen.

A pulsor fired again and a shout drew them toward the external hatch. When they rounded pod three, they found Mark Bonham clutching a box in his arms.

"Stop!" he gasped. "Or we'll all die together."

"Your mission is over, Bonham," Kellen said, keeping his weapon leveled on the injured man. "There's not going to be any evacuation. We circulated that rumor to draw you out, and it worked."

"No!" Bonham shouted. "The pad is infected and the atmospheric generators are corroded! I did it myself."

"But we found the key to the virus," Cecine said, also holding his weapon on the man. "Both Ketrok and the pad have healed, and only two of the generators were destroyed."

"No!" he screamed. "Not yet! You're supposed to die. This ship is supposed to be ours! We deserve this ship after you destroyed all of ours!"

"You're Narthani?" Tiber asked, surprised. He seemed too young.

"My mother is," he said, wiping sweat from his eyes. When Kellen ventured closer, he yelled, "Stop or I'll set this off!"

"Why would you risk the safety of your mate and unborn children?"

He hesitated, and then said, "There are things greater than the needs of my family, like the needs of our entire race."

"Your race!" Cecine thundered. "Your race is prospering with our help."

"You lie! First you tell us that you destroyed our homeworld, and then you claim you did not! Pret explained how you ruined Narthan for generations to come with *our* wealth and your weapons."

"Pret deceived you for his own gain. Do you not see that? Pret and Gillim were against our mating with Terrans from the beginning. They used you to sabotage this mission."

"I don't believe you!"

"I'll let you speak to Lord Sals himself."

"I do not know of this Lord Sals," Bonham said defiantly. "And it's too late. If what you say is true, I have nothing to lose."

He hit the activator on the box before anyone could fire. They all hit the deck, but the blast containment system confined the explosion to a blinding bubble of light.

"Holligan, is Gillim in custody?"

"Yes, Commander."

"Has Lieutenant Shauss reported in?"

"No, Commander."

He looked at Tiber. "Let's go get him."

* * * * *

Ragan King's hand slid down her forearm in a gesture so blatantly sexual, it made her want to vomit.

"Go ahead, my dear," he urged. "Slice off that offensive organ he used to torture you. He can't move, but he will feel every bit of pain you can inflict."

She swallowed bile. Shauss' genitals were shriveled with the cold and his eyes were wild as he looked up at her. Surely he knew she wouldn't do this.

His sudden scream said otherwise. "No!" he sobbed. "Please don't cut it off! Please!"

"What's the matter, Daughter? Don't you want your revenge?" He grasped her hand. "Here, let me help you get started."

He slowly exerted downward pressure and she resisted. God, she hated him. "No."

"Yes."

"I said, *no*." Pivoting, Jasmine shouted her *kiai* as she slammed her other hand down on his forearm, knocking the scalpel away.

King stumbled backward and then steadied himself. "Is that any way to treat your father?"

"You're not my father!" she shouted.

"Oh good, I'm glad we've got that out of the way," he said, crouching as he sidled around the table. "I've got plans for you that aren't very fatherly."

Jasmine followed him, unsure of what she was going to do but determined to keep herself between Shauss and that disgusting creep.

"You're sick," she spat.

"No, I'm just very sexually frustrated," he explained matter-of-factly. "Terran women don't react well to spurs these days, so I haven't had sex since Dayree died. Since her death is your fault, you can damn well take care of that problem for me."

"My fault?" she demanded.

"Yes, your fault. If she hadn't become so bloody attached to you, I wouldn't have had to kill her."

"What?" Jasmine froze.

"She was on her way to tell you about your heritage, to encourage you to join the Garathani and find *happiness*." He spat the word like a curse. "That was all she ever thought about once she had you in her arms. Her stupid brother was hired to kill you both, but instead he thought, why let an infant go to waste when his sister had always longed for one? The fool gave you to Dayree as a happy little *bon voyage* gift for our mission, and she took you, of course, promising it was only to keep you alive."

Skirting along the wall, King never took his eyes off her. "She swore she'd give you up to a Terran family when we got here, but by that time she'd grown attached to you and I couldn't break her heart by taking you away." He gave her a dark look. "That was the biggest mistake of my life. I should have slit your little throat right then—she would have gotten over you and we would have continued with our lives as planned."

Jasmine's head was still ringing. "You killed my mother?"

"She wasn't your mother," he growled. "I killed *my mate* because of you, you ungrateful little bitch. I've had reports of how easily you submit to this Garathani offal, and now you can submit to me, for once."

That was it. Ragan King was a dead man.

An arm looped around her neck and Jasmine reacted instinctively, throwing the man over her shoulder. He landed with a heavy thud and groaned. She kicked him in the face until he lay still.

Ragan's eyes widened. "Impressive."

"You're next," she promised coldly.

"I don't think so." Siri aimed Shauss' ray gun at her.

Jasmine dropped into a crouch and shoved her father's legs out from under him just as the weapon discharged. He landed on her back like a sack of cement, knocking the breath out of her, but she rolled him off her in a massive surge of adrenaline and leaped on him again, punching him in face with enough force to split his nose.

A wave of hot energy buzzed past her head as the woman fired once more, and Jasmine rolled, pulling Ragan King's limp body in front of her.

"Siri," another male voice gasped. "Mark is dead!"

"No!" she screamed. "No!"

"The mission has failed, Siri," he said. "We must leave here before they come."

She turned and fired. Clutching a burning hole the size of a fist in his chest, the man gasped and fell over.

Then Siri refocused on Jasmine. "You Garathani bitch, you will die for this."

Jasmine glared back. "You first."

"Die!" Siri screamed, firing again.

Jasmine shoved Ragan King toward the woman just as the weapon's discharge blew a huge hole though him. Shaking with fear, she dived into a barrel roll and tumbled across the floor. Her fingers brushed the scalpel and she paused mid-crouch to grab it up. Before she could stand, a hand grabbed her by the hair and shoved the weapon under her chin.

"Now you die," Siri ground out.

Jasmine brought her arm up with a loud *kiai* and buried the scalpel in the older woman's face. Siri fell to the ground, twitching, and Jasmine grimaced when she saw her—she'd driven the thing right into her eye.

Terrified panting grabbed her attention. "Shauss!"

"Help me!"

She scrambled for the table. "I'm here, it's okay," she breathed, kissing his face and his lips. "They're gone. They can't hurt you."

When he took a shuddering breath and quieted, she grabbed his hand and kissed all his fingertips. Then she looked around and snatched up his uniform, which was crumpled in the corner. Draping it over as much of his trembling body as it would cover, she wrapped her arms around his neck and breathed hot, moist air on his cold cheek.

"Don't leave me here," he whispered.

"I'm not going anywhere," she said soothingly. "Everything will be fine, I promise."

A moment later Kellen pivoted through the entrance, his weapon raised. When he saw her, he gave a jerk of his head and Tiber slipped in behind him, also pointing a weapon. They scanned the room, taking in the carnage with wide eyes before venturing farther into the mine shaft.

"Are you all right?" Tiber asked.

"Help him! There's some kind of a neural trap holding him."

Kellen looked around and then fired at a box mounted in the corner. Sparks flew as it exploded and the lights went out.

Shauss jerked and then his cold arms closed around her. "J-Jasmine?"

"What, Shauss? I'm here. Everything's fine."

"You d-d-disob-beyed me."

She chuckled, nuzzling his ear. "Damn right I did, and I'd do it again to keep you safe."

Tiber and Kellen worked in the near dark to haul him up off the table, and then Tiber wrapped his arms around them both. Just as the flare bubble engulfed them, he planted a loud kiss on her temple, and said, "Remind me never to back you into a corner."

Chapter Twenty

"How is Shelley?" Jasmine asked Monica over lunch in the minister's dining room.

She and Shauss had slept through breakfast. He hadn't made love to her but she could hardly complain, considering what he'd been through yesterday. He *had* kissed her and held her body tightly against his in those precious five seconds before he passed out and slept like the dead for eighteen hours. And their quick shower this morning, during which he'd soaped and rinsed her without a word, had held all kinds of dominant promise.

A promise she wasn't taking for granted just yet.

"She's completely out of it." Monica shook her head in sympathy. "She had no idea he was Narthani."

"How could she not know?"

"He didn't have a spur." At Jasmine's wide-eyed look, she said, "I know, I know, but apparently the spur is a recessive trait and boys with Narthani mothers and human fathers don't have a spur."

"Wow."

"Yeah. She's freaked out and keeps trying to go into labor. I don't know how long we can hold it off. The nurses are giving her lots of TLC, but I'm going to go back and check on her as soon as I'm done here." Monica polished off a big glass of milk and then wiped her mouth with the sleeve of her suit. At Jasmine's arch look, she said, "What? If they can't give me a napkin, I'm damn well going to use my sleeve."

Jasmine could only smile and hope that Monica never changed.

"Oh, and did you hear?" Monica tossed an arch look of her own across the table at Kellen. "Turns out that Empran was *hacked*. By Mark. That's how he could get around without being detected by Empran. Of course it made opening doors and turning on lights a bitch, but I guess that was a small price to pay for being invisible."

"Empran wasn't hacked, my love. Bonham simply uploaded some additional code."

She rolled her eyes. "What the fuck do you think hacking is, Kellen?"

"The deficiencies in Empran's sensory protocols and the cerecom system have been rectified and I'm confident there will no further breaches."

"Yeah, whatever. I'll take my iPod, please."

Zannen stepped behind Monica and she shivered when he trailed a huge hand over her neck and shoulder. "You might want to be nice to him, Dr. Smart Mouth. We have plans for you tonight and if you piss him off, he may not even try to keep me in line."

"You don't scare me, you big, bald cream puff."

He leaned down and his breath ruffled her hair for an instant before he rose and continued on his way.

Deep pink stained Monica's cheeks and she stared at her plate, speechless.

Confused, Jasmine asked, "Are you okay?"

Monica looked up at Kellen. "Why did I hear him in my head?"

"Because your cerecom implant has fully integrated into your nervous system. I've been hearing you all week," he told her with a grin.

"Say what?"

"I heard you the first time when you were shrieking about the block that ate Ketrok. That's when I hear you most often, when you're shouting out loud as well. You should have heard what you were thinking when Zannen claimed you," he added.

"Thanks for the bulletin, asshole." Her glare should have set his head on fire. "So that's how you knew about, um, Hastion."

He just smiled as her face turned red again.

"So who else has been listening to me?"

"Only Empran and I have had access to your cerecom transmissions, and after we bonded, Zannen. You'll need to learn to control and direct your transmissions as soon as possible so that you can send and receive from the rest of the crew as necessary."

"I'll get right on that." She blew a raspberry at him. "So did Jasmine get an implant too?"

Jasmine started—she'd been wondering the same thing. Maybe hers was transmitting to Monica already.

"As a matter of fact, yes," Tiber said. "Although, thankfully, hers hasn't integrated enough to transmit yet. If she'd transmitted yesterday within range of Ragan King's neural trap, he'd have captured her cerecom signature and used neural restraints on her as he did Shauss."

Her stomach twisted. "That wouldn't have been good."

"So, Miss King," the minister began from the head of the table.

Jasmine shuddered. "Would you mind calling me Jasmine, Minister? I've developed an intense aversion to that name."

"An understandable reaction," he said. "According to our protocol, you are officially Jasmine, third house Andagon."

She tested it on her tongue. "Jasmine Andagon."

"Can you live with that?" Shauss asked.

She smiled at him. "I can live with that."

"Getting back to my original query, Jasmine," the minister continued, "what do you plan to do with the rest of your life?"

She looked to Shauss for some input, but he just watched her with intense eyes, saying nothing.

"I want to be wherever Shauss is," she said tentatively, hoping he wanted that too.

"Females are not allowed to accompany their warrior mates on military missions," Cecine said.

"Oh." Well that sucked.

"However, I believe you could serve Garathan in a unique and vital capacity."

Jasmine eyed him doubtfully. "You do?"

"I do. The general council convened this morning and your name came up. The consensus was that you've demonstrated all the most admirable qualities of a warrior. You exhibit both an ability to follow orders and a willingness to ignore them and take control of a situation if the need arises. You display an aptitude for combat but you are not ruled by your need to fight. You have excellent instincts but you don't act without thinking. Most importantly, you don't hesitate to risk your life when you feel others are in jeopardy. You are a fierce defender of those you care about."

Stunned, she could only blink back tears, her heart beating unevenly.

"Furthermore, you are a Garathani who was raised on Terra by Narthani parents, and you've demonstrated a rare capacity to embrace and act in the best interests of all three races without bias toward one over another.

"With all these factors in mind," he concluded, "the council has voted to appoint you as our new Terran ambassador on the condition that you complete an abbreviated officer training session aboard the *Heptoral*."

Jasmine swallowed hard. "I'm...honored. Flabbergasted, really."

"You should be," he said with a smile. "You will be the first female in the Garathani fleet."

Monica hugged her. "Oh my God, Jas, I'm so proud of you!"

"My sister, the warrior," Hastion quipped. "And I was her first victim."

"It will be a challenging mission to rebuild trust among three worlds, but I believe you are more than equal to the task."

Lips trembling, she looked at Shauss. "Aren't you going to say something?"

"What do you want, Jasmine?" he asked. "I may dominate you in our bond, but you are your own person."

She hesitated. "I want both. I want to stay with you and I want to be ambassador."

"The *Heptoral* is assigned to the Terran ambassador for the duration of this mission." He contemplated her for a moment, and then said, "I will allow you to accept the post on two conditions. First, you will accept a full-time security detail and follow the directions of the security officers. Your life may very well depend upon being able to react without question."

Jasmine nodded. "I can do that."

"I hope so since I'll be heading your security team."

Tears prickled in her eyes as she nodded again. Yay!

"Second, your commission will last only five years, at which time we will retire to our farm. I believe Boydon will be ready for a much-needed vacation by then. At that point, we will begin producing young. I find I desire your children very much indeed." He hesitated before adding, "I assume you desire my children?"

The tears finally fell. Her vision was going to come true—she was going to have her baby and her garden with Shauss. Whether or not she'd get the curly hair remained to be seen.

"Of course I do," she said, wiping her eyes. "What about Tiber?"

"Tiber will do what I tell him to."

Jasmine held her breath as she glanced at Tiber but he simply smiled. "Where you both go, I go."

Well, that was a relief. "But don't we have to have a third?"

"In light of both your heritage and your heroism," Cecine said, "the council has allowed Lieutenant Shauss to reserve third indefinitely, as Commander Kellen has."

Monica frowned. "Hey, wait a minute—if you all retire to the farm, what am I going to do for toys?"

"Zannen owns half that farm," Kellen said. "I'm sure he'll want to stop in to make frequent inspections."

She sighed. "I guess that'll have—"

"Dr. Teague, please report to Infirmary Three for a patient in labor," Empran ordered.

Monica started to stand up and then froze. "Empran, did you just say please to me?"

"Yes."

Grinning, Monica opened her mouth to speak but Empran preempted her. "But don't get used to it, Monica."

* * * * *

Jasmine stopped into Infirmary Three that afternoon. Shelley was holding one of her tiny babies in her arms while the other slept peacefully in a bassinet.

"Hey," she said. "They're beautiful."

"Thank you." She stroked the little boy's bald head. "It's a miracle they're so healthy. If it weren't for the treatments Dr. Tiber gave me, their lungs might not be so well-developed."

"What did you name them?"

"Nothing yet. I'd planned to name him after his—" She swallowed and looked away.

"I'm so sorry, Shelley."

"I was married to an alien," she whispered. "How could I not know that?"

"There was no way you could have."

"What am I going to do? How can I go back to Earth now? My babies are aliens, Jasmine. They're part Narthani, and now everyone knows it was Narthanis who blew up those bases. My God, Mark probably helped," she sobbed.

"Oh honey!" Jasmine leaned over and rubbed her back.

The door opened and the minister walked in.

When Jasmine rose, Shelley grabbed her wrist, and whispered urgently, "Stay."

Jasmine settled back on the bed beside her.

Cecine hovered for a moment and then moved into the room.

"Please allow me to express my deepest sympathies, as well as those of the council."

"Thank you," she whispered without looking at him.

"If you require anything at all, you have but to ask."

She didn't say anything and Cecine peered into the bassinet. "May I?"

She hesitated and then nodded. Cecine could have picked up the baby girl with one hand, she was so tiny and his hands so large. He cradled her against his chest and rocked her. If the look on his face was anything to go by, he was smitten.

"So very beautiful," he said, brushing a light kiss in her hair.

"Could you put her down, please?" When he looked at Shelley, she repeated in an almost hysterical voice, "Put her down."

"Of course."

He laid the baby in the bassinet and bowed. "As I said, if you require anything at all, you have only need ask."

After he left, Shelley broke down. "Oh God, what are we going to do?"

* * * * *

Shauss entered his quarters, fully expecting to find Jasmine waiting for him in his bed. What he didn't expect to find was Tiber there too, every bit as naked and holding her in his arms while he delved in her mouth with his tongue.

He paused in the doorway, breathing in the delicious bouquet of her pheromones. "Starting without me?" he asked in a deceptively mild tone.

Jasmine started but Tiber went on as if he hadn't heard him and she relaxed back into his hold, running her hands up his arms and into the pale yellow sprigs of his hair. Unwilling arousal speared him—they were beautiful together and he wanted to fuck them both.

After he'd taken care of some business.

Tiber eased away from her mouth and focused on him. "Why don't you get undressed and join us?"

Shauss raised a brow. "Excuse me, but are you forgetting who the Dom is here?"

"Not at all." Tiber kicked away the blanket and stood up. His cock stood, as well, pointing straight up his belly. "But I think you have a lesson to learn, Shauss, and Jasmine and I are probably the only ones you might be willing to learn it from."

"Think again," Shauss said shortly. "Jasmine disobeyed me yesterday and is due a substantial punishment for placing herself in mortal danger. As will you be if you continue to forget your place," he added with a ferocious frown.

"Jasmine saved your ass yesterday, and you're only postponing the inevitable." He smiled, but his gaze was ruthless. "Now get undressed, Shauss, or I'll undress you."

"You and whose army?" Shauss asked incredulously.

"I'm the ship's psychiatric officer, remember?" Tiber strolled toward him, his hands hanging loosely at his sides. "If I deem it necessary for you to be naked and restrained as part of your healing process, I'm sure the commander and Zannen won't hesitate to lend me a hand."

"Healing process," Shauss snorted. "What have I to heal from?"

Tiber gave him a scornful look. "Do you think I'm blind, Shauss? I saw the look in your eyes when we pulled you off that table, and I see it there still. You're haunted by the way all control was stripped from you."

Shauss turned away. He didn't remember all of what had transpired yesterday, and that alone troubled him endlessly. To lose control of his body had been trying enough. Losing his ability to reason and being reduced to a blubbering child...

He opened his toy cupboard and gazed unseeing at the collection of floggers hanging there. Was that truly what was deep inside him—bloodcurdling fear?

"All your life you've fought giving up control."

"That's why I'm the Dom," Shauss explained with exaggerated patience, taking out one of the floggers and trailing the thongs over his palm. "And you're the subs."

"No, you're the Dom and Jasmine is the sub," Tiber corrected. "I'm the switch."

Shauss raised his brows. "Switch, eh?"

"Yes. Now put that thing away and undress or I'll call Kellen and Zannen to help strip you—then I'll use it on you."

"You wouldn't dare." Shauss nearly rolled his eyes at the clichéd reply because of course Tiber would dare.

After trying to stare him down for a moment, Shauss hung the flogger back in the cabinet.

"Strip, Shauss. Now."

His heart thumping unevenly, Shauss pulled off his boots and unzipped his uniform. Both Tiber and Jasmine watched him with dark, hungry eyes, and despite the unnerving situation, he felt a whisper of power shimmer through his veins.

"I don't want to strip control away from you, Shauss," Tiber said gently. "I want you to give it to me the way Jasmine gives it to you. The way I give it to you. It doesn't have to be ugly and invasive. You know that. Surrender can be a beautiful thing."

"I can't."

"Shauss, yes, you can," Jasmine urged. "You already did it with me, out there on the mountain—remember?"

"I was in control of that situation," he said firmly, though something in him squirmed. He *had* given her power over him. A lot of it. More than he was comfortable with Tiber being aware of.

"Were you?" Her blue eyes pinned him. "Really?"

"Well, you're not going to be in control of this one," Tiber declared, looking pointedly at his uniform.

Even as he repeated "I can't," Shauss pulled the uniform off his shoulders and stood up, stripping it off the rest of the way mechanically.

"You must." Tiber's eyes followed his every move. "According to the BDSM playbooks I read, no Dom should require a sub to do anything he wouldn't."

Shauss tried to stare him down again. "The ones I read said subs like you should be punished severely for trying to top from the bottom."

"I'm not topping from the bottom. I'm topping from the top. You just have to make up your mind that for tonight you're the bottom."

Shauss' jaw tightened. "Why are you doing this? The way we were going suited all of us just fine. I know you enjoyed taking my cock up your ass."

"Yes I did, although there's no reason to be crude about it." Tiber's reproof was gentle but a reproof nonetheless and Shauss was shocked to feel his ears begin to burn. He was actually embarrassed!

"As to why I'm doing this..." Tiber stepped closer until they stood face-to-face, cock to cock then he took Shauss' face in his hands and kissed him tenderly. "I'm doing it because I love you. Enough to give you what you need, not just what you want."

"How do you know what I need?" He'd tried to make the question belligerent but it came out hoarse, almost desperate-sounding. "Just because you're a psychiatrist doesn't mean you know everything about me."

Emotion was an enormous boulder in Shauss' throat, restricting his breathing as Jasmine rose from their bed and slipped behind him.

She wrapped her arms around his waist and kissed his back. "I'm not a psychiatrist, but I think I know you well enough to agree with Tiber. You need to let go and let us love you, Shauss. You're so beautiful. Please let us have you however we want to," she begged softly. "Can't you trust us enough for that, just once?"

He looked down at the floor as he thought about it for a long moment, breathing hard.

"Don't you love us enough for that?" Tiber pushed.

He couldn't deny it. "Yes, I do."

"Then look at me, Shauss."

Raising his eyes had never been so difficult, but once he met Tiber's warm brown eyes, he couldn't look away.

"You trusted me enough to name me as your bond mate even when we were at odds," Tiber said, grasping his neck with both hands and leaning in until their foreheads touched. "I think you've always known, somewhere inside you, that I made you vulnerable. That's why you fought to get away from me."

Shauss agreed but he couldn't say it.

"I always knew you needed me, though I wasn't sure why until you showed me how much I needed you." Tiber kissed his lips and then continued. "I truly thought I was content with my lot—and I was certainly happy enough with your magical probe," he added with a grin. "I'd had my soul mate in Nelina, I have my healthy sons at the academy, and my daughter is happily mated, and I thought I was...done. I thought what was left belonged to those who hadn't already been as fortunate as I."

He paused before saying, "You showed me otherwise by sharing your most valuable possession with me."

"Jasmine."

"Yes, Jasmine. And now we want to share our most valuable possession with you."

Shauss' brow furrowed in puzzlement.

"Trust, Shauss," Jasmine said, slipping between their bodies to lay her head on his chest. "Absolute trust in another person. It's the most freeing sensation you'll ever experience, and once you do, you'll never doubt how we feel about you again."

Taking a deep, shuddering breath, he nodded.

Jasmine took his hand and led him to the bed while Tiber went to the wardrobe and started digging in Shauss' treasures.

Shauss looked nervous, so she pushed him back on the bed and kissed him in the same leisurely way Tiber had kissed her earlier, sliding her tongue over and around his, sucking it like a ripe fruit and then letting it draw hers into his mouth. She loved kissing, especially now that she was bound to men who were so good at it.

Tiber's knee sank into the mattress and Jasmine watched out of the corner of her eye as he reached out for Shauss' arm. He fastened one of the leather cuffs around it and then attached it at the head of the bed. Shauss took a deep, shuddering breath but continued kissing her.

When Tiber came around behind her, she moved to allow him access to Shauss' other arm, and soon he was bound with his hands far apart. She pulled away and he tested the links.

"They won't hold you if you really want to get away," Tiber said.

Jasmine frowned. "They certainly held me."

Shauss gave her a tight grin. "They were meant to."

She started kissing her way over his broad, lean chest, burrowing into his chest hair. She was pleased when Tiber followed suit. Together, they played with his stiff little nipples, drawing gasps at first, and then a deep, "Oh yeah."

Tiber chuckled. "You're supposed to be fighting this to the bitter end."

"What's the point? You've got me where you want me, so I might as well enjoy it. Besides," he added, "I know you saw my collection and are fully aware that any discomfort you put me through will be returned a hundredfold."

"I have no taste for pain," Tiber said with narrowed eyes.

"You will."

Jasmine shuddered with arousal at Shauss' quiet promise and watched a dozen different expressions chase across Tiber's face before he smiled ironically.

"Then I guess I'd better get my licks in while I can," he murmured.

True to his word, he began licking his way down Shauss's taut stomach, and Jasmine followed suit eagerly. Together they both lay between his spread legs and nuzzled the flesh between his hair-roughened thighs, tickling him with their breath accidentally and then torturing him with it on purpose. He writhed as they put their mouths everywhere but where Jasmine knew it would feel best.

"What are you waiting for?" he cried.

"What do you think?" Tiber asked in a silky voice.

"You want me to beg, is that it? Well, I won't do it."

After two more minutes of their attention, he ground out, "Suck me. Please."

It wasn't much as far as begging went, but apparently it was enough. Shauss whimpered in gratitude when Tiber's mouth closed over his cock, and Jasmine slid to the side and watched, mesmerized by Tiber's approach. He was fearless when it came to caressing Shauss' testicles. *Caressing*, she snorted. More like manhandling.

Abusing.

Her eyes grew wide with alarm. He was really squeezing them hard, until the flesh bulged out between his fingers, and Shauss was groaning like he was genuinely in pain. She bit her lip, wanting to break in but trusting Tiber not to hurt him.

"Fuck me, I'm going to come if you keep that up. Either that or rip these rings out and ream your ass."

Without responding, Tiber eased his hold and then let go altogether. Jasmine let go of the breath she'd been holding while Shauss groaned again, this time with relief.

Tiber pulled away, licking his lips. "Can't have that."

Then he leaned lower, leading with his chin and nudging Shauss' sac with his nose. When his mouth opened and his tongue disappeared between those firm cheeks, Shauss went rigid.

"Peserin's hell! What the fuck…"

He arched off the bed, nearly knocking Jasmine over with his leg, but Tiber followed him, looping his arms under Shauss' thighs and holding him in place. Shauss' eyes were tightly closed, his face contorted with need. His expression was eerily close to the one he'd worn yesterday in the mine, and the awareness of just how much control he was giving up filled Jasmine's heart to bursting.

It also twisted the knot of desire in her belly until she wanted to scream.

She reached between her legs and found the hair there slick with moisture. Without hesitation, she slid a finger between the plump outer lips and directly into her nook. Shauss had left her dangling on the edge of arousal for days and she felt no compunction about releasing the pressure herself. The knowledge that Tiber was exploring Shauss with his tongue set her world on fire.

When Shauss keened and jerked against the restraints, Tiber drew back.

"What do you want, Shauss?"

Shauss howled unintelligibly.

"I'm sorry, I didn't quite get that," Tiber said, amusement plain in his voice.

Shauss opened his glassy eyes and stared at the ceiling, the muscles of his jaw bulging as he ground his teeth. Her poor, proud warrior!

Jasmine drew her hand from between her thighs and trailed a wet finger over his lips. He sucked it into his mouth hungrily.

After he'd licked her clean, he said clearly, "Fuck me. Please. Now. Anybody. Everybody. Please."

Tiber bit his lips as he sat up and his belly jerked with silent laughter. Once he had it under control, he released Shauss' wrists.

"Make love to Jasmine."

Jasmine squealed with delight as Shauss snagged her leg and dragged her under him. Pinning her wrists to the bed he all but mauled her in a clash of teeth and tongues. His furry chest turned her nipples to fire as he kissed her and she writhed beneath him, desperate for release.

He released her mouth and dove to her breast.

"Oh God, yes! That's—" She gasped as he drew her nipple out to the point of pain. "That's what I want. More. Please. Harder."

Pulling back, he panted, "They're so beautiful now—real, soft...edible."

They were real and so much more sensitive, she was about to come from his mouth on them. She pulled his head back down, anxious to find out if she could.

Maintaining suction on her breast, Shauss arched his back and speared his cock into her, and she shot over the edge with a scream of pure bliss. *Finally!*

"Shauss," came Tiber's command, "don't move until I tell you to."

Shauss wanted to kill Tiber, but he obeyed, holding himself taut as Jasmine's cunt contracted around him.

"You're fucking cruel," he snapped.

"No, I'm fucking you."

Warm, slick fingers pressed against his anus and he gritted his teeth as they gained entrance.

Leaning on one elbow, he looked over his shoulder, tense with nerves. "This shouldn't bother me," he said in a rush. "I've done it to you. I've done it to Jasmine. Hell, I even used the probe a time or two before we bonded."

She blinked up at him. "Really? Why?"

"Because I didn't mate with Monica after the initial claiming," he ground out. "Peserin, but that's a little tight!"

"It's supposed to be." Tiber's voice held humor and not an ounce of compassion.

"Why not?" Jasmine persisted.

"Two reasons," Shauss said through gritted teeth. "First, my spur didn't fit her nook, so I couldn't mate with her properly. The one time I took her, I took her ass."

"Now that's interesting," Tiber murmured. "So you really never claimed her."

"I claimed her ass."

"What's the other reason?" Jasmine persisted.

Shauss hesitated for a moment before saying, "Because she wasn't you."

Tears welled in her eyes. "Really?"

"Really," he grunted. "Oh, fuck me, that hurts."

"I intend to."

He threw a dirty look over his shoulder before explaining, "I wanted what Monica and Kellen had, and I think something in me might have known I could have it with you. You intrigued me, appealed to me...you called to me on some level."

"Oh Shauss," she whispered. "I felt the same about you from the moment I saw you."

"You're soul mates," Tiber said smugly. "I figured as much."

"I'd sneer at the idea, but I'm afraid you're right."

"I am. Females have excellent intuition, and Garathani females have a preternatural ability to sense their mates."

"I always thought that was just a fable," Shauss said.

"Not at all. Nelina knew me before she ever met me. She said she heard my name and knew I was the one."

"That's like Monica!" Jasmine gasped.

Shauss raised a brow. "What about Monica?"

"All right, quiet, you two," Tiber ordered. "You can trade secrets after I've had my way with this ass."

Without another word Tiber braced his hands on the bed and pushed the full weight of his cock into him, setting his fears to rest once and for all. The feeling was incredible. Painful and powerful, and so mind-stealing that he could only breathe through his nose and take it when Jasmine pulled his head down and kissed him. Just breathe and take it.

Breathe.

He was taken.

Kiss.

He took.

Breathe, kiss and take more. Breathe, kiss...

Take. He needed to move. The thick, repetitive intrusion of Tiber's cock was energy, building hot and urgent at the base of his spine, and he needed to move, needed to fuck —

"Don't do it."

Shauss roared with frustration.

"I've got you," Tiber promised in his ear. He laid all his weight on Shauss' back and Shauss grunted, propping them both up on his elbows so Jasmine wasn't crushed.

Then Tiber drove into him, pushing him into Jasmine again and again. Shauss absorbed it all — the pounding thrusts, the hoarse cries, the fingernails scoring trails of fire down his ribs — until sweet, searing energy boiled up his spine and down through his balls.

The resulting explosion nearly blew his eyeballs out of his head.

He didn't know how long he'd rested his damp forehead on Jasmine's when he felt Tiber's tongue on his shoulder. Had he come too?

The feel of a softening cock sliding wetly from his ass answered that question. He must have used the probe.

"You're both mine now," Tiber said smugly.

Jasmine shook her head. "No, you're both mine now," she wheezed. "And you're incredibly heavy. Could I have some air, please?"

They both rolled off her at once and Tiber ducked into the shower to clean up.

While he was gone, Shauss opened the cabinet to take care of an overdue task.

"Your neck is still very slender, but I added a few links to this thinking—hoping—you'd gain some more weight." He frowned. Jasmine's lips were trembling as she stared at the collars he held. "Is something wrong?"

"You're giving it back?" she asked.

"Of course I'm—" His eyes widened and his heart squeezed. "I never took it from you, *aramai*—I removed it during your transition so it didn't choke you and resized it while it was off. It's always been yours. It always will be."

Her smile was blinding as she held up her hair. "Please?"

He refastened it around her neck and snapped the lock shut with finality.

"I'm yours," she whispered.

He brushed a tear from her cheek. "Yes, you're mine." Spying Tiber, he added, "And so are you. Come here."

Standing, he showed Tiber the beaten gold band he'd acquired for him. "Like hers, this one locks and I hold the key. Once I put it on you, it stays. Are you mine?"

After a long, solemn look, Tiber nodded. "I'm yours."

Shauss closed it around his neck and locked it. "You're both mine. You always will be."

"What about you?" Tiber asked.

"What about me?"

"You're ours. Aren't you going to wear one?"

"Doms don't wear collars."

"You do when you're ours," Tiber promised.

Seeing the determination on his two favorite people's faces, Shauss grinned and said his two favorite words. "Make me."

Also by Robin L. Rotham

☙

eBooks:
Alien Overnight
BIG Temptation
Carnal Harvest
Seniorella

Print Books:
Alien Overnight
BIG Temptation

About the Author

A bookworm from the age of ten, Robin L. Rotham lived vicariously through daring, romantic heroines for nearly twenty years, dreaming all the while of one day writing her own romance novels, as well as her own happily ever after. When she finally found her real-life hero, he wasn't quite what--or where--she expected. Undaunted, she chased him over three states and four years before he finally swept her off her feet. He's been more than worth the effort.

The realities of home and family kept her from fulfilling her other dream for ten more years, but Robin finally succumbed to the writing bug in 2005 and cranked out her first novel on a used laptop from eBay in less than seven weeks. Alien Overnight is her second completed novel.

Robin welcomes comments from readers. You can find her website and email address on her author bio page at www.ellorascave.com.

Tell Us What You Think

We appreciate hearing reader opinions about our books. You can email us at Comments@EllorasCave.com.

Why an electronic book?

We live in the Information Age—an exciting time in the history of human civilization, in which technology rules supreme and continues to progress in leaps and bounds every minute of every day. For a multitude of reasons, more and more avid literary fans are opting to purchase e-books instead of paper books. The question from those not yet initiated into the world of electronic reading is simply: *Why?*

1. ***Price.*** An electronic title at Ellora's Cave Publishing and Cerridwen Press runs anywhere from 40% to 75% less than the cover price of the exact same title in paperback format. Why? Basic mathematics and cost. It is less expensive to publish an e-book (no paper and printing, no warehousing and shipping) than it is to publish a paperback, so the savings are passed along to the consumer.

2. ***Space.*** Running out of room in your house for your books? That is one worry you will never have with electronic books. For a low one-time cost, you can purchase a handheld device specifically designed for e-reading. Many e-readers have large, convenient screens for viewing. Better yet, hundreds of titles can be stored within your new library—on a single microchip. There are a variety of e-readers from different manufacturers. You can also read e-books on your PC or laptop computer. (Please note that Ellora's Cave does not endorse any specific brands.

You can check our websites at www.ellorascave.com or www.cerridwenpress.com for information we make available to new consumers.)

3. ***Mobility.*** Because your new e-library consists of only a microchip within a small, easily transportable e-reader, your entire cache of books can be taken with you wherever you go.

4. ***Personal Viewing Preferences.*** Are the words you are currently reading too small? Too large? Too… ANNOYING? Paperback books cannot be modified according to personal preferences, but e-books can.

5. ***Instant Gratification.*** Is it the middle of the night and all the bookstores near you are closed? Are you tired of waiting days, sometimes weeks, for bookstores to ship the novels you bought? Ellora's Cave Publishing sells instantaneous downloads twenty-four hours a day, seven days a week, every day of the year. Our webstore is never closed. Our e-book delivery system is 100% automated, meaning your order is filled as soon as you pay for it.

Those are a few of the top reasons why electronic books are replacing paperbacks for many avid readers.

As always, Ellora's Cave and Cerridwen Press welcome your questions and comments. We invite you to email us at Comments@ellorascave.com or write to us directly at Ellora's Cave Publishing Inc., 1056 Home Avenue, Akron, OH 44310-3502.

Cerridwen, the Celtic Goddess of wisdom, was the muse who brought inspiration to storytellers and those in the creative arts. Cerridwen Press encompasses the best and most innovative stories in all genres of today's fiction. Visit our site and discover the newest titles by talented authors who still get inspired - much like the ancient storytellers did, once upon a time.

Cerridwen Press
www.cerridwenpress.com

Discover for yourself why readers can't get enough of the multiple award-winning publisher Ellora's Cave.

Whether you prefer e-books or paperbacks, be sure to visit EC on the web at www.ellorascave.com

for an erotic reading experience that will leave you breathless.